Betrayal and Escape

Betrayal and Escape

Dr. John M. Hall

VANTAGE PRESS
New York

This book is based upon the true life story of the author. Names have been changed to protect the privacy of those involved. Any similarity between the characters appearing herein and any real persons, living or dead, is purely coincidental.

Published by Vantage Press, Inc.
516 West 34th Street, New York, New York 10001

Manufactured in the United States of America
ISBN: 0-533-13228-2

Library of Congress Catalog Card No.: 99-94926

0 9 8 7 6 5 4 3

To my dear Mama, who not only gave me life on May 25, 1941, but also planted in me the seeds of strength that sustained me in my early childhood and eventually led me to my dear Savior, Jesus Christ

Foreword

Dr. John Hall is one of the most courageous people I know. As a small child growing up in a large family locked in abject poverty, he learned to cope with all kinds of losses by looking to the adults around him for guidance and direction. His biological mother functioned almost as a single parent, providing for her many children as resourcefully as she could. Her religious faith enabled her to persist in keeping the family together and resolving issues one day at a time. Much of John's strength and resourcefulness came from this wonderful woman who not only gave birth to him but also literally saved his life on several occasions. When Dr. Hall began putting his life together, he came to appreciate the rich legacy his birth mother had left him during the four and one-half years they lived together. The recognition of this contribution meant a new life for John in his late forties.

When his father's sister, Beulah Howard, adopted John following the death of his birth mother, he was faced with a different set of expectations. Previously, the family had lived in a survival mode, depending many times on the generosity of local people who believed in the Lordship of Jesus Christ. There were few restrictions and structures because everyone in the family was trying desperately to survive. However, when Jim and John moved into Beulah Howard's house, this all changed. She provided well for their material needs. However, she micro-managed the lives of these two young boys. Her rules and perception of reality prevailed at the expense of their feelings and thoughts. It didn't matter how they experienced events. The only thing that mattered was Mrs. Howard's perceptions. This posed a problem for both boys. Jim rebelled and used charm interspersed with defiance to cope. John absorbed his adoptive mother's affronts and internalized them, feeling increasingly cut-off and alone. Ultimately, this could have proved fatal to John's emotional and physical development as a person. However, John had inherited his birth mother's spiritual vitality. He persisted in believing that God was good and He would give those who were faithful the necessary strength to survive and eventually prevail. This is the only explanation that makes sense in the context of the various abuses John suffered: at the hands of his adoptive mother; humiliations around normal developmental issues; isolations by his peers in a hostile school environment; and resentments in his church relationships when he had to parrot Beulah's eccentric admonitions to placate her. John was caught between a rock and a hard place and yet found a way to survive. In an ironic way, both brothers helped each other survive. I'm not sure either brother could have made it without the consolation and relief their relationship provided.

John's courage and strength were manifest in his ability to absorb these many assaults on his personhood while equipping him to function as a health care provider. These academic and professional accomplishments enabled John to prove to himself and others that he was worthwhile in spite of his adoptive mother's condemnations that would have crushed most people emotionally. John developed a very high threshold for physical and emotional pain. This gave him a sense of inner victory over those who tried to hurt him. While this shored up John's inner sense of self-worth, it also cut him off from some of his warm human feelings. He would not let himself cry or show emotion toward those who were trying to hurt him even when he felt he was being purposely victimized. This is what contributed significantly to John's growing depression. This occurred concurrent with his midlife reassessments after leaving the church of his childhood. He pondered the ultimate questions of life: Was life really worth it? Did anyone really care? Was he an effective dentist? Was he a good father? For him everything was a big effort, and he questioned his adequacy in many areas of day-to-day functioning. This was the point when John began his pilgrimage of putting together and developing "remnant theology." Over a twelve-year period of time he went back to the formative events in his life and reflected on what they meant. He dared to ask soul-shaking and -shaping questions, which only a pilgrim in pain would dare to raise. During this long, tedious process, he did not back down. He persevered. He reminded me of Jacob on the Jabbok

River, who was in great pain but would not let the angel go until he had received the blessing. This is Dr. Hall's story. It is a story that only a man of faith and courage could write. Each of us who reads John's story might well ask him- or herself, "Given the events he had to endure, would I have had the courage to write what he did with such candor and trust?"

JOHN M. MACKEY, D. MIN.,
September 1, 1988

Betrayal and Escape

1

It was October 23, 1945. Beulah Roberts had been confined to the bed for about a week. A tired and worn body such as hers had very little resistance. Therefore, it was not difficult for her to develop a fatal case of postpartum infection. Thick black curls framed her small doll-like face. Smooth ivory skin made even paler by her condition gave no true indication of her age. Her slight five-foot-three frame hardly made any impression beneath the covers. As the fever raged in her poor body, Beulah Roberts talked very little. A fishing-tackle box became a coffin for the last little baby she had brought into the world, who was laid in that box and returned to the earth from whence it came. There was no ceremony or words of love for the little thing, as if it were something to be discarded like a broken toy. Beulah Roberts was only thirty-six years old and had brought eleven babies into the world, eight of whom had survived. That was a tremendous task for such a tiny, delicate body such as hers.

The family knew she was sick but had no idea of the severity of her condition. The muted conversation of those sitting around the bed was interrupted when Beulah looked at her husband, Josh, with kindness and a tenderness born of true Christian love and said to him, "Son, I'm going on to rest and I want you to meet me someday." The family members continued talking quietly among themselves as they sat in chairs surrounding the bed, not realizing how soon Beulah would actually leave them all. Suddenly she lifted her hands above her face and began to clasp and unclasp them, as if rejoicing with praise, then ever so slowly she laid them gently on her chest, and as she gave a gentle sigh her life was gone.

When those sitting around the bed realized she was gone, in desperation they fell on their knees around the bed all praying at once with a loud voice, begging that a miracle would happen and she would somehow live again. "She can't be gone . . . She can't leave us . . . What will we do? . . . ," "We are ruined!" they said when it was apparent that she truly had passed away. Beulah Roberts had been their spiritual mentor, their guide, their inspiration, their strength in times of trouble. She had been like a shepherd to all of them. When they needed someone to confide in who would understand their trials, would guide them back when they had gone astray without condemning them and making them feel less of a person, it was Beulah Roberts. Always so kind, compassionate, loving, and understanding, never judgmental or critical, never belittling. Everyone was always referred to as "little children," for she loved them so dearly. She always encouraged each of them and gave them so much inspiration, guidance, and hope, in their times of deepest distress. There was just no one else like Beulah Roberts.

There was also another Beulah present that fateful night. She was my aunt Beulah Howard, my daddy's sister. Beulah Howard requested a Bible be brought to her, and taking it in her hand she stood up and began to preach to all who were present in the room that God would give her the spirit of the departed Beulah Roberts. She would then continue the work that my mama had begun. That proclamation brought some consolation to all those present, for they believed that it was possible, just like in the story in the Bible of the two prophets, Elijah and Elisha, in which the spirit of Elijah, when he was taken up to heaven, was passed to Elisha, who remained on earth. Because the relatives believed in the passage of the spirit of one to another and had so much spiritual confidence in my mama, Beulah Roberts, it was to them as if the spirit of my Mama now lived in my Aunt Beulah. That was the means through which she was able through the intervening years to gain so much power over them and so much control, not only over their lives but also even over their very souls.

I know it is so very confusing to have the most important people in one's life both have the same name, but in my case that was the truth. My birth mother and later my adoptive mother were both named Beulah. Looking back now over my entire life, I can see how at that moment when Beulah Howard accepted the responsibility of carrying on the spiritual work that her sister-in-law Beulah Roberts had begun, a seed was planted that grew through the years to become like a great tree under whose branches everyone could find shelter, but then as time passed, almost as if it mutated, the great tree would turn into a monster that would put such a stranglehold on the entire congregation that people's lives would be destroyed by it.

Life had always been hard for Beulah Roberts. Having been orphaned as a child herself, she was reared by adoptive parents who were harsh and even cruel at times. The hot, humid summer days and cold winter months were filled with hard manual labor on the farm. Many times at the end of a toilsome day in the fields, with every fiber in her tiny body screaming for food and rest, she had to kneel on the floor, remove the boots and socks of her stepfather, and bathe his dirty feet as he relaxed in his chair.

In those days sharecroppers would often swap work with other sharecroppers. In that way the work could be done without an expenditure of money, which was in very short supply.

It was a beautiful sunny summer day. Some sharecroppers from another farm had come to help Beulah's stepfather. Among those who came was a handsome, nineteen-year-old blond-haired, blue-eyed young man named Josh Roberts. At the time, Beulah was a tender eighteen years old. As they worked that day hoeing the tobacco plants to rid them of weeds, they began talking together. Their interest in each other made the day go by faster and the work seem far less boring.

They were immediately attracted to each other. As they sat in the cool of the shade eating lunch, he was already making plans to see her again. He was kind and gentle, and it didn't take much persuasion for Beulah to go out courting with him. They spent many happy evenings sitting in the tobacco barn talking together. It seemed so wonderful to have someone warm and strong whose shoulder she could lean on.

In those days there were no theaters, bowling alleys, concert halls, or amusement parks and certainly no shopping malls. Life was so very simple. Many times courting took place in a mule-drawn wagon going to visit another relative or taking your sweetheart to church. How romantic it was for Beulah and Josh walking slowly along those country dirt roads hand in hand, sharing all those sweet little nothings in their conversation on the way back home from church on Sunday afternoon. Soon the two were deeply in love.

They were married not long thereafter in a simple ceremony performed by a justice of the peace. About a year later her first child, Chris, was born to Beulah Roberts. From then on until the end of her short life, Beulah Roberts gave birth to a child about every eighteen months for a total of eleven, eight of whom survived her death. She did not have the luxury of a hospital with doctors and nurses in attendance during her deliveries, but bore all of her children at home with only the help of a midwife. Beulah's earlier years of toiling in the fields had developed the needed strength in her body that made giving birth much easier for her than many.

Quickly the years passed and soon there were many of us children, just like doorsteps. Mama lost a child between Chris, the firstborn, and Dana, my oldest sister. Then there was another one who died between Marie and Eva. When we children were small, my daddy performed chores around the house such as rocking us children to sleep and washing dirty diapers in the old galvanized tub to help Mama, but as time went by my daddy changed and his family was not as important to him as it once was. He was not always a good provider for Mama and us children, either. Hunting and fishing were a passion of his, which he pursued to the extent of sacrificing a good-paying job. If he was painting a house and the notion struck him to go fishing, he laid down the paintbrush and went fishing. Other times he squandered his wages on alcohol and prostitutes, then would tell Mama he had not been paid. Mama was left alone many times to fend for herself and us children, which demanded she become resourceful.

During the summer months we made trips into the neighboring woods, battling mosquitoes, risking the danger of snakes, struggling through briers and thick underbrush to gather blackberries and blueberries (or huckleberries, as we called them). I looked forward to those days when Mama would go to the kitchen, call us children, and give each of us an enamel bowl to carry. We knew what was coming: blueberry picking! It was such fun for us to get away from home and go to a different place, there was so little else to do.

I can still remember the excitement I felt upon discovering a beautiful bush loaded with big, plump blueberries or a thicket of

4

brier-berry bushes hanging with succulent black fruit. "Look, Mama! Look what I've found!" I'd call. "Try to get them all, little Johnny," she would say.

To pick the berries, one had to snake his or her hand and arm through a maze of branches bristling with sharp thorns. The thorns grew toward the stalk of the bush, so after you picked those glistening blackberries, letting them roll into your hand, it was almost as if the bush wanted to prevent your taking them. The thorns would dig right into your hands. Those berries protected by leaves from the direct sunlight were much bigger, better, and sweeter, but also much harder to reach.

A pailful of plump blackberries was a wonderful reward, though, for scratched hands and arms. We children were always proud of what we could pick in our little bowls and pour into Mama's big pail. Mama always bragged on us, for she, too, was proud of what we could do to help her.

We worked hard in the garden also. Mama gave us children the job of ridding the vegetable plants of insects. "Little children, I need you to go pick the bugs off the bean bushes for me," she'd say, and we almost jumped for joy. It was fun for us to pick off the worms and bugs. They didn't frighten us a bit.

Our jobs were the fun stuff, but poor Mama had all the real work to do. Gathering the berries and vegetables was the easy job. Later Mama spent long tiring hours toiling at a hot stove canning them. The luxury of air-conditioning wasn't even in existence in those days. Freezers were not available then to poor country folks like us, so everything had to be canned. I always enjoyed watching Mama fill her sparkly clear glass jars with all those beautiful multi-colored fruits. I was fascinated with the colors, and my, oh, my, how delicious they were on my plate at suppertime! In spite of Mama's efforts, however, we still went hungry many times.

When she really became desperate, Mama was not too proud to beg for food from her neighbors for us children when there were no other means available. She would do anything for her children. Often suppertime came late at night after Daddy came home with some groceries. I can remember eating raw oatmeal out of the box. It was *sooo* good. Josie, my sister who was next older than I, ate some lard out of the lard stand. She said that was delicious, too. You can know from that just how hungry we were, when lard by itself tasted good.

The obtaining and preparation of food were not the only difficult tasks for my dear mama. Ordinary chores such as housekeeping and laundry in those days were major undertakings. Without the luxury of central plumbing, an outdoor pump was our only water supply. The pump had to be kept primed all the time, else you couldn't get any water out of it. We always kept some water handy in a large wooden or galvanized tub to use in case we had to prime the pump. For those who have had no experience with hand pumps: when the water level in the pipe dropped down below the pump valve, an air space developed between the water below and that solid valve above at the top. When that happened, no water would come up. There had to be a continuous column of water from the water down below in the ground all the way to the top of the pump for it to work.

In order to prime the pump, we had to pour water down the pipe until it ran out the mouth of the pump, vigorously pumping the handle up and down as we poured in the water. Once a solid column of water was formed by expelling all the air, the valve could then lift water out of the ground.

We pumped our water for cooking, washing, and cleaning into a large galvanized bucket, then carried it into the house. We kept larger containers inside for storing water in the house, which prevented so many trips to the pump. That was especially important in the cold wintertime.

Pumping water was fun for me. I was intrigued by the clear stream of water as it flowed out of the spout, and a drink of cool water in the hot summertime from the big metal dipper felt so good to a thirsty mouth.

Mama cleaned the wooden floors of our house by scrubbing them with a cotton mop and lye soap water. She scrubbed them until they gleamed bright and clean. Our house was plain, but we kept it very tidy. Unpainted boards covered the walls, floors, and ceiling. We didn't have extras like pictures and other pretty things to hang on the walls. Many houses in those days had no insulation, either. There were cracks between the boards in the floor where we could peek through and see the ground below. Simple cotton curtains hung from slender metal rods at the windows. The furniture in the house was also very plain. Our home had only the barest of necessities.

Washday! That was a major undertaking. Washing clothes was a real task, for one had to heat water on the stove to boiling, then pour it into a large galvanized tub or cast-iron wash pot and stir the clothes with a wooden stick to wash them. Sometimes the clothes were actually boiled to ensure that they were really clean. After you poured the hot wash water out, fresh rinse water was poured into the tub and the clothes were then rinsed by hand, twisted as dry as the hands could wring them, and then hung up to dry. It was an all day job, and quite tiring, too.

The danger of being burned from scalding water was ever present. I remember dear Mama was burned one time and I felt so much pity for her. Her arm was red as a half-ripened tomato. "Little Johnny," she said, "it hurts so badly. I don't ever want to go to hell." Folks didn't wash clothes as frequently as we do nowadays, either. When my mama said she washed clothes, she indeed really did, not like it is nowadays, when the machine washes, rinses, and slings them dry so they are ready to hang out.

Life was hard for Mama, but for us children it really was not that bad. Amusement came easily to us, for we had great imaginations, which we put to use every day. Our wood-frame house stood on unusually high foundation pillars. The bank of the Black River was only a few hundred feet away from the edge of our back porch. The foundation had been built high so that when the river flooded and overflowed its banks the water did not come into the house. In our house, too, there were cracks in the floor where we could peek through and see the ground below. We had us another whole world under that house. During the hot, sultry months of summer, we could play in the cool comfort of the make-believe world we imagined down under there. We had our own house, our church, and a hiding place as well. I remember the feel of that cool sand in the hot summer. It was so refreshing. We didn't worry about getting dirty. We played in it, lay down in it, and sometimes poured it on one another. We spent a lot of time in our secret safe little world away from anything else.

In addition, a wonderful front porch extended the entire length of the house. The porch railing gave us another place to play. What time we weren't playing under the house we were playing "birds." Yes, that wonderful high railing on the front porch gave us a perch from which we could jump off, flapping our arms up and down like a bird does with its wings, actually hoping we would be able to fly. It was always such a rude awakening when we hit the ground if we didn't land just right, though, for our knees smacked quite hard against our chins. Sometimes the breath would nearly be knocked out of us. I had always been fascinated with the flight of birds and would spend hours jumping off the porch railing, pretending I could fly.

Mama had two rocking chairs she kept on the front porch. We liked nothing better than turning those chairs upside-down, and pushing them all over the porch as if they were our cars. It was so much fun. As we pushed them slowly along, we made a sputtering noise with our lips like a motor, making the "car" seem more alive. To us little fellas who had no toys, ordinary things like that were simply wonderful. Once when our dog Shep died, we played church and gave the dog a burial service. Chris even preached its funeral. You can believe our days were never boring.

Sometimes, however, our childish ideas got us into trouble. Once we were playing a game with some passing motorists, trying to see how many times we could cross the road before the car arrived. There was only one problem with that little game: one of the drivers just happened to be a neighbor. Being concerned about our safety, he stopped and told Mama what we had been doing. She promptly lined us up in a row, and beginning with the eldest, she switched our legs in good fashion. I remember waiting in line. I can still see the others who were ahead of me as I waited. I wasn't scared, just waiting my turn. Mama was so dear. She switched us just enough to teach us a lesson

One summer day my oldest sister, Dana, wanted to see little Johnny, as I was called, float in the river. So she put me in the big galvanized tub she used for bathing us. She thought quite innocently I would float in the tub and that would be fun for me. Galvanize tubs are very unstable on the water. No sooner had she pushed me out into the river than the tub capsized, dumping "little Johnny" out into the black water. Of course, not knowing how to swim, I began to flail around frantically. As I was screaming with my mouth wide open, my head went under and my mouth filled with water. I couldn't breathe. I couldn't touch the bottom. I began to choke and cough as I strangled on the water. I was terrified. Desperately I fought for my life.

It seemed like forever while I was in that awful black water. Dana and the other children, seeing I was in trouble, ran screaming for Mama. Dear Mama came running from the house and pulled me out just in the nick of time. Because of that childhood experience, throughout my life, up until I learned to swim when I was in college, I had a recurring dream about being out in a huge expanse of black water up to my chin, struggling desperately to reach the distant shore. In the dream my eyes were on a level with the water, and far in the distance I could see trees on the shoreline. I felt the same desperation in the dreams that I had the day I almost drowned. Even today I still have a morbid fear of the water and have to constantly remind myself to relax, that I can swim. I tend to fight the water, and I'm sure the fear stems from the past.

We had never heard the word trampoline; they didn't exist for us. But being like most children, we loved to jump up and down, too. So we used one another to jump on. Some of my siblings jumped on me. The worst problem with that game was that I suffered a slight hernia and had to wear a truss for a short time. I remember going to the doctor. That was a most exciting event for me. I had never been to the doctor before. In fact, we never went anywhere. The doctor's office was so fascinating with all those shiny chrome tools, and the clean white jackets everyone wore were so different from anything I had ever seen before. The visit to the doctor made me feel important for a short while.

Natural disasters also brought excitement to our otherwise-quiet world. One summer the Black River flooded its banks and our entire world was underwater. The only means of transportation was by boat. We had never seen a power-driven boat before. I very well remember the first time it came to the house bringing us food. I took one glance at that huge monster of a thing coming toward the house at such a speed I thought in the next minute it would land right on the porch. It was spraying two huge arches of water out each side of it as it plowed across the surface of the river. Those walls of water on each side almost looked like the wings of a monster or some kind of strange bird. It was making such a dreadful noise as I had never heard before in my entire short life, and screaming with terror I ran inside the kitchen where Mama was, slamming the screen door behind me. "Mama, Mama, there's a motorboat coming! There's a motorboat coming!" I cried. Mama's calm, soothing words of reassurance that it would not hurt us just took away all my fear, and I stopped trembling right away. I felt so small and helpless before such a terrible-sounding thing.

While the front yard was still underwater, Eva, my second-oldest sister, and I decided to go exploring in Daddy's rowboat. With all the excitement of doing something we shouldn't be doing and the adventure of a totally new experience, we began paddling slowly out into what was once our front yard. Not having much strength in our young arms for using the paddles and with no knowledge of how to guide a boat, we drifted up against an old oak tree.

To our horror, there was a huge black spider crawling on the rough, bumpy bark of that tree. To my little mind that spider was about at least six inches long. It was crawling down the trunk toward us. Its body was so fat and heavy-looking, with long, hairy legs. Just the thought of that creature getting into the boat with us frightened me so much I do believe I would have jumped right out of the boat in order to escape, forgetting at that instant that I could not swim. Our terror was so great, we didn't even scream but began to paddle that boat as fast as our scrawny little arms could work those oars. The inside of that boat never saw us again. I knew I would never get myself in such a predicament as that again.

One unique experience relating to an unfortunate deer hunter remains forever etched in my mind. Laws to protect wildlife had not been passed at that time. Hunters could hunt all year long. Game was very plentiful and, besides, poor folks needed the meat. Late one warm summer afternoon my sister Dana was giving my younger brother, Jim, and me a bath in the galvanized tub on the back porch. Suddenly we heard a shotgun go off in the woods nearby, followed immediately by desperate cries for help. Those haunting cries still resound in my mind even today. They were so mournful, so pleading, and seemed to hang as if suspended in the still, humid air of that fateful afternoon. We were so scared. *What was wrong?* we wondered. *What had happened?*

This is what had happened; In those days some hunters set a string gun trap for deer. Strong twine was attached to the trigger of a shotgun that had been securely fastened to a tree. The twine was then stretched between two other trees in such a manner that when an unsuspecting deer walked into the twine, it would pull the trigger, shooting and, the hunter hoped, killing the deer. The only problem this time was that the poor farmer had forgotten exactly where he had placed the twine and accidentally walked into the trap he had set for the deer. He became the prey. A short time later a mule-drawn wagon came by the house. Lying in the bed of the wagon was the body of the poor man who had been shot. He was so pale and lifeless. I realized some mistakes can be very bad. I have never forgotten that body lying in the wagon. That was my first experience with death, and it made a lasting impression on me.

Life was rather interesting at times for us. I remember a few occasions when Mama left us children alone in the house for a short while at night. The house creaked sometimes like all older houses, and with our childish imaginations we heard things, too. I remember being so scared and hiding down on the floor behind the sofa. We were always so glad to see Mama come home.

Mama's life here on earth was a full one as long as it lasted. She became a born-again Christian early in her married life and immediately began to spread the Gospel of what God had done for her and to show love and compassion to all she knew. Many days were spent fasting, even when she was pregnant with us children. She didn't worry about material food but was most concerned about God's work for her to do. Her trust in God was so great she had no fear for us or for herself.

Once when the doctor was attending her during a serious illness he said to her, "Lady, if you knew your condition it would scare you to death."

Her frank and honest reply was, "Sir, I'm not afraid of anything except God and hellfire."

Years later that same doctor spoke of Mama's great faith and what an impression it had made on him. She never turned away anyone who sought her out for prayer or comfort. Many hours in

11

the night and day were spent on her knees praying, and I am sure those prayers have followed me.

We were living in Curry when Mama died. Daddy had moved us there from Whiteville, where all of us children, except the last little baby, had been born. His reason: he was tired of someone else trying to run his life and even tell our mama what to do. That someone else was his sister, Beulah Howard. As a child she had bossed her brothers around, and as she grew older her controlling personality continued to develop.

I remember the night Mama died. There were so many people in the house, and we had to sleep on the sofa. I just wondered why all those people were there but didn't realize that Mama had died. I'm not even sure a child of only four and a half years of age understands what death really is.

Oh, but that day when Mama left for the last time, that is a picture forever etched in my heart and mind. I was standing on our front porch looking down the lonely dirt road in front of the house. As I stood there feeling so sad and bewildered, I watched an old pickup truck with a two-wheeled trailer attached to it driving slowly away into the distance. On that little trailer was a wooden box. I knew my mama was in that box. They were taking her away, and somehow I knew I'd never be able to see her again. Children at the age of four and one-half don't really understand death. I just knew Mama was gone.

An overwhelming sadness always fills my heart when that picture comes to my mind. It unfailingly brings tears to my eyes. Even now, more than fifty years since that day, it's still hard to believe she's gone. On that day I did not know it, but my simple and tranquil world was soon to change and life for me would never be the same again.

2

At the time of Mama's death my daddy was having an affair with another woman who was pregnant with his child. He had apparently lost his former affection for mama, because he brought his girlfriend along to visit Mama while she was on her deathbed. The two of them even used a fishing-tackle box as a crude coffin to bury the tiny stillborn baby Mama had given birth to a week or so previously.

Shortly after Mama's funeral Daddy sent word to his family that he was planning to put us children in an orphanage. If they didn't want that to happen, they should do something right away or else not say anything to him later about what he did with us children. Mama was gone and he was in love with another woman who was carrying his child and obviously didn't want the responsibility of caring for eight children, so he gave us all up for adoption.

Aunt Beulah Howard, my daddy's sister, instigated the adoption of us children by his brothers and sisters. Aunt Beulah told them God showed her that if they took us children and were good to us, God would bless them, but if they mistreated us, God would curse them just like He cursed those people who mistreated the Israelites in the Old Testament.

The family members were made to feel pressured into taking us and even guilty if they didn't want to take another child to rear when they already had several children of their own. Chris stayed with Uncle Joshua and Aunt Ruth for a very short time but then joined the navy. Dana also stayed with them for a while. But Grandmother wanted to adopt her. Aunt Helen and Uncle Moses took Marie but did not adopt her. Eva was adopted by Aunt Esther. Josie was adopted by Uncle Kevin and Aunt Rosie. Aunt Beulah adopted Jim and me. Uncle Aaron took Tina, but she died six months later of pneumonia.

My daddy had been promised by Aunt Beulah he could visit us

after the adoption, but as soon as he signed the papers releasing his legal right as our parent he was more or less told to get lost and never come around us again. At that tender age I didn't know my daddy had fondled his sister Beulah through an open bedroom window when she was a child, but I learned about it years later. I believe that occurrence had some bearing on my Aunt Beulah's shutting our daddy totally out of our lives. From that time on he could have absolutely nothing to do with our life. I didn't see my daddy's face again for thirty-six years.

Jim and I stayed with Grandmother for a short time while Aunt Beulah waited for Uncle Ron to come from California. Those memories are such fond ones for me. It was so much fun playing in the yard and watching the chickens while they wandered around clucking contentedly as they scratched in the dirt, looking for little seeds and bits of grit. Sometimes, if I wasn't looking where I stepped, my bare foot would land on top of a warm patty of chicken poop. I still remember the feel of the poop as it squished between my toes. A blob would be stuck on top of my big toe and some between my toes. I would have to kick my foot to sling it off. It sounds yucky now, but then it was not bad at all.

All country folks had chickens in those days. I loved to go with Grandmother to the henhouse to gather the eggs. The henhouse seemed such a cozy place to me. It was like a little home. I would even imagine how secure it would feel to have a little place where you knew each night you were safe inside. It would always be there for you. It would never go away. I was already feeling the loss of my own home and of my mama. Now those eggs! It was so fascinating to me that eggs came out of a chicken. How did it happen? How did those big eggs get out of that chicken? Sometimes the eggs were still warm. The eggshells were so pretty, too, round, smooth, and such beautiful colors. I especially liked the brown ones. But I was scared of those chickens, too. Sometimes Grandmother would tell me to go gather the eggs. It was fun to pick the eggs out of the nests that were empty and when the chicken let out a loud squawk as she flew off her nest and the egg was still warm. But if a hen had decided she wanted to "set the eggs," it was a different story. If you reached your hand toward the nest, she would puff her feathers way out on her neck to frighten you and peck you viciously on the hand. One try was all it took for me to decide that I should let Grandmother get the eggs from under that old hen.

One day I was outside at the water pump playing. As was quite often the case, I was doing something wrong. But it was fun. I had taken my hat off and was pumping water in it. Uncle Ron, Aunt Beulah's husband, saw me, walked over, and told me to stop. Would you believe I can remember today exactly what came to my mind? *You don't have anything to do with me and I don't have to listen to you*, I thought to myself. So I continued pumping water in my hat.

When he saw I wasn't going to stop, he thumped me very hard on top of my head. The thump hurt my dignity and my feelings more than anything else. Feeling sorry for myself, I turned and walked into the house, crying as I went. I had no idea at the time that very soon this strange man I knew very little about would be my stepfather and I would be calling him Daddy.

I also developed a very serious ear infection during that time while at Grandmother's. We were not carried to the doctor for anything, nor did we have medicine to take. I remember hurting so bad at night, tossing and turning, crying for what seemed to me like hours from the pain.

The infection became so bad my ear began to drain. Grandmother had me sit in a chair with a towel draped over my shoulder to catch the puss as it dripped out of my ear. I was too sick to go out and play. The drainage actually made my ear feel better, however. It is a miracle I can hear as well as I can today. I know God was looking out for me.

The most profound impression left in my mind from that short stay at Grandmother's was formed one night while I sat by the fireplace in the kitchen. I was all alone. A fierce wind was howling outside. It was cold. There was a warm pile of glowing coals in the fireplace with a soft flame flickering above them. As the coals popped and cracked and the tiny flames flickered up now and then, a small mantel clock slowly ticked away the passing time: *tick, tock, tick, tock.* I can still hear it, though now it seems so very far away. I guess it was the loneliness of the hour that made such an impression on me. I think of it now, and I feel the same way, so lonely, sad, abandoned, everyone so far away from me, almost as if time had stopped. And in one sense, my world at that time had stopped. My dearest possession had been taken away from me, my dear mama. As much as I could understand at that time, I knew she was gone and I would never see her again. I missed her so much. Even now as I think of it that same lonely feeling comes to me, one of abandonment, of being far away from something that means more to me than anything else in the world.

Very shortly my life was to take a totally different turn and would never be the same again. We were going to a faraway place called California, so far away that we had to ride there on a train. Aunt Beulah had come and told us about all the wonderful things in California; the big city lights, the tall buildings, something we had never seen before. We would be able to see the ocean, the big zoo where all those animals were kept, animals we had never heard about, let alone seen.

When she described the train ride to us, it sounded so unbelievable. Then we began to feel excited. We had never seen a passenger train in our entire lives. Just think—we could sleep and eat on the train. We couldn't imagine anything like that. The anticipation of the ride to California began to build, and when the time finally arrived that everything was ready to go we could hardly control ourselves.

On the train ride to California Jim was the center of attention everywhere we went. The waitresses in the dining car soon learned Jim's name and looked forward to waiting on us. Even at the tender age of two and a half, Jim would wink at the waitresses; they got such a kick out of that. He also amused those around him with his mimicry.

The pantomime I remember so well was his imitation of someone trying to light a cigarette. Jim would take the pack of cigarettes out of his pocket, take out one cigarette, put the pack back into his pocket, take the cigarette between his thumb and index finger, and tap it on his knee as he had seen men do. Then he would place it between his index finger and long finger. Next he would take out his matches. Now for the real show! He would tear one off the pack and strike it, and it would burn out. He would tear another one off and strike it as before, with the same result. After several attempts he would finally succeed in getting his cigarette lit. Then he would very deliberately put it to his lips and commence to puff on it, doing the entire scene with his eyes closed. All those watching thoroughly enjoyed the show. He really was fascinating to watch.

It was fun to go to bed at night. The sleeping berth was more beautiful than anything we had ever seen before. There were colorful curtains at the windows. The floors were either stained brown or covered with beautiful rugs. And bunkbeds! I had never seen beds like that before. I opted to sleep in the top bunk. It was so much fun climbing the ladder up to the top, then being able to look down on Jim and Aunt Beulah while I was up so high. I can in my mind still hear the clackety of the wheels of the train as it ran over the joints of the track, *clackety, clackety, clackety,* until it would lull you right off to sleep.

The landscape was so interesting to us little country kids who up to that time had never been outside of Columbus County, North Carolina. After all the green trees in North Carolina, the mountains out west amazed us. All those huge rocks with virtually nothing on them.

Unfortunately, the trip ended too soon. Before we hardly knew it, we were leaving the train to begin a very new and quite different life in San Diego, California. Uncle Ron had gone ahead of us on another train because he was in the process of buying a home in Bay Park, one of the many residential areas of San Diego. Uncle Ron was employed at the naval base there, working for Civil Service.

He had spent almost thirty years in the navy, Aunt Beulah said. There were years she didn't see his face for twelve months at a time. Now he had been planning to retire, and he and Aunt Beulah were going to travel, but he had to start all over again to raise Jim and me. Aunt Beulah said Uncle Ron had to start all over again to raise us boys. That was repeated to us over and over again through the years, and it instilled a tremendous sense of guilt in our hearts for ruining their lives. If it weren't for us, they could have been happy.

When I first saw the house, it seemed unbelievable that we were going to live there. It was a white stuccoed house with a red tiled roof. There was a garage, a garage! I had never heard that word before, let alone known what it meant. But it was where Uncle Ron kept his car so it wouldn't be damaged by the sun and bad weather.

The streets were paved with black asphalt, and there were

cement sidewalks all along the streets. All our lives we had only been accustomed to dirt roads. And we had never seen a cement sidewalk.

Back home our yard was white sand, which we kept clean with a broom-straw rake, but here even the yards had beautiful green grass, with lovely flowers of every imaginable color blooming along the edges of the yards. There were oleander bushes ablaze with pink, red, and white blossoms lining the streets, too. Roses trailed up little wooden fencelike things called trellises. And there were flowers, prettier flowers than I could have ever imagined. Those daises were Shasta daises, the size of saucers, with the edges so frilly, as if they had been cut with scissors again and again until they looked like shredded confetti. It was such a different place from anything we had seen before.

I suppose it was the things that were soon to follow that caused the memory of that house to have left such a clear picture in my mind, but today, almost fifty-two years later, I can draw a picture of the house and a floor plan, too. The front door opened into the living room. To the left and beyond the living room space was the kitchen with the dining table. There was a spare bedroom immediately behind the living room. As you walked to the back of the living room and to the right, you entered a small hallway that separated Beulah and Ron's bedroom from our bedroom. The bathroom was situated between the two bedrooms. A little stoop opened outside the kitchen door toward the garage. It was a nice house. We liked it very much.

We were soon settled in and life began to have some routine to it. Jim and I had our own separate beds and didn't have to sleep crowded together in a small bed like we had done back home. There was a pretty white bathtub in which we got a bath instead of the old galvanized tub we were used to. There was the strange thing called the commode to use instead of the outside toilet or the enamel slop jar we were accustomed to using. And to eat we had all kinds of things we never knew about until then, cantaloupe, cereal for breakfast, just wonderful food, so much of it, and all we wanted to eat.

But lessons were soon to be learned. The first one had to do with that commode thing. I had never seen a commode before. Like I said, we were accustomed to using an outside privy, or when the weather was bad and at night, we used an enamel pot called a slop jar. I suppose Aunt Beulah thought us little country bumpkins would play in the commode, so she was going to teach me a hard lesson. I was already sort of afraid of it, that round bowl where all that noisy water went swirling around and around, then disappeared. First Uncle Ron showed me how a cloth would get sucked right down that hole. He flushed the commode and the water sucked the rag right out of sight. I was watching in amazement.

Before I knew what had happened, he picked me up by the ankles, held me headfirst over the bowl, and then flushed the thing again. I had seen that cloth going down the hole and only Uncle Ron holding onto it keeping it from completely disappearing, and in my childish mind I did not know that I was too large to fit down the hole. I just knew I would also go down that hole. In sheer desperation, I grabbed the sides of the bowl, held on with a vicelike grip, and screamed as loudly as I could. The terrifying noise of the water swirling around in that strange thing right in front of my eyes made it seem like a monster to me. I was never so glad to be put back down on the floor. Needless to say, I never, but never, played in the commode.

These experiences that happened to me were as if they had been burned into my subconscious with a hot iron. They seem as real to me today as they did over fifty years ago.

I remember our first Christmas in California. It was the only Christmas I had ever experienced at that time in my short life. Back home we were so poor, Christmas just came and went. It was just another day. We were rather bewildered on this Christmas morning. We knew nothing about Santa Claus or presents and were just kinda wandering around the living room. Aunt Beulah had told us about Santa Claus, but until you experience it, you don't know what to expect. I remember Aunt Beulah finally had to tell us to look behind the sofa. When we walked around behind the sofa and spied shiny brand-new red tricycles, we couldn't believe our eyes. There was one for each of us. We had never seen anything like them. We were so tickled. We had to be shown how to ride them. Of course we were eager to go outside to play. We had a long wide cement driveway where we could ride our tricycles. The driveway was on an incline, with the higher part being out by the street. Our yard did not have any grass in it yet. The grass seed had been planted but had not had time to come up. Our yard was one big field of red clay.

Aunt Beulah gave us very explicit instructions that we must not ride our tricycles into the clay yard. She was a very fastidious housekeeper, extremely clean and orderly, and didn't want her house or our clothes soiled with red clay. You know how kids are when they play—they really don't think about what they are doing until it is too late. We pedaled around the drive awhile, and after becoming more accustomed to our new toys we became a little braver, going a little faster. We were at the top of the drive headed downhill toward the garage when, before we realized it, we were going so fast we couldn't control our direction and ran right off the drive into the red clay dirt, turning over as well, getting that red clay all over our clothes.

We were concerned but not really that scared, because we had not intentionally run off the drive. We told her we did not ride our tricycles into the yard on purpose, but it made no difference. "Come on," she said. "I'm going to whip you for being disobedient to me." No amount of pleading would do any good. I ran to Uncle Ron, whom by that time we called Daddy, and begged him not to let her beat us. We had not done anything to deserve a beating, I pleaded. But he just threw his head back, laughed, and said, "You are getting just what you worked for."

When those words came out of his mouth, it was as if something inside me were squeezed very tight into a knot, as if I were being crushed in a vise, and I knew I would just have to hold myself together and take what was coming. I was alone. There was no one to help me. There was no way out. I was trapped. There was no escape. She held us down on the floor and beat the living daylights out of us. From that time on I began to fear this woman who was once our aunt but whom we must now call Mother.

She was a pretty woman, too, about five feet, one inch tall, of medium bone structure, but with decidedly bowed legs. She had rather large knees for her size, and her right one swelled and became quite stiff because of an injury she sustained on a city bus. The bus driver slammed on the brakes just as she stood up to leave, and her body twisted around while her foot remained stationary, tearing the ligaments in her knee joint. The pain was so great she fainted, and the bus driver thought she had been drinking. Mother had a small rather delicate face that tapered slightly down to her chin. Watching her powder her face always intrigued me, for it was so interesting to see how the powder transformed her pale, smooth skin into a beautiful palette of the faintest pink. Her cheeks were then the color of a delicate rose, and her small, slightly upturned nose no longer had an oily sheen to it, for the powder took care of that, too. But her lips. She didn't have much lips. They were thin and almost like a straight line. She would purse them tightly together as she viewed herself in the mirror when she powdered herself up before going out. She held those lips in that thin line and would flip her hand by her hair on each side of her face. Then she was usually satisfied with her appearance. I was fascinated with the clothes she wore. I had never seen such fancy clothes as hers. Being so poor, my mama had always just worn very simple dresses, but Mother had beautiful suits with big square shoulders that made her look strong and powerful when she stood in her high-heeled shoes. Ah! Such shoes. The heels of some of them were so high I was amazed that she could walk in them. But they were pretty, and they made her look so fancy. When she got ready to go somewhere, she made sure everything about her person was just right before she went out. She was our mother now, and I was proud of her.

Mother was good to provide us with material things, and we had many wonderful times and experiences we would never have had if she and daddy had not taken us in. I remember the time when I first saw the ocean. I just stood there in utter amazement and said, "My, my, all that water." I just couldn't believe there could be so much water in one place. Also, our first visit to Balboa Park, one of the most famous zoos in this country, stands out in my mind. We got all dressed up too in pretty suits and patent-leather shoes. Daddy was dressed in a suit and tie, and Mother had her fancy suit on with those really high-heeled shoes. It was not like we were going to the park where stinky animals were, but more like we were going to church.

Mother had stressed to us the importance of staying close to her and Daddy so as not to get lost. And she said whatever we did, not to go looking for them if we became separated. I had already developed a bad habit of looking at anything that interested me so I could absorb all the details of it. Everything about people was worth noticing to me, their eyes, the shapes and sizes of their noses, their ears, the shapes of their faces, and I could go on and on, for I observed every single tiny detail of the complete person. Mother would always say, "Johnny, quit staring." My answer was always the same: "I'm not staring; I'm just looking." Anyway, we were at the zoo standing by the huge cage where the monkeys were kept. As I never had seen a monkey before, they were enough to keep my attention. But in addition someone had put a long piece of rope inside the cage with them. Those monkeys were just like a school-yard full of children: they were chasing each other up the bars, down the bars, swinging across from limb to limb in the trees in the cage. One monkey would get the rope away from another one and run as fast as he could. Even the mother monkeys with babies cling-ing to their backs were playing the game. Those little babies would hold on for dear life as their mother streaked all over the place try-ing to keep the others from getting the rope away from her. It was a sight to see.

I was like someone rooted to the spot. I couldn't keep my eyes off those monkeys. After a while I looked around for Mother, Daddy, and Jim, but they were nowhere to be seen. Remembering what Mother had said, "If you get separated from us, don't leave that place to look for us, but stay right where you are and we will come back and find you," I did just that. I turned back around and proceeded to watch the monkeys play. In a short time Mother came back for me just as she had promised.

Going to the zoo was so much fun even if we did have to dress up like we were going to church. We wore suits and patent-leather shoes. I guess Mother wanted to show us off to others who were there. A pretty girl named Darlene, who also lived in our suburb, would go with us sometimes. We three children would play games, slide on the tall slide, and swing in the swings. Mother and Daddy carried a picnic dinner, and we ate at the tables placed around the park for that purpose. There was nothing quite like those trips to the zoo.

There were the fun times during the summer when we played in the yard. I was perfectly content if I had construction paper, pencils, crayons, a pair of scissors, and some straight pins. I could sit for hours drawing airplanes, cutting them out, and putting them together. They were made to have wings, wheels, and even propellers on the wings. I would fasten the propellers on the wings with the straight pins. Jim would always beg me to make him one. I'd say, "Make one yourself." But if he begged hard enough, I would relent and make him one, too.

Mother bought us little planes made out of balsa wood at the store. There was a vacant lot near our house where we went to play with them. That lot still stands out so vividly in my mind. It seemed so immense to me then, as I was accustomed to our small yard at home. It was a sandy lot with small scrubby bushes scattered here and there and wild grass growing on it, too. Little hills made excellent places on which to stand and launch my planes. I remember how the grass swayed in the soft breeze that blew over the field on the best days for flying. It was the perfect place for our planes.

The balsa planes had a strong rubber band that attached to the propeller at the front and to a notch cut in the back of the body just below the tail. You would twist the propeller until there was lots of tension on the rubber band. Then, holding the propeller, you would throw the plane forward, releasing the propellor at the same instant. With a steady buzz the little plane would soar out into the sky. It was surprising how far it would fly before crashing, especially when a gentle breeze was blowing to help carry it along. We would spend hours flying those planes.

Jim and I were so different. I could amuse myself alone. I liked doing things with my hands. Jim needed someone to help keep him entertained. He was an outdoor person who loved hunting and fishing. He dreamed of someday going fishing with Uncle Max, whom he adored. When we were outside, Jim would beg Mother to make me play with him so he could play fishing. To go fishing, he would sit in our little red wagon and throw out a piece of old rope he had found. The rope was his fishing line. He had already placed some boards around in the yard. They were the fish. When he threw out the line, my job was to tie the rope around the board nearest where the rope had landed. In that way he pretended he had caught a fish. I would dutifully play with him for a while; then, becoming bored, I would quit. But for that short space of time, I had made Jim very happy.

Our neighbors behind us, I remember very clearly, had a very ugly place. There were lots of dead spots in the yard, and all kinds of litter were lying around the place. A big hole in the middle of the yard provided a place for their children to fill with water and splash around in like ducks.

In comparison, our house and yard always looked so pretty. Mother kept everything orderly and neat, and her flowers were gorgeous. One summer we had a plague of snails. They were eating everything green and especially Mother's flowers. The best method of ridding oneself of snails was simply picking them off the flowers and dropping them into a pail of strong brine solution, made by mixing lots of salt into a bucket of water. She gave us the job, and what fun it was! We didn't mind those old snails one bit, even though that bucketful of dead snails looked rather nasty. But best of all, we were doing something for Mother. We were making her happy.

Mother was strict, however, and had very little patience. I remember the first time we went shopping downtown. I was awestruck by the size of those tall buildings reaching up into the sky, all those cars going up and down the street, and my, oh, my, so many people. Never had I seen anything like that in my short life. You must realize we had lived in a very isolated rural area of North Carolina and had never been anywhere else until that time. As was usually the case, I was looking at something that had caught my eye, not paying attention to the fact that Mother and Jim were leaving me behind as we were crossing the street. Mother reached back, grabbed me by the hand, and pulled me forward to catch up with them. Then, I guess to teach me a lesson, she took a little piece of skin on the back of my arm between her thumb and long finger, pinching the skin so hard it felt like it would cut right through the flesh. It hurt so bad, I winced in pain. At times like that, her tone of voice was always harsh and impatient. Along with the good times, there was the ever-present fear of being punished, even for something I did not do intentionally or even realize I had done.

There were other events that intensified our fear and reverence for her. Poor Jim ran from her once when she was going to beat him for something. He was halfway through the living room before she caught him. I'll never forget what she said: "I'm going to beat you first for what you did and then again for running." He never ever tried to run from her again. Another time Jim and I were outside playing. There were some clothes hanging on the line. Jim, even at a very young age, was fascinated with women's underclothes. He pointed to a pair of Mother's underpants and said, "Kacky dooky." It seemed to me at the time what he had said was like cursing, and knowing we weren't supposed to say ugly things like that, I told Mother. She mixed up a soapy suds solution, made poor Jim open his mouth, and filled it with that horrible stuff. I can still see her holding one hand over his mouth and the other hand under his chin to prevent his opening his mouth to spit the suds out. He was suspended off the floor in her strong grip with his feet dangling down as he kicked and tried to scream, but without success. She held him until he swallowed the nasty stuff. When I saw what Mother had done to him, I never told on him again, never.

One afternoon we were outside playing. Mother called me to the kitchen door. When I stepped inside, she said, "Look what you caused me to do." It was then I saw her finger. She had been cutting rutabaga turnips for supper. The knife had slipped, almost cutting the last digit of her little finger off. It was bleeding quite profusely, and the piece of finger was just hanging by a thread of skin. *How could I have caused her to do that?* I thought to myself. *I was out in the yard.* At the same time, I felt like all my blood had drained down into my feet. Then I said to myself, *I guess if she said it, there must be some way I don't know about that I caused her to do that.* I really expected her to beat me, but I guess a cut and bleeding finger prevented it. I pondered over that, though, for a long time, trying to understand how I had caused her to cut herself. She went to the doctor and had it sewn back together. She was left with a very little scar.

Jim was such a cute child back then, and being two years younger than I, he was much more gullible. As I have said before, we did not have electricity in our mama's house back in North Carolina, so we were not even familiar with the light switches on the wall. Jim had an intense fear of policemen. I'm not sure why. Maybe it was because he remembered the time a policeman stopped by the road when we lived in Currie and picked up someone on the roadside and carried him away. All Mother had to do to make Jim burst into tears was go stand by a light switch on the wall and pretend she was calling the police. Little Jim's mouth would fly wide open and he'd start bawling at the top of his lungs. It seemed to amuse Mother, for she did it quite a number of times. It would take a lot of reassurance then to get him to stop crying, too.

At that time in our lives, Jim loved to talk and I was the shy, silent one. Mother would get so aggravated at Jim for talking so much. As she had been accustomed to living alone with Daddy, I'm sure it was nerve-racking to have a little child chattering all the time. When she had had enough, she would seize him by the shoulders, lift him off the floor, plop him down hard in a chair, and say with that stern exasperated voice, "You sit here and don't you say another word until I tell you to. Is that clear?" He would sit there just a very short time, then would raise the index finger of one hand, point to it with the index finger of the other hand, and say, "Mother, I have an idea." If that didn't work, he would wait a few more seconds, then say, "Mother, can I talk now?" He just found it very difficult to remain silent for very long at a time.

When we went shopping, Jim being younger than I, Mother usually asked me to stay in the car with the packages she had bought while she and Jim went inside to run a quick errand. One day, though, Mother told Jim that I should have a turn going with her and he should take a turn sitting in the car. She promised him if he wouldn't pout, she would bring him an ice cream. He liked to pout if he didn't get his way. When we came back to the car, Jim was sitting in the backseat with his mouth all puckered up like a toad. Mother said, "Well, just because you are pouting, I'm going to eat your ice cream myself." And she did. Mother ate his ice cream right there in front of him. I felt so sorry for Jim. Poor little fellow couldn't hold it in very long before bursting into tears. Mother continued eating the ice cream while he bawled his heart out. I was hoping she would relent after a while and at least let him have some of it, but she ate the whole thing.

I remember pouting, too, a couple of times. The second time while I was pouting, I thought about what I was doing; I didn't feel good being all puffed up and hateful and it was not changing anything, either, so I said to myself, *Pouting is not fun. I'm not going to be that way anymore. I'll just learn to take disappointment and not let it bother me so much.* Years and years later I asked Mother about it and she said it was indeed true that I had only pouted once or twice.

Jim was always trying to decide what he wanted to be when he grew up. When he first saw a fireman on the pretty red fire truck, he said, "I want to be a fireman when I grow up." Then he saw some cowboys on horseback. "I want to be a cowboy," he said. The one that really tickled me was when Jim saw an old man walking down the street with a long white beard. "That's what I really want to be when I grow up; I want to be Santa Claus," he proclaimed.

Jim had a problem wetting the bed, probably brought on by the trauma of losing his mama and then being taken to a strange place with people he hardly knew. In an effort to control the bedwetting, Mother gave us only a small amount of liquids at suppertime. And that was all for the night. No water or anything to drink before going to bed. The only problem with that is certain foods make you more thirsty than others. After certain meals we were still thirsty. We did not dare ask for more to drink. She had told us over and over, "If you won't drink too much before bed, you won't wet the bed."

Even little tots like us were ingenious. We discovered a way to get some water without her knowing about it. We knew if we turned the water spigot on she would hear us, and if she knew we were drinking water she would beat us. So we would wait until Mother left us in the tub to get our bath. At first we would soak our washcloth in the water and suck the water out of the cloth. It was sooo good. But that took too long to satisfy our thirst, so we learned to put our lips to the surface of that beautiful clear blue water and drink our fill. Oh, it was so delicious! The urge to drink when one is thirsty is a basic instinct, so we did just that. Mother never found out about that, either.

Poor Mother, in an effort to help train us to use the bathroom at night, would try to wake us up at a certain hour to go pee. We were both extremely sound sleepers. After trying repeatedly to wake us up, she would become impatient and exasperated. Then she'd go get the toaster cord from the kitchen, come back, and swing that thing hard down across our backs, shouting "Wake up! Wake up! Put on your slippers!" Those precious slippers! We weren't allowed

27

to walk on the floor without our slippers. I recall so well sitting on the side of the bed and, in a sleepy stupor, sliding my hand across the bottom of my foot over and over thinking I had put my slipper on my foot. When she hit me with the cord, I would jump and holler at the same time, then rub my hand over my foot again. I'm sure it was very frustrating to her. After many attempts and more blows from the cord, I would somehow manage to wake up enough to get on those slippers and make it to the bathroom.

Another time, Jim, in his sleepy state, thought he was in the bathroom and pee-peed all over my coloring book that was lying on the bottom shelf of the nightstand between our twin beds. The next morning when I discovered it, I was angry with him at first. I said, "You silly thing, you peed on my coloring book. It's ruined."

"I'm sorry," he said with a truly plaintive tone in his voice. "I thought I was in the bathroom. I wouldn't have done it for anything if I had known it."

So there was no way I could be upset at him. After all, it was only a coloring book.

I was the bad person, too, sometimes. Jim being quick as a cat, would always get the best of the boxes Mother threw out the back door for us to play with. One particular time, he jumped up and got the box I wanted so badly. That time it was more than I could take. I jumped up, seized him by the arm, and bit him hard. The poor fellow started crying, went in the house, and told Mother, who then told him to bite me, which he wouldn't do of course. I realized then it was not his intention to hurt me by getting the boxes. He was just faster than I. That realization made me regret what I had done. I sat down in the garage and cried and cried for a long time. Mother said I had punished myself enough, so she wouldn't beat me that time.

I suppose in desperation to get Jim to stop wetting the bed Mother would try anything. One night right after we had gone to bed, Mother came to the room and called for Jim to go with her. He stayed gone for a few minutes, and when he returned, always being afraid as we were now, I asked him what had happened. He told me she had led him to the kitchen by his penis, pulled a big sharp butcher knife out of the drawer, then told him if he didn't stop wetting the bed she was going to cut off his penis. Knowing the things she had done already, I really thought she would do just that.

28

The most frightening experience for Jim, however, came one night right after we had gone to bed. I was almost asleep. All of a sudden in a frantic voice, Jim whispered, "Johnny, is that you?"

I couldn't imagine what he was talking about. I said, "No, go to sleep."

A few seconds later he repeated the same question, only that time his voice carried a more urgent tone. I responded as before. The third time he asked me, he did not whisper and his voice sounded desperate: "Johnny, is that you?"

By then I was getting irritated. "No, you silly thing, it's not me; go to sleep."

The very next second, Jim jumped out from under the covers, landed on his knees, and began to flail wildly with both hands at the body beneath him on the bed, all the while screaming as loudly as he could, "Mo-other , Mo-other, there's a policeman in my bed."

What Mother had done was get in the bed with Jim, lie down beside him, take hold of his penis, and very softly in a low, threatening voice say to him, "I'm a poliiiceman." Each time she said that to him, he would ask me, "Johnny, is that you?" After the third time, he couldn't take it any longer. He went into action. After beating her in the face and on the chest with both fists for a few seconds, he jumped up and ran off the bed right onto the floor toward Mother's bedroom, screaming as he went, "Mo-other, Da-addy, there's a policeman in my room!"

As soon as Jim started beating her, she had tried to tell him it was she, but the poor child was so terrified he didn't even hear her.

Daddy was coming to our bedroom door to see what was happening, and Jim collided with him in the hallway outside our room. Daddy put his arms around Jim just about the time Mother got there and he then saw it had been she who was in his bed. It took a while to calm his frayed nerves. The next morning Mother had bruises on her face Jim had inflicted with his little fists. Needless to say, he was quite sorry he had done that to her. Can you imagine a mother doing such a thing to a child?

It was in our home in California that religion first took root in my life. The events that occurred during Uncle Sam's visit to our home were all connected to the church. Uncle Sam was the preacher in our church back home in North Carolina. The words Mother said

29

to us before his visit and the things that happened after his arrival instilled firmly in me the belief that Mother was truly a person of God and one with whom God communicated.

The night before Uncle Sam was to arrive, I had two very strange dreams. In my first dream, a huge bull as black as coal came into our living room and died in the middle of the floor. In the other dream, there was a witch sitting on the vanity stool in Mother's bedroom combing her hair. I'll never forget how Mother reacted when I said to her the next morning, "Mother, I had a dream last night." We were in the hallway outside her bedroom. She stopped in midstride, turned to me, and with a very serious expression on her face said to me, "Son, what did you dream?" I somehow realized she put a great deal of importance in what I was going to say.

At that time I had no recollection of having heard about it before, but I had almost died as an infant. Mother, who was then just my Aunt Beulah, and my biological father had taken me to the doctor while my mama stayed home and prayed. The doctor, after examining me, had told them to take me back home and that I probably wouldn't live through the night. I had a severe kidney infection and was passing pus in my urine. Aunt Beulah stopped by the roadside on the way back to our house to pick some flowers to put on my grave. She was that certain that I would die. When they arrived back home, my dear mama met them at the door to tell them her good news. She had prayed earnestly while they were gone, and God had shown her that little Johnny would live and would grow up to be a preacher of righteousness.

Mother seemed to have a certain kind of respect for me, as if I, too, had some special relationship with God. Her treatment of me at that time planted the seed of a bond between us that over the years would grow so great that nothing or no one but she herself could ever break it.

Before Uncle Sam arrived, Mother told us he was coming and that he would offer us some candy, but that we should not accept it because he was in a terrible spirit and if we took it something could happen to us. That knowledge made us afraid of him. I wouldn't have taken that candy for anything in the whole world. So, sure enough, he arrived the next afternoon and, just as she had said, offered us some candy, which we refused. We were really afraid. Mother sent both of us off to bed right away.

I remember he and Mother stayed up all night long. Uncle Sam had come out there, among other things, to convince Mother that she should visit other churches and let other preachers visit our church. Mother claimed that after her family had been put out of one church God showed her they should be separate from the world and not visit other churches.

While my mama was still living, she and all the other members of the family except Beulah Howard had been put out of the Baptist church they were attending at the time. The elders of that church had agreed not to put Beulah Howard out because she gave a considerable amount of money to the church fund. Mother told me Granddaddy had voted against a certain lady in the church being given the position of church pianist, because she was having an affair with the pastor. He didn't believe such conduct was appropriate for elected members of the church. Also, Mother said that some of the church members were displeased and annoyed with my mama's praying. They said she was disturbing them next door. For those reasons Mother's family was put out of the church. Mother owned a piece of property, and a small, simple A-frame wooden church was erected on the property. That was the founding of what became known as the Roberts Church and the Roberts religion.

Where my family went wrong was in not forgiving the people *if* they had treated the Roberts wrongly by putting them out of the church. Christ taught that we are to love our enemies, do good to them who despitefully treat you, and pray for those who mistreat you, but the Roberts never did; rather, they held onto the grudge over having been put out of church their entire lives. They never set foot in that church again, either, and they never had anything at all to do with any of its members but treated them as if they were infidels.

So Beulah Howard then proclaimed that God showed her they, meaning her parents and brothers and sisters and their wives, were called out from the world and should remain separate from the world and have nothing to do with other churches or pastors, either. They were to be like the Children of Israel, called out of the world to be different, to be God's chosen people. I suppose that was why we didn't attend church in California. We went to church only twice the three and a half years we lived in California.

The next morning, Mother and Uncle Sam were still talking. They had been up all night. Mother would not be persuaded to change her mind. She wouldn't budge. She maintained that she was right and he was wrong. He must repent. She was a stronger person than he, so she prevailed. Already the seed had taken root that would grow into the monster of control over the entire family. It was her way or no way at all. She was right and everyone else was wrong. But to us at that time in our lives it was almost as if we had been delivered from something terrible that could have destroyed us. Our confidence and trust in Mother were greatly strengthened. Many years must pass before we learned the truth.

From the very beginning of our stay in California, Mother had made it very clear to us we must never get out of bed until she came to our bedroom and gave us permission to get up. So I well remember Jim and I lay there in those little twin beds that Sunday morning, growing hungrier and hungrier by the minute. We tossed and turned, singing a little ditty to pass the time away. It went like this: "Mother, come get us up; it's ten-thirty." We sang that little tune over and over and over. Finally, at about 3:00 P.M., Mother came to the door and said the magic words: "You can get up now. It's time to eat."

She had prepared a wonderful dinner. I won't ever forget how delicious that meal tasted. Jim was so hungry, though, he just crammed the food down, making himself sick, and then had to throw up. He tried eating again but was only able to hold down a small bit of food. Then we were allowed to take the candy Uncle Sam had brought, which we thoroughly enjoyed.

Something else happened that day that stands out in my mind. Someone had sent Mother a beautiful bouquet of roses. She put them in a vase of water. The next morning all of the roses were fresh and beautiful except one. It had wilted, and the bud was bent over like someone dead. Mother told us God had shown her that a soul in the church back home was lost forever. In other words, that soul would go to hell, without any hope of redemption.

Thinking of a person up walking around who was going to hell was so frightening to me. I imagined such a person to be something

32

like a demon, like someone possessed with a terrible spirit. I would have fled in terror at the sight of him or her. And I did just that after we had moved back to North Carolina. I spied the poor woman from a distance approaching me on the sidewalk. I began to tremble with fear and fled into the nearest available door and remained there shaking until she had passed by. Our religious brainwashing had already begun at the tender age of three for Jim and five for me.

That was exactly how the other members of the congregation regarded this woman, too. She was a complete outcast from everyone. She was put out of the church, and a member of the congregation was instructed by Mother to tell the poor woman that she was lost forever. Mother said it took five men to hold her on the bed she was so frantic with fear. She lived in torment for months, until her friends and other loved ones convinced her it simply was not true.

Mother said she had to accompany Uncle Sam back to North Carolina kinda like his ambassador. The folks back home were afraid of him, and without Mother actually being there to speak on his behalf, they would not accept him back into the church. She also had to bring that new revelation about the lost soul to the church. You must remember there were few telephones back then. So with Uncle Sam flying back home it was necessary that Mother accompany him on his arrival in North Carolina.

That left Jim and me to stay with Daddy in California. Those events occurred in the month of May. My birthday is May 25, and that day arrived while Mother was away in North Carolina. I don't know what got into me, but I decided I wanted to have me a birthday party. I had heard some of my classmates at school talking about their parties. It sounded like so much fun, getting all those presents, having all those people at the house, and enjoying the good cake and ice cream. I had never had a birthday anything, let alone a party. We simply were too poor. You can imagine just how much I knew about things, too, when I invited a lot of my classmates to my party without first having said a word to Daddy about it.

The mother of one of the children who had been invited called Daddy to inquire about a gift for me. It was then Daddy learned of my plans. Kind, good Daddy went right along with everything. He hastily ordered a cake, some balloons, and some ice cream for us. I had even promised Jim I would give him some of my presents, which I did. I didn't want him to be left out. He enjoyed the party very much, especially the presents. One present was a little kitty. Jim and I loved that kitty. Apparently, it was a bit too young to leave its mother, for it meowed all night long in the garage. The next morning Daddy made us take it back home. He said he couldn't stand that meowing another night. We begged and pleaded with him to let us keep it, but to no avail. We were so sad as we walked a long way carrying our little kitty back to its original owners.

When Mother returned home, I was so afraid I would get a beating for having the party, but that time Daddy talked her out of it. That was a very interesting little chapter of my life.

Our vacation trips back to North Carolina were also rather eventful times for us. We were always excited to be going back home to see our sisters. Once our older brother, Chris, came to see us in California. I think he was stationed at the naval base there. He just visited for the day. That is the only time we actually visited with him. We were usually kept away from him, never being allowed to visit or spend any time with him.

Traveling by car that long distance was boring to us children. We entertained ourselves very quietly in the backseat. Mother didn't want to be bothered with noisy children so we learned to talk very quietly between ourselves and to this day we both speak with calm, quiet voices. In fact, by the time I started school I had developed such a soft-spoken voice that the teachers always had difficulty understanding. Going through the desert where the heat was so oppressive left its impact on us, too. We called it sticky heat because our legs would stick to the seats. When we got one of those first air conditioners, we thought we were really fancy. It was a metal box that attached to the driver's window. You bought dry ice and placed it inside the box. There was a fan inside that blew air across the very cold ice. This then gave us a deliciously cool breeze, which lasted until the ice had evaporated. For us, that simple accessory was as fine as you could get.

We had a little stuffed monkey we played with on the trips back home. We lived very quietly in our make-believe world with that little monkey. It talked and we talked to it. Tiring of playing with the monkey, I used my hands, putting them together with my

34

index fingers and thumbs near one another to form a bird. My two index fingers were the bird's head, and my two thumbs were the legs. My make-believe bird flew all around, alighting on the car seat, flying far away, then returning to its nest. We really could entertain ourselves quite well.

Ah, but when we had to pee! Being afraid of Mother already, we didn't want to bother her, so we waited until it was actually an emergency to ask to go. Then we were expected to be able to relax out by the car on the shoulder of the road with cars coming by making all kind of noise and with Mother telling us to, "Hurry up! Hurry up!" Her yelling at me just made me more afraid, which in turn made it more difficult for me to relax. Several times I was not able to relax enough to do one little trickle but had to get back into the car knowing things would get much worse. After a short while I reached the threshold of pain. My bladder felt like a balloon stretched to the bursting point. If a pin were stuck into it, it would pop. Reaching the point of desperation, I would tell Mother again that I couldn't hold it any longer and we'd again stop. The fear of wetting my pants and getting a beating for that was so great in my mind, too. Somehow the second time I was able to relieve myself, and what a relief it was! Today I simply can't understand why an adult didn't have enough understanding to know little children, like adults, need a more private place to be "excused." It just seems to me Mother resented having to be bothered with us in the first place. There definitely wasn't much maternal love shown in those situations.

A couple of events stand out in my mind from those trips. One evening at the motel, Mother was giving us a bath. I had never used a shower before and was actually a bit afraid of it. We had always used the tub to bathe in at home. There I was, a little child standing far below that huge powerful stream of water pouring down on me and I was simply afraid of it. I hadn't wanted to get under it, either. Mother had pushed me under the water. In addition to my fear of it, the water was so hot I thought it would scald me. I screamed, "It's hot! it's hot!," as I leaped out from under the stream of liquid fire, trying desperately to escape from beneath it.

"No, it isn't; get back under the water!," she shouted as she pushed me back under the scalding hot water. She thought it was my fear that made me jump out from under the water. Then when she was finally finished, she said, "Well, it *was* hot. You look like a boiled shrimp." I pondered over things like that and wondered why Mother didn't know the truth. But being a child, I forgot the bad experiences very quickly.

Because we didn't attend church in California, we looked forward to going to church again in North Carolina. Our church was out in the country where Uncle Max and his wife, Maggie, lived. It was a plain rectangular A-frame wood building, which stood on a small sand hill. The windows were not even etched glass but just plain ordinary glass. Our only means of lighting was a Coleman lantern that hung from the ceiling in the middle of the room. I remember in the summertime huge bugs would fly in the windows, fall on the floor under the light, and spin around and around. They were funny, but we didn't dare laugh. That would have brought severe punishment when we got back home.

One time I was tired and fell asleep during church and Mother beat me soundly when she got me to the house. Our benches were stained wood benches that became very hard after sitting on them for a long time. There was a small table that stood at the front of the church on which lay the Bible and a bottle of olive oil used for anointing the sick and those who were saved so that the spirit would come to dwell within them. There were no additional rooms other than the rectangular space inside the church where everybody sat on the pews. Against the front wall of the church were placed two long benches that had no back to them, and these small benches served as the altar. There was ample space between the altar and the front pews for everyone to kneel when we went to prayer, for in our church we all knelt together at the altar to pray. Just behind the last pew on the left side of the church were a few chairs that were used for us children to sit in while my oldest sister, Dana, taught us the Bible stories out of a Bible-story book. I'll never forget one Sunday morning Dana was teaching about the Ten Commandments and after going over the lesson, she asked each one of us to tell her one of the commandments. When her turn came, one of my cousins said, "Thou shalt not die."

Dana had to smile really big to keep from laughing and answered very kindly to the child, "Honey, you meant 'thou shalt not kill,' didn't you?"

"Yes, ma'am," was the meek reply.

I almost got tickled myself, but such an infraction committed in church would have brought severe punishment, so I stifled the urge to giggle.

Outside and to the left of the church was the cemetery where my mama was buried. We didn't believe in having tombstones, and for years the only means of knowing where anyone was buried was the mound of dirt where the grave was. For a long time there was only the one where Mama had been buried. Six months later was my baby sister Faye's grave. Then there was Granddaddy's grave, then Aunt Linda's. Years later small grave markers were placed to identify where each person had been buried.

In those days people weren't so persnickety about dress for church, and in the hot summertime we went to church barefoot. Being barefoot was fine and dandy until we had to walk across the church yard. Then it was sheer torture. The grass was full of sand spurs, a type of wild grass that grew little round seeds that had needle-sharp thorns sticking out from them. The green ones were bad enough, but when the seeds had dried, the thorny needles became stiff and would stick into the bottom of our feet. They hurt going in, but pulling them out was even worse, almost like pulling out a small dry nail. The pain of it would make you tremble. We dreaded those sand spurs like the plague. You can imagine to what lengths we went tiptoeing across the yard in an effort to avoid those dreaded sand spurs.

Grandmother's! Ah, Grandmother's! There was no place like Grandmother's. She was so kind and sweet to us boys. I can still hear her say in that voice so filled with love and concern for our health, "Beulah, don't you want to give these boys a glass of milk? They need it to help them grow." We were so scrawny at that time. Bless her dear old heart, she meant well, but I always dreaded to hear those words. The milk was good, but there were globs of rich yellow cream floating on top. When those blobs of cream went down my throat, I gagged every time. Such a chore! I was so glad when we finally got enough meat on our bones that she didn't insist on us drinking milk. Grandmother made the most delicious raisin-nut pound cake you ever put in your mouth. I can still taste it right now and would love to have a piece, too.

Once we made a trip back home in the wintertime. One Wednesday night at church, after we had sung a few songs, we had prayer requests; then after that, we all went forward and knelt at the altar to pray. The adults went ahead of us children. As I was kneeling down, before I had put my head down on the floor, I noticed Granddaddy had knelt down, then immediately raised his head and trunk up, turned around, sat on the floor, stretched his legs out in front of him, and fallen backward flat out on the floor. Next he began to turn all different colors.

I was intrigued. I had no idea what was happening, but I kept my eyes glued on him. First he turned red, then purple, then blue as a huckleberry, and finally he became as white as a sheet. By the time Granddaddy had turned purple, Daddy had noticed him and nudged Mother to bring it to her attention. She frantically crawled over to him, calling out loudly to the others near her to pray with all their might. "Papa's dying," she said. Everyone began praying very earnestly all in a loud voice at the same time.

After a few minutes, when they realized there was no hope for his return, they ended the service and carried him out. I remember he had wet a large round spot in his pants as he was dying and Mother put her sweater over the spot to cover it. He was already stiff like a board when they took him out of the church, because I remember he didn't even bend when they picked him up and carried his body out. I was amazed! They placed him over the seats in somebody's car and carried him to Grandmother's, and his body just lay there exactly like a board. That was my second experience with death, only this time it was very close to me but not frightening at all. When I looked at him in the coffin, I remembered that same feeling of sadness at knowing he was gone and I would never see him again.

During another of our vacations back home in the summer, something happened in church that really frightened me and made me realize how serious religion was. It was during a Sunday-morning service. There was a great-uncle of mine, Uncle Charlie, who many times would give long testimonies in church. He talked very slowly and deliberately. That morning something strange was going on, but I don't remember all of it. I do remember sensing that Mother perceived the poor man to be evil and was able to convince the congregation of that as well and that he must also be put out. Mother stood up before the congregation and asked the people who in there would be willing to obey the Spirit and put Uncle Charlie out of the church. Uncle Moses would have nothing to do with it. Mother focused her attention on Uncle Sam and told him if he would be willing to obey the Spirit, God would heal him.

Uncle Sam had a hernia that had bothered him for years. I remember seeing him press his hand against his lower abdomen when he preached in church, especially when he preached in a loud voice to dramatize his point or when the Spirit really came to him greatly. Sometimes his face became very pale from the pain he was experiencing. So he and Uncle Kevin picked that poor man up bodily, carried him out the door, and set him down on the front steps. I'll never forget it if I live to be a hundred years old.

I was very frightened. My thoughts were confused. By that time I believed in Mother. I believed God told her to do these things. She had prophesied about the candy in California. If God told her to do something like put someone out of the church, then it meant he was an evil person. Deep inside my heart I felt sorry for him, yet at the same time I was afraid of him. The poor man sat on those steps for a long time, crying so mournfully. He never entered the church again.

And in addition his wife was commanded to live separate from him; in other words, they were not to live as husband and wife. She wasn't even supposed to sit at the same table with him to eat. Mother's power over the people was already firmly established at that early time after my mama's death. My mama didn't believe in such harsh, judgmental treatment of others, but she was gone and unable to do anything about it. Poor Uncle Charlie died years later after spending such a long time separated from many of his people. I remember Mother speaking about it in church, rejoicing that God had delivered Aunt Melinda, Uncle Charlie's wife, and had kept her soul from falling.

I had also been taught by Mother to fear my own daddy. We were taught we must never go near him, lest his bad spirit possess us. It was also preached in church that the only way our Daddy could be saved was for us to remain separated from him. We should pray for him, and *if* he would acknowledge that we were righteous

39

and he was sinful, then God could save his soul. Whenever his name was mentioned, it carried a sense of danger and foreboding with it. If I had seen him, I would have run from him in terror. It didn't take long to instill that intense fear in us, only a few years. When a child is so young as Jim and I were, it is not difficult to brainwash him into believing anything. Think of it; we had seen an adult being carried out of the church bodily. She had foretold us about the candy, and it came true. We also had no avenue of escape if we wanted to. We loved Mother, too. She had rescued us when our own father had abandoned us. She was good to us in so many ways. Put all these things together, and I hope you can understand how she was able to get into our minds so deeply and exert such control over our lives for so long.

Except for those frightening experiences, vacation time brought us a lot of happiness. We got a chance to play with our sisters. One incident stands out clearly. I guess Josie was playing mama one day, but she spit in my hair and combed it to make it lay down flat. My hair was curly. She didn't mean any harm. When Mother saw it, she was livid. She told Josie if she ever did such a thing like that again, she would wear her out, meaning she would beat her with a switch. To this day Josie says she never forgot how frightened she was of Mother that day.

Another time we pulled Granddaddy's mule wagon out from under the barn one day and pulled it down the dirt road a short way. I'm sure we few little scrawny kids couldn't pull that big wagon fast at all, but I remember it seemed to me we were flying. It was so exciting until that night when Granddaddy questioned us about it. We were so scared he was going to beat us. And he did, but it was not bad. He just laid us across his lap and spanked us with his hand. The suspense of waiting for it was worse than the punishment itself. We were always getting into some kind of mischief, us little city boys come back to the country.

I was a very impressionable child even at that early age. In the state of California damaging trees in any way, i.e., cutting one down, climbing one, or breaking the branches off, was against the law. One afternoon as we were leaving the school I saw an older boy climb the tree that stood at the edge of our playground. His weight was too much, and a large branch broke off. The teacher asked if anyone had seen who had done the damage to the tree. Of course, thinking I was doing the right thing, I volunteered the information.

How that boy found out who had told on him I don't know, but a few days later on our way home from school, he met us in the vacant lot between our house and the school. He pretended he had something to give us. At the start I was distrustful of him, but he was very persistent. Then, I reasoned, maybe he was going to be nice. "Hold your hand out," he said. "I have something for you." I extended my hand out to him, and he took a tube of bad-smelling glue and smeared it all over my hand, then quickly turned and ran away.

A few days later, on the way to school one morning, that same boy knocked me down with his bicycle and ran over me. It did not hurt me as much physically as it hurt my feelings. I went on to school crying as I went, sat down on the steps at school, and continued to cry awhile. It felt good to me to feel sorry for myself, but I soon learned it didn't change a thing.

That encounter left me with two very important lessons; one doesn't tell on anyone even if it seems the right thing to do, and you can't trust people; they aren't willing to admit their mistakes and take responsibility for them. I would carry those lessons learned there on that old grassy vacant lot in Bay Park, San Diego, back east with me buried deep inside, never to be forgotten. I didn't realize it at the time, but those experiences laid the foundation for my strength and self-reliance that would carry me through many dark trials in my future life.

3

We moved back to North Carolina in September of 1949. Daddy didn't want to move because he had such a good job at the shipyard there at the naval base in San Diego, California. He knew there were very few good jobs in the town where we would be living. But Mother wasn't happy living so far from her people and said God wanted her to move back to lead and guide her people. They needed her spiritual guidance. The church was having problems, and it was hard for her to help them while so far away. She must move back to do the work God had put on her for her people. Her word prevailed over Daddy's. We packed all our things into a huge van and moved back to rural North Carolina, where I had been born.

Our first home in North Carolina was a rental house in town. We got settled in and then it was off to school. That first day at school left such an impression on me I've never forgotten it all these many years. Since Jim and I didn't arrive in North Carolina until September, we were late registering for classes. I was in the third grade, having completed two years of school in California. When I went to my classroom door to be introduced to my new classmates, the teacher asked me a question, which I cannot remember. While living in California, we had developed an accent similar to that of people from the North. When I answered the teacher's question, the entire classroom burst into laughter. "He sounds funny," they said, and mocked the way I talked. If that incident had been the only negative one, I would have forgotten it quite easily, but from that fateful day until the last day I spent in the school system of the town in which we lived, the ridicule and harassment never ceased; it only grew worse.

The teachers didn't help, either. As was often the case in small towns, most of them showed partiality to the children of prominent members of the community. I'll never forget the day in the third grade a classmate sitting next to me jerked my books off my desk. Of course, the books being mine, I immediately jerked them back on my desk. After the second or third time, the teacher came marching over to my desk with a ruler. She swung it to hit me. I jumped aside. She struck the desk and broke the ruler. Inside I laughed with glee that she had broken the ruler. It was good enough that she had broken her ruler. I hadn't done anything wrong.

I asked, "Why are you beating me?"

She was short and fat with dark black hair. With an almost wild look on her face and with her nostrils flaring she said, "You were jerking those books off his desk."

"They were my books; why don't you beat him?" I answered, and actually with a bit of indignation on my voice. If I had done something deserving of being struck, I would have taken the punishment without a word, but I wasn't going to let her beat me for nothing if I could help it. She kinda snorted in disgust and marched back to her desk. I was afraid to tell Mother about that incident at school for fear she would beat me herself.

That same year while I was in the third grade I got a C in math. We were studying fractions, and I didn't understand the concept of how to work them quite yet. We had a hedge that grew next to the vacant lot behind the house, and Mother broke a long switch off that hedge and beat me black-and-blue with it. I begged. I desperately pleaded with her not to beat me, that I didn't understand the math, that I was trying as hard as I could, that I would do better. "Please Mother, please, don't beat me. I'll try harder," I begged. That made no difference to her. So much was expected of me. So many sudden and dramatic changes were taking place in my life in a very short time. I was having to get adjusted to a new school and new classmates, most of whom regarded me as an odd outsider with a strange way of talking. Then having the very one I most needed to understand me flogging me for something I didn't understand made life very difficult. That day I fully realized how powerful this woman was. The pain of the switch as it wrapped across my naked back was like a knife cutting me. I tried to jump out of the path of the switch as she swung it at me, but she seized me by the arm with a vise-like grip and held me as fast as was possible, for I continued to jump about. After leaving California, she

43

didn't wear the pretty clothes like she had then but wore very plain cotton dresses. She had a stern, harsh, demanding look on her face as she brought that switch down across my back as hard as she could swing it. There was an expression of resentment on her face, too, as if she was angry that she had done so much for me and that in return I was repaying her with such an unacceptable grade. I was quite literally terrified. The cutting pain of the switch was so sharp, and it seemed to last so long. And such blessed relief when she was finally satisfied. The beating didn't make me study any harder; it only made me scared to death on each and every report card day for the rest of my school life, all through grade school, high school, and yes, even dental school.

On report card days my stomach would be upset, I'd have to go to the bathroom several times, and I would be nervous all day long. My mouth would be dry, swallowing was difficult, and my heart would begin beating with a slow, sickening thud every time the thought of my report card entered my mind. I dreaded those days; they seemed to last forever. I found no relief from the sickening dread until I got my report card and saw my grades. If any of them were bad, then those horrible feelings only worsened until after I got home and had received my punishment. It was actually a relief when it was over. Her cruel treatment of me at a time when I most needed her love and support made those days a living nightmare, especially during my grade school and high school years. Fortunately, I managed to get good grades most of the time.

The fourth grade went by rather uneventfully. The girls liked me a lot and I liked them, too, but not as girlfriends, because there were several with whom I wanted to be friends. That didn't always work, however. Reba Mitchell liked me first. Reba had started giving me quarters with which to buy ice cream. Of course I didn't refuse them. The ice cream was so good. We hardly ever got ice cream, and certainly not at school. I became bold enough to write her a note asking how much she was going to give me that day. I would think to myself, *Well, she's going to give me some money so I'll find out how much.* Sometimes it was a dime and other times a quarter. Back then an ice-cream sandwich only cost a dime.

Then a new girl named Betty Ann Arp came to school. Right away she liked me very much. The kids at school picked on her because she was poor. But she was nice to me, and I liked her, too. So Betty Ann wrote me a note in class saying she didn't have money to give me, but she loved me more than Reba did. What was I to do? I liked both girls. Then one night Reba called me at home to tell me if Betty Ann talked to me another time, she was going to get a bloody nose. That really put me in a pickle. I certainly didn't want to be the cause of Betty Ann getting a bloody nose. I tried to explain to Reba that I just liked them both, but she hung up on me still in a tizzy.

Reba stopped giving me money after that incident, which was fine with me because then I didn't have to feel obligated to her, even though I missed the ice cream. I guess both girls realized I wasn't going to commit myself to either one of them, and the turmoil stopped. After all, we were only in the fourth grade and just children.

My artistic ability, which began to manifest itself in California, had developed pretty well by the time I was in the fourth grade. In California in the first grade I drew a picture of my teacher, Mrs. Yettman, with all the students sitting around in a circle on the floor in front of her. I put lots of minute detail in it, too, like the teacher's high-heeled shoes, her glasses, her particular style of dress, and so forth. My teacher was impressed and gave me lots of construction paper to use for drawing. I loved Mrs. Yettman so much.

My fourth-grade teacher asked me to draw a manger scene using colored chalk on the black board in our room for Christmas. After I finished it, another teacher saw it and asked me to draw one for her blackboard, too. I felt quite honored. One of her students, who was also very talented at drawing, became quite jealous because she didn't ask him to draw the scene. I guess she liked my work better. The only difference between his work and mine was its neatness. He could draw just as good as I but was not able to draw freehanded. He always had to prop the heel of his drawing hand against the blackboard, which caused him to smudge the colors together. His work just didn't look neat and crisp like mine did. I told him I couldn't help it that the teacher had asked me instead of him and that I thought his drawing was as good as mine, which was true except for the smudges. That seemed to make him feel better. I certainly didn't want enemies.

I always enjoyed recess time. I loved the outdoors, where I was free to run and play. We played softball at school, and it was fun except I made mistakes that brought me more ridicule. I would try very hard to throw the ball and to catch it. Not having a glove at home to practice with made it difficult. And I wasn't very coordinated and had no self-confidence. Being left-handed didn't help, either. Soon it became obvious that I wasn't a very valuable player. It became very painful always being the last one to be picked for a team. Sitting by watching the others play, seeing how they accepted one another, even when they made mistakes, made my pain even greater. I never remember getting any encouragement from my classmates, only jeers and laughter. Those jeers were the seeds planted in me that grew to make me feel so inferior to everyone else. My mode of survival was to avoid playing unless the teacher insisted upon it. And more than anything else in the world I wanted to be like the other boys, to be accepted by them, to be one of them, not some creep.

Now Jim, he had no problem whatsoever. He was scared of animals but not people. Being more coordinated than I was, and having more confidence, he did fine at sports. He could play ball or anything else he wanted to. I remember seeing him with a group of boys running across the playground like wild horses. If anyone bothered him, he wasn't afraid to jump right into a fight. He would fight anybody. We were so different, he and I. He was afraid of animals, and I was afraid of people. I knew people couldn't be trusted. You could learn about animals and their behavior was quite predictable, but not people. You never knew what they might do.

My sister Eva, who had been adopted by Aunt Esther, also lived in town and would walk to school with us. Those gray cement sidewalks hold vivid memories for me. As we walked along those many city blocks to school, there were times we would meet other children who walked along with us. Eva would embarrass me so. She was always saying she looked like a witch and that she had such ugly lips. Hers, she said, were like a straight line, with no shape at all, but mine were so beautiful. She'd say, "Look at his lips; aren't they beautiful? Look how pointy they are. Mine are so thin and flat. I wish I had lips like that instead of my old ugly ones." Feeling like sinking into the ground, I would tell her if she looked like a witch for just ten minutes, she would change her tune.

But she didn't mean to cause me any grief. I never told her until years later how this made me feel. I loved my sisters so much. I wanted them to be happy.

Once while we were still living on Franklin Street, I spent the day at Aunt Maggie's house. She lived in the country on a farm. I loved to go to the country. I enjoyed watching the cows, Uncle Max's mule, and the chickens. On that particular day, Mother had instructed me to not go anywhere but to stay right there at Aunt Maggie's.

Well, her daddy had a cow barn right down in front of the house not more than a hundred and fifty feet away. I thought nothing of going down there to see the cows. It was not away from Aunt Maggie's. To me "away" was down the road out of sight of Aunt Maggie's house. But the barn was in sight of her house. I had me a good time studying the cows. I absorbed every detail of them, their huge noses with their large openings. Ugh! Sometimes they would lick all the way up their noses with their long tongues. I suppose they were cleaning their nose. After all, they had no hands. But it did seem a bit nasty to me, and I was fascinated. I could have drawn a very detailed picture of one. I even watched Mr. Randy milk the cows. I was amazed how he took those teats in his hand and squeezed them just right and out came the milk in tiny streams. It was still warm, too. He had to be very careful, for sometimes the cow would shift her back legs, hitting the milk bucket, turning it over and spilling that precious milk.

That evening Aunt Maggie told Mother about my going to the barn. When she got me back home, she got me down on the floor in our bedroom between our single beds, put a pillow over my face so I couldn't holler, and beat the daylights out of me. I kicked and tried to scream, but to no avail. I couldn't understand why she was beating me. It seemed so unfair. "I didn't go anywhere. I didn't leave or go down the road. The barn was right in front of the house," I said. Then she told me why she was beating me. Aunt Maggie had informed Mother that her daddy was fairly drunk that day at the barn. I had no idea he was even drinking. I suppose she thought I might like to be drunk myself; who knows? It was another one of those times when she beat me and I really hadn't done anything to deserve it.

47

Rudy, Uncle Moses's son, developed cancer while we lived in town. There was not much known about the disease at that time and certainly very few treatment options. The most anyone could do was pray. It seemed to me Mother took Aunt Helen, Rudy's mother, to our church in the country every day and prayed for him. They would lay him on the altar as they knelt in front of him to pray. Sometimes he would pick pieces of the cancerous tissue out of his mouth and put it on the altar. It was really a very sad situation. The doctors had given up hope. There was nothing they could do. He was slowly wasting away, becoming thinner by the day.

We loved to go to Aunt Helen's. She lived in the country in a big old farmhouse with a large porch that wrapped around two sides of the house. There were chickens and turkeys wandering around the yard and lots of places to play. And besides, she was a wonderful cook. She made the best cakes I had ever eaten. Sometimes Mother would let us stay at Aunt Helen's house while she and Aunt Helen took Rudy to church to pray for him. My sister Marie had been taken by Aunt Helen and Uncle Moses to bring up. They just didn't adopt her, though. On one of those days while they were gone to the church, I grew tired of playing around the house, so I decided to go exploring on their farm. I meandered through the cornfield enjoying the freedom of being where I felt completely safe, taking in all the details of how the corn grew on the stalks, and how the beautiful morning glory vines entwined themselves around the stalks of corn. After a short while, I came to a clearing. In the distance I could hear voices, some laughter, and someone talking. As I peered down through the corn leaves in order to see better, way across from where I was standing, I could see two people. After a few seconds of intense staring I realized they were naked. At about the same second I realized they were naked, they turned and saw me. Having no desire to impose on their privacy and stare at them, and being very frightened as I had been detected, I left immediately. I didn't take another glance in their direction. I didn't even recognize who it was. I most certainly learned from Mother that it was my sister Marie and her stepsister Lisa. They had been swimming at the pond. They told Mother I was looking at them. Mother tore a huge switch from the hedge at Aunt Helen's house and took me out to the tobacco barn, and in spite of my earnest pleas that I

48

wasn't just standing there staring at them but had just accidentally stumbled out onto the clearing and out of simple curiosity was merely trying to determine what was going on, you *know* what happened next. She beat me black-and-blue with that switch. Ah, but it hurt so bad! Another time I had been beaten for nothing at all. But being resilient as children are, I forgot the incident very quickly. Still it left a very strong message deep in my subconscious mind; i.e., naked women were not even to be viewed from a great distance without dire consequences. Later on another incident would occur to strengthen that message even more.

At those times it would scare me to death when Mother was going to beat me. She was a strong woman. When that switch came down on my back, it felt like it would cut the blood out of me. I guess I had sensitive skin, because it felt almost like a knife cutting my back. I would raise my arms to try to stop the switch from hitting me and would get stripes on my arms. She would tell me it was good enough for me for getting my arms in the way. "You had no business getting your hands in the way," she'd say. "I can't help it if you get stripes on your arms." It was embarrassing, too, going to school with stripes on my arms and legs.

Poor little Rudy didn't get any better. One evening as Mother was preparing for us to eat, she reached up to get plates out of the cabinet for supper. I can see her as she reached into that cabinet, then turned toward us and said, "God has put it on my heart to fast so that Rudy will be healed. Do you want me to fix you some supper?" Of course we said no, we weren't going to eat if she wasn't. So we all fasted that night. She had also told Uncle Moses about the fast. Uncle Moses didn't believe God was behind many of the things Mother said God had put on her to do. Mother told us he disobeyed the Spirit and didn't fast. I'll never forget hearing Mother tell Aunt Helen that if she and Uncle Moses had been obedient to the Spirit, Rudy would still be alive. Poor Aunt Helen was weeping so pitifully. They were sitting on the sofa in the living room of our house on Franklin Street. Mother knew how to make people feel very guilty and remorseful.

Aunt Mary, Uncle Aaron's wife, died, too, while we were living on Franklin Street. She was pregnant and became deathly sick after eating seafood with ice cream for dessert. They called it ptomaine poisoning. Uncle Aaron took her to the doctor to get some medicine to stop the vomiting. They were afraid she would lose the baby. She didn't get any better after going to the doctor, however, only worse.

When her condition grew critical she was rushed to Sidberry's Hospital in Wilmington. Mother rode along in the ambulance with her. When the doctor in Wilmington saw all the bruises on Aunt Mary's thighs, he asked what had caused them.

Mother said, "The shots."

"Shots for what," the doctor almost shouted in an alarmed voice. It was then he suspected what had caused her death, an overdose of paregoric, an antiemetic used to control the vomiting. That fact was later confirmed by an autopsy.

My poor uncle had a rough time after his wife's death, for he was accused of being the cause of it. After Aunt Mary's death, there was a big stir in the family. Her sister, Beth, had it put in the local newspaper that Uncle Aaron didn't take his wife to the doctor and was responsible for her death. Of course that caused my family to turn against her. They never again had anything to do with that woman and never forgave her either. Uncle Aaron had indeed taken Aunt Mary to the doctor, but the doctor's treatment was the cause of her death. That knowledge was hushed up, and not until years later was the truth finally uncovered by Betsy, one of her daughters.

My family at large also were viewed askance because our religious beliefs forbade our seeing the doctor. We had been very fortunate up until that time in that none of our family members had ever had a life-threatening illness. It is easy to have faith when one is not faced with those kinds of situations.

I remember how scared Jim and I were when we went through the hallway at Uncle Aaron's to get to the kitchen. As you went down the hall, you had to pass by the room where Aunt Mary's body was lying in the coffin. It was dark in the room that night. I think if anything had moved in that room, I would have screamed and run as fast as my skinny little legs would carry me. We were glad when that coffin was gone. It made it a lot easier to go to their house and we loved to visit them because they had six children and, as we had grown up for a time with eight in our family, we were right at home among them. They had taken my baby sister Faye to bring up, but she died six months later of pneumonia.

It was in the fifth grade that I was chosen to play the role of George Washington in our school play because I could memorize lines easily. George Washington's character had the most lines to learn. A big problem arose, however, when Aunt Mary's sister, Beth, offered to let me borrow her son's George Washington costume. We were in class together. When I told Mother about it, she said, "It would be the most awful thing for you to wear that suit. That woman is wicked and there is no way on earth you could wear that costume. If he brings it to school, you must refuse to try it on. If the teacher insists, just tell her it is for personal reasons." I knew I must obey Mother or bear the consequences, which in this case would be very severe.

I dreaded the next day. I had never before refused to obey the teacher, but that was exactly what Mother was commanding me to do. Sure enough, Beth's son had brought the costume. Mrs. Ward asked me to try it on to see if it fit. It was such a simple request. It was so embarrassing for me not to be able to try the suit on. When I said, "No, I can't," every head in the classroom turned toward me. I'm sure my face turned pale. My heart was beating so fast I could hardly talk. After her asking me twice and my telling her I can't, Mrs. Ward then asked me why. By that time I was about to choke, but I managed to mutter that it was for personal reasons, somehow hoping that only the teacher could hear me. It was so humiliating. My refusal did not make the class think very highly of me, either. It only gave them more fodder to feed on about my being different from them. They began to say, "You go to that Roberts church, don't you?" That was the name given to our church by many people in the community. People resented the fact that we lived separate from them and at the same time were prosperous and quite self-sufficient. Like I have said, if we had all been "poor as Job's turkey," as the expression goes, then nobody would have given us a second thought. But there was a lot of envy and jealousy involved for them to make the sarcastic and cutting remarks that got back to us.

Later in the afternoon of that same day, Mrs. Ward asked me if I had any sisters. Mother had strictly told me that if anyone asked me that question I was to say I had a brother. I always felt like it was being dishonest, as if I were denying my sisters, whom I loved very dearly. But Mother felt quite different. She thought it was just fine to say that because she didn't want anyone to know we were adopted. I never could figure that out. Anyway, I answered Mrs.Ward just like Mother had told me to do. She repeated the question twice, getting the same answer from me. *Then* she said, slowly and emphatically, "John, did you know that Dana, Marie, Eva, and Josie are your sisters?"

"Yes, ma'am," I answered very calmly.

You should have seen the expression on her face. To say the least, she was shocked.

That night Mother went to her house to settle the matter about the costume. Mrs. Ward informed Mother that the reason she had told me about my sisters was because she knew of a case in which a child did not learn of his adoption until he reached adulthood and then the revelation was devastating. She also said she had never seen a child like me before in her life. He didn't tell a lie but said exactly what he had been told to say. Mother explained to her about the family conflict and promised that she would make a costume herself. Mother was a very good seamstress. She made a lot of her own clothes. I remember how proud I was to play that role. At the end of the play, I had to stand like a statue, with my sword by my side. My sisters complimented me on my performance.

I remember in the fifth grade an ordinary student, Lew Tuner, like myself, and Reg Colder, a student of socially prominent parents, had committed an offense requiring punishment. As Reg was leaving the classroom, the teacher told the entire class, "I can't beat that child because of who he is." So she sent *him* to the principal's office. She took poor Lew before the class and beat him with a yardstick. He was humiliated before all the other students, but the other child's only punishment was going to the principal's office. I remember saying to myself that Reg could just as easily be beaten as anybody else. Another day, that same Reg started kicking dirt in my face on the playground during lunch recess. It made me angry, so I kicked dirt right back in his face. When Mrs. Ward saw us, she came running over but jumped on *me* for kicking dirt at him. "He started it first," I said. But that didn't matter to her. She took our heads, one in each hand, and cracked them together. I resented being punished for something I had not started, so I made my neck as stiff as I could, which made it very difficult for her to crack our heads together very well.

One day, Mrs. Ward stepped out of class for a few minutes. She left us on our own to behave ourselves. Unbeknownst to the rest of us, Reg was playing with the radiator safety valve at the back of the classroom. It broke. With a tremendous roar like the sound of a rocket being launched right there in the classroom, the steam escaped out of the radiator. Reg fainted dead away and collapsed on the floor. The entire class en masse rushed toward the door, screaming at the top of their lungs. I didn't scream, but I was halfway to the door before I realized what had happened. We all went back to our seats. Almost immediately, bossy Mrs. Grant from upstairs came barging into our classroom, demanding to know why we were making so much noise. How could she expect us to sit there like knots on a log with all that was happening? For heaven's sakes, it scared us half to death!

Years later poor Reg spent time in prison for armed robbery. After serving his term, he went back to school, learned a trade, and got a good job. A few years later he was caught with cocaine. While in jail awaiting trial, he hanged himself with a belt. It was really very sad.

Back to the subject of ridicule. Mother didn't help with it at all, either. She had certain notions about what she wanted us boys to wear. I think she must have read some books about Charles Dickens. She wanted us to wear clothes from way back in history— knickers, those strange corduroy pants that billowed out like some kind of baggy sack and had an elastic band that gripped the leg very tightly just below the knee. As the pant legs rubbed together while walking, they made a squeaking noise that brought everyone's attention to you.

No one else in our entire school had such clothes. In addition, during the winter when the air was dry, the skin on our legs became so dry it would flake off like dandruff. Sometimes the kids would say in a mocking tone of voice, "Look at your legs; they look like you have dandruff." It was so humiliating. At times like that, I wished I could disappear. I hated those knickers. I said I would never make a child of mine wear such weird clothes, and I didn't, either.

Mother's lack of sensitivity to our needs as young children made my life so much more difficult. It seemed all she thought about was what she wanted. She wouldn't let us wear clothes like everyone else. She forbade us getting on our knees to play marbles, too. She didn't want our pants to get stains on the knees. We had to squat when we played. This was another thing that nurtured the growing feeling of inferiority inside me.

One day during recess I was leaning against a large oak tree on the playground. Bobby, an older student whose father was a doctor in town, came up to me and with a contemptuous sneer in his voice said, "Where did you get those bloomers?" Mother had made me wear some old flimsy-legged white shorts to school that day. I had begged her over and over, "Please, Mother, please, don't make me wear these things." I felt like an idiot with them on. They were almost like underwear. When I got out of the car, I could feel everyone's eyes on me. I felt so exposed, almost half-naked.

The sixth grade passed fairly quietly, except for a few events that further traumatized me. I was a very shy and quiet child, as I've said before. One grade period that year, I received a B in conduct. I had no earthly idea why Mrs. Finch had given me that grade. I still remember how terrified I was to go home with that report card. Mother took one glance at my report card, saw the grade in conduct, and asked me in a cold, menacing voice, "What on earth possessed you to get such a grade? What have you been doing to get such a grade?"

I began to beg, to plead, "Mother, I didn't talk. I haven't talked. I always behaved in class." It made no difference. Once again, she got a huge switch and beat me black-and-blue.

The mortifying thing, however, was that she made me go up to the teacher at the end of each day and ask her if I had talked, if I had behaved. I felt so stupid, but I didn't dare disobey Mother. That would have called for another beating, and probably a worse one than the first. Every day she asked me, "What did the teacher say? Did you behave today?"

I did not learn until later that poor Mrs. Finch's husband was an alcoholic. I'm sure that's hard to live with. He may have been abusive, too. Many days she seemed irritable and impatient. Probably on one of those days she had seen me turn to another student and say one single word or ask one simple question. For that, she gave me a B. Thank goodness I never received another bad grade on conduct.

One day a Blondie and Dagwood movie was going to be shown to the school in the auditorium. Our class was included. I wanted to go but was afraid, because going to the movies was against our religion. I'd never been to a movie before. My class-mates begged and begged and finally persuaded me to go. When the movie started, I began to laugh. As it continued, I became quite hysterical. I had never seen anything so funny in my entire life. In one scene they showed someone smiling and when his lips parted his teeth were the size of horse teeth. That was almost too much. I burst into squeals of laughter. I was laughing so hard I could barely see. Tears were streaming down my cheeks. I could hardly catch my breath. The kids in my row of seats quit looking at the movie and started watching me. I can still see their heads leaned over, watch-ing me like I was crazy. I was having the time of my life.

They just didn't know what it was like, living in such a plain and severe world as I did. We were rebuked for laughing, were informed that all foolishness is sin. Our life was very serious. I *really* enjoyed that movie. I was in dental school before I ever went to another one, and that time with very grave consequences.

The events surrounding Aunt Mary's death, all the peculiar religious beliefs we practiced, the strange clothes we had to wear, and especially our belief that we must live separate from the world had begun to have their effect on the way the kids at school treated me. We lived apart from the world, much like the Amish. We didn't drink bottled drinks, we didn't go to the movies, we didn't listen to the radio, the girls couldn't cut their hair, shave their legs, wear makeup, or wear jewelry, and men couldn't wear watches or grow a mustache or beard. The list could go on and on.

I was a quiet, shy child who stayed by myself. When one is so different, the other kids many times will pick on that one who is not like them. By this time, some of the boys in my class had developed an intense dislike of me. One day as I stood out in the hallway out-side my classroom, a boy came by and with all the force he could muster hit me in the middle of my thigh. It was painful, but I did not flinch. I had endured beatings much more painful than that. I had seen other boys get the same treatment, and they would fall on the floor writhing in what appeared to be agony. I would not give my attackers the pleasure of knowing it even hurt.

Ideas of what I wanted to be were already being formed in my mind. You see. They were calling me queer and sissy. I didn't understand what those names meant, but I knew they were bad. But when they had to endure a little pain, they acted like babies. Yet they called themselves tough. They considered themselves to be men. I grew to have contempt for what they represented. It was disgusting. As we would say back then, they were "big talk and do little." I wanted to be a totally different kind of man from that. I wanted to be like the real men I knew in my life, mainly my daddy and my uncles. They were strong and courageous, not whimpering babies like those boys at school who hated me and made my life so miserable. There was no one who would be my friend. I tried obtaining friends by helping them with their homework, but I soon learned that made no difference at all. As soon as they had gotten what they wanted, I was treated just as bad as before. Then in order to survive, I withdrew from virtually everyone at school. My inner strength to cope with life began to develop during those early years. Living without friends was easier than the pain of being rejected and humiliated in front of others.

My parents bought a lot in a new residential section, just outside the city limits. The prospect of building a new house was very exciting. We enjoyed clearing the lot, cutting down trees, piling them up, and burning the debris. We had lots of relatives to help us, too. We always loved having company. They were a guarantee that we wouldn't get a beating even if we did something wrong, at least not until they were gone. Jim and I would comment to each other how glad we were that "so and so" was there with us, that Mother wouldn't beat us while he was present.

We would have workings, as we called it. Lots of relatives would come to help with nailing down subflooring, putting up the stud walls and other parts of the construction. Mother would cook piles of good food for them to eat. Such fun! We played a lot until the time came to clean up the trash. That was about all we knew how to do well. But cleaning the scrap boards out of the way, keeping the workplace clean, was very helpful. We were like little elves scurrying around picking up boards and all kinds of scraps and piling it up to burn.

Soon the house was finished. It was a beautiful home. We even had two bathrooms, and no one else in the family but us had that luxury. Mother had extremely good taste. The kitchen cabinets were a beautiful blue, trimmed in yellow. She loved colors and was very particular and demanding of the painter, Mr. Phillips. He was Whiteville's best. A beautiful bow window extended out from the kitchen, and as we sat at the table to eat we could look outside, see flowers, birds, and whoever came up to the house without having to go to the door. Everything was brand-new. It was so nice living there, if only . . .

I was such a bean pole of a kid back then, just skin and bones. You could count every rib in my chest and every joint in my backbone. My hip bones protruded up like those of a bony milk cow when I lay on my back, and my stomach was so thin and flat you could have poured water in the depression in the middle of my stomach. And I had a neck like a giraffe, so long and skinny. My neck looked like it was two feet long. As I had not participated in sports very much, my muscular development was lacking. Without muscle tone, I was stoop-shouldered. And Mother hated a humped back.

One day during that first fall in our new house, we were out in the backyard raking leaves. All of a sudden, before I knew what was happening, Mother grabbed the rake out of my hand and, gripping it with both hands, began to beat me all across my shoulders with it, shouting at me all the while, "Hold up your shoulders! Hold up your shoulders! I despise a humpbacked man. You look like a camel." That scared the daylights out of me. But the rake didn't hurt me as bad as she hurt my feelings and my sense of self worth. For a while the fear of getting a beating for being stoop-shouldered kept me in a state of tension and apprehension. It was not easy, but as I have said before, children are resilient. We are just like the grass that waves back and forth in the wind as it blows over us and like the sapling tree, which also bends before the violence of the wind but does not break. For an adult to have to endure such treatment would probably be disastrous. Adults cannot bend but break under the strain. Oh, the wonders and beauty of youth. It is truly amazing.

I tried to consciously hold up my shoulders. I realized this was something else I was expected to do whether it was possible or not. Consciously holding my shoulders up worked for short periods of time, but then I'd forget. Panic would grip me, for I feared she had seen me relaxed and would beat me later. And she did. She even called me into the house once and beat me with the toaster cord. It was terrible living in so much fear.

As if that weren't enough, the boys at school hated me because the girls liked me and because I made good grades. They had begun calling me names. I was called a sissy, queer, and teacher's pet. I assumed a sissy was someone who played with girls, because that's what the boys would tell me to do when I wanted to join them in games. Other times they would ask me with such contempt, "What do you do to make the girls like you? Tell us so they will like us, too." "I don't do anything. I'm just nice to them," was always my reply. I had no idea what a queer was.

The worst insult, however, came when they accused me of going down to the dead end and helping "niggers" change their rubbers. The dead end was the street in our residential section where no homes had been built yet. I had no idea what they were talking about at the time, but somehow I knew it was something very degrading.

Not only was I having to endure the scorn and ridicule of my classmates at school, but now Mother didn't like the way I looked, either. It was like I could feel her eyes as they viewed me with disgust when I was walking around in her presence. And I would tell her I couldn't help it. I didn't want to be hump backed. "You can help it; just hold up your shoulders," she'd say.

It was then I grew to love the story of the ugly duckling. It always filled my heart with joy when the beautiful swan flew away from all those who had tormented him, driving him away from their presence. He was free! Free! Never to have to endure their mockery again. I would dream of being able to fly away, high in the sky far away from everything that was after me. I would wish I could be like the swan, that I could turn into something everybody would admire. Such a wistful longing filled my heart each time I read that story.

It hurt so to see other kids have friends who would horse

around with them, pat them on the back, or grab them around the chest in play. I wanted a friend, too, so bad. But nobody wanted me for a friend. The only way they wanted to touch me was if they were trying to hurt me. I was "queer," they said. I knew in the right circumstances they would all turn on me. Even the girls who once liked me had changed as they grew older, and they, too, had contempt for me. In order to survive I withdrew from everybody at school. There was no one I could trust. I began to live a lonely life. Living alone was easier than enduring the humiliation by my classmates. Yet deep inside I wanted to be accepted like everyone else. My strength took roots in those years of emotional hardship, and that strength would take me through many more hardships as well.

Ah, dear me, my poor little body reached puberty that same year. With many little boys, a short time after reaching puberty their sex glands produce too much secretions. The body, in order to rid itself of the excess, ejects the stuff at night during sleep. This phenomenon is called wet dreams. My very first one really didn't make much of an impression on me. I wondered why my pajama pants had that sticky wet spot on them.

But oh, dear me, I'll never, never forget that first time I got beaten for it if I live to be a thousand years old. Uncle Kevin and Aunt Rosie lived in the country a short distance down a dirt road behind our church. They had given Mother a key to their house so she could look after it while they were on vacation in the mountains.

I'll never forget. It was on a Saturday morning. She came into my bedroom and told me to come on. We were going out to Aunt Rosie's. From the tone of Mother's voice and her aggravated mood, I knew she was going to beat me. I just didn't know what for. I was scared to death as all of us drove out into the country. Jim and I didn't dare even talk to each other in the backseat, but we both were wondering what was going to happen. My fingers were cold as ice; my mouth became dry; my heart began to race. I felt the urge to use the bathroom. I could hardly keep still in the backseat. I began to rack my brain, trying to recall what I might have done to get a beating. But nothing, I could think of nothing.

When we finally arrived at Aunt Rosie's house, Mother went out in the backyard and broke the largest switch I had ever seen. It was about four feet long and as big around as her thumb in diameter. It looked huge to me. She had left me waiting in fear in the kitchen. Mother had beaten me other times, but this time I was more afraid than I had ever been before. There was a vengeance and an anger that I had never encountered in her. Since we had moved back to North Carolina, Mother had become fatter than she used to be. Her shoulders had become broad and thick, with large, powerful arms. Hard work had made them that way, she said. She was rather large overall, with a thick waist, large hips, and big, heavy thighs. The stony expression on her face was one of anger and resentment, and her approach to the situation was, *I'll beat this evil out of you if it's the last thing I ever do.* "Pull off your shirt," she said with a steely cold tone in her voice that struck sheer terror in my heart. "You know what I'm going to beat you for, don't you?" she asked.

"No, ma'am, I don't. What have I done?" I replied with a tremor in my voice.

"Yes, you do," she said in anger that I had already denied having done anything wrong, and with that the switch came down with a vicious hard whack on my bare bony back and shoulders, once, twice, on and on. I hollered out in pain and fear each time the switch cut into my back and tried to jump away from the cutting blows of that awful switch. "Come back here!" she would yell at me while her eyes looked so intense with steely determination to accomplish her task.

"What have I done? What are you beating me for?" I pleaded over and over.

"You know what I'm beating you for," she'd repeat.

The only thing that came to my desperate mind was that I had told Jim that same morning that Daddy used too much toilet paper. When I told her that, it seemed to infuriate her, for she flew into me with the switch with renewed vengeance. For what seemed to me like an eternity she continued to flail at me with that thing. As I've said before, she was very strong. The main body of the switch landing on my upper back and shoulders brought a burning pain like someone hitting you with a stick. The outer part was flexible and would flip all the way down to my pants and sometimes around to my bare stomach. As it did, that flexible tip felt just like a knife cutting me. I simply couldn't help jumping every time it struck me.

I suppose she realized I wasn't going to confess or else she was getting tired, but she finally told me what she was beating me for. "You were playing dirty tricks on the bed last night, weren't you," she said.

Dirty tricks? I had no earthly idea what she meant. *Dirty tricks? What was that?* raced through my mind. I had never heard of such a thing. Of course I denied the charge.

She began beating me again, and now she seemed even angrier. The pain on my back was increasing by the second. As the switch struck me over and over again, it lashed over the same places more than one time and the repeated injury increased the pain. I didn't know how much longer I could endure it.

Finally, out of pure desperation to get her to stop, I lied. I admitted to the dirty tricks, still being totally ignorant of what that was. Then she beat me for a while longer. I even told her I wouldn't do it again. Finally she was satisfied and stopped. Was I ever relieved, too! Now as I relate these terrible events, I wish it were possible to go back in time, put my arms around that skinny little twelve-year-old child, and comfort him. Those memories are so very painful.

Somehow, I put the two things together and realized it was about the wet places on my pajamas. It is really very difficult to relate these events. It hurts now so deep, because I can see that skinny little kid being flogged unmercifully for something he had absolutely no knowledge of at all. What a cruel woman she was! My back was sore for days. After that dreadful day, my first waking thoughts were about my pajamas. That's the first thing I would do when I awoke. I would feel them. If they were wet, I would hurry and make my bed, hoping against hope she would not find out.

I can still see her another fateful morning when she came into our bedroom, and with one swift jerk of the covers, exposed my sheets. There was the dreaded wet spot. She let out a snort of disgust and strode swiftly back to the kitchen. I heard the cabinet drawer being jerked open. I knew she was getting the toaster cord. I felt sick to the pit of my stomach; my palms turned sweaty; my heart began to pound. She was so provoked that time she didn't even wait to make me take off my pajama shirt but began to lash me with the toaster cord. As she swung it on me, it wrapped around my body, leaving purple and black loops on my back or anywhere else it struck the flesh. One of those times it wrapped completely around my back and across my hips and came down right across my poor little penis. I screamed in terror and pain, "You hit me! You hit me," I yelled. *Am I going to get my penis cut off with the toaster cord?* I thought. A brief frantic glance told me it was still intact. That was a relief. But it turned purple as a plum and swelled so much I could hardly use the bathroom for over a week. Fortunately, she stopped beating me right then, but there were many other times I got a severe beating for the same thing. As I said before, the terror of getting a beating was so intense that it even pervaded my subconscious mind so that many times just as I was about to ejaculate I would awake enough to grip my foreskin and hold it tight so that the semen collected inside the skin and didn't get on the sheets. Then I could put it in a handkerchief. The reader can't even begin to imagine how it is to live in such fear. You can read the accounts of my past experiences, but there is no way in the world you can know what it's like unless you have experienced it yourself. It just isn't possible. At that time in my life I didn't know the word *masturbate*, but that's what Mother thought I had done onto the bedsheets. It was not until three years later that I even learned to perform the act.

Mother, at those times, could strike sheer terror into your very heart. She was a very attractive, if rather simple-looking, woman in her early forties. She had thinning dark brown hair, which she always kept very neat. I watched her many times as she took a section of hair, wound it around her index and middle finger, then took bobby pins, and pinned it to her head. It was kinda like a roll at the base of her neck. She wore no makeup and no jewelry, not even a wedding ring. She was blessed with beautiful smooth fair skin. She had a small, slightly upturned nose and thin, straight lips. She was five-feet-three at the most, stocky, with large rather muscular-looking arms. Her muscles had developed from much hard work on the farm, she always told us. She was very full in the bust and fairly stout all over. Cold steel blue eyes looked out of a stern impassive face. When she was provoked at us, her already thin "Roberts" lips were drawn even tighter. With only a fleeting glance into that face, we knew what was coming.

One evening we were all sitting in the den, just lounging around talking. I was lying on the sofa with my head propped up in my hand. Mother sat in a recliner across from me. All of a sudden, with words that struck terror into my very heart, she jumped up, yanked open the cabinet drawer where she kept the toaster cord, and said in her stern, provoked voice, "Come on in the bedroom." My heart sank to my feet. My throat tightened with fear. My heart began beating wildly. Again I didn't know what I had done. When she got me in the bedroom, she cut into me with that hateful toaster cord. Over and over she brought that thing down on my back as hard as she could swing it. It would leave large blue loops wherever it struck. I jumped all around hollering as usual, throwing my hands in the air in an effort to deflect the lash from my poor back. After beating me a few minutes, she asked, "What were you doing looking up my dress?" Looking up her dress! Looking up her dress! Such a thing had never entered my mind. I wasn't interested in her dress, let alone looking up the stupid thing. A reinforced message: Women are untouchable; nor can you look in their direction without grave consequences. Mother beat the daylights out of me for having just glanced at Marie from a great distance beyond the cornfield. Mother's treatment of me left a distrust of women buried deep in my subconscious, but I didn't become a psychopathic woman hater because of it. I just learned to cope and to realize that all women were not the same, but it still made life much more difficult than it should have been. She never admitted she was mistaken but left me with the impression that she didn't believe me, always thinking the worst.

Whenever she laughed, however, her face lit up like a light. She was really a pretty woman, and we loved her in spite of all the terrible things she was doing to us. It was wonderful to see her laugh. So long as she laughed, it was OK, we could laugh; otherwise we were being foolish, and the Bible taught that all foolishness was sin. We got beaten for that, too. That ever present fear of being punished always lurked in the back of our minds.

But we still loved her. She had been the only mother we had for so long. She and Daddy had taken us when we couldn't help ourselves. And Daddy was having great difficulty finding work he could do. One of his first jobs was loading heavy bags of fertilizer onto trucks at a fertilizer plant. As he was not accustomed to such hard work, many times, Mother said, he was so tired at night, his legs and his back ached from carrying those heavy bags. Then he got a job at a furniture store, but one of the other employees there disliked him, making his life very unpleasant. Fortunately, he wasn't employed there but for a short while.

His next job was driving the Merita bread truck. What a wonderful thing to do, drive a truck full of all kinds of delicious cakes and cookies! I looked forward to riding with Daddy on his bread route because it always ended at the storage building on Highway 701. In addition to the breads and snack foods, there were stacks of boxes of oatmeal cookies. Delicious cream-filled oatmeal cookies! Ummm, they looked so good. It seems I was always hungry. We could have the stale cookies about to be discarded. There was nothing better to us. I ate every cake I could have. Those were the most delicious things in the whole world to me. Times were hard, so we didn't get any special things like that; we only had the bare necessities, peas and beans, rice, and the good staple foods. Soul food, as it's called today.

Daddy was a good provider for us. He did his very best and never, ever complained. I have absolutely no memories of his saying a single word about having to work hard, about his job being difficult in the heat and cold or anything else. I have an image of him sitting at the table not having much to say, just being there. Mother did most of the talking and certainly almost all of the bossing.

One quality about him was his punctuality, and I'm sure that had been instilled during his many years in the military. In addition, he was a little hard-boiled, which is also a trait of military personnel. When he came to our rooms to wake us, he only called once. If we didn't respond, then it was our fault, and he never changed. Occasionally Mother, I guess in her impatience and frustrations with us, would come into the room, jerk the sheet back, and lash across our bodies with the toaster cord, shouting all the while, "Get up! Get up! You were called to get up!" That happened only once or twice, which was enough for us to become more attuned to hearing Daddy's voice when he called.

Mother complained enough for both of them. He always kept

our shoes polished clean and shiny until we grew old enough to do it ourselves. As she informed us how difficult his life was, Mother reinforced in our minds how Daddy had started all over again to raise us boys, making us feel so indebted to them. We felt so sorry that we had ruined their lives. They could have been happy if it were not for us.

There were times we left the table hungry but would not have asked for more food for anything, even though it would have been soooo good. I felt sorry for Daddy, having to work so hard, especially doing jobs he did not know well. Sometimes when Mother talked about Daddy's plight, I felt guilty, like it was my fault. I would wish I could vanish so that I no longer was a burden to them. After all, if they hadn't taken us, their lives would be so much better.

Other events that remained vivid in my mind occurred while we lived in the new house in the residential area. Two aunts of mine who had married my daddy's brothers would often get in a bad fix. I do not know what they had done, probably nothing more than disagreeing with Mother on some spiritual matter, but whatever it was, they were made to believe their souls were in jeopardy of being lost unless they repented. Those were such harrowing times for everyone involved.

Even though the congregation loved and trusted her, many times their life was in turmoil because of Mother's continual minding of other's affairs. Arriving home from school, we usually knew what was taking place when we recognized Uncle Bob's car at the house. I would think to myself, *Oh, dear! Not again.* I knew Aunt Alice was in a bad fix again. She and Mother would spend hours, sometimes a day, on the floor praying, trying to help Aunt Alice find repentance for something she had done that was displeasing to God. We had to show respect for the works of God, too. We couldn't just go waltzing into the room where they were praying. We had to tiptoe, being very quiet. Talking was absolutely out of the question. While they were there, our life, Jim's and mine, seemed to take second place. We'd be so hungry, too. We'd just go into our room and do our homework, hoping supper would come before too awfully late. Sometimes we didn't eat until late, way past our mealtime. Everyone received open rebuke in church for their wrongdoings.

These aunts of mine got the same kind of treatment right before everyone in church, and if Mother still didn't feel free about them, she went to their homes during the week and prayed with them there. Other times she called for them to come to our house. We dreaded those times. They spent hours on the floor praying, mourning, weeping, and begging God to have mercy on them, to help them to see where they had failed. Our life was put on hold until Mother had straightened their lives out, or at least until she had them under control again. Now I fully believe it was the latter.

It was a wonderful thing when they found repentance. Most of the time they would shout all over the den. I remember once when Uncle Roger was rejoicing over Aunt Alice's deliverance, his head broke the shade on the ceiling light in the den. Mother said she didn't care that the light was broken. She was so happy for her dear sister. Enduring the long waits for supper and just learning to tolerate the intrusion into our lives taught us patience.

Looking back on it now, I'm sure they did nothing worthy of such intimidation. The fear instilled in them was powerful. They actually believed she knew whether they would be saved or go to hell. Mother was like a god figure to them. Sometimes she said to them that God had shown her that their names had been blotted out of the Book of Life. That fact was so frightening to them, they truly believed they would be lost and go to hell. It is terrible to do such things to poor people in the name of God.

Mother got a lot of her inspiration from the Old Testament. She did exactly what her daddy told her not to do. When she was saved, her daddy told her to not read the Old Testament, that it would confuse her. She recounted that story many times to us in church and would always say she thanked the Lord she had never been confused. The truth of the matter is she has never realized just how confused she has been all through the years.

Mother believed in ritual cleansing. Once in the dead of night, she got Aunt Alice and told her God had put it on her for the two of them to wash the church. Aunt Alice had taken a dress belonging to my mama. Because it belonged to my mama, the dress was considered to be sacred. Using the dress of my mama was supposed to purify the church of the spirits of adultery, as if there were divine power in the dress. The two of them spent the better part of the night washing every square inch of the inside of that church. I remember so vividly Mother telling me how unconcerned Aunt Alice seemed as she cleaned. Mother said Aunt Alice was just hurriedly flipping over the walls and pews while she herself made sure she cleaned each tiny spot on every single thing: walls, pews, windowsills, moldings, backs of the pews, just everything. Mother went on to say she knew Aunt Alice could never serve the Lord faithfully. She was not particular enough. Just think of passing that kind of judgment on another person.

Mother set herself up almost like a god. Everyone was always required to come to the things in *her* heart. I heard Mother say many, many times to the people in the congregation, "If you can't come to the things in my heart, there is no way you can get to God." I have come to realize many of them truly believed that.

In those early years, however, Mother was a wonderful person, one whom everyone loved dearly, even though she struck fear in the hearts of everyone when she stood in the church and rebuked the congregation, for we were rebuked openly before everyone present. But back then she had a sweet, humble spirit about her. Her face looked like the face of an angel to us when she stood in the church to preach. Even though Uncle Sam was our preacher, she was our spiritual leader, the one who guided us and had the last word, as it were, from God. No one was supposed to question her judgment, for God spoke and showed her whatever she brought to the congregation. At least that's what we believed at that time.

Special events had taken place that endeared her to the people, including me. These acts of love and kindness were truly inspired by God, which increased the confidence everyone had in her. Once, years ago, when Uncle Bob and his wife, Alice, were having a financial struggle, Mother said God bade her to send them $300, which she did. Aunt Alice has stood in church on more than one occasion with tears of gratitude streaming down her cheeks and told us how much that $300 helped them out. Without it they could not have survived. Another deed concerned Uncle Sam. God bade Mother give him $500 to start his cabinet shop. The cabinet business grew to be a thriving enterprise, providing employment for many of those in the congregation as well as outsiders. Each time those events were recounted in church, my eyes also ran over with tears of love and gratitude, for it seemed to me that Mother was the most wonderful person in the whole world to do such loving deeds for those in need.

I loved to go to church to hear the words that came out of her mouth when she stood. She was like my mama back then. Mother gave hope and joy, strength and understanding, to everyone. You could confide anything to her, and she wouldn't make you feel like a terrible person but would help you to get your life back in order again. I had so much confidence in her that the terrible things she was doing to me at home, the horrible beatings, had nothing to do with God or her goodness. To me, they were two separate entities, not related to each other at all. It really never entered my mind that she was anything but a wonderful person. She was never judgmental or condemning to anyone. But at the same time, too, none of the members of the congregation had any idea what was happening to me and Jim at home. She was trusted totally by almost all of the congregation except two of her brothers, well, really three.

As I grew older, I realized there was a division between these two brothers and Mother, and as time went by the struggle between her and these two brothers became more and more intense. It was really a power struggle, with Mother being the strongest of the three. The third brother was my real daddy. My oldest sister, Dana, said Daddy told her he had moved his family to Curry because "I am tired of someone else telling me and my wife what to do." Apparently he was stronger in some respects than any of his siblings. But Mother was able to manipulate everyone who remained within her grasp. She had the power to convince others to follow her and to oppose those brothers. If either of the two brothers tried to make a break with any of the "laws" of our religion, Mother would have convinced everyone else to oppose them, so rebellion was quickly squelched.

We revered her as if she were one of the prophets of the Old Testament, like Samuel. When she came home from Charleston and called for a special church service, people actually trembled with fear, for they believed God could show her the thoughts of their hearts and minds. In fact, I have seen her in that light myself many times.

She was once a true and wonderful leader of the people. But as the years went by and the people didn't need her as much, she began to lose control over them and then began to change, little by little, until she became a source of damage, pain, and destruction. She resented their independence and became critical and judgmental toward them, instead of sharing in their newfound freedom and independence. I remember how she criticized my sister Marie and her husband when they built their second home, simply because they didn't ask her advice about different aspects of the construction process. But that's the strategy of all who seek to control others: keep your subjects ignorant and very dependent so they will always need the controller. Because she was so deeply entrenched in the hearts of the people, she had the power to either lift them up or cast them down. It was like she had an invisible umbilical cord attached to all of us and we found strength from her. We had all become too dependent upon her, but that was her own doing. She had created our dependence upon her. She was always the one who had to have the last word about repentance, about our salvation, whether we were actually saved or not. In other words, the life and spiritual well-being of the entire congregation revolved around her. Many believed Mother held the keys to their entrance into heaven. I've heard her say many a time in church to certain individuals that God had shown her that their name had been blotted out of the Lamb's Book of Life. That proclamation brought abject fear into the hearts of those to whom it was said. Many years had to pass before they were able to break away from the grip of that fear and realize that God doesn't show mortal beings such things. Once an aunt of mine said to me, "What will we do when Beulah is gone?" My reply was, "What do you think we'll do? Keep on living. It won't be the end of the world!"

About that same time, my sisters Eva and Josie trimmed their hair. They didn't cut but a few inches off, mostly to get rid of the split ends. When Mother found out about it, she got two black scarves. That night during prayer meeting, she rebuked my sisters before the whole church as if they had done something terribly sinful, and according to Mother they had. They had to go to the altar and repent, and Mother put those scarves on their heads to cover their shame. Mother said God put it on her to get the scarves for that purpose so the shame of their sin wouldn't be exposed before the world. They left church with the scarves on their heads. I later learned Mother was going to demand they wear the scarves out to school, but after much pleading and promises that they would never, never cut their hair again, she relented. They told me how relieved they were. I can imagine! It was humiliating enough for them to go to school with their hairy legs for everybody to laugh at and make fun of. They couldn't put on a gym suit or shorts of any kind to play in PE, either. All these peculiar things expected of us made our life very difficult.

Branden Gross entered our lives about the time we moved into our new home. He was Grandmother's sister Bell's boy and had been a prisoner of war in Germany during World War II. When he was liberated, he weighed only eighty-seven pounds; his normal weight was around two-hundred pounds of solid muscle, no fat. Before being drafted, he used to preach in our church when I was an infant. My family never forgave him for not being a conscientious objector. I've heard Mother say many a time that instead of Branden refusing to take up arms, he became a sharpshooter, even winning a medal for it before he went off to the war. Somehow Mother learned he had befriended a German girl before being captured. Mother accused him of having an affair with this girl. "Such a thing was awful," she said, "because Branden had a wife and child back home."

Mother told me a dream she claimed God had given her. In her dream she saw Branden's bed sheets, which had spots on them. "Those were spots of adultery," she said. The dream, she maintained, was God's way of letting her know that Branden had committed adultery.

Because of his adultery, Mother also bitterly accused him of being self-righteous. In other words, if he had committed adultery, he should not have read the Bible to his buddies in prison but should have spent all that time, I suppose, repenting for his sin. How did she know he had not repented? Mother was just so judgmental. After his capture by the Germans and during the time he spent as a prisoner of war, he would read the Bible daily to the other prisoners to inspire them, give them hope, and boost their morale. He would also dump the lice out of their boots after the men became so weak it was impossible for them to do it themselves. He

70

was there every day for them, watching as they died one at a time.

It seemed so unfair to me for her to pass judgment on him for showing compassion on those poor souls, no matter what he might have done. How, but how, could his reading the Bible to those poor dying men and doing those deeds of kindness be self-righteous? I wondered about it even back then.

Branden had come to church a couple of times. Both times he stood up and preached. He delivered a good sermon, too, and without preparing for it beforehand. He certainly had no notes to refer back to, for there was no pulpit in our church on which to place any kind of material. He was one of those called by God to preach, and without being educated for that. I enjoyed hearing him very much.

One Wednesday night as he preached, he called me by name, asking me directly if I wanted to be saved. Of course I did, and I began to weep. I'm sure he noticed my reaction to the first question, and then he said to me, "I believe if you will get on your knees, God will save you." Believing what he said, I stood up to kneel at my bench. As I was turning around to kneel, it seemed to me the whole congregation, like one body, was coming toward me. I can see their hands even now as they were extended out toward me. Everyone was reaching out to touch me. I knelt down, put my head on the bench, and simply said, "Dear Lord, have mercy on me." That was all I had time to say before somebody was telling me the Lord had saved me, to stand up and the Spirit would bless me. People were shouting all over the church. All I knew to do was thank the Lord for saving me.

I had never quite realized until that night just how much the church thought of me and how they had looked forward to that day. It goes back to the promise God made to my mama that I would live to grow up to be a preacher when the doctor had said I wouldn't live through the night. I truly felt a peace I had never known before. It was like everything would be all right, no matter what came or went. That has been so true in my life ever since that day. God truly has taken care of me. That's the reason I was not afraid when Hurricane Hazel came through. I knew I wouldn't be killed in the storm, because the promise to Mama had not been fulfilled: I wasn't a preacher yet. Josie and Eva came to my classroom the next day during recess to speak to me. I remember telling them how peaceful I felt inside, that it was wonderful to know I was saved.

Soon, however, Mother began to pressure me *to work*. She would come to me in church as we were on our knees praying and say, "God doesn't save us to be idle; He saves us to work. Let God put something on you to do." One Sunday my older brother, Chris, came to church, something he rarely ever did. We were having prayer at the end of the service as usual. Mother came over to me, began to slap me on the back as she prayed, and said, "You need to let God put something on you for your brother's soul." It seemed to provoke her that I didn't do anything. I didn't know anything to do. I thought, *What could I say to him. I am only a child.* That very day the struggle began in my heart over what I really believed God saved me to do and what *Mother said* God had called me to do.

She continued rebuking me for being idle, pressuring me to let God put it on me to warn some of the elders in the church who, according to Mother, were not living as God would have them live. I was left with a sense of guilt that if I didn't do as she said, I was displeasing God. Mother's influence over me began during those tender years right after I had been converted to Christianity. When I was at that early age of twelve she began to enter my mind to steer me in the direction she wanted me to go. I was to be her successor in the church. That fact and the fact that I was told over and over again God had spared my life to be a preacher and I was to lead my people were how Mother was so able to enter my mind to influence me so dramatically. That's how brainwashing is accomplished: the continual repetition of an idea or principle so that the hearer takes the idea to be his own and then acts upon it. I began to honestly believe I was doing God's will as I fulfilled the wishes of my adopted mother. But at the same time, the silent struggle began in my own heart about what I actually believed God wanted me to do and what Mother said I should do. I read the Scriptures diligently, poring over them, asking God to help me to understand them, and indeed, some of the beliefs Mother imposed upon us were contrary to my understanding of what the Bible said. For example, Mother said we were not to own ostentatious cars such as Cadillacs. We were to be examples of humility before the world. But the Bible said to me that God judges the heart and if the heart isn't proud, then whatever we have isn't a sin to our souls if we don't go about with

72

an arrogant attitude about what we possess. After all, Solomon, the king, was one of the wealthiest men who ever lived, and his downfall was not his wealth but, rather, turning to worship strange forbidden gods. It was God who had given the wealth to Solomon in the first place.

But children trust their parents. I trusted Mother. I loved her. Many times I had doubts, but I trusted her because she had rescued me when I was totally helpless and dependent upon her. I suppressed my own doubts and followed her commandments. She was the only mother I had ever known. My real mother was gone. At that very tender age of twelve the religious brainwashing began in earnest. But I was not aware of that at all. Looking back on it now, I find it all very plain and easy to see.

One always asks the question: how does an individual become victim to such control by another person? For me and Jim, it began while we were still very young, even before age twelve. Mother had exerted an iron fist over us from the very beginning, and in addition, she began weaving religion and the fear of hellfire itself into everything she brought to us, which planted in us a great awe and respect for her. We had been rescued by her when our own daddy abandoned us. She was very good to provide us with all the material things we needed in our new life. We had also witnessed an adult being carried out of church and set on the front steps of the church. That in itself gave us fear bordering on awe, for at that time we truly believed God guided her in everything she did. After giving my heart to God at the age of twelve, she began to brainwash me even more relentlessly. A twelve-year-old is still very much a child and quite vulnerable to brainwashing. It began in earnest then, very slowly, insidiously, and the person, myself in this case, doesn't realize what is happening. Experiencing the practice, and/or belief that blessings came to the obedient, but punishment came to those who failed was also a factor. In my case, as I complied with the demands she placed on me, which she always termed obedience to the Spirit, there followed the reward of her love and acceptance of me. As long as I did exactly what she expected of me, the love was there, but when I failed to comply, then the love was gone. I would not learn that lesson until years later, because in the early years I was such a compliant child. I wanted more than anything else to please her. And the lack of trust in my own judgment also played a part. It would not be until many years later that I would doubt her judgment, but by that time my own would have been developed through my trust in God and God alone. That display of love over the years caused a bond to grow between Mother and me that became so strong nothing or no one but she herself could ever break it. I would have followed her through the fire. She became the dearest person on earth to me. I had more confidence in her than any other living being. The only greater bond than the one between Mother and me was the bond I had in God, and that trust and reliance on Him was what ultimately gave me the strength and the courage, years later, to escape from the religious prison in which I lived.

After having those expectations repeated to me relentlessly, I finally began to accept that maybe she was right. Maybe I *was* supposed to rebuke people. So I began to pray to God to show me what He wanted me to do. It was not long before I felt moved to rebuke one of the elders for some mistake he had made. That pleased Mother. She continued to nurture me for other works of God. We became very close over the years and would sit for hours at a time discussing the faults and weaknesses of the members of the congregation. Mother's intentions were good. She wanted to help them become better Christians, and during those early years she really helped everyone. It was not until she began to lose control that she became so extreme and started to destroy what she had built, by finding fault with virtually everything and everybody. Her desire to control became more important than showing true Christian love, which she had done in the years past. And that was so sad.

With the abuse at school continuing and my feeling of inferiority increasing, the place I held in church gave me a sense of fitting in. At school I felt like an outcast. I had withdrawn from everyone. Nobody wanted to be my friend. I lived alone.

Being alone was not fun. I longed to be accepted like everyone else. Watching the other kids as they laughed and played made my pain even greater. In church, however, I was safe. I was among those who loved me, and there was never any reason to fear. I knew I could trust God. He was always the same. There was a place for me in church, a purpose. I was actually somebody in church, not some creep whom nobody wanted to have anything to do with. My purpose was to help my people serve God, bring them the Word of God, and lead them back to the right path when they went astray. Going to the altar, kneeling down with my face on the floor, humbling myself before God, and praying to Him about everything in my life gave me great strength, for I learned that I could tell God anything without His lashing out at me and making me feel small or stupid. Sitting in the pew singing the beautiful hymns made all the pains of the week just vanish away. I looked forward to attending church so much. It was so comforting and uplifting.

Our religious beliefs gave me a sense of belonging, a sense of identity. To keep them was to know who I was and what I was doing. I was doing God's will. That gave me peace inside. Our beliefs that to the other people in our community were so peculiar did not seem so to me. By not going to the movies, not drinking bottled drinks, not smoking, not buying anything on Sunday, the girls not wearing pants, not wearing jewelry, and not cutting their hair, and even not going to the doctor, all these things made our life simple, and peaceful. We didn't have a lot to worry about. We left all our worries to God. It was truly a wonderful life. I was totally loyal to Mother and listened to all the things she had taught us to do or not do.

There developed a wonderful bond between the two of us during those years even though at the same time she was beating me for the "dirty tricks," of which I was completely innocent and totally ignorant as well. I do, however, remember thinking to myself after I had been saved that surely Mother would know now that I was telling her the truth, because she would know that since I was saying the same thing I said before, I was telling the truth, because now I certainly wouldn't lie. I even sat next to her in the church pew and said to myself, *If she would only ask God, He would let her know I was telling the truth.* But it didn't work that way. My only comforting recourse was to pray to God as I knelt at the altar and wept, realizing that He knew I was being truthful. That was the beginning of the relationship between myself and God, which sustained me through my darkest hours, for I knew God always understood me and saw me exactly as I was, even when no one else seemed to understand and trust me.

I always tried to please her, to do exactly what she wanted of me, both in the church and outside as well. Those were the good years, or so it seemed at the time. Looking back now, however, I see Mother was never content to let peace reign in the church but always had to bring judgment or a rebuke to someone about something. If only Mother had not destroyed it with her religious fanaticism, the church could have grown to be a very large congregation of people with a boundless amount of true Christian love.

Our interpretation of the Scriptures was that God's people were to be different from the world. That gave me a feeling of pride that I was different from the world and that pleased God. We had been taught that we were the saved of the world and everyone else was lost. I heard it preached all my life growing up that we were like the "Children of Israel, God's chosen people." We had been called out of the world to be different, to live separate from the world, and to pray for their souls. When one believes such a thing as that, it has a mystical air about it to the believer, almost like a fairy tale. It seemed so to me at that time.

It was not until many years later that I could see the fallacy in that belief. How can anyone know he is loved if no one ever tells him or has anything to do with him? It's not possible.

After I was saved, I thought surely Mother would stop beating me for the wet spots on my pajamas, but no, it didn't make a bit of difference. I even sat in the church pew beside her and said to myself, *Why doesn't she know I'm telling the truth? If she would ask God, He would let her know I was telling the truth.* I guess she never asked Him. I knew God was good and had nothing to do with these bad things she was doing.

To find peace and happiness during the week, I began to spend lots of time in the woods surrounding the house. Hours and hours I wandered through the trees and underbrush. I liked nothing better. I was alone with nature. There was nothing to fear. The thought of snakes rarely entered my mind, and I'm sure God looked out for me on that account, for there were many poisonous snakes indigenous to the area. I learned all of the North Carolina songbirds, their distinct songs, their nesting places, the colors of their eggs, how many they laid, etc.

One Christmas Jim and I got a BB gun. We were so excited. It was fun to go hunting. The challenge of shooting birds was great. However, you know how boys are. There was a pasture not too far from our house that had hogs in it belonging to our neighbor Max Cutler. Jim and I got the idea that it would be exciting and funny to shoot the hogs with our BB guns. They were a good distance from us, so we figured it wouldn't hurt them. When the BBs hit them, they would jump and let out a little squeal. It was funny until the owner told Mother about it. She wore us both out with a big switch and took our guns away, too. I don't remember hunting anymore after that.

The same farmer had a dog. That was the most beautiful dog I had ever seen. Her hair was raven black and so clean it just glistened in the sunlight. She had the face of a German shepherd, with tall, pointy ears and extremely intelligent eyes. Those ears were always standing straight up to catch every sound. She seemed to be on the alert at all times. Occasionally, when Max first got her, she would wander across the street to our house. I would put my arms around her, holding her tight. She would follow me around until Max called for her. I loved her from the very first time I laid eyes on her and longed to have her as my own.

All went well until she developed mange. She lost all the fur on her body except the hair on her head and face. Poor thing, her beauty was gone, but my love for her was not. She didn't even look like a dog, rather like some strange pink creature with a black head and black pointy ears. I inquired around among my relatives about a cure for mange. I was told a copper collar would do the job. I got a piece of copper pipe and fashioned her a collar to wear around her neck. Then I began to beg Mother to please let me have her. I saw that Max didn't take care of her. My pleas became even more urgent after I came home from school one afternoon to find the poor thing had no water.

It was a hot day in September. As we walked by the place where she was tied with a chain, she was pacing back and forth at the end of that chain trying to bark. The only noise to come out of her throat was a raspy squeak. I was horrified. I couldn't believe anyone could be so cruel, so careless. I knew then Max didn't care about the dog. Running to the house as fast as my skinny legs would take me, I put my books up, told Mother where I was going, and ran over to give her some water. When I put the pan of water down before her, she lapped it up in great gulping mouthfuls like she was dying of thirst, and I'm sure she was. When she had enough, she wagged her tail thankfully and licked my hands. I loved her so much. Mother would not relent and let me have her, though.

Later that fall Max was raking leaves and burning them one day. He shot the poor dog, threw her on a pile of leaves, and burned her up. It made me sad but at the same time glad, because I knew she would never have to suffer anymore. She would never spend a hot, dry summer day barking for water or going hungry or be kicked around and yelled at by some unkind person.

My sister Eva, who had been adopted by Aunt Esther, first lived in an area at the outskirts of town called the Brickyard. Eva spent many lonely days in the house with no one to play with her. Aunt Esther had divorced her husband, who had mistreated her rather badly from what Mother had told me, and worked every day in town for one of the clothing stores as a seamstress. She became one of the very best, too. She and Eva had moved to town and lived in an upstairs apartment off Main Street. Jim and I went to their home on Saturdays to stay with Eva while Mother, Aunt Esther, and Daddy went off somewhere.

Jim and I absolutely loved to go there. It was so much fun. Evie, as we called Eva, would make French fries. There Jim and I could eat all we wanted without feeling guilty or afraid to ask for more. We were like birds out of a cage. While we three were together, we made up all kinds of silly things to say that weren't even words, so we could laugh and have fun. For example, Evie would say "finch" whenever we made a statement. We all laughed. Jim and I would say such things as "ross-a-thoss-a-yeeb-yeeby." Then we would go into hysterical laughter. We would not have dared to do such a thing in Mother's presence. We would have been rebuked, then beaten for being foolish. When we went for a walk down the street, if our elbows as much as barely touched as we walked along, just that would send us into peals of laughter. I know it sounds stupid, but we would have the silly giggles the entire time we spent with Eva. It was wonderful! I have such fond memories of those days with my dear sister, and she and I became very close as the years went by.

78

I know this sounds silly as you read it, but if in your world there was no laughter and, besides, you were chastised for it or even beaten, then you can understand why we were foolish when we were away from that world. You know, children have a lot of joy and mirth inside them and it needs to come out. For me it was like the laughter had been kept inside, restrained, and when the opportunity arose it came out like a fountain spraying out water. It was good for us, too. We went away feeling much the better for it.

Hurricane Hazel came in the fall of 1954. Satellite weather forecasts were nonexistent in those days. We barely had enough warning to get out of school and go home. It was announced over the radio that a hurricane had struck the beaches in Wilmington and was headed our way. School was closed early. We were no sooner home than the hurricane struck us with its full fury. Mother and Jim were scared to death.

I wondered why Mother was so afraid. She would say to me, "How can you stand there at the window looking out? Aren't you afraid?" Yet she had stood in the church over the years and told me that my life had been spared so that I could grow up to be a preacher. That had not happened yet, so my faith in God told me that I would not die. There was no need to have fear, yet it seemed to me she had doubts, and that didn't make sense to me. I was fascinated with the storm. It was beautiful at the same time that it was so powerful and destructive.

We were very fortunate. Our house sustained no damage, just a lot of trees were blown down. Two of the largest oak trees I've ever seen were blown over. Their trunks were so huge that it took three men holding hands to reach around the circumference of the tree. As they fell, they took at least a dozen trees down with them. I was watching in utter amazement when it happened.

My sister Josie learned to play the piano that same year. We didn't listen to the radio, so I had no previous contact with music. I had never heard music before, other than the songs we sang in church, where Aunt Esther led the singing. We had no instrument to accompany us. I guess there was no one to play, and a piano was expensive, too. The most beautiful sound I had ever heard in my life came out of that piano when Josie played. It reminded me of the sound of angels. I could discern the different sounds made by the various keys as she struck them. It was divine. My mama's love for music had been passed to me, but I didn't know it at that time. All I knew was that I had never heard anything so beautiful in all my short life and I wanted to hear it over and over again. I would beg Josie to play for me. Sometimes she would play a little, but most times she'd say, "I can't play. I make too many mistakes" Of course I knew she could play. I'd seen her do it. No amount of pleading, however, would persuade her to play for me. So I said to her, "Well, you can rest assured of one thing. If I ever learn to play and someone asks me to, I'm going to play for them even if I do make mistakes." And I have always done just that.

So I began to beg Mother to let me take piano lessons. "How do you know you can learn to play?"

I said, "Give me lessons and I will learn."

Then her next question was, "Where will you practice? You don't have a piano."

"I'll practice on Mrs. Dobson's piano," was my response to that question. You can see I was a very determined child, and that determination has come in a good stead for me through the years.

Mrs. Dobson was a friend of ours whom Mother had helped to learn to drive a car, a widow with an only child, Sharon. Mother felt sorry for her and, to help financially, would buy eggs and butter from her. She lived about a good city block from us and had an old upright piano in her living room. That could be my practice instrument. After some continued pleading, Mother inquired in town about teachers, and I started taking piano lessons from Mrs. Doll Smith. She taught out of her home on Lee Street. It was so wonderful learning to play.

Sometimes when I went to practice at Mrs. Dobson's, she and Sharon would be gone to town. I stood out by the highway for an hour in the cold watching the headlamps of the oncoming cars, hoping the next set of lights would be those of Mrs. Dobson's car and would turn in her driveway. Then I'd be able to practice. Many times I practiced the piano in her living room when it was so cold my fingers were so stiff I could hardly play. But I was very determined to learn. Mrs. Smith took me all the way to John Thompson's third-grade book in a year and a half. I loved it. Music opened up a whole new world for me. It was wonderful! Later in my life, music would sustain me when situations in my life became even more difficult to bear.

The last two years spent in that school were the most traumatic for me emotionally. By then the boys' animosity against me had reached a level that made my life very unpleasant.

The first day of school was a nightmare. I dreaded it like the plague. I would have rather had Mother beat me black-and-blue than go to school on the first day. At least a beating stopped hurting when the lash or switch stopped hitting my back, but I had to endure the humiliation all day long at school. The students congregated in the gym in order to learn who their homeroom teachers were. When my name was called, those certain students would start hissing, booing quite loudly, and calling me sissy and queer right there in front of all the other students. It was so humiliating. I wished the floor would swallow me up, but all I could do was look down at the floor and continue walking to my homeroom group. Other students, who didn't know me, began to recognize the kid who was called names.

There was nobody to be my friend. The girls who at one time liked me now had about as much contempt for me as the boys did. Then in the eighth grade something happened that made matters even worse for me. One of the students in my room took the paint we were using to color leaves with for a class play and vandalized the classroom. Our teacher tried unsuccessfully to learn who had done the deed. No one would tell her.

Suddenly her eyes lit on me. My heart sank. I wished I could have vanished. I dreaded her question. She knew if she asked me, I would tell her the truth. I told her several times I didn't want to say, but she was very insistent. I knew she knew I knew, and I was afraid she would punish me if I didn't comply. When I gave her the student's name, his buddies were furious. I knew they had it in for me. His girlfriend said to me with a sneer, "John Hall, if I were you I would get on those skinny legs of yours and start running and I wouldn't stop, either." She was the same girl who, in the fourth grade, had given me the quarters so I would like her. I responded by saying that I wasn't afraid of him. That afternoon on the playground he and his buddies ganged up on me. One got down behind me on his hands and knees. The other two kept pushing me hoping

I would lose my balance and fall backward over the one behind me. They continued hitting me, trying to start a fight. I believed and tried to practice what Jesus taught, to turn the other cheek. So I did nothing in my defense except to ask them, "Why don't you leave me alone? What have I done to you?" They just glared at me with contempt. When they saw I wouldn't retaliate, they finally left me alone.

My name became so notorious that one day during lunch a high school student came up to me as I leaned against the railing by the gym door and with a sneer, asked, "Are you John Hall?"

I answered, "You know what my name is."

With that he turned and sulked off. I felt like I was some kind of freak. I was already scarred for life, but fortunately, at the time I didn't know it, at least not in those terms. Life was very lonely for me, to say the least.

Most of our summers were spent working in tobacco. In the summer of 1955, a small pimple about the size of the head of a pin developed on the inside of my left leg immediately above the ankle bone. The skin around it was red and the center was filled with yellow pus. I thought nothing of it until it continued to get worse. Within a few months the small yellow pimple had turned into a bad sore. The surface ruptured and began to ooze fluid. It grew steadily larger until it reached the size of a silver dollar. The top of it projected above my leg about an eighth of an inch. A clear reddish fluid seeped out of it all the time. The surface appeared like the color of ground beef and glistened in the light due to the continual seepage of plasma. The surface was exquisitely tender to touch. The outer edge was like a lip that was curled down, just as if it had been rolled. It was quite dreadful to look at.

Many times it ached at night after I had gone to bed, especially if I had been on my feet a lot that day. Sometimes as I walked, the heel of my right foot struck right against the sore. Oh, it was so painful, just like touching raw flesh, and that's exactly what it was, raw flesh. When I stood at the tobacco barn bench handing tobacco, as we did in those days, my leg throbbed so bad. I had to prop my foot up on a small wooden crate to lessen the pressure on it, which helped. Mind you, we didn't believe in taking medicine for pain or for infection or for anything else, either, for that matter. Our religion forbade it and also forbade our seeing a doctor, so I had only God to trust in to help me.

The next summer another sore came on the other leg in the very same place. Fortunately, it never grew to be as large as the first one, only about the size of a dime.

I'll never forget the Christmas I was riding in the front seat of my sister Dana's car on the way to Fayetteville on a shopping trip. The older of the two sores had, without my knowing, begun to smell rotten. All of a sudden Dana said, "I smell a dead rat." I held my breath. *Would they find out about those sores?* I thought frantically. *What would they say? What would they think?* I was so afraid they would discover the truth, that it was I who was stinking. I didn't want to be treated like a freak by my dear sisters, so I remained very still and silent. You can't imagine the pain it would have brought me had they discovered the truth and then recoiled from me in horror. I don't know if I could have borne that sorrow; I really don't. Fortunately, the stench was weak and they forgot it right away. And such a relief for me, too!

The summer of my junior year in high school I spent in North Carolina. All my summers were spent there really. There was nothing that would take the place of those summers in North Carolina. They were a few weeks of freedom for me. I didn't realize that fact at the time; I just knew it meant more than anything else to me to spend the summers in North Carolina. I said to Mother once when it seemed she wasn't going to let me go, "Well, you'd just as soon chop my head off as to not let me go." She didn't appreciate my comment one bit.

Those sores were still on my legs. I wanted so much for them to be healed. They had been on my legs for so long, one for three years and the other one for two years. I had to wear white socks all the time because Mother had been told they were better since they had no dye in them. Every day it was necessary to dress these sores with a gauze bandage. They wet the bandages, and then the fluid soaked through to my socks. I had to be so careful not to bump them. It was quite painful if I did.

As I knew I had no other source of help, it came into my heart to fast and bring my sores before the church, so maybe God would look on me with favor and heal them. I knew He could if it was His will. At that time I was extremely thin, almost like a skeleton; I was five feet, ten and one-half inches tall and weighed only 126 pounds with a twenty-six inch waist. On that Thursday I neither ate nor drank anything the whole day until after church. I worked in tobacco, too, just like I usually did. That night in church I stood before the congregation and brought my request for my legs to be healed. We practiced what the Bible taught: the King James Version. "When there is one among you who is sick, let the elders pray over him and anoint him with oil and he shall be healed."

Everyone was touched by my having fasted and came to the altar to pray for me. Uncle Bob anointed my legs. I was so happy in my spirit. I shouted all around the altar. Others were shouting, too. Someone had embraced me, and the next thing I remember, I heard a loud noise like the roar of a waterfall. My first conscious thought was, *What is that noise? Where am I?* For a split second I had no idea where on earth I was. As consciousness returned, realizing where I was, I attempted to sit up, all the while gasping for breath, great heaving gasps as if my very life depended upon it. I was pushing everyone away from my face in an effort to get some fresh air. It seemed to me if they didn't get away from my face so I could breathe, I would die. I've never felt so desperate for air.

Many had knelt around me to pray, for they feared I was dying. Eva later told me my legs had started drawing up into a fetal position. And Mother told me I would never be any colder even if I were dead. When they saw I was living, everyone moved away from me, which helped so much.

When I finally caught my breath, I asked for a glass of water. Mother came immediately and whispered in my ear that I should get up or the church would doubt me. I said, "I'm too weak. If I try to sit on the bench, I'll faint again," but she persisted, so I managed to pull myself up on the bench. The next thing I knew, I was back on the floor. I was simply too weak to sit up. Even after lying there on the floor for the remainder of the service, I couldn't stand up so Uncle Bob carried me out to the car. He drove me down to Grandmother's house. She and Dana lived a short distance down a dirt road behind the church where Aunt Rosie and Uncle Kevin used to live. After eating, I finally regained enough strength to go home. But the sores didn't heal. I accepted it was not yet God's will for them to go away. I must be patient, endure them a little longer, and wait.

Sometime later that winter, someone told Mother that if the sores were covered with a mixture of Vaseline and sulfur that would cure them. So she got some and put it on them for me. A couple of days later, she woke me up in the middle of the night crying. I'll never forget it. She came to my upper bunk bed and told me she was sorry for putting that sulfur on my sores. It had been a moment of weakness in faith that caused her to do it. She washed it all off as she wept. It broke my heart to think she would repent to me for something she had done in order to help me. Those sores would remain on my legs for a few more years before finally healing.

We moved to Charleston, South Carolina, in the summer of 1955. That was a blessing for me in more ways than one.

4

We were so excited about moving, because Mother said Daddy would have a good job again with the shipyard there in Charleston. That meant he didn't have to work such long, tiresome hours, doing things he wasn't really trained to do. We were so glad for him. Our first home in South Carolina was a rented two-story house in a residential section in Charleston across the Ashley River. My, it seemed wonderful when Mother went grocery shopping. The bags of groceries she brought home! It was unbelievable. It reminded me of how it was in California. The last two years in North Carolina had been very lean. Jim even said "Daddy makes rich money now." That entire summer seemed like a celebration. We had lots of company from back home. The dinners Mother cooked were delicious.

Since Mrs. Dobson's piano was no longer available and there was money to buy one, Mother found a nice used upright piano for me. Now I was really uptown with my own piano. It was as good as a brand-new one to me! I could practice all I wanted to now. We kept the piano in the basement, which had a smooth cement floor. We had skates and could skate inside in all kinds of weather. I can still see us as we went around and around on that basement floor. Occasionally we would grab the steel posts that supported the upstairs as we passed by them, which made our feet spin around and almost slid out from under us. Sometimes I even got blisters on my fingers, too, from holding onto the posts so tightly. It was such fun, though. That was a nice place to live, but we stayed there only a few months. Then we moved back across the Cooper River to Mount Pleasant, South Carolina. The house there belonged to a Mrs. Zurich, a German lady who had immigrated to this country many years ago. She still spoke with an obvious accent and was also quite contentious. Mrs. Zurich made Mother put down a deposit for damage to the house, which Mother resented highly because she had to spend hours cleaning the place just to make it livable. The house really was filthy. Mother was an excellent housekeeper; in fact, I think she might have been one of the best. There was something rather foreboding about the place, too. It was a low cinderblock house painted white. The trees and shrubbery around the house were overgrown. Black mildew grew on the cinder blocks near the ground and up the sides of the house in places.

As I said before, I loved to spend time wandering through the woods. Even the woods behind the house were the same way, kinda scary, spooky, and foreboding. Thick, dense vegetation grew everywhere. Not much sunlight could penetrate the forest floor, not at all like the sunny woods I was accustomed to wandering through back home. There was even an element of fear in them too. And mosquitoes. Millions of mosquitoes infested the place during the hot summer months. I didn't spend much time in the woods, either, like I wanted to do, for those reasons just mentioned.

One event from our time in that old house stands out so vividly in my mind. One Saturday, Mother was sitting at the table as I stood in the doorway leaning against the door casing. The subject of her beating me for the "dirty tricks" had come up. I can see her face now as she looked up at me as I began to talk. Her eyes, which at times could be warm and loving, became cold and hard. Her expression became one of impassive stony disbelief. I looked her square in the face and said, "Well, you can beat me to death, but I'll never again tell you another lie. I haven't done anything, and I don't know what you're talking about. You can beat me all you want to, but I'll never lie again." My eyes filled with tears from the emotion of my resolution, but I meant exactly what I said. It made her angry, but she never beat me again for that. Looking back now, I can see that with my facing off with her, my resolution actually set me free. Escape from the terror of those awful beatings had finally come for me. Soon, however, things would become very bad for poor Jim.

One of the most profound events of my life happened while Jim and I were living at Mrs. Zurich's and still attending Mount Pleasant High School. It has affected my life ever since that day. Mother had instilled in us the importance of being modest, of dressing in private. It was almost a sin to look at another person naked. Remember, I had great fear of Mother's wrath if I didn't do as she said. I knew she would find out, too, if I had not been obedient to her.

So, I was so nervous on that first day of PE in the locker room before changing. My heart was pounding so hard I could barely keep still. I kept waiting and waiting, hoping the other guys would hurry and change and leave so I could change. We had been warned by the gym teacher if we were late, we had to run laps around the football field. That would have been easy punishment compared to getting a horrible beating for disobeying Mother's orders. I feared the wrath of my mother more than I feared the teacher. I was getting rather desperate by the time most all the boys were gone. I thought everyone had left the locker room when I began to change my clothes. I was shaking so from nerves and tension that I could hardly get dressed. As I pulled my gym shorts on over my tennis shoes, my spastic movements caused the toe of my shoe to get stuck in the pant leg. I almost lost my balance and fell.

Suddenly an older student came walking out of the shower area naked as a jaybird. Had I known he was naked, I wouldn't have looked in his direction. What I saw in that instant has affected my life ever since. I had thought everyone was like me. I did not know that some men had such large private parts. I did not know at the time that being nervous and scared makes one's member shrink up even more, all I knew was he looked wonderful as a male and I looked pathetically small. At that moment I would have given anything to be like him.

It was as if the realization struck me that maybe that's why the boys in Whiteville had called me queer. I was so small compared to them. I assumed then that all other boys had such big private parts. I had always wondered what was wrong with me that made them call me those terrible names, now I assumed it was related to that. It made me sick. I felt more inferior than ever. I had physical evidence of it. Now in addition to the pain of being rejected by them, I had to deal with the pain of knowing I was inferior to them in a way that made me feel much less of a male. It was really a profound and painful revelation for me at that young age, considering the scars that had already been put in my mind from all the mistreatment by my peers.

For years I carried that weight around with me, feeling so inferior to all other boys. I fought it so hard. I wanted to be like everyone else, to be accepted by the other boys and not be treated like there was something wrong with me. If only I could change like the ugly duckling did in that story and turn out to be like them that would be so wonderful.

I finished changing and as we did our exercises I thought to myself, *If only I could be like them*, but somehow knowing it would never be. My peers' rejecting me earlier in my life had instilled in me the intense inferiority complex I had to fight all my life. Most of the time it's not a problem anymore, but occasionally it still tries to assert itself even now, after all these many years.

Mother began looking for property right away to buy to build a house on. Whenever she found something interesting, she would first check it out herself. If she liked the place, then she would get her favorite brother, Uncle Swift, to come look at it for her. She placed a great deal of importance on his judgment. The two of them would pray over it, and if they felt it was God's will, then that's the property she would buy. She found a lot there in Mount Pleasant, made a $350 deposit on it, and then began to feel disturbed about it. She tried to get her money back, but to no avail. After the ordeal was over, it was just a relief to know she had not purchased the lot.

Next she found a lot in Berkeley Hills, a nice, fairly new residential section in North Charleston. Uncle Swift went with her to look at it. They both felt this was the place for Mother to buy, which she did.

Then we moved to North Charleston to a small house in a rather run-down housing project named Woodbine. Mother decided to have Uncle Swift build our new house, for she knew no building contractors in Charleston. He was an excellent builder, one Mother could trust to do a good job. Uncle Swift made plans for W. J. Fisher, a cousin of ours, to come help him with the construction of the house. The two of them would stay with us during the week while working on the house, then go home to their families on weekends.

Having them build the house was a good plan, with one major drawback: the extra company posed a problem with sleeping arrangements because the house was so small. The solution was making Jim and me sleep up in the attic on a mattress laid on the floor. At bedtime we climbed the disappearing stairway and Mother closed it after us, leaving the two of us in complete darkness. It was rather scary at first. We would say to each other, "What if they didn't open the stairs for us in the morning? What would we do?" We took a bucket up there with us to pee in, too. It was there as the two of us lay talking before going to sleep that I learned how to masturbate. A cousin of ours had taught Jim how to do it, and he told me how. Just think—those three years Mother had been beating me for those "dirty tricks," and now I had finally learned how to do it.

We enjoyed Uncle Swift and W.J. being there, for as I have said before, as long as someone was with us, Mother wouldn't beat us. Unbeknownst to them, they were our insurance against a beating. It was also fun to go out to the construction site and see the progress being made on our new home. But, there was no way on earth we could have had any idea of the horrors that lay ahead for us in that house.

5

Soon we were moved into our beautiful new home. It was a ranch-style house with charcoal gray cedar siding. There was a large plate-glass picture window in the center of the living room. Mother used lots of color in this house just like she did in the house in North Carolina. Our kitchen had beautiful stained-wood cabinets. Red and white linoleum tiles covered the floor in the kitchen. The other floors were finished oak. They were beautiful. Ceramic tiles were used in both bathrooms. A bow window extended from the kitchen table. We could look out at the birds and flowers while we ate breakfast. In our new home we even had a separate dining room, a living room, and a den. There was another picture window in the den. Plate-glass windows were very popular in those days. Almost every new house had one. The view was so spectacular looking out of them. From the den we had the view of the creek behind the house.

Jim and I had our bedroom at one end of the house with our own adjoining bathroom. Mother and Daddy's bedroom was at the other end of the house with their adjoining bathroom, and their bedroom had wall-to-wall carpeting which seemed wonderful. It felt so soft and luxurious to our feet when we walked over it

Mother had very strict rules to follow in this house. We always had to take off our shoes before entering the house so as not to take in dirt that might be on our shoes. And we had to turn the cuffs of our trousers inside out to remove any dirt trapped inside them. Without fail, she reminded us of those trouser cuffs every single time we entered that house. She was a very fastidious housekeeper. Every morning it was our duty to take the dust mop and go over the floors so they would be free of lint. It was done every day except Sunday of course. We did no work at all on Sunday. These practices kept our house sparkly clean. I enjoyed dusting the knickknacks that sat around on shelves and tables. I liked having a clean house, myself. I was always a very neat and tidy child. Even when I worked, I didn't get my clothes dirty like most people

We were happy in this new house until things began to turn upside down for us. While we were still in North Carolina, Jim had fallen in love with one of his cousins. Since we were not allowed to wear engagement rings, he had given her a hope chest made of cedar. There were even plans of marriage in the future. Then at one of our church services back home, Mother stood as she did many times and told us something God had shown her. This time she told a dream she had. In her dream she had planted two pine trees. One had grown tall and stately; I was that tree. The other one was all dried up so that it was nearly dead. That tree was Jim. Realizing it was dying, she fell down on her knees and tried desperately to press dirt around the bare roots with her hands where it appeared the rain had washed all the soil away.

The dirt didn't want to stay; it seemed to disappear as soon as she would put some in place, and as she continued trying to pack dirt at the roots, a hand appeared out of the branches. As she looked at the hand, it was all mangled as if someone had chewed it. She said a voice spoke to her saying that her brother's daughter had bitten Jim's hand. It was a wound unto death. Mother knew it was the cousin.

When Mother awoke, she believed God had visited her. I could have never known that day in church, but from that time on Mother began with uncompromising zeal to do everything in her power to terminate the relationship between Jim and the poor girl. Mother began to poison his mind about the girl, portraying her as some kind of evil, sensual person, whose spirit could even possess him. You must understand that by this time in our lives we had grown to trust Mother completely and believed whatever she said. *And, moreover, even if we had not believed her, there was nothing we could have done in protest.* In my heart of hearts I wondered how the girl could be as bad as Mother made her out to be. It just didn't make sense to me. Mother put the girl's parents through a living nightmare, going to their home all hours of the night and day to "bring them the truth" about their child. Mother's powers of persuasion at that time were very great, but looking back on those events now, I realize neither my aunt nor my uncle had a strong relationship with God, but relied upon Mother to tell them what to do. Their awe, trust, and reverence for her blinded their ability to put their trust in God themselves. They would believe things Mother told them about their child even though they knew it was not possibly true. That was the extent to which some of the congregation had been brainwashed.

The poor girl had to return the hope chest to Jim, and he gave it to Mother to keep for him. After having the dream, she took the ax and chopped the hope chest in pieces and threw it into the creek behind the house. It was as if Mother believed she had to destroy everything associated with the girl. Moreover, poor Jim was made to help the girl's daddy bury her clothes. Jim was required to dig a hole out by the church cemetery just outside the fence. The church grounds were considered sacred, so with Jim burying the clothes there God would help to terminate the relationship between the two; that's what he was made to believe. That poor girl went through torment because of Mother. Once Mother stood before the entire congregation and said the girl should be taken out and stoned. Another time the poor girl's father beat her in the bathroom in the church because Mother told him she needed to be punished. I can still hear her as she fell against the walls in her efforts to escape his belt. The rest of us were in the sanctuary on our knees praying. I cried and cried. It was so horrible to me. Mother had begun to change at that time, but many years had to pass before my trust in her could be broken. I was busy with my studies in college and did not have time to dwell on these events very deeply, and Mother was still a very powerful figure in my life. It was only deep in my heart that I questioned the things that were being done. I still only saw Mother as one who wanted to help the people become better Christians.

Mother used religion to achieve many of her goals. Jim had been told so many times that if he couldn't come to the things in Mother's heart, there was no way he could get to God. She would be standing before him in church with the Bible in one hand, touching her chest with her other hand, as she spoke. That was enough to frighten him into doing anything she demanded of him, no matter how difficult it was emotionally or otherwise. The congregation was told that same thing, and many of them believed it literally, too.

Jim did for years and years. Those who did actually viewed Mother as their gateway to God, and without her they felt lost and ruined. That's how much control she had over them.

Mother used poor Jim many times in other ways, too. There was a creek that flowed right behind our house. The water rose and fell with the tides. There were marsh weeds that grew on the water. Sometimes they grew so thick they covered the entire surface of the creek. Mother wanted to be able to see the water. So she would make Jim go out in a boat with a bush ax and cut those water grasses so they could float out with the tide. I don't see how he did it—sheer strength, I suppose. He always has been exceptionally strong for his size. He risked being bitten by water moccasins, cutting himself with the ax, and falling out of the boat and drowning, for he could not swim at the time.

It seemed Mother now became obsessed with Jim's masturbating, and with anything having to do with sex concerning both of us. We did not realize it at the time, but when Jim and I reached puberty it was almost as if Mother wanted to destroy the male part of us. I know now that my biological father had tried to molest her when she was a child, which event she certainly couldn't forget, but she took out her anger and frustration at her brother, our daddy, on us. We were these terrible male creatures that were the product of the one who had tried to molest her as a child. She was going to beat that male "stuff" out of us. Understanding the issues as I do now makes the past clearer. The rage I felt from her the first time she beat me for the "dirty tricks" makes sense now, but then I had no idea why she was angry at me. Now her anger focused on poor Jim. He had confessed to her that a cousin had shown him how to masturbate. After that she began to beat him, but even worse than she had beaten me. And she told poor Jim that God had put it on her to beat him so he would not become an adulterer like his natural father. I wonder now if in order to ease her conscience she convinced herself that God had directed her to beat Jim. I now have two dear daughters, and I would kneel before anyone and allow them to beat me to death before I would stand on my feet and do to them what was done to Jim and me. I couldn't even do those horrible things to a complete stranger. I cannot comprehend the kind of love she claimed to have for us. It makes no sense to me. Many times he

94

would ask her, "Mother, what have I done? What are you beating me for?"

"God has put it on me to beat you so you won't be an adulterer like your daddy," was always her reply.

Think of that for a moment if you will. Jim was only thirteen years old at the time, and would a child at such a tender age, especially during the decade of the fifties, really understand what an adulterer is? I think not. In addition, we were kept isolated from the outside world except for the contacts we had in school and when we went to town. We had no friends to visit us, nor did we visit anyone. And there we were, two scrawny little kids struggling with our identity, too, as males, with this terrible ruthless woman beating us for the natural functions of our little bodies, keeping us in a constant state of fear and terror. We both wanted to be like the other boys and be allowed to play sports at school. It's so difficult to explain on paper the pain of feeling so much an outsider, an outcast, someone nobody is interested in. I remember once Jim and I went in the locker room after the football players had gone out on the field to practice. It was as if we pretended for that short moment in time that we, too, were football players. We each found a discarded athletic supporter, put it on under our other clothes, and wore it home. Somehow that seemed to help us to feel a part of that world we so wanted to be included in. I also remember the sheer terror we both felt when Mother noticed the supporters under our clothes and questioned us about them. We had forgotten to be certain our shirt was over them. I'll never understand why she didn't beat us, but that time we escaped with only a verbal reprimand. There was no part of our world that escaped her.

The constant fear of getting a beating turned our world upside down. We talk about teenage crisis today. Jim and I had a crisis, but it was not like those of teenagers of the nineties, but was one of escaping the rod of correction. We never knew when she was going to beat him. When she did, she would tell me, "Johnny, you go in the living room and play the piano while I beat him, so the neighbors can't hear him hollering." I dreaded those awful words. I would be sick to the pit of my stomach. My heart would be pounding so hard it seemed it was in my throat right below my ears. Fear made my throat feel dry and tight, and swallowing was difficult. I felt like I would choke. My leg would be trembling as my foot pressed on the piano pedal. As I listened to them going down the hall, my stomach drew up in knots. When the sound of the lash hitting his back came to my ears, I could almost feel it myself. It was awful. Then I slowly began to play hymns, and the sound of the piano drowned out the sound of her beating him, but when I turned the page to another song in the hymnbook, I could hear him hollering so pitifully. Poor Jim. I felt so sorry for him. I couldn't understand why he was getting beaten so much.

Just imagine having to go through that over and over again. And the fear of my getting beaten again was ever-present, too. She had beaten me many times for absolutely nothing. I never knew whether she would beat me next after she had finished with Jim. It was horrible. I dreaded those times for both of us. We had to get ourselves together afterward in our bedroom all alone. A strange thing, too, that we didn't talk about it much then either. We were just so glad when it was finished. We wanted to forget it, if that were possible. Resilience is the beauty and strength of youth—a child is like a sapling in the wind; it bends when the wind blows but doesn't break. When we grow older, we break, because like the tree, we have become hard and rigid. Our resilience is gone. There is no way I could go through those horrible events today.

There is one day in particular that stands out most vividly to me. It was one afternoon after school. We could always tell when we arrived home from school if a beating was forthcoming. One glance at her face told the story. We even commented about it to ourselves on the way home from school that day; we had said to each other, "Wonder if she'll beat you today." Our reason for pondering over it that particular day was because she had beaten him the week before and his back was still black-and-blue and very tender.

When we entered the garage, she met us at the door. Sure enough, one fleeting glance into that cold, almost marblelike, impassive face told us what was coming even before she said a word. "Jim, come on into the bedroom; I've got to beat you," she said in that dreadful voice that made all the blood seem to run into my feet. With the most pitiful pleading tone in his voice, Jim began to beg, "Please, Mother, please don't beat me today; please, my back is still sore." He had not even healed from the last beating. That fact made no difference to her. She beat him anyway, and I had to go play the piano. It made no difference. My eyes fill with tears even as I'm typing these words. I can hear his voice even now. I think on it now, and it's really more than I can comprehend that a mother would beat the back of her child again when it was already black-and-blue, and seemingly without any compassion at all. I hurt just thinking about it. And her claim that her actions were according to God's instructions seems incredible. She had truly become very, very misdirected, far from the will of God.

As I said earlier, like most boys that age, our bodies just produced too much secretion. We were afraid that if we didn't do something to relieve ourselves, we'd have wet dreams, and I had already experienced the punishment for that. We were scared to masturbate in the bathroom. She wouldn't let us lock the door, and we really thought if she caught us in the act, she would probably beat us almost to death. Mother gave us a certain amount of time in the bathroom for the natural functions of the body, and if we ran over the time *she thought* was necessary, she was banging on the door wanting to know what we were doing in there. For a short while she even had me stand at the shower door to watch Jim while he took a shower. We even laughed about it. It was really funny, my standing at the door watching him, as if he would do something while I was watching. Can you, the reader, even comprehend what it's like to live in that kind of world, where every act you perform is policed and you feel like even the thoughts of your mind could be perceived? A world in which you have absolutely no privacy, that any time Mother deemed it necessary she would enter your room? Jim and I felt as if we were naked before her, as if she could see right through us. Is it any wonder that while living in such a state of fear and tension it became an impossibility for me to urinate in a public bathroom unless I was in a stall where I could lock the door. The amusing thing about it all was that Mother tried to control everything about us, but we were a little bit smarter then she was. We did it in a handkerchief at night after we had gone to bed, then hid the hankie beneath the mattress. Can you imagine, we were afraid to go into the bathroom for that purpose after Mother had gone to bed? She could have heard the door open or close, so we hurriedly did what was necessary and caught it in the hankie. Those reading this account of our adolescent years may find it hard to believe, but that was the depth of our fear. Our entire life was ruled by Mother with an iron hand. Our home was a virtual prison. No room was safe from her. We were OK with the hankie-thing until that dreadful Saturday morning when she washed the mattress cover and turned the mattress over. There lay the hankies. She picked one up and smelled it, then threw it down in disgust. We were scared to death. I just knew she was going to beat us half to death, but something even worse than that would take place. Her ruthless mind began a plan that very day.

Then the unspeakable happened. She was bound and determined to prevent Jim from masturbating, so she had Daddy get her a pair of handcuffs. She made my poor brother put his hands behind his back. He was only fourteen. Then, just like one does with a convict, she locked those handcuffs onto his arms right before he went to bed. He had to sleep with those things on his wrists. Can you imagine that?! Sleeping in bed with your hands handcuffed behind your back! Just think about the pain and discomfort, not only to your wrists but to your shoulders as well. He had to back up to the bed and literally fall onto it; he had no control and not much balance. It's more than I can comprehend now to think someone would become so misdirected as to do such a thing as that to a mere child and, of all things, believe she was doing God's will. It was absolutely heinous.

We had bunk beds. I slept on the top bunk. Jim slept on the bottom. I felt so sorry for Jim, and actually felt guilty that I didn't have to wear handcuffs myself. After all, he had not done anything more than I had. Night after night I would lean over the side and call down to him, "Jim, are you doing all right? Can you sleep?" I was so concerned about him. It was so horrible to see him go to bed with his hands behind him like that. This went on night after night. I remember his calling up to me one particular night and saying, "Johnny, my shoulders hurt so bad I can't sleep!" I can still hear his pained and pleading voice as he said those words. They wrenched at my heartstrings. It took me a long time to go to sleep, too, lying there thinking about him down below me in that dreadful fix. The only position he could get in was on his side. But by morning his shoulders were so sore from being twisted in that contorted position that it took a while before he could even move them freely.

However, out of pure desperation to survive the horrible ordeal Jim learned how to wiggle his butt and legs through his manacled hands. It took several attempts before he mastered the trick. Then he was able to rest his hands on his stomach and sleep so much better. With his doing that, however, he had to be on the alert for Mother the next morning. Had she found him with his hands on his stomach, there's no telling what she might have done. When he heard her coming, (he could hear her through the heat vents), he quickly flipped his legs and butt back like they were when she last saw him. What one can do when the situation becomes so desperate!

He wore the handcuffs at night for several weeks. They began making raw places on his wrists, and for that reason alone, she stopped his wearing them for fear of being discovered. She said to me, "I'm going to have to quit making Jim wear the handcuffs because the teachers will see the sores on his wrists and will be asking questions." Thank God for that!

Another time Daddy got her a riding crop. That's the thing jockeys use to beat racehorses. I suppose since there were no switch bushes, as we called them, here, Mother needed something to use in its place, thus the riding crop. Daddy twisted Jim's arm behind his back and held him over a footstool while Mother beat him until she was exhausted.

When he came back to the bedroom, his arm was hanging at a grotesque angle by his side. He said to me, "Johnny, I believe my arm's dislocated. I can't move it."

I felt so sorry for him. God surely was looking out for us boys, though, because Jim's arm was better the next morning. Mother probably didn't even notice the condition of his arm. We always had to get ourselves together after those beatings without her help. We were strong emotionally or we never could have endured such horrendous abuse without cracking, or running away or taking some other drastic action.

After what seemed like forever, she quit beating him. A period of time passed without a beating, but we continued to live in fear for months after that. Finally, it was over. And those memories we buried deep in our subconscious, never to think of them again for years and years, in fact, for almost thirty years. That's how children survive such horrors. I know. I've been there. As soon as the horror is over, you bury the memory as if it never happened so you can be happy again and life will continue, or else you keep the memory alive and let it destroy you. But Jim and I both are survivors. We meant we would not be destroyed by anything.

At that time, we were attending school at North Charleston High. There was no high school in Hanahan County, so the county had to pay Charleston High School $350 per student for us to attend their school. The kids there resented our presence and were ugly to us. But their mistreatment of us was mild compared to the scorn and ridicule I had been accustomed to in North Carolina. The tenth grade here left no bad impression on me.

Across the street from the football field at school lived a man who had racing pigeons. I fell in love with them. They were so beautiful. It was so much fun to go over during recess and watch them in their loft as they went about the duties of nesting and caring for their young. Their owner was one of those people who right away recognized my intense love for them. He promised me two little birds that had fallen out of their nest. I was tickled to death. One of them had been pecked almost to death by the other birds. Of course I had a special love for that one. But baby birds fall out of the nest, that's their fate unless someone rescues them.

Then my job was to persuade Mother to let me have pigeons. I had to beg and plead with Mother for several weeks, until, out of pure desperation, she agreed to let me have them. My excitement was hard to control. I prayed for the little injured bird. It soon got well. It turned out the two were a pair, male and female. A cousin of mine built me a nice round pigeon house with screen wire across the front one-third to allow for fresh air. There were three shelves with partitions, which allowed the birds privacy while they were nesting. A foot-wide landing perch outside permitted the birds to come and go, and the door was suspended by a hinge. I could hook the door open, allowing them free access inside and out, or I could leave it free to hang, which only permitted the birds to come in but not go out. I was so proud of it. Soon they had mated, made a nest, laid two eggs, then had two little babies, called squabs.

I loved those birds so much. I was so attentive to their every

100

need. I always fed them in the morning before I ate a bite of breakfast myself. I kept their house neat and clean. Scraping the poop off the shelves where they slept didn't bother me in the least. To me it was no different than a mother cleaning a diaper for her child. When you love something, nothing you do for it seems difficult or unpleasant.

I spent many hours watching them fly over the house. They represented an escape for me from the reality of the things going on in my life. Watching those birds gave me a sense of freedom, almost like I could fly away, too. As I watched them wheel and dip in excited flight over the house, I was there with them high in the sky, far above everything that tormented me.

For years I had the same recurring dream. I always appeared in the same forest, where the trees were so huge I could stand on the branches. When the dream began, I was always so happy to be there in the forest where I knew I could fly. All I had to do was extend my arms and *wheee!* I could sail through the air. In my dreams, it was such a joy to fly high above the ground, far beyond the reach of anything that could harm me. It is truly amazing, when you think about it, how the subconscious mind through dreams, sets one free from the pain and cares of life. I actually looked forward to those dreams. I can remember just like it was yesterday that when the dream began, I was actually glad that I was in that forest again. For that brief moment of time I was so free. It was wonderful, sailing through the air over housetops and trees, high above people who were after me. In other dreams I had about flying, when some evil person was after me I could close my eyes and have faith, and then all I had to do was extend my arms and I could fly away and escape from him. I flew so high and so fast. Oh, it was wonderful and so exhilarating.

Back to my pigeons. I was so hurt when, on the first day of duck season, several of my pigeons never returned home. I think whoever killed them did it for the sheer fun of it. Surely a hunter could tell the difference between a duck flying with its long neck sticking straight out in front of it and a pigeon, with no obvious neck at all when seen from the ground. I knew hunters were the culprits because two of the other birds had holes shot in their wing feathers.

When I went off to dental school, I had to give my pigeons away. Mother didn't want the responsibility of caring for them. The few I had left I gave to Aunt Esther. She kept them shut up for three weeks. They had laid some eggs, and I felt like they would be OK and would stay there at their new home. So, that weekend I opened the cage and out they flew. They went straight up, circled twice, then headed south. With no experience at long-distance flight, I'm sure they probably got lost and ended up with someone else's birds. That was better than being shut up in a cage. I cannot bear to see animals imprisoned. I wanted them to have their freedom, and that's exactly what they got.

Next, Hanahan County negotiated with Rivers High School in Charleston for us to spend the last two years of our high school education there. It was a predominantly Jewish school. We were treated very well there, not at all like outsiders. I enjoyed going to school there. All my memories associated with Rivers High were good ones.

I have one little incident I'll share that stuck in my mind. Jim and I resembled each other some, but not as much as one teacher seemed to think. We both had this same English teacher, Mrs. Costen. One day I was feeling a bit mischievous. We were taking turns reading Shakespeare aloud in class. When she called on me to read, she said, "Jim Hall, read." I didn't say a thing. She repeated her request again, and with no response from me. Then she looked at me and said very emphatically, "I said, 'Jim Hall, read.'" Very calmly I replied, "I'm not Jim Hall."

That made her furious. She bellowed out, "You know I can't tell you two apart and from now on when I say read, whether I say Jim or John, you read! Is that clear?"

"Yes ma'am," I replied meekly. But it was still fun, and it seemed a bit childish that the teacher took it out on me because she couldn't tell me and Jim apart. We didn't look that much alike, and I felt she should be able to tell us apart. After all she was the teacher.

While still in high school, I gave a lot of thought to what I wanted to be in life. My first love was music, but Mother said I couldn't be a professional musician because that would not be right in God's sight. A career in music would require that I perform before large audiences. Jim and I had been taught the world was our enemy. We must be separate from the world at all costs. I would also have to play on Sundays, and that was against the teachings of the Bible. The Sabbath must be kept holy—no work of any kind or, any pleasure either, only church and talking quietly with family members and relatives. So I racked my brain for something to be. I had determined years ago that I was going to be somebody someday and then nobody would make fun of me and call me names. I would have a name, and a good one too.

After much thought, I finally settled on dentistry. It was a respectable occupation. Dentists were looked up to. They made a good living, and they were always clean. I didn't like getting dirty. Oh, I didn't mind work. That didn't bother me. It was being so nasty that I hated. Helping other people was part of their job, too, and already I was developing a love for those who were unfortunate and needed help. Another very important aspect was not having to get up so early. I hated when we had to awake to an alarm clock at 5:30 A.M. to be on the job at 6:00. And the heat! One summer while I was working for Uncle Kevin building a house in the country, I almost had a heat stroke. The temperature was ninety-five degrees and the humidity was 100 percent. I became so hot I had to stop working and go sit in the shade. Ever since that day, I haven't been able to tolerate extreme heat. I determined that summer I would have a better job one day where I could work inside where the air was cool and fresh, not hot and stifling with humidity.

Desiring God's blessing and assurance that He would be with me, I prayed over my choice of dentistry for an occupation, and peace came to me concerning it. The next Sunday morning I stood in the church and told the congregation that God had shown me He would bless me to be a dentist and that Grandmother would live long enough for me to do some work for her. It was like a revelation for me. I knew without a doubt that Grandmother would live until I finished dental school. That prophecy filled the hearts of my people with joy, because many times they had feared Grandmother would be taken away from them. My faith never wavered from that day on, even when she was sick. I was perfectly confident of God's promise. And it was true. She lived thirteen years after I had gone into private practice.

Before I settled on an undergraduate college, I wrote a letter to the Emory University School of Dentistry to see if credits from the College of Charleston would be accepted at Emory. A reply stated that by all means I could do my undergraduate study at the College of Charleston, that even though the College of Charleston was small, it had an excellent academic curriculum.

Mother didn't seem to have much confidence in my ability to go to dental school. She would ask me, "How do you know you can make it?" My answer to that was, "If others can do it, so can I." It was very exciting to begin my college education in the fall of 1959. At that time, I was the only member of my family who had ever gone to college. I was doing something no one else in my family had ever done before. That first day at the College of Charleston was so exciting for me. I can still see the crowd of students waiting in line to buy their books. It was such a wonderful feeling. At last I was on the way to becoming somebody.

That same summer before college began, Mother took me to a navy doctor about those sores on my legs. I guess she was afraid maybe the school officials would ask questions and she needed something to show I had been to the doctor. During the examination I remember his asking me if I had always been so thin. I really did look like a skeleton with skin stretched over it; you could count every rib and every vertebrae. I looked awful. He mentioned something about sickle-cell anemia, but I never really learned what caused the sores. If any medicine was prescribed, none was ever mentioned to me.

In college we were required to take gym. I remember how concerned I was about taking a shower in front of all those guys. The shame of exposing my inferior self before them was great enough, but now I had those awful sores on my legs, too. How did I cope with the situation? I would go to my locker and stall for time as I watched the others go to the shower room. Then I would dress quickly, putting my clothes on over my hot, sweaty body, hoping no one noticed what I had done. It would have been so embarrassing, so humiliating. I couldn't bear to expose my legs with those horrible running sores on them. What would the guys say if they saw them? Even though I had been treated like a normal person in the schools I had attended in Charleston, the subconscious fear of being ridiculed still lurked in my mind.

Sometime later that same fall my sores finally healed without my having done anything. That was the most wonderful thing in the whole world to me. You just can't even begin to imagine! No more bandages. No more pain at night. No more fear of someone seeing them and recoiling in horror from me. Truly escape had come to me that year. I gave God complete and total credit for it. He had healed them. I knew they had simply been left to test my faith and to teach me patience. Scars were left on my legs from the sores, but I don't mind them. Every time I am examined by a doctor, he or she thinks they are burn scars. When I tell them they are from a sore, the next question is always, "Sore! What kind of a sore?" Then I have to explain all about the sores, how they started etc., but what a testimony of what God did for me.

The first year at the College of Charleston I found a friend in Larry Crosby. He had a twin brother named Larson. Larry and I were in math class together. It was so good to have a friend, someone I could talk to, someone to share things with. We were getting along well when I made the mistake of telling Mother about him and our friendship. She immediately began to poison my mind, telling me how he was of the world and that we must be separate from the world in order not to fail God. Jim and I had been taught the world would lead us back into sin. At the time, deep inside my heart, I wondered how Larry could be so dangerous to me; it just didn't make sense. I wanted our friendship to continue, but I was afraid of Mother. Whatever she said we had to do. So I began to terminate our relationship, but with a sad feeling in my heart. It was back to living separate and all alone again.

And now for a most interesting account. Aunt Carol's only daughter, Linda, had married twice. The second husband was a nice chap named Robert Packer. They had two children, a girl and a boy. Linda and Robert were both tired of city life in New Jersey. The peace and quiet of the country were calling them strongly, and Linda wanted to be back home where she could attend church.

So they moved back to North Carolina. Not too long after moving back, we were in church one Thursday night during prayer meeting when Mother stood up and told Linda she and Robert were living in adultery and that God had shown her the only way they could live right was for her and Robert to separate. Linda was given the Bible, and we then went to the altar to pray. At times like that, whenever a decision of any magnitude was to be made, the Bible was almost always given to the person in question. The Bible gave us courage to make the right decision. It seemed to reinforce in our minds that we were choosing between life and death. I can still see her as she knelt there on the floor weeping and praying for what seemed like hours. As she knelt there in her anguish, she clutched the Bible that had been given to her.

I knew it was a monumental decision she was trying to make. Being so young myself and having never married, I had no idea just how difficult her situation really was. She was torn between her love for her husband and her fear of being lost. The fear of going to hell had been instilled so deep into our hearts—yes, our very souls. That was the most awful thing that could ever happen to a person. Today as I write this, it is difficult for me to understand how anyone would accept such a requirement, especially if there were any doubts at all in his or her mind. But Mother had stood in church through the years and told the congregation that unless we came to the things in her heart, there was no way we could get to God. I believed that only to a point, but I have come to realize many of the congregation believed it literally. They saw Mother as their only access to God, which is really quite sad. Years later one church member even said to me, "If something happens to Beulah, what will we do? We'll be ruined." I was amazed that he made such a statement. I responded by saying, "Hugh, we'll just keep on living. It won't be the end of the world."

The poor thing chose to leave her husband, even though she loved him dearly. She and her two children moved into an apartment in town. Robert would visit her now and then. Mother frowned on that very severely. I remember how Mother talked about it to Linda's mother all the time. Linda was not to have any contact with him at all. Looking back on it now, I realize Mother was trying to force them to accept something they didn't really believe in themselves. They were only doing it out of the sheer fear of the torment of hellfire. Linda's life became a living nightmare, I'm sure.

Not too many months after their separation, her poor husband was given an ultimatum one Sunday morning in church: if he did not repent of all his sins, he had to leave the church. He had been accused of having an affair with another man's wife and of visiting prostitutes, probably neither of which he had ever done. That was a Sunday to be remembered. We stayed in church all day and on into the night. We got so hungry and thirsty, but that didn't make any difference. In our church we got on our knees to pray. If we knelt on our knees too long, our feet would go to sleep, in addition to the pain to our kneecaps. We children and even some of the adults would stretch out on the floor and go to sleep after a while. I think of it now and I am sure God grew tired, too, of hearing the same things repeated over and over again.

Robert had prayed and prayed and prayed, confessing to all kinds of sins, many of which I don't believe he had even committed. Sometimes in his frustration, he would pound on the altar with his fists as he cried out for mercy. I remember about ten o'clock that night the poor fellow went outside. I wondered where he had gone. After a few minutes he came in the door with a piece of burlap wrapped over his body. He had gone next door to his mother-in-law's house to get a piece of burlap out of her storage area. He had cut a hole in the closed end and draped it over his head. He said he wanted to be humble and come in sackcloth. Aunt Esther got tickled, laughing right there in the church. It was not funny to me. I realized in that moment how great his desperation to be accepted was. He was willing to endure such humiliation in order to be accepted. Mother never would accept his repentance as true. And she always had to be the one to confirm whether a person had repented or not. Unless *she* acknowledged it, then there was no repentance. I felt sorry for the poor man, but there was not a thing I could do to help him.

Finally, at about eleven o'clock, all those still remaining in church left. Robert was all alone at the altar. I can see him now as we walked out the front door. I looked back, and he was kneeling down with his hands and arms resting on the altar. His head was face-down, resting on his hands, like someone dejected and lost. At that moment he seemed frightening to me. The way things were said and done in church at times such as that made Jim and me afraid. It was not until we grew much older that we realized there was a great deal of mind control going on. He left the church early the next morning. Later everything that he had given to anyone was taken to his apartment in town and piled up on the street. When a person left the church, we were led to believe a person like that was defiled, and if we kept anything from him, it would also defile us. Realizing there was no way he could win, the poor fellow moved back to New Jersey.

Linda moved into a little house out in the country right next to the church. There she was expected to take her brother's two children, and look after them as well as her own two children, while she was working at the same time. Not too long after Linda moved into the house in the country, Mother said God had shown her the only way to get rid of adultery in Linda's life was to burn everything she had. That meant all her personal belongings were defiled with adultery. The poor woman felt ruined, but she had to comply with Mother's commands or be put out of the church.

A huge fire was made out behind the church. Linda's car was parked behind the church, and everything the woman possessed was piled on it and burned; the clothes on her back, all her furniture, all her pots and pans, the dishes, all her other clothes, the stove, the refrigerator. Even the cats she had brought from New Jersey were shot and thrown on the fire.

Mother had such power over the people. It is difficult for those reading this to even comprehend. The church members perceived her as Samuel in the Bible. In the Bible, when Samuel came to a village, the people trembled with fear. I also saw her in that light. She had done so many good things for the church and really did have a heart full of love. I can remember in years gone by when she stood in the church and told us how God had put it in her heart to give Uncle Sam $500 to start a business. Another time she gave Uncle Bob $300 when he and his wife desperately needed the money. It always touched my heart when she told those stories to us. She had just become misdirected and confused exactly like her daddy had told her she would. She was mixing the Old Testament with the New Testament, and the two are quite different.

Hysteria seized many of the church members. They went through their belongings trying to reason whether they had anything that was contaminated with adultery. My sister Dana even went to her sister Eva's house, got her wedding pictures, and burned them. It was years before Eva got over losing her wedding pictures. A rotisserie Dana had won at the grand opening of a new store in town was burned because she feared it had been handled by an adulterer. She was going to burn some things of Grandmother's, but Grandmother told her to get out of her stuff, that she wasn't going to burn anything she had. Dear old Grandmother had a lot of wisdom and good common sense.

I was not allowed to help with burning of the accursed things tainted with adultery for fear that the adultery would get on me. I remember questioning what Mother was doing at the time. It didn't make sense to me that getting rid of someone's possessions could eradicate something like adultery. To tell the truth, I really didn't understand the whole meaning of adultery. We have to change from the inside, not the outside. And, too, it seemed like such a waste. And anyway, God does not expect us to ruin our lives like that. Of that I am very certain.

After the burning, the church members all chipped in and replaced all of Linda's belongings. We truly understood the meaning of love for one another and put our beliefs into action. And Mother had love, too. She just became misdirected and overzealous with her religion.

On the way home back to Charleston from Whiteville after all the burning, I was so tired and drifted off to sleep for a few minutes. A vision came to me while I slept there in the car. I was standing in the doorway of a very large room with a tall ceiling. There was a beautiful chandelier hanging from the ceiling, and the light from it filled the room, making it as bright as day. Pale blue curtains hung gracefully from tall arched windows. Chairs covered with rose-colored fabric sat in the room beside a blue sofa. In that instant it seemed my real mama's spirit was there, almost like her radiance filled the room. It was such a beautiful sight to behold. I awoke immediately. I described the dream to Mother and told her it was like a vision of what my home would be like in the future and that I would dedicate my home to my people: little did I know that it would not only be dedicated to my people but even more to all my dear friends and patients who had helped me to achieve that goal. That dream gave me something wonderful to look forward to for the future.

That was the last profound event that occurred before I went off to dental school. I remember the day I received my letter of acceptance from Emory University. My excitement could hardly be contained. I jumped up and down for joy. I was also accepted by the University of Alabama and was quite proud of that accomplishment. Usually an undergraduate degree was required, but the board of admissions was so impressed with my interview and my grades were such that they accepted me without the degree. I chose Emory University, however, since it was much closer home. How good it was, too, that I chose not to attend the University of Alabama, for all the civil rights crises there would have been so frightening to a country boy like me. Soon I was off to Atlanta, but still I was not able to escape the shackles of religion that were firmly bound around my ankles.

6

I was looking forward to dental school with great anticipation. As I had never been away from home before except to spend the summers in North Carolina with relatives, a whole new world was waiting for me. It would be so much fun. I would have freedom that I had never known before, I thought. But I just didn't know how much Mother's control would follow me all the way to Atlanta. I would remain in an invisible prison for many years to come.

Mother had been concerned about me before I ever left home because of a dream she had. She told her dream in church one Sunday morning. In her dream she had packed my trunk to go off to dental school. In the trunk she had put meat for me to have. The meat, she said, was the things of God for me to have. But I was taking the meat out, throwing it away, and in place of it I was putting the things of the world. The dream didn't trouble me. The true things of God were firmly planted in my heart, and I had no intention of throwing them away. I knew God was going to take care of me and I was going to live according to the teachings of our religion. Looking back now, I think the dream probably meant I was throwing away the bizarre beliefs we had been taught, replacing them with the true teachings of Christ.

I guess in a desperate attempt to ensure that I would not go astray, she told me that God had shown her if I would be willing to put my glasses aside while going through dental school that would be something to keep my soul from falling away from God. Mind you. I had been wearing glasses ever since the eleventh grade in high school. In the depths of my own heart I didn't believe God expected that of me. But I trusted her and was willing to do as she requested. Still in the back of my mind was the guilt of having ruined her and Daddy's lives, and now he was going to send me to dental school. The least I could do was obey whatever she expected of me. So I put aside my glasses those four years in dental school. To

111

ensure that I not be tempted to wear them, I left them home in Charleston. That was another religious shackle placed around my ankles for me to wear day after day. It was not easy, either, but I learned to survive that, too.

In spite of all that, nothing dampened my enthusiasm for the future that lay ahead. I was so excited. I could hardly wait, but I had no way of knowing the things I must face there in the big city of Atlanta.

Why Mother didn't take me to Atlanta when I moved to campus I don't know. Aunt Rosie, Uncle Kevin, and their son Daniel took me. We stayed at the Atlanta American Hotel. I'll never forget that Thursday night. By that time all my previous excitement had vanished. I thought, *This is my very first time away from home among complete strangers,* and we had been taught to fear strangers. What faced me began to sink in as the time drew near when my relatives must leave me. The realization struck me how alone I would be when Aunt Rosie and Uncle Kevin were gone. I had an overwhelming sense of being abandoned in that huge city to make my own way in a world totally foreign to me. I felt ruined.

I saw, too, that all my people back home could never know the pain I was going through. They were safe at home in their secure world. There was no way they could feel my pain. They had no idea. Daniel and I had a room together, and I begged Daniel over and over through my tears to please tell everyone to remember me when he got back home. Somehow it was comforting to know I would be in their thoughts. I finally cried myself to sleep.

The next morning at breakfast was even worse. It took every ounce of concentration I could muster to eat without breaking down. I could barely talk. My lips were trembling so I could barely form words. The muscles of my chin were jerking spastically. I had to fight to push out of my mind the fact that they were leaving me there in this place I didn't know.

Each time that thought presented itself to me again, I would almost break and burst into tears. The knowledge of their leaving me was almost more than I could bear. No previous experiences away from family made the transition extremely traumatic. My family, relatives included, was all I had ever known. They were everything to me. It was as if I were losing the dearest things in my life. Finally, they said their good-byes and dropped me off at the dental school on Forest Avenue and drove away, back into their own safe little world, and I was abandoned there to make the best of life. I can say now that parents should never, never shelter their children to such an extreme extent. It makes the transition out into the world too painful for them. I know from my own experience. It's absolutely devastating. Had I not had the strength acquired years earlier, I would never have survived the ordeal.

The first day of school we had to check in our equipment. Each one of us had to buy $950 worth of dental supplies and $250 worth of books and $150 worth of other book supplies. As the instructor called out the instruments, each student checked to see if all his supplies had been delivered to him and then marked each one off the list. As we checked them off one at a time, we all wondered how we would ever learn what to do with all those different tools and instruments. It was quite overwhelming.

At the end of the day, I was standing in the entrance hall wondering to myself how I would ever find my way back to campus, which was situated in Decatur, when one of the doctors approached me and asked if I would like a ride back to the dorm. I'm sure I must have looked like a poor lost puppy to him. I had never been so relieved. I had no idea even which bus to take to get back to the dorm. I don't know what I would have done, probably asked someone on the street how to get back to Emory campus, I guess. I'm sure God was looking out for me, though.

That first weekend was the most devastating for me. My dorm roommate had gone home for the weekend so I was left all alone. I would lie in bed at night and, as I looked up at the stars through my tears, I would picture those I loved back home as they slept. The same stars shone on them, but I knew they did not think of me. Only those going through the situation at the time know what it's like. [Again, I would say to parents: Please don't shelter your children too much. When they do have to be separated from you, then it won't be so traumatic for them. Give them some freedom. We had none, and even then in dental school at Emory, I was imprisoned by my religious beliefs.] I lived totally separate from all my classmates; I never participated in any of the social activities that went on during the entire four years of dental school. Living alone was difficult and at the same time easy, because the fear of the world would have made it frightening even to go to one of the frat houses. My natural curiosity to learn about different things, and my complete trust in God to take care of me would have enticed me to go to some of the campus functions, were it not that I had such a great fear of Mother. Therefore, staying away from these functions was not that difficult for me. The lonely hours I spent and Mother's treatment of me for the harmless things I did do were difficult and very painful, however. Her lack of trust in me and her cruel treatment left me deeply scarred for life. I will come to that later and in great detail.

The next night, which was Saturday, I called Mother. I was so homesick. I told her I would stop payment on all the checks and go back home, but she reminded me what I had said in church about God blessing me to become a dentist. That gave me the courage to dry my tears and go on.

Soon we were engrossed in our studies. One of our instructors said the amount of knowledge we were expected to learn that first year was comparable to having a bucket of water thrown at us with nothing to catch it but a teaspoon. Our vocabulary would increase by about three thousand words that first year, too. We believed it! Such detail; it seemed to us we were expected to remember everything. But even though it was so difficult, it was very interesting.

Right away Glenn McClane, one of my classmates, and I struck up a friendship. Because his parents lived in the city, he was not required to live in the dorm but was allowed to live at home. His home was very much like ours, very clean and neat. I liked his parents, too. He begged me to come live with them. I wanted to more than anything I had ever wanted to do in my whole life, but I knew Mother would never agree to it. At last I had found someone who accepted me for who I was and didn't treat me like I was a freak. The friendship was wonderful even though I had the constant fear that I would commit some sin, and most of all, Mother would find out about it. I have so many regrets now. It would have been so wonderful to have stayed with the McClanes. All those lonely hours in the dorm could have been avoided.

Glenn and I began doing things together. He had his own car, which seemed great to me. Then one weekend he persuaded me to go to the movies with him. I had told him we didn't go to movies, that it was against our religion. But he said this was not a Hollywood movie, just a documentary film made in New Guinea. And he also explained that watching a movie was similar to reading a book, except you didn't have to read it. That made sense to me. So, with some trepidation I went. The film, *The Sky Above and the Mud Below*, was quite interesting, showing how the natives lived as they had for thousands of years, still untouched by civilization. However, when we got back to the dorm, the instant I entered my hallway someone called out to me, "John, you had a phone call." My heart sank to my feet. I felt sick. I knew it was Mother.

When I heard her voice on the phone, I knew she was very upset. "Where were you? I called and you were not there," she said. I told her where we had gone and tried to explain that it was only a documentary film. That made no difference to her. I had failed God and my people. "What are your people going to think of you? They have confidence in you, and now you have let them down," she said. She went on and on. From that day on, she never ceased to reprimand me both on the phone and in letters. It made my life miserable. I grew to dread the sound of the phone ringing.

In spite of all Mother's preaching, Glenn managed to persuade me to go to another movie with him. You see, my curiosity took charge again. I had been enlightened. I used my common sense. And my knowledge of the Bible also helped because it plainly says that God looks on the heart and I knew that my interest was pure and simple and not at all evil. Glenn's point about seeing a movie being very much like reading a book made sense to me, and probably the reason Mother was so upset at me was that she no longer had complete control over me and my mind. This movie was a military comedy. I really enjoyed it too, only I didn't laugh quite as much as I did in grade school at my very first movie, with Blondie and Dagwood. Mother found about this, too. Our friendship continued and would have become much stronger had I not been harassed so much by Mother. Like I said earlier, I have many regrets. What would it have hurt for me to stay with Glenn? Not a single thing. We could have had such a good time together. But the fear of Mother and those religious shackles were still weighing me down. She was able to use her mind control again, for one night Glenn and I were on the way to a movie when he had an accident. It was not his fault, but Mother with her power of persuasion over me convinced me that God was warning me to terminate the relation with Glenn before something worse happened. There was no escape yet.

Then to make matters worse, since I was afraid to do much with Glenn, I started watching TV on weekends. When Mother learned about that, she was even more upset. There I was in dental school, being expected to live totally separate and alone from my classmates, except for the time we were together in classes. And that was difficult. So many times I longed to go with them and do some of the fun things they told me about. The loneliness at times was almost unbearable. And I grew tired of watching the monkeys at the zoo. I tried to explain to her that as long as I had studying to occupy my mind, I was fine. But when Friday came, it was like the sky fell in. The loneliness was almost unbearable. If I were home with everyone else, I wouldn't have any desire to watch TV. That didn't appease her a bit. She said there was no justification for failing God and turning to the things of the world. Her lack of compassion and understanding for my situation made me bitter and hard at times and made life very difficult.

On campus there was the Emory student film series. Each weekend a different classic film was shown free of charge to the students. Sitting there in the auditorium trying to see the picture was really a problem without my glasses. I discovered if I would take my index fingers and press against the inside of my lower eyelids, my vision would improve enough so I could see clearly. Otherwise the picture was so out of focus I couldn't enjoy watching the film. The pressure against my eyeballs changed the shape of my eyes, thus clearing my vision. I have vertical astigmatism, a condition in which the eyeballs are oblong instead of round. After trying to watch a few films, though, I quit going. It was not worth the effort. I would grow tired of holding my fingers against my eyeballs, and without that I just simply couldn't see well enough to enjoy the films.

Equally difficult was having to develop a sense of the passage of time in my head. In dentistry there are certain procedures that require specific time periods to accomplish. For example, impression materials for making crowns required three minutes to set. If they were disturbed before the time limit, the material would distort and the impression be ruined. Filling materials required a certain curing time, and if we did not allow for the proper time, the material would not work. Therefore, I had to learn to time things in my head, because I wasn't allowed to wear a wristwatch.

I tried so hard explaining to Mother the need for a wristwatch. Why was it OK to wear a pocket watch with a fancy gold chain, but we couldn't wear wristwatches? It didn't make any sense to me. When you have both hands in someone's mouth, you surely can't reach into your pocket for a stupid pocket watch. She wouldn't listen. As with other things, it was her way or no way at all. I always tried to remain loyal to all the teachings of our religion.

As most people read these accounts, the question always arises: Why did we let her rule our life to such an extent? We loved and trusted her. She was the only mother we had now. She had rescued us when our daddy had abandoned us. She had been so good to us. We had ruined their lives. They were sending me to dental school. Shouldn't I be grateful? Why should I not be willing to endure whatever she imposed on me? It still seemed so contradictory to say having a pocket watch was OK, but wearing a wristwatch was not. I couldn't understand why God would make such a small difference so important. And deep in my heart of hearts I knew that God didn't mind my wearing a watch. It was Mother that minded. And I was loyal to her religion. And I know now that in the depths of my own heart I didn't believe that her demands were truly of God, but there was nothing I could do.

There was never any relief from her relentless chiding, week after week after week, calling me on the phone, writing long letters admonishing me to return to God. I feared her trust in me was broken, and very soon that fear would be made a painful and bitter reality.

We did not have a break from school until Thanksgiving. I wanted to go home to North Carolina. I missed church. We did not go to church anywhere else, either. I had heard all my life that all other churches were synagogues of Satan. All other ministers were wolves in sheep's clothing, soothsayers, satisfying the itching ears of the unrighteous. When the time to go home for our Thanksgiving break finally arrived, to make things easier for Mother I was to ride

117

the bus from Atlanta to Columbia, South Carolina. Mother and Jim would meet me there. We would travel on from there by car to North Carolina. That meeting in the bus station would impact my life forever. Thinking deeply on it now, I realize what happened in that bus station in Columbia, South Carolina, was actually the very beginning of my ultimate escape.

I can still visualize the interior of that old bus station. The overhead lights were bright, making the stark white walls seem even brighter. Drab brown wood benches, faded from much use, were lined up in rows to sit on. The place was full of travelers of every age and description.

As I said, I feared Mother's trust in me was broken. I dreaded meeting her. I dreaded looking into that face. I feared what I would see.

I arrived a good while before Mother and Jim did. Sitting there alone on that hard bench, I went over and over in my mind how it was going to be when Mother arrived.

When I saw her coming through the door, my heart began that terrible pounding just like it had all those times when I had been beaten so severely. Even from that distance I could see the expression on her face. It was one of stony disapproval. Gone was the tender look of love she used to have for me. I knew she no longer felt the same about me. I could sense very definitely that the place I had once occupied in her heart no longer belonged to me. She was looking at a stranger. I felt like someone standing outside the door of his home desiring to come in, realizing in that instant I was a stranger in their eyes.

Always before when she hugged me, it was with warmth. Now she was cold and stiff. She barely touched me. My heart sank, only this time it sank in despair. In my heart of hearts I knew it would never be the same between us again, never. And why? Why? What had I done that was so awful? I felt so hurt, so wounded deep inside, almost like I was slowly dying.

It was like being abandoned all over again. My own precious mama was gone. She couldn't help leaving me. She had no choice. Death had claimed her. Her poor little body was worn out. But Mother, why was she abandoning me? Why didn't she love me anymore? I had been so honest with her and had kept nothing back

118

from her. I had not stepped aside from the religious beliefs we were brought up with except for buying food on the Sabbath day, going to the two movies, and watching some TV to pass the lonely hours. I could see too that watching a movie isn't sin. It's no different from reading a book, just like Glenn had told me. And I didn't believe God expected me to fast every Sunday, either. Why were those things so awful? And just for that she was treating me like a stranger, so cold, so unwelcoming, and so unloving. It hurt so deep, really much worse than the beatings she had inflicted on me, because it lasted long after she was gone.

That day in the bus station the question began in my mind, *Does she love me any more?* More than anything else, I wanted that love back like it was before I went off to dental school. I wanted that place back in her heart.

As you read this account, I am sure it is hard to understand or grasp the emotional devastation brought by her detachment from me. Try to imagine, if you can, your life without outside friends, your entire life revolving solely around the church, your family, and your relatives. School only played an educational role for us. We were not allowed to play sports of any kind, nor did we attend any games or other school activities. The high school prom was also forbidden. No class rings. No banquets. Nothing. Then imagine the single most important person in your life rejecting you just for those simple reasons I previously mentioned. Your world was not complete anymore. Whom could you turn to for support?

When we arrived at Grandmother's, Mother took me in the bedroom alone and talked to me for hours about how I had failed the church.

Other times I would be sitting in a chair just looking at nothing in particular and she would ask me, "What are you thinking about? Are you longing to be back at school?," insinuating I wanted to be there so I could watch TV. Her saying such a thing to me hurt me more than ever, and I realized it was true, she did no longer trust me, even though in my heart I was the very same.

When I stood in the little church, I knew she was afraid of me. When confronted about it, she denied that she was afraid of me, but that didn't change the fact. She believed it was hypocritical of me to stand in church as if nothing had happened, yet she didn't want me to confess to the church what I had done. I was willing and ready to confess to the congregation, but Mother said, "No, no, you must not do that. They will lose confidence in you if you do that."

But I knew if I let everyone know what I had done, they would understand. After all, it wasn't that awful. But now I understand why Mother didn't want me to tell them. She would have lost more control over the congregation because all of them had a lot of confidence in me and if I had gone to the movies, then going to the movies wasn't so bad after all. That was her fear that I would confess to everyone openly in the church about going to the movies. At the time I did not understand why she was so afraid, but now it's quite clear to me she would have lost so much control.

But she did say she would rather I never stood in church again if I was going to continue doing the things I had been doing, namely, watching TV and going to movies.

Mother became obsessed with trying to figure out what had caused me to fail God, as she said. She pressured me into fasting on Sundays if I couldn't buy my lunch tickets in advance. I tried to reason with her that God didn't expect me to fast every Sunday. God would understand my circumstances. But it was her way or no way at all. One Sunday night I was about to perish with hunger, so I bought a candy bar from a snack machine in the dorm. When Mother discovered I had done that, she gave me a sermon. I was expected to keep the Sabbath day, and all buying was forbidden no matter how hungry I was or anything else.

In spite of all Mother's relentless chiding me, I still enjoyed being home with everyone and going to church. The church had been my life for so long. I had missed it so much. It was so good to see my sisters and other relatives, too. Thanksgiving vacation just didn't last long enough, though.

I continued to study hard in school and didn't watch any more TV that year. In place of it, I went to the zoo. I watched those animals in Grant Park enough to write a thesis on animal behavior. Other times I would wander around downtown walking through Riches Department store and Davidson's Department Store.

Then luckily one afternoon I found an Allen organ in the student auditorium on campus. It was unlocked, so I turned it on and began to play. It was the next best thing to a real pipe organ. I bought a book about organ stops and organ technique and taught myself how to play the organ. I spent many an hour at that organ. I would sit on that organ stool for five hours at a time. I only stopped then because my butt hurt so bad I couldn't stand it any longer. The music always lifted my spirits up and filled my heart with joy. That organ was an escape for me there in the big city. I had not been able to escape from Mother's long arm, nor from the shackles of religion, but the beautiful sound of that organ let me forget everything for a brief moment.

There are some very fond memories tucked away in my heart from dental school that first year. Between Thanksgiving and Christmas vacation, a group of the guys and I were talking in the dorm. Different subjects were being discussed. When they learned I had never studied on Sunday, they were flabbergasted.

"You mean to tell me you have never opened a book on Sunday?" one of them said. "How did you make it? What did you do if you had to study for an exam?"

"I just studied until midnight on Saturday and then remembered it until Monday," I answered.

They just couldn't believe it.

Next, the subject of drinking alcohol came up. When I was asked if I had ever drunk a beer, of course my answer was no.

The same kind of response: "You mean you have never drunk a beer?"

"No."

"Not even tasted it?"

"No."

"Not even a drop?"

"No."

"I can't believe it. You're twenty-one years old and have never even tasted any alcoholic beverage of any kind?"

"That's right," I said.

They just shook their heads in disbelief.

Then someone said, "Well, I know you grew up in one of those old Victorian homes in Charleston , didn't you?"

"No, we don't have a Victorian house," I said. In my naïveté, I thought they were talking about the style of house we lived in.

They began to laugh. "Well, you certainly led a sheltered life."

"No," I replied. Again I misunderstood the meaning. My thoughts went to a tobacco barn. That's the only shelter I knew anything about. When they all burst into derisive laughter, I demanded what on earth was so funny. With that statement they went hysterical. I couldn't imagine what on earth was so funny. Someone made the statement, "You're the last of the good guys. That's just all there is to it."

I got the same response when they discovered I didn't even know what BO or VD meant. I look back with fondness now and realize they could see right through me. They knew I had indeed been extremely sheltered, was very naive, and knew nothing about the world. One of them jokingly said I lived in "Plum, plum out of the city and nearly out of the country." The first time I heard a joke, I went hysterical. They got a big kick out of seeing me laugh so much over something so simple. I have good memories associated with all of them, not like the memories of grade school.

That first year passed quickly. One of our final projects in dental morphology was carving something different from teeth. I decided to carve a camellia blossom for Mother. I wanted to express my feelings of love, devotion, and loyalty to her. When it was finished, not having experience with packing fragile things, I didn't put enough insulation in the box. When the plaster flower reached Charleston, it was badly broken.

To make matters worse and increase my sense of loss and failure, she wrote me a letter. In the letter she told me when she opened the box and saw the broken and crushed flower something said to her that the bond between us was broken. Just as the flower could never be put back together again, so the bond between us would never be mended again. The contents of the letter only confirmed what I already knew anyway. But I was to face an even deeper hurt in the very near future.

Time passed quickly. Soon May arrived and school was out. I had been promoted to sophomore standing. That was so exciting. In the beginning Mother had doubts about my being able to make it, and now I was a sophomore. How wonderful! That first year had been murder; gross anatomy and biochemistry almost did us in. But my joy was soon completely crushed on the way home to Charleston.

The Friday Jim and Mother were to arrive in Atlanta to pick me up, I packed my trunk and suitcases. I remember saying to myself, *Maybe if I'll lie down on the bed and go to sleep, when I wake up it will all be a dream and Mother won't be angry at me.* Such a childish thought! I also knew when Jim came he would be afraid of me. I was certain Mother had poisoned his mind about me. That hurt very deeply also.

Anyway, I lay down and fell asleep. When Jim woke me, the very first words I said to him were, "You're afraid of me, aren't you?"

"No, I'm not," he whispered fearfully.

"Yes, you are. Mother has talked to you about me, that I'm evil and bad," I said again. "You think I'm awful, don't you?" I asked.

"No, I don't," he replied, but I knew he was lying in order to protect me. It was obvious. He was afraid. He would hardly touch me. It was not as painful for me that he was afraid of me, because I knew Mother had brainwashed him, but I still had to deal with feeling like a dog in comparison to him. I knew his place in Mother's eyes had not changed as mine had. He told me later that Mother mourned and prayed so much around the breakfast table he thought I had slept with a whore. We both laughed when I told him the simple truth of what I had actually done.

Anyway, Mother came in with her cold, detached attitude toward me, barely speaking, still treating me like a stranger. My trunk and suitcases were loaded into the car and we were on our way home to Charleston. I was glad to be going home for the summer, glad to see them, and began a conversation. Imagine my shock when neither of them would answer my questions and I realized they were not going to talk to me. I had wondered why I couldn't sit in the front seat with them. I had been made to sit in the back all by myself like I was a convict. Mother and Jim sat in the front. Think of it! I was twenty-two years old at the time. Whatever conversation went on was between the two of them. They didn't say a single word to me the entire six-hour trip home. I had been expected to live alone, separate from all my classmates, and now the very ones I loved and trusted the most were not accepting me. Rather, I was being treated worse by the one who claimed to have the love of Christ and who was the spiritual leader of our church than by those out in the world who were supposedly my enemies.

Overwhelming despair filled my heart. That was the one time in my life if I had known someplace to go, I would have run away. But I knew I couldn't roost in a tree. I had to have food and clothes. There was no escape. I had no choice but to brace myself, take what was coming, and hope for better days. That's the beauty of being a child. Children are so resilient. They can bend. Even though I was twenty-two at the time, in heart and spirit I was still very much a child. I had been so sheltered and suppressed that my emotional development was stunted. As you read this, you can't begin to imagine how it felt to be put in the backseat and treated as if I were a convict, a total stranger. It amazes me now how I was able to survive these terrible ordeals, but my tremendous will to survive, which God gave to me, made it possible.

That summer we took a few days' vacation in Gatlinburg, Tennessee. Aunt Rosie, Uncle Kevin, Josie, and Daniel met us there. We all stayed at the same motel. During some of the conversation there, Josie mentioned how afraid she was of getting VD from a toilet seat. In order to protect herself, Josie said, she squatted over the toilet seat to use it. Well, I thought I would be helpful. So, I informed her in front of Aunt Rosie that VD couldn't be contracted in that way. I noticed Aunt Rosie acted a bit peculiar but thought nothing of it. The next day Mother gave me a sermon about modesty, about how awful it was for me to talk about such things in Josie's presence, how mortified she was. I was really disgusted. I thought to myself, *Well, if they fall off the seat into the commode, I don't care. I'll never tell them anything again. I was only trying to help.*

When Aunt Rosie and their family left, I felt abandoned again. As long as they were with us, Mother acted like nothing was wrong. I knew what was coming. The minute they were gone, Mother started her preaching with renewed vigor. One night she came to my bedside weeping, telling me she had been so hurt by what I had done that she had toyed with the idea of jumping off the back porch of the cottage down into the black water and ending her life.

Of course that made me feel horrible. But at the same time, it made me as bitter as gall. I felt as hard as stone. All she seemed to care about was herself and how she had hurt. She made no attempt to understand my circumstances at school. No matter how hard I tried to convince her that I wasn't interested in TV except as a means of passing the lonely hours on weekends, it didn't make the slightest difference. It was a no-win situation with her. It was her way or no way at all.

I flunked bacteriology that first year in dental school. It's the only subject in all my schooling I have ever failed. I hated it. That's why I failed, I guess. It was the study of bugs we couldn't even see. The only way to see the things was under a microscope. Putting those dangerous invisible things in petri dishes, allowing them to grow, and then returning to count the number of colonies of bugs growing in the medium was not the least bit interesting to me.

Anyway, Emory located another university that offered bacteriology during the summer, the University of Michigan, in Ann Arbor. I had to repeat the course in order to enter the sophomore year. Once again my relatives took me. When they left, however, there was no trauma associated with their departure as I had the first time I was left in Atlanta.

I stayed in the men's dorm. The three classmates of mine who also had to repeat the course rented an apartment together. Still being so loyal to my religious upbringing, I lived totally by myself. I went my way and they went theirs. They asked me to accompany them a few times, but I was actually afraid to go with them for fear they would do something that I wasn't supposed to do. We had really been brainwashed into believing the people of the world were terribly sinful. I felt safer living by myself. By then I was strong enough it didn't bother me so much except during the lonely hours after classes.

That summer I enjoyed my food to the fullest. Potatoes and whole milk were served at every meal. Boy, did I eat! My stomach was poking out like a barrel every time I left the table. But it was soooo good. I put on some weight, too. When my sister Josie saw me, she went hysterical with laughter. "Child, you're fat as a butter ball!" she exclaimed excitedly. "Your face is so round." Another fit of laughter came rolling out. "I can't believe you're so fat." Then we both laughed some more. She had never seen me with any fat before. I had gone up to 185 pounds. I did look a bit plump.

The sense of loneliness was even greater in Ann Arbor than it had been in Atlanta. I was farther away from home than ever. To pass some time I went to the swimming pool. As I went to get in the water, I noticed that everyone was looking at me with strange expressions on their faces. Without my glasses I couldn't see well at a distance and couldn't make out that everyone was naked. The lifeguard on duty came to me and informed me I had to remove my bathing trunks. Everyone was required to go swimming naked. The purpose of that was to prevent the transmission of VD

You can imagine how a country bumpkin, John, felt going swimming naked. I crept into the pool as quickly as I could, so I hoped nobody noticed me. I didn't stay long, either. A few days later I went back one more time. But when some man I had never seen before showed an unusual interest in looking at me down there, I was afraid. So I never went back again.

There was no Grant Park with the animals to watch, so I began watching TV again to while away the lonely hours.

Of course Mother called to see how I was doing and asked the usual questions. I was always honest with her. I told her everything. I would not have had peace inside if I had been dishonest. The torment began with renewed vigor when I told her I was watching TV again. I grew to hate the sound of the phone ringing in my room. It reminded me of a death knell. There were times I wouldn't even answer it. I dreaded to listen to the same reprimands over and over again. The summer passed quickly, however, and I passed bacteriology. Uncle Kevin and Aunt Rosie came to get me from Ann Arbor. On the way home, we stopped in Lexington, Kentucky, and went to a rodeo. We really enjoyed it, too. But, when Mother found out about it, we got a sermon about going out to the things of the world. We had to repent. I really couldn't see the harm in it, myself. At times like that, I said I was sorry when deep inside I really wasn't.

7

The remainder of the summer passed quickly. When fall arrived and it was time to return to Emory, Mother took it upon herself to take me back to Atlanta. She wanted to find me a place to live so I could be separate from the world. When we arrived in Atlanta, she bought a newspaper to check the ads for boardinghouses. She found one right away run by Mrs. Kay Buck, on Fairview Road, a beautiful tree-lined street with lovely old homes on both sides.

The boarding house on Fairview Road was a large red-brick two-story house with a jalousie windowed sunroom at one end. A red quarry-tile terrace extended across the entire front of the house. The original owners of the house were the founders of the Atlanta Bakery. The corner lot on which the house stood was like a hill, for as you rode by in a car you had to look up to get a view of the house. A very narrow brick drive led up to the garage apartment behind the main house. It was a fine mansion in its day.

Inside, the rooms were actually small, considering the overall size of the house. As you entered the front door, you stepped into the foyer. The living room was immediately to your left through a pair of French doors. The stairs ascended in front of you, and to the left of the stairs through a narrow hallway you entered the kitchen. Mrs. Buck's bedroom was the old dining room, which was right behind the living room and to the left of the kitchen.

Mr. Hallsworth's bedroom was the small room behind the kitchen. He was an aristocratic old man in his eighties, and as straight as a stick. He always ate a poached egg for breakfast. He had made a fortune in Ford Motor stocks.

All the other bedrooms were upstairs. As you reached the top of the stairs, the first room to the right was Mrs. Waters's room. Behind her room was a small, narrow sunroom occupied by Mrs. Hamilton. She had Hunt's syndrome, an extremely rare brain disor-

127

der that causes spastic involuntary muscle contractions. At night, when everything was still and quiet, you could hear her dentures clattering together as her jaws jerked all the time. Once I saw her walking down the sidewalk. I'd never seen anything like it in my entire life. I was amazed that she could even walk without falling. As she walked along, every few steps she would rise jerkily up on her tiptoes while the rest of her body would bend so far backward I thought surely she would fall. Just as it seemed she would topple over backward, she would straighten up. It was unbelievable to see her walking.

The second room on the right was taken by Mr. Hayes, another elderly gentleman in his eighties. He was afflicted with rheumatoid arthritis. An event occurred later that caused him to become totally bedridden. I will give the details of that later.

As you turned the corner to the left, my room was next on the right. The room directly across from mine was occupied by Rachel Carson, an elderly woman who claimed an English heritage. Her room was the largest in the house except for the living room.

She was a character. The first time I saw her at the dining table, she was putting sugar in her coffee cup. She poured about half of the sugar in the cup and the other half in the saucer. My first thought was to let her know she had spilled the sugar, but I decided that would not be the best thing to do. I realized she was just about blind but was too vain to wear glasses.

She surprised me once, too. We were talking about people's appearance, size, etc. Without any reservation, she stuck out one of her legs and said, "Look at my legs. Don't you think I have pretty legs? Don't you think I have a nice figure? And I have never worn a girdle." I didn't expect such questions from a woman. I was kinda shocked, but of course I agreed with her. She did have a good figure and nice legs for her age.

Another time around the table after the meal we were talking about people putting tombstones on graves with the person's birth date and date of death on them. Rachel piped up and with some indignation in her voice said, "Hugh, I certainly don't want my birth date put on my tombstone." Someone asked why. She said, "Hugh, I don't want anybody to be able to say, 'I sure didn't know that old bag was that old.'" I thought to myself, *Bless your heart, you look like you're a hundred now.* She had the most wrinkled face of any person I had ever seen. But she was a nice lady. I enjoyed her company quite a lot.

She liked to dress up and go out to tea with her friends. I felt sorry for her, though. Once when she was all dressed up, she called me to her room door to see her in her finery, as she called it.

Not being able to see well, she apparently didn't know there were spots on her clothes where she had spilled food on them. I wondered why her friends had not told her about the food spots, but I guess for the same reason I didn't. We didn't want to hurt her feelings. Her clothes I am sure were very stylish in their day—that was obvious at a glance—they were just very old and soiled.

Another time she called me to her room to show me her clothes she had collected from around the world. As she handed me a shoe or an article of clothing, she told me where it came from. She threw me a hat and said it came from France. Being curious to see how things were labeled in France, I looked inside the hat. The label read: ATLANTA, GEORGIA. Everything else she said after that I took with a grain of salt.

The first meal I ate at the boardinghouse was rather tasteless. I'll never forget it. Mrs. Buck had fried pork chops. They were black, and I mean black. She had used the same grease over and over until it had lots of burned particles in it. That's what gave the meat the black color. I had eaten fried pork chops before, but they didn't look like those things. I was spoiled by Mother's cooking.

As I sat at my place at the table, picking at the food on my plate, Mrs. Parker, the little lady who rented the apartment above the garage, said to me, "It won't bite." That broke the ice for me. I couldn't help but laugh. Still being loyal to my religious teachings, I was practicing living separate from everyone else. Up until she cracked the little joke, I had not said a single word. Her little bit of humor brought me out of my shell, and I never went back into it again, either. It was much more fun being outside than inside that lonely shell.

I began to see that there were other good people in the world who also had good hearts. There was no need to fear them. They were not a threat to me, as were my classmates, for I feared they would lead me into something I was forbidden by my religion to do. Everyone out in the world was not wicked. They were quite harmless. It was a revelation for me. I became attached to all those dear folks there. It took a while to become accustomed to the food, however.

That first year at Mrs. Buck's passed rather uneventfully. I grew to enjoy living there. I would do everything I could to help her. Many weekends I cleaned the whole house for her. I didn't mind. I didn't have my mother to do things for, so I did things for Mrs. Buck.

In a way I became a confidant of sorts to Mrs. Buck. She confided in me once that first year on a rather personal level. Her son Wills was an alcoholic. He had lost his license to practice chiropractics. She said many times she feared that Wills, in one of his drunken states, might kill her while she slept. She said, "You know people many times kill the person they actually love the most." She really had no privacy. Her bedroom was the former owner's dining room. It opened onto the living room through a large and quite graceful archway. Wills could have entered her room without any effort at all. He slept on one of the living room sofas not more than fifteen feet from where his mother slept. Mrs. Buck really had no protection from him entering her room, for there was not even a door to lock.

Wills and his mother didn't get along very well. He was raving and cursing about something all the time. He was never content. Once while cleaning the house, I overheard part of a conversation between them: he had asked for money, and she refused him. In a voice dripping venom and pure hatred, I heard him say to her, "Yes, doll, I've never given you a g——d——thing in my entire g——d——life." With that the door to the kitchen slammed shut with such force the dishes rattled in the cabinets and Wills stormed out of the house. I thought to myself, *Gracious peace, he nearly tore the door down*.

It always felt so good for him to leave. Peace and quiet could reign in his absence. Poor Mrs. Buck told me Wills was breaking her with his drinking habit. I tried to encourage her to put him out, but she never did.

When I cleaned the house, I found bottles of Old Crow under

just about every cushion in the living room. That's what he drank, Old Crow whiskey. The trash cans outside had empty bottles by the dozen in them. She said his habit cost her several hundred dollars a month. I couldn't understand why she put up with him. I knew my mother would kill me for such a thing.

Rachel stayed only a short time then moved to another home. A rather strange retired lawyer rented Rachel's old room. When prospective boarders applied, Mrs. Buck never required character references. All anyone had to do was present himself and have the money, and he or she got the room. This lawyer's first appearance at the supper table made quite an impression on me. His entire demeanor was quite stilted and aloof. I remember asking him a question about law. By then, I had come out of my shell quite well. I had learned to make conversation easily and was only trying to make him feel at home with the rest of us. His answer was curt, blunt, and actually rather rude. I started to say, "You don't have to be so hateful," but I didn't. I thought to myself, *Well, you can keep all your lawyer stuff to yourself if that's what you want.* After missing him at supper for several nights, I asked Mrs. Buck where he was. In a hushed voice, she asked me to go upstairs to his room and check on him to see if he needed anything.

What I saw, when I opened his room door, shocked me so I can see it plainly right now. As I said before, the room was quite large. It had a beautiful dark blue floral carpet on the floor. Twin beds sat side by side against the outside wall. Two upholstered armchairs sat at an angle on each side of a table on which sat a large lamp with a beautiful shade.

The poor man was sitting in one of the armchairs smoking a cigarette. Scattered all over the room were his soiled boxer shorts. They were lying on the floor, on the chairs, on the bed. A bucket sat on the floor in front of his chair. He had used it for a toilet. A hideous brown fluid almost filled the bucket, and what looked like hundreds of cigarette butts were floating on top. The stench was overpowering. I was appalled. How could a human being live like that? I didn't understand how he endured it.

He gave me some money and asked me to get him a sandwich and a carton of milk. When I returned with the food, he gulped the food down like a starved animal.

A few nights later I was awakened around two or three o'clock in the morning by his reciting poetry in the hallway outside my room. I assumed he was still drunk. Another night he was arguing a court case in the same manner in the middle of the night.

His last night at Mrs. Buck's took place while I was on campus practicing the organ. Before I entered the front door, I knew something was amiss. A police car sat out by the street in front of the house. That aroused my curiosity and alarmed me at the same time. Why would a policeman come to the house? What had happened?

Upon entering the kitchen where Mrs. Buck was, I inquired what was going on. She told me the lawyer had gone into DT's, the abbreviation for the medical term *delirium tremens*, a state an alcoholic goes through when coming off a binge. The person sees things and even hears voices. Mrs. Buck said Fred was yelling at the top of his lungs, pacing the floor, and throwing shredded undergarments at the wall or, more specifically, at the demons he thought he saw in the wall. Poor fellow, the cops hauled him away to the jail I suppose. I really felt sorry for him. Mrs. Buck made a big mistake by having him as a boarder.

Very shortly after he left, Mrs. Buck rented his room to some "hillbillies," one of whom was almost seven feet tall. His name was Jack. Mrs. Buck was not always up-front with prospective borders. She had led the folks from Tennessee to believe she provided room service; i.e., their room would be tided up and the beds made. When Jack returned at the end of his first day of work and discovered that was not the case, he wanted a refund of his money. Mrs. Buck didn't refund anything, most of all not money. Of course Jack was very upset with Mrs. Buck.

While Mrs. Buck and the hillbilly were arguing, Wills butted in and started giving Jack some flack. I heard Jack tell Wills, "Look here, you little scrawny runt; if you don't shut up and get out of my face, I'll string you up on that chandelier." There was not another word out of Wills. He left the scene. Wills told me later how scared he was: "Man, I went up to my room, took a drink, and went to sleep. I wasn't crazy. I knew that man meant what he said." Those fellows were so angry they didn't even stay out the month but moved out just as soon as they had found another place.

132

With no air-conditioning in the boardinghouse, we slept with the windows open at night during the hot summer months. One night I was awakened in the wee hours of the morning by the sound of feet running down the street. It was so eerie, like a deathly calm. Not another sound could be heard except the *tap-tap* of the shoes as the woman ran down the street calling, "Help, help! Somebody please call the police!"

My heart was pounding. I was trembling. *Was I going to witness a murder?* I thought to myself. I raced to my window and looked out. Windows were being raised across the street, and heads popped out. Then I could see the fleeing woman. She had come back onto our lawn and was being chased by a man. The two went around a large cedar tree on the front lawn a couple of times, then, to my utter amazement, calmly walked hand in hand back in the direction of the garage apartment. The entire episode lasted only a few minutes, but at the time it seemed like forever before I realized the poor woman was OK.

I learned from Wills the next morning it was the man who lived in the apartment. The poor fellow suffered from schizophrenia and sometimes battered his wife. Apparently that night for those few minutes he was one of his violent personalities. What a scare for a country boy like me. This was another case of Mrs. Buck not being selective enough when choosing her boarders.

Henrietta, the French teacher, was plagued with an ulcer. She rented a room at Mrs. Buck's on the one condition she be served a glass of milk at each meal. Everything went well until Mrs. Buck began buying milk from someone in the country. Cows' milk, as we country boys called it, was OK unless the cows had been eating onions. Then the milk tasted terrible, just like onions. I just closed my mind to the thought of the taste and gulped the stuff down. I was developing an ever greater degree of discipline and self-control. I needed the nourishment and the protein, so I drank it. And there was no need to argue with Mrs. Buck about it or try to get her to change. She was getting the milk at a better price than she found in the grocery store and was not about to switch.

Henrietta was outraged. When she took the very first swallow, she let out a grunt of disgust, set the glass aside, and never touched the milk again. She kept a record, however, of all the meals at which she had been served a glass of milk she could not drink. Between Thanksgiving and Christmas, she found a better place to live. One Wednesday night she began moving her things out to her car. Mrs. Buck came storming up to Henrietta's room, demanding she not move another thing from her room that night, simply because she thought Henrietta wouldn't pay her bill. Soon as Mrs. Buck left her room, Henrietta hurried to my room all in a flurry, asking me what she should do.

Mrs. Buck had no right to stop her, so I said to Henrietta, "You fence, don't you? "

"Yes," she said.

"Well, I'd take my fencing sword in one hand and my suitcase in the other. If either Mrs. Buck or Wills approached me, I'd wave my sword and tell them to get out of my way."

Henrietta loved it. She did just as I told her, and it worked. Not a soul bothered her. She moved everything except what she needed to spend one more night there.

To ensure a safe departure the following night, Henrietta brought a friend along as a bodyguard. He was a towering six-foot-four, 250-pound behemoth who stood outside the front door hoping Wills would come outside so he could teach him a "lesson or two."

When Henrietta made her last trip to the car, she left her final payment on the hall table with a note explaining how she arrived at the total figure. She had deducted ten cents for each glass of milk she didn't receive at each mealtime.

Mrs. Buck was livid. She hit the ceiling. "Why, you SOB, I'll wring your neck for that!" she bellowed. But Henrietta was out the door by then.

She and her friend waited outside for a few minutes. Wills paced the floor like a caged animal. He said he would break them in half and banged his fist against the wall like a crazed idiot. Mrs. Buck had the presence of mind to restrain Wills from going outside on the porch where Henrietta's friend was waiting for him. She knew what would happen if Wills antagonized Henrietta's friend. Mrs. Buck wasn't a fool. She knew others wouldn't control themselves as I had done.

But I was a bit mischievous, too. The house there at Mrs. Buck's was filthy. I was appalled the first time I saw the dishwater with all those pieces of food in the sink. At home, we had been taught to throw out the food from the plates before we put them in the sink to wash. Mrs. Buck dumped everything in the dishwater. There were pieces of bread and meat in the sink. It looked so gross to me. I had to learn to block those things out of my mind or it would have been impossible for me to eat a single bite in that kitchen.

In addition to the filth, the place was infested with roaches. Roaches! There were armies of roaches in that house. During our evening meal roaches crawled up and down the door jambs and on the floor, and at times little ones even crept around on the table while we were eating. All of us complained to Mrs. Buck.

She claimed the Orkin man had sprayed for them. But, a few nights later, as we were eating supper, I spied a big roach crawling up the door jamb. Just to let Mrs. Buck know we were aware the problem had not been corrected, I said in a loud emphatic voice so everyone could hear me, "My, there's a roach!"

You've heard the expression "if looks could kill." Mrs. Buck gave me that kind of look. The other boarders sitting at the table all laughed devilishly. We were all convinced she had not had the place sprayed for roaches at all.

Another thing. I always wished a zoning inspector would come by while I was there. Mrs. Buck ran the boardinghouse outside the proper zone. She was legally allowed to rent rooms only, not provide board, too. She had told the others numerous times that if anyone ever came by asking questions, they should simply say they were renting a room. Mrs. Waters didn't like the idea of lying about anything. She always said if anyone asked her, she was going to tell the truth. She would have exposed Mrs. Buck if the inspector had come by, but he never did. I would have defended the dear souls there at the boarding house.

Another evening as I was finishing my supper at the table, Mrs. Buck was tidying up the kitchen. She had put some water in the pressure cooker to loosen the chicken stuck to the bottom of the pot. She was bent over with her back to me looking for something in the refrigerator when the safety valve on the pressure cooker blew off with a tremendous blast like the sound of a rocket being launched.

With one continuous motion, she jumped straight up, turned around, and raced across the room. When she reached the kitchen door, she stopped, wheeled around, and looked straight at me with the most peculiar expression on her face. I really believe she thought I had shot her. It was so funny to me; I still laugh about it today. The day I left there a year later, the grease and bits of chicken spewed out of the pot that night were still clinging to the ceiling.

Wills did a stupid thing while I was home for Christmas holidays. I had stressed to his mother the importance of not allowing anyone in my room. There were $300 worth of dental tools in my toolbox. I just wanted them to keep the door locked. On my return trip, I had somehow managed to take the wrong bus schedule which put me arriving in Atlanta around 2:00 A.M. I climbed the stairs to my room and alas, the door was padlocked. I couldn't believe my eyes. I was locked out of my room. There was no other alternative but to wake Wills to get the key. He stumbled out of bed and amid much raving and cursing located what he thought was the correct key. As he stumbled up the stairs, he began to blame me for the problem, saying it was my fault for wanting the door locked. But I explained that I only wanted my room locked, not a padlock put on my door. I only wanted my door locked with the key. We each had a key to our rooms. After discovering the key wasn't the correct one, the silly thing took a hammer and broke the lock off the door. He was raging like a maniac. Beating and banging, making enough noise to wake the dead, he finally opened my room door. I remained as calm as a cucumber. It was funny to me. I said to him, "Maybe it will teach you a lesson, not to put padlocks on people's doors." He muttered some more choice curses under his breath, clomped back downstairs, and went back to bed.

Mrs. Buck's true character came out that fall when I returned for my second year of dental school. Frugal as she was, she coerced Mr. Hayes into mowing the grass for her. Remember he was a skinny, eighty-year-old man with rheumatoid arthritis. That yard was rather large, and much of it was on a steep incline, the house having been built on a hill. Mrs. Buck had a gasoline-powered push mower that Mr. Hayes used. By the time he finally finished mowing, his clothes were soaking wet. He sat down in the cool shade under the large oak in the backyard to rest, and when he tried to get up he was almost rigid. The arthritis had almost cemented his joints together. Walking was almost impossible. He had to be helped upstairs to his bedroom.

What happened during the next few weeks was like something out of a horror movie. Rheumatoid arthritis is a severely debilitating disease that causes intense burning pain, soreness in the joints, and sometimes complete rigidity of the skeleton. There are several cases in the medical literature in which the patient's entire skeleton became fused together and was completely rigid, and totally unable to move a single limb, finger, or toe. Mr. Hayes became bedridden, unable to go downstairs to eat. Being busy with my studies, I did not realize at first the severity of his condition. I noticed his absence at the table for several days and would hear Mrs. Buck talk about him.

Wills was given the responsibility of taking Mr. Hayes's food to him. Ah, the ravings, the cursing we had to endure at the table. "I'm not paid to take his d—— food to him. Let him come get it himself," is what Wills said every time his mother asked him to take Mr. Hayes's food to him.

I only wish I could be there again. I would take it myself. I had not given much thought to the situation and had no idea what was going on until the second week of Mr. Hayes's confinement to his room. One afternoon as I walked by, going to my own room right down the hall, Mr. Hayes's room door was open. He called to me as I passed his door, "Mr. Hall!" I stepped inside the room. "Mr. Hall, I hate so much to ask you, but would you please empty this bucket for me? They won't do it and I can't do it myself." To my horror, it was the same enamel bucket that the retired lawyer had used in his room during his drinking spree. Again it was almost full of human waste. Mr. Hayes had a tin can in which he urinated and then poured it into the bucket. The poor thing had to grapple the solid waste out of his pajamas and dump it into the pail, too. There were crumbs of food all on his sheets where he had eaten in bed. It was horrible! It almost makes me weep now to even think he had to endure such dreadful conditions. Getting up was so excruciatingly painful he had simply lived out of his bed. I assured him not to worry, I didn't mind emptying the bucket one bit, and I would be sure to check on him every day and keep the pail emptied for him.

137

On a little table at the end of his bed were all the dirty plates from the week before stacked on top of each other with the leftover food still on them. It's incredible to think Wills was too lazy just to take the dirty plate back downstairs to the kitchen after bringing up the warm food. Never had I seen such degradation of the human body, and that being done by one person to another.

I continued to keep a check on Mr. Hayes, empty the pail, remove the dirty plates, and even shave him. The first time I tried that, I was a bit apprehensive. After all, shaving an eighty-three-year-old man with loose paper-thin skin under his chin isn't your everyday chore. I wouldn't have hurt him for anything. But I was very careful and kept asking him if I was doing OK. From then on it wasn't difficult at all.

What really disgusted me was the fact that Mrs. Buck neglected him during the month, but on the day his check was to arrive she would go in his room and sanctimoniously pretend to clean it up, sweeping around the floor with a broom and moving the chairs a bit. One Saturday morning I couldn't take it any longer, so I confronted her about it. "Why do you let him rot during the month, yet on the day his check is to arrive, you come up here and pretend to clean his room?" I asked her. She made no reply. She had no answer. She just glared at me with an evil look in her eyes.

His plight continued until one Saturday afternoon Mrs. Parker, who used to rent the garage apartment, dropped by to visit Mr. Hayes. Boy, did she go ballistic when she saw his condition. She was like a human tornado. She flew into a rage at Mrs. Buck, and the fur was flying. "What in God's name do you mean, leaving that poor man up here in such a mess?" Mrs. Parker screamed at Mrs. Buck.

Of course Mrs. Buck retorted with an impossible statement. "He could have come downstairs to eat if he wanted to," she answered.

"What are you talking about?" Mrs. Parker yelled, "The poor thing can't even get out of bed, let alone go downstairs." She told Mrs. Buck, "I want an ambulance brought over here, and I'm not budging one inch until I see him taken out of this dump and carried to the hospital." She called the ambulance immediately.

I saw Mr. Hayes for the last time as they led him painfully

down the steps. He was so pitiful. His poor body was so thin he looked like a skeleton with skin stretched over it. He could only walk on his very tiptoes. His feet were locked in that position. He just hollered as he crept along. Back then stretchers were not brought into the house like we do nowadays, so he had to walk out himself.

I learned later from the other boarders that his brother in Bremen, Georgia, had been notified and had taken Mr. Hayes home with him. I was so glad he had someone to care for him. I'll never forget that poor man's plight there at Mrs. Buck's.

Feeling sorry for Mrs. Buck, I offered to clean her house for her on Saturdays. I enjoyed cleaning, and in addition, it made me feel good to do something to help her. After all, Wills certainly did nothing to help her.

Anyway, Wills had a pet canary that he totally neglected. I don't understand why he even had it. Loving animals as I did, I requested Mrs. Buck's permission to care for the bird. I promised to keep the cage clean, feed the little thing, and give it fresh water every day. While I cleaned the cage, I would let the canary fly around the living room to get some exercise and, more important, to have a little bit of freedom.

One Saturday as I was upstairs cleaning my room, I heard a commotion downstairs. I could hear Wills swearing. Then I heard him say, "What in the hell's going on in here?" A sixth sense told me something was very wrong downstairs. Just about the time I reached the landing at the bottom of the stairs, the canary came flying through the living room door immediately followed by a sofa cushion. The distraught little bird was in desperate flight to its cage. The bird barely made it inside when the cushion hit the cage, knocking it off the stand onto the floor, leaving the bird reeling from the shock. Wills strode through the living room door, reached down, picked up the cage, stuck his hand inside and took the canary out. He took that tiny thing by the neck, held it between his thumb and index finger, and squeezed it several times as if he were trying to choke it.

As I was standing there on the landing watching the scenario unfold before me, violent thoughts entered my mind. I was trembling with rage. Every fiber in my body screamed for me to lunge at

139

Wills and try to break his neck. But I knew better. Self-control was my friend in a situation like this. I laugh now when I think of what I said to him, but I couldn't think of anything else to say. "I've never seen such an unreasonable person in my whole life," I said.

"I'm glad you finally met one," Wills retorted with cutting sarcasm, and with that he threw the bird back into the cage and strode out with the cage, bird and all.

"Did you see that?" I asked his mother, who had just come out into the hallway. "It's *his* bird," she answered rather disdainfully.

Never before had I wanted so much to give someone a karate chop to the neck. I'm sure if I had lost my self-control and vented my rage, I probably would have broken his scrawny neck.

At the time I did not understand the source of my rage, but looking back on it, I now know it was actually rage against Mother for all the times she had victimized me and Jim, controlled our lives, and humiliated us. I was witnessing the same kind of thing being acted out right before my eyes again with Wills and the helpless little bird. I knew that in reality Wills wanted to squeeze my neck, but being afraid to attack me, he took it out on the poor bird.

He hated me because I had more privileges in the house than he did. He saw that his mother trusted me entirely, allowing me to have free reign in the house. I also knew if I so much as touched him, his mother would have me thrown in jail. Those experiences taught me self-control to the *nth* degree. My first priority was to finish dental school. That was foremost in my mind. I knew I couldn't let anything derail me from that goal, nothing, no matter how difficult it was or how badly it upset me. After all, nothing lasts forever.

140

8

The summer of 1964 went by without any major events occurring. I returned to Mrs. Buck's in September to begin the fall term as a junior. I was soon to learn things were not as I had left them in May.

First of all, the other boarders began addressing me as Dr. Hall: initially as a joke to aggravate Wills because they had lost respect for him. But it became a habit. The envy of my new title began to eat on Wills. Very soon I was to learn just how much.

The first incident occurred one Saturday afternoon while I washed my clothes. Mrs. Buck had given me permission to use her washing machine. Washing my clothes saved a laundry bill, and I did everything I could to cut costs. I was so grateful to Daddy for sending me to school, the least I could do was wash and iron my clothes. Anyway, I was on the small porch just outside the kitchen minding my own business when Wills came storming in looking like some deranged maniac.

The noise of the machine had awakened him. His eyes were wild and bulging, like frog eyes, all bloodshot from a drunken spell the night before. "What in the hell are you doing with the d—— machine?" he yelled in his harsh, raspy voice.

"I'm washing my clothes. What do you think I'm doing?" I answered.

He continued to rave at me, accusing me of tearing up the machine and demanding that I leave that d—— washer alone, to never use it again. As before with the bird episode, rage filled my entire body. Trembling all over, I informed him quite emphatically that his mother had given me the privilege of using the machine, that I would continue to use it as long as his mother said it was OK, and that I also knew quite well how to use it properly. After I stood my ground with him, he sulked off to his garage apartment like an old cur with his tail between his legs.

A week or two after that outburst I was late coming home from

141

school one Friday evening. We had been studying for an upcoming exam. The school had been left unlocked until 9:00 P.M. for that purpose.

The very second I entered the foyer, the negative vibrations in the air let me know something was wrong. Upon entering the kitchen, I was shocked to see Wills was helping his mother wash the dishes, something he had never done before. The table was empty. There was no plate of food left for me. I had given Mrs. Buck explicit instructions not to wait up on me if I was late, to simply fix me a plate of food and leave it on the table, and I would eat it cold. I didn't mind the cold food. I was willing to do that because I didn't want to be any trouble to her.

"May I have something to eat?" I asked.

While she reluctantly went about fixing me a plate of food, Wills began his little speech. "What's this coming in so late? Where in the hell have you been?" he asked with utter contempt dripping from every word.

"I was studying late," I said to him.

"Awh, don't hand me that bull. I've been in school before, too, and I was never late," he answered.

That remark affected me like striking a match and throwing it on gasoline. I began to tremble all over inside, and my heart pounded in my throat. By that time Mrs. Buck had fixed my plate of supper which I took to the table to begin to eat. Just as I sat down at my place at the table, Wills went over to the wall switch and cut the light off over the table, leaving me in the dark. Such an insult! Such absolute contempt!

"May I have the light on, please?" I asked, directing my request to his mother. "I can't see very well."

She turned the light back on.

Again with utter disgust hanging from each word, Wills spit, "Aw, Mom, he's not worth that."

After hearing that remark, I was so upset I knew there was no way on earth I could have eaten in that room with them, so I took my plate, went up to my room, and ate my cold food. At least I was away from my tormentors and found some peace. It took a while, however, for the trembling inside me to cease.

So interesting! Each time those totally outrageous outbursts of his occurred, I focused on his scrawny neck. I don't know why, but that's the one thing I always wanted to do; give him a hard karate chop to that skinny little neck of his and teach him a lesson. Thank God for giving me the strength and self-control to never touch him. I would always say to myself, *I can't touch him. I can't end up in jail for assault and battery. I've got to finish school no matter what. I can't let anything derail me from that goal.* I had a strong feeling that something was brewing there in that house and things would get worse and I would soon realize why.

A few weeks later, one Saturday morning, the storm came to a head and Mrs. Buck lowered the boom. I had slept late as I usually did on Saturday mornings, being tired from studying until one and two o'clock in the morning all during the week. When I came downstairs, Mrs. Buck was fumbling around in the kitchen doing some tidying up but there was no food at my place at the table again.

"May I have some breakfast?" I asked.

Without saying a word she began to dig around in the drawers for the pots and pans, obviously resenting having to cook me anything to eat.

I thought to myself, *It's your fault for not doing as I have told you over and over*, but I said, "You don't have to be so hateful. I've told you over and over to fix me a plate of food and leave it. I would eat it cold."

She made no reply and I thought maybe everything was OK. After finishing my breakfast of bacon, eggs, and toast, I was leaving the kitchen when she informed me that she wanted to talk to me in my room. It was then I sensed something foreboding in the tone of her voice.

My room at the time was not the nice, cozy room I had once occupied upstairs, but rather the jalousied sunroom downstairs off to the left of the living room. In order to help her out so she could take on another boarder, I had foolishly agreed to move downstairs into that room. It was never meant to be used for a bedroom. Having glass walls on three sides, it was extremely cold in the winter months. We had snow that winter, and the outside temperature dropped down in the teens. I am sure it was in the forties inside. The only heat I had came from a small portable electric floor heater with a tiny fan to direct the warm air. I remember being so cold I had to

143

get up in the middle of the night, put all my clothes on and sleep fully dressed, and with only two thin blankets she had given me I was still cold. In the morning I would be stiff from sleeping curled up in a ball in order to stay warm. It was dreadful to say the least.

In addition to the cold, the lighting was extremely poor. Not wearing my glasses I had trouble seeing well enough to study. When I first took residence in the room, there was only one small forty-watt bulb in the ceiling light. Persons with my type of eye deficiency require bright lighting in order to read without severe eye strain and subsequent eye fatigue. I placed three sixty-watt bulbs to increase the illumination. At least then I could see fairly well.

Feeling nervous already, I dreaded what was coming but had no idea it would be such an ordeal. When Mrs. Buck got to my room, she started in on me, practically shouting out her words. First off, she said, "You promised to change those lightbulbs," waving her hand in the direction of the ceiling light as she spoke.

"Change the lightbulbs! I never thought of such a thing. I need them to see with," I said most emphatically and with utter disbelief in my voice. I began to rack my brain to recall any conversation we had had concerning the lightbulbs. But nothing! Nothing! I felt exactly like I had the first time Mother beat me for playing the "dirty tricks." I had no earthly idea what Mrs. Buck was talking about. Next, she informed me I had been drinking the cream off the milk.

It was then, at that instant, I knew it was her son Wills who had poisoned her mind against me. "Cream! What cream? I've never seen any cream, let alone drunk it," I said with even more disbelief.

"Don't lie to me. I'll slap your face," she answered with a low, threatening tone in her voice.

"I'm not lying, I'm telling you the truth," I almost pleaded.

Imagine this now for a moment if you will. In front of you stands this short, very stout lady with evil flashing in her cold blue eyes, which, like those of her son's, bulged out, and in addition had bluish bags under them, reminding you of a toad. There she stands, waving her arms about, accusing you of things that never entered your mind. I was totally dumbfounded. I wondered in that split second what I would do if she did indeed slap my face. But I knew I

144

could only stand there and take the abuse, for there was nothing, absolutely nothing, I could do.

Next she said, "I've never had anyone talk to me like you have before in my life. I could have you locked up for talking to me that way."

I suppose maybe no one had ever stood up to her before. I certainly had not shown any disrespect, just made a simple statement of fact. I simply stood there saying nothing in response to that statement. By that time Wills had come to the door. "It's OK, Mom. I've already called the cops," he said.

"That's fine with me. I happen to know a few things myself," I answered. Wills thought he could intimidate me by pretending to call the police. I knew there was nothing any policeman could do to me. I had done nothing amiss. Mrs. Buck turned and walked away. I guess that time I was a little gutsy myself!

It was then I knew I had to find another place to live, but how? My studies occupied all my time. I had no car. I couldn't ask my classmates to help me find a place. I couldn't walk, that would take forever. Atlanta was a huge city. I would be like an ant looking for a crumb in a haystack trying to find another room to rent in that big city.

Then a godsend happened. Phyllis Maple, one of Mrs. Buck's friends who visited occasionally, came by one Saturday. We talked a bit in private, and I described both incidents to her. She told me Mrs. Buck had changed, that she wasn't a good person like she once was. After giving some thought to my dilemma Phyllis said, "John, I have an idea. I will scour the newspaper each day for you. If I see anything interesting, then in the afternoon when you get out of school, I'll take you to look at it." Never was anything such a blessing. She truly rescued me. She was an angel in disguise.

The first place we went to see reminded me of an insane asylum. The room for rent was in the basement down a narrow, dimly lit hallway at the back of the house. The room was OK, but to reach it I would have had to pass through the living room. There in that living room sat a group of the most pitiful-looking people I had ever seen before in my life. Most of them I could see at a glance were mental patients. Some couldn't even talk coherently. One was severely disabled. I would have been scared to live there, never knowing who might enter my room and when. That place was totally out of the question.

Thank the Lord the next week she found a room at 1095 St. Charles Place, which was only about three city blocks from Mrs. Buck's. It was run by a Mrs. Mattie Mae Neville James, a fine lady who was quite proud of her southern heritage as a gentlewoman. She required a character reference, which Phyllis provided for me. Mrs. James had only rooms, not board, but I would have the privilege of using the refrigerator. I was tickled to death to find her place.

My next step was to get someone to move me. I wrote Mother a letter describing my circumstances at Mrs. Buck's to see if anyone there could help me out. Sure enough, dear Uncle Kevin and Jim came to move me.

Jim amused me. When Mrs. Buck came to my room door that Saturday morning, trying to push her way in to tell Uncle Kevin to have me tell my dark side of the story, Jim became so scared and nervous. When she left, he said, "My, she's awful."

I laughed and replied, "You don't know anything. All she did was step in here and say that, and you are all scared and upset. What if you had been here when she jumped all over me accusing me of all those ridiculous allegations?" But I was glad he didn't have to know. It wasn't pleasant at all.

When I settled up with her that day, I think her conscience was bothering her. She said to me, "I've given you the best of everything. I fed you like feeding a dog." Well, feisty me, I retorted, "What best? I haven't seen any best."

She just sat there and glared up at me from her desk. If looks could kill, I would have dropped dead right then, but thank goodness they don't.

Well, Uncle Kevin and Jim moved me in at Mrs. James's. Compared to Mrs. Buck's, it was a haven. Mrs. James's home was clean, tidy, and quite beautiful. The house was furnished with antiques that had been in her family for generations. She had a maid named Claudia, who came each week to clean. The smell after she had done her work was always so fresh. Every few weeks Claudia baked bread, too. Mrs. James was from the old school, having grown up when people made their own bread. You insulted her if you offered her store-bought bread.

Once Mrs. James invited me to dinner with her one Sunday. Ah, the food was so delicious. There was country-cured ham, green sweet peas, steamed carrots, and homemade bread served with real butter and spiced apple preserves. With ham she always served a seedless green grape salad, made by rolling the grapes in just enough Philadelphia cream cheese to cover them. It was wonderful.

Oh, but life there was soon going to take a very interesting turn too. Mrs. James was Presbyterian. That spring she went with her church to their retreat in the mountains for a few days. She left me in charge of the place. She informed me there was to be no drinking in the house while she was gone, as if I could stop anybody.

Anyway, there was a gentleman upstairs who, Mrs. James said, was trying to get back together with his wife. She might come to spend a night or two with him. But that was OK. He was to leave for another place at the end of the month.

Another young man who was to occupy that room when it was vacant was sleeping downstairs on a daybed in the sunroom.

The second day of Mrs. James's vacation, I noticed a bottle of vodka in the fridge. Hmm, I thought to myself, what's going on here?

That night I was awakened out of a deep sleep by the sound of someone being struck hard on bare flesh. Immediately my heart was beating so hard I was almost ready to choke. I tiptoed to the door, and placing my ear up against it, I listened. The sound grew closer and I realized they were coming up the stairs. As the person was struck, a stern commanding voice said, "Get back in your room." That let me know it was the man and his wife. My first thought was, *Dear Lord, is that poor woman being battered by her husband?* I was sure the vodka belonged to him, and I had heard of alcoholic men beating their wives.

Just as I was about to go outside to see if she needed help, they went into the room, I heard the door close shut, and all became quiet.

The next morning, I learned the interesting details of the past night. The new boarder sleeping in the sunroom downstairs had been awakened in the middle of the night by someone climbing into the bed with him. It was a naked woman. He climbed out as she was climbing in. As he was getting out, she said in a low, seductive voice, "It's OK; you don't have to leave." He hurried upstairs to inform the husband that his wife was downstairs in his bed.

That's when the beating took place. The husband hit her with his belt and barked at her to get back in the room. When I learned all that, I was quite relieved she had not chosen to come into my room. With my past experiences regarding women, it would have frightened me half to death.

The next morning her suitcase was packed and she was sent on her merry way. I suppose her husband had enough of her for one night.

Overall, my stay at Mrs. James's was a very pleasant one. I have only good memories associated with her home except that one scare, and it wasn't anything compared to the demons I faced at Mrs. Buck's.

Life at Mrs. James's was great, but the rigors of dental school were hard, to say the least. Coupled with the magnitude of material we had to consume, trying to function without my glasses really made life difficult. Remember, Mother had told me that God showed her if I would be willing to lay them aside through dental school, it would be something for which God would look upon me with favor and my soul would be kept from falling.

Almost every Monday that rolled over my head I had a splitting migraine headache. It would start about ten o'clock, and by 5:00 P.M. when school was out, my head was throbbing so hard it was difficult for me to concentrate. And we didn't believe in taking medicine for pain, so I had to endure it. I wonder now how I ever survived it. Through trial and error, I learned that if I tilted my head back as far as I could, it seemed to relieve the pressure inside my throbbing head. The only way I could go to sleep was by sitting propped up in a chair until my headache had subsided, then very carefully tiptoeing to bed. If I exerted myself the least bit in such a way that my heart started to beat a little harder, my head would start pounding all over again. Then there was no need to even lie down. I had to get right back up, sit in the chair until my head stopped throbbing, then try once more to slowly creep into the bed.

My optometrist has explained to me why I had headaches almost every Monday while I was in dental school. Over the weekend and especially on Sundays, when I never, ever opened a book, my eyes were totally relaxed. Then on Monday morning starting at eight o'clock sharp, having to focus my eyes so intently on reading material for long periods of time brought on muscle fatigue, which in turn triggered the headaches. Even now, with my wearing my glasses, I have to wait until after lunch or at least up into the morning before I read anything or I will still develop a migraine headache.

My loyalty to the things we believed made Mother's treatment of me even more painful. I could have taken an aspirin and not told her, and I could have gotten some other glasses and worn them. But I didn't. However, I didn't receive any credit for that. Instead, she was always preaching at me about what I did wrong and for me to come back to the Spirit. Never any praise or recognition for the things I did right. Only chastisement for watching TV and going to the movies. I was truly trying to be faithful to God.

At that time I trusted Mother, even though in my heart of hearts, there were doubts. I read the Bible very intently and sought understanding of what I read. Some things Mother said just didn't make sense. But Mother had not done anything yet to break my trust in her; that would come later. So there was a struggle that went on deep in my heart every now and then, the question of what was truly God's word and what was Mother's. It would take many more years and many more events before my confidence in her was broken, however.

Ah, food, wonderful food! Buying food on Sunday, Mother seemed convinced, was one of the reasons I had failed God. Therefore she had arranged to get me the room at the boardinghouse, so I would not have to buy my meals on Sunday. That first year while I was in the dorm, I even had to buy my lunch tickets in advance or else I was expected to fast on Sunday. I remember one of those Sundays. In the dorm, when I was so hungry from fasting, I had gone to one of the snack machines and bought a candy bar. She rebuked me very severely for that. And I was so honest with her I told her everything. It made no difference that I was so hungry. Like I said earlier, it seemed she no longer had any compassion but was only concerned with her precious religion.

Mrs. James didn't serve meals, so I had to get food some other way. I kept milk and orange juice in the fridge for breakfast, but for the other meals I had to make other arrangements. Sunday meals were the problem. A solution for that was coming. One day stands out very sharply in my mind.

It was a beautiful spring day. I had been home for spring break and was returning back to school. I see that street so clearly, St. Charles Place. The flowers were blooming everywhere, and their fragrance filled the air. The dogwood trees were white with blossoms, and the birds were singing so sweetly. It was such a beautiful time of the year, but I was sad, and in my heart lay a heavy stone much like the weight of the canned food stacked in my suitcase. I didn't matter. My feelings were not important, only the religion Mother imposed on me. There was no thought or consideration given to me. I was expected to endure any kind of hardship, no matter how difficult it was. I knew men had to eat out of cans during the war and that would be OK with me if I were there, but I did not want to have to be so different from everyone else.

As I trudged along carrying my suitcase loaded with canned food (which Mother had bought for me to eat on Sunday), it was so heavy, I had to stop every few feet, put the suitcase down on the sidewalk and change arms. The weight was so great it felt like it would pull my arms out of their sockets. I could carry it only a few feet at a time. It was such a relief to finally make it to Mrs. James's and put that suitcase down for the last time.

Believe me, Chef Boyardee spaghetti doesn't taste good cold straight out of a can. Neither do boiled potatoes or string beans. There was no microwave oven in those days and I didn't have kitchen privileges, so there was nothing to do but eat the food cold. Such experiences really teach you self-discipline to a very great degree. Sometimes, though, I would feel a little self-pity. It just seemed bad that I had to eat old cold food on Sundays while everyone back home was eating good warm food. It really seemed to me that Mother didn't care one thing about me and what I was having to endure, only her religion. That was everything. And truly in my own heart I didn't believe God would have punished me for buying food on Sunday. He understood my circumstances, but it was Mother I had to deal with.

But life sweeps one along and you don't have time to ponder over things when there is so much to do all the time. During the last two years in dental school, there were eleven academic courses we had to study as well as six clinics in which we had to treat patients. There was an operative clinic where we filled teeth and a prosthetic clinic where we made dentures for those who had lost some or all of their teeth. In Oral Surgery we extracted teeth. In Orthodontics we studied how to straighten teeth, except that I got the distinct impression that orthodontics was only for the privileged few who went into that speciality. In crown and bridge clinic we replaced missing teeth with fixed bridges and made crowns for badly broken down teeth. In pedodontic clinic we worked on children's teeth. We had the job of not only treating our patients but also calling them, making all our appointments, and doing the work without assistants. Only occasionally did we have an assistant and only in our senior year. As you can guess, the work kept us very busy all the time.

As the time for graduation approached, the excitement and tension heightened. The question foremost in our minds: Would we receive our diplomas or would we have to repeat the year? At Emory Dental School, just because one had completed all his clinical requirements didn't necessarily mean he would be promoted from one grade to another or, as in our case now, that he would receive his degree. If the instructors thought a student wasn't prepared to graduate, then he had to repeat the senior year.

When the day arrived for us to receive our letters stating whether we would graduate or not, we were all so nervous. But oh, the cheers, the hugs and the laughter when we learned those precious diplomas would be ours. It was truly a wonderful time.

Then I began to plan for graduation. It was such a thrill to get my two invitations. They were so expensive and I wanted to help out all I could, so I only bought the two. One was in white leather, and Mother still has it, I guess. The other one was on white paper. I told Mother to pass the white paper one around so everyone could see it and if anyone wanted to come he was welcome.

I still could hardly believe I was going to graduate. The years had been long and hard, the studies rigorous, and worst of all was the loneliness I had to endure those four years. It was so hard for me, having been so sheltered and then leading such a separate life all to myself.

At last, I was going to be somebody. I would have an identity. It seemed so wonderful. No longer would I be ridiculed and called names, but I would have a real name, a title, Dr. Hall. It seemed I would be free at last. But ah me, I just didn't know that in only a few days there would be another great stone that would crush all my joy and happiness and leave me with a bitter, sad disappointment and more pain.

June 13, 1966. It was a Friday. That was the grand day we had all been waiting for. Graduation! Degrees! Liberation! When that weekend finally arrived, there was a mixture of excitement and dread inside me, excitement about graduation, dread about seeing Mother. She had never ceased preaching to me, reprimanding me, all through the four years of dental school, for having departed from God, which simply was not true. I dreaded to face her. I tried so hard to hope that somehow she would be happy, that things would be better, that at least for a short while she would give me the benefit of what good I had accomplished instead of always dwelling on the negative. I was graduating from dental school! I had proven I could do it, even in the face of her doubts. I had not let Daddy down. I had shown him my appreciation for his sending me to school by doing my very best. Maybe Mother would be proud of me for that, too. But it was not to be.

Jim and his wife Betty, Uncle Sam, my sister Josie and her husband, Carl, came to my graduation. They stayed in a motel in downtown Atlanta, but I was still at Mrs. James's place. None of them were accustomed to the big city, so it was a pleasure to show them around. On Thursday night we ate supper in a restaurant on Peachtree Street. We had to wait quite a while to be seated. Then there was another wait while the food was being prepared. Finally our food was brought to the table at ten o'clock. Uncle Sam had never eaten so late at night in his entire life. I really enjoyed giving him that experience. I remember laughing about it to him, and he took it quite good-naturedly.

I was dating a very beautiful girl named Brenda, who was a secretary at the dental school. She ate with us that night, too. Josie was so taken by her beauty, I'll never forget her reaction when she first met Brenda. The expression on Josie's face said a lot, but when she was alone with me, she declared, "Boy, that's the most beautiful girl I've ever seen in my life. She's gorgeous, but she's way out of my class." I let her know Brenda might be beautiful, but she was not arrogant or stuck up, as we say in the South. At the dinner table that night Josie learned for herself what I already knew about Brenda. There were some good memories associated with my graduation, but only a few. That was one of them.

Mother and Daddy arrived late Thursday night. I had enjoyed being with the others of my family, but I didn't look forward to seeing Mother. As soon as I saw her face, I knew she was in one of those terrible fixes. She had that awful expression she always carried when she was troubled spiritually. At times like that she hardly spoke but was always very cold, stiff, standoffish , and not at all like a true mother would be. She was so hateful and cold to Mrs. James, who had been such a wonderful landlady to me after the nightmare I had endured at Mrs. Buck's. Mother's attitude put a lot of strain on me in addition to the pressure and excitement of graduation day at Emory University Dental School. There was no warm welcome, no congratulations for having completed such as rigorous task. Instead, I had to deal with something that was tearing my world apart again. In my wildest imagination I couldn't have conceived what the next few hours would hold for me then and even for the rest of my life.

As we were leaving Mrs. James's house on the way to the university campus, Mother stopped on the steps at the front of the house, turned to me, and began picking at the collar of my shirt. Then she lowered her boom of destruction. Looking at me with that dreadful expression on her face, she said, "Son, don't let it make you feel bad, but I hate your education. It's separated you from God."

When I heard those words, my heart fell to my feet. All the blood and the emotion seemed to drain out of me. As that statement sank down into my heart, it was like a burning weight that seared everything as it settled down until the part of me that had been alive and vibrant with expectation and joy was numb and dead. Something inside me truly died. I was in shock. Thoughts raced desperately through my mind. Why? I had not departed from God. I loved Him as much as I ever had. All I had done was watch some TV to pass the lonely hours on weekends and go to a few movies.

All my efforts to do my best to show my appreciation for Daddy sending me to school didn't count. I felt like something swept aside by some huge thing as if I were trash. My accomplishment, having graduated from Emory University School of Dentistry, meant absolutely nothing. I was of no importance at all. The only thing that mattered was her *precious religion*. It was very much like the time I was put in the backseat of the car and excluded from the conversation like a criminal. I was an outcast again.

There I stood before her, all my emotions slowly being destroyed. The four years I had spent hours and hours studying hard to do my very best so they could be proud of me were nothing. They held no value. All the hours of loneliness I had endured, eating cold food out of tin cans, being willing to lay aside my glasses, being willing to do whatever was necessary to finish school, all that was for nothing.

Once again I had been betrayed. Once again it was like being put in the backseat like a criminal and being excluded from the conversation. What I had to say or do had no value, only what she deemed valuable. I was an outcast again.

In my despair, I had to reach deep inside to find the strength and courage to go through the graduation exercises in the same manner I had found the strength to go on when I thought of running away at the gas station on the way home from school that first year. That's when God takes over and carries us and we are not even aware of it.

As I sat among my classmates listening to the graduation speech, I felt so alone. It was like in those dreams I had all through the past years when I would be in the black water far from the shore, trying so desperately to get back to the bank of the river, where I would be safe. I was alone to make it back to the shore the best way I could.

After the graduation address by the university president to the entire graduating body, each school went to a separate place on campus to give out the individual degrees. The graduates from the school of dentistry went to the same auditorium where I had learned to play the organ. Think of it, the same room where I found so much consolation at the organ. There in that room I received my D.D.S. degree.

I think of it now and my eyes fill with tears, for I only wish I could go back in time and congratulate John Hall for his achievement. Somehow it would help to wipe away the pain of the past. For then, on that day, it was as if nobody cared, and nobody was even there to applaud me for what I had accomplished. What I had done was nothing. Anybody could have done the same. For years, and even today, there are times that I still have the same feeling of emptiness and failure still grips my heart with its iron claws. The most important aspect and there was nobody to take a picture, to say, "I am proud of you," or anything else, instead Mother standing there with that horrible look on her face, sooo cold and hard, just like she hated everything there, and I guess she did. That's what she had said.

Mother had been so cold and withdrawn toward Mrs. James I didn't even bother to introduce her to Glenn McClane's parents. I assumed she had no desire to meet anybody. Later she accused me of being ashamed of her and said that was why I didn't introduce them to her. Nothing was ever further from the truth. I would have been happy to do so if I had known she even cared. I just didn't want a repeat of what had happened at Mrs. James's.

Deep down inside I was disappointed and ashamed of Mother that day because of the way she treated Mrs. James, who had been so good to me. I had been happy for her to meet my parents. After all, I was proud of them as my parents and especially proud of what they had done in sending me to dental school. That was no easy thing for them to accomplish, even in those days when tuition was only a tenth of what it is today.

Somehow I managed to get through graduation day. There is much about that day that is still not clear in my mind, and I suppose it is because I was in a state of shock. The times through the past years I have visited Emory University campus since that day, I invariably went and stood at that same place on the quadrangle looking out over the lawn where the commencement exercises were held. I could see all the caps and gowns of my classmates and of the other graduates, too. I saw the speaker on the platform in front of us as he stood to make the graduation address that day. The pain and emptiness of it all comes right back to me even today, thirty-two years later. I wonder if it will ever go away. And it is impossible to relate fully all the pain of that day and the impact it had on my life. Sometimes words are simply not adequate to describe the hurts that can be inflicted on one's heart and mind. For years I could hardly bear to look at my diploma and degree I had received from Emory. At that time I didn't understand why, but now I know it was the emotional pain I felt each time I looked at them. It brought back the memory that the most important person in my life didn't care a thing about the fact that I had successfully graduated from Emory University School of Dentistry. I didn't want to even think about that day. The thought of it hurt too deeply.

I dreaded to go home that summer, but fortunately there was a position open at the dental school as a clinical instructor for the summer, which I took. Summer school lasted for six weeks and I was paid $1,000. That seemed like a lot of money to me.

Those few weeks working at the dental school were like a short-lived dream. At last I had a car of my own, my very first, a brand-new Buick Skylark coupe. It was a beautiful cream color with a black vinyl top and white bucket-seated interior with a shift console and automatic transmission plus air-conditioning.

I had finally succeeded in something. I had a degree, which no one could take away from me. It was mine regardless of what Mother said or did. I had earned it all by myself. I had a respectable job of some importance, not as a hired helper, but as someone of position, who had knowledge that others needed. It was a joy and pleasure to share that knowledge with the students on the clinic floor. I had been in their place just the summer before as a junior myself, and I remembered how I felt. I was so glad to help them all I could.

I enjoyed that summer so much. Traveling to and from Charleston and Atlanta or just driving around in the city and to work each morning was sheer pleasure. I savored every moment I was in the car and everything about the car: the radio, the air-conditioning, the beautiful interior, the gear lever in the console, and just the fact that I had a car of my own.

I was out of school! It simply didn't seem possible. I was so happy. Finally I was free. Every morning the sun was always so bright. Work was not work but a pleasure, a pure joy. The rigors of school were behind me forever. I was somebody at last. It's hard to describe the happiness I felt those few weeks. The ugly duckling had turned into a swan and had flown away, high above all that had tormented him. That wonderful flight into freedom would be very short-lived, however. The hunter was not far away and would soon shoot me down. The summer was just too short, and soon all my joy would be turned into a burden of pain and sadness, which I would have to carry for years and years and years.

I'll never forget what happened when I arrived home in Charleston after the end of my summer job at Emory. Mother arrived back home from a visit in North Carolina at the same time. She was driving a compact station wagon they had bought. It had no air-conditioning. I had just gotten out of my car when she drove up in the station wagon. When she got out of her car, I went over to greet her. She wouldn't even hug me but pulled away. She had that bitter hard look on her face. "Yes, you are all cool and dry and I'm all hot and soaked with sweat," she said. "You rode in air-conditioned comfort and I had to ride in the heat. Every thread on my body is soaking wet." Bitterness, resentment, and jealousy dripped from every word she spoke. She definitely didn't display a mother's love in any way, fashion, or form.

Again the shock, the disbelief at what I had heard, hurt, the disappointment. I wished at that moment I had only the most pathetic car available, a pure rattletrap, as we called such a vehicle. Then she wouldn't have anything to throw in my face. It was as if I should apologize for having my car, for being educated, for being successful. She hurt me so very deep. It would not have hurt any worse if she had stabbed me in the back. I have survived both emotional abuse and physical abuse, and emotional abuse is much more intense and long-lasting. When the physical abuse stops, the pain ceases immediately or very soon thereafter, but emotional abuse leaves the scars inside that never go away. Never! And this was truly an omen of what lay ahead for me. I have looked back at times with deep sadness, wishing I had stayed on as a clinic instructor there in Atlanta at the dental school. Then I would have escaped the nightmares that were to come later.

9

Where should I go into practice? That was the big question. The last few months of school, I had asked Mother to pray that God would direct me to the right place to go in practice. I knew she had the time to go check out different cities, and I still trusted her that God would give her peace concerning the right location. I wanted to go to a larger, more metropolitan area where it would be easier to practice what we had learned in school. We looked at Florence, South Carolina, first. I really wanted to go there. We looked at Fair Bluff, North Carolina, and gave a little thought to Chadbourn, too. I remember the little building the mayor of Fair Bluff showed me that was available for a dental office. We also considered Mullins and Conway, South Carolina.

Mrs. James was also very concerned about the location of my practice. As we looked at different places and I returned to school and told Mrs. James about them, she would always ask me where each place was in relation to our former hometown, for she knew the church and all my relatives were there. I'll never forget what she said to me when I told her we had finally decided on Clarkton, North Carolina. Upon realizing how close Clarkton was, the dear soul said to me, and with a hint of exasperation in her voice, "I knew you would get right under their noses. I knew you would be as close to your people as you could get."

That particular time I felt a bit defensive and answered her with, "If I do, it's my own business."

"I suppose it is," she answered back, and she never mentioned it to me again. So many times she had said to me, "You have so much to give to the world. You need to go out in the world and not back with your people. I know they're good people, they're bound to be for you to be like you are, but the world needs people like you." She was a wise old soul.

At the time, I didn't understand what she was talking about.

Now I do. She recognized how sheltered my life had been and how separate I lived from everyone, and it concerned her very much. I remember how exasperated she became with me after encouraging me to take my visiting relatives to see *The Sound of Music* that weekend. After they left, she asked me if I had taken them to see the movie.

I said, "No, ma'am."

With raised voice she retorted quite emphatically, "Why not? There's not a single thing in that movie that any minister would object to."

I made no reply but realized somehow she knew it was my religious beliefs that kept me from going, even though I had never said anything about it to her. But she was right. When I did see the movie years later, I saw exactly what she meant. It was a story about escaping from the tyranny and mass murder of Nazism and of good triumphing over evil. Oh, if we could live parts of our life again!

Mrs. James saw that Mother had a very strong control over my life and that I was influenced a great deal by her. I have many regrets. Mrs. James tried to get me to attend church with her, but I never did. Looking back, I wonder what it would have hurt for me to go to church with that dear old soul. Not a single thing, and in addition, it would have done me a world of good. I loved the church. I loved music. She was Presbyterian and her church had a large pipe organ, too. I would have been in "hog heaven" listening to that fabulous organ every Sunday morning. Regardless of what Mother said, I had not been separated from God. I loved music, and hearing the beautiful hymns on Sunday morning would have given me so much courage to face my daily trials. I was still in that religious "prison," for we had been taught that all other churches were "synagogues of Satan." But there was more fear of Mother than of going to church. I would have committed the worst "sin" if I had gone to church with Mrs. James. I would have probably been thrown out of my church back home.

I'm sure those regrets I held deep in my heart were the grounds for the recurrent dreams about Mrs. James I had for years after leaving her place. The dream was always the same and always in black and white. I would appear in her house, going all through the rooms looking for her. I was always weeping like a child whose heart was broken. For years those dreams occurred now and then until the night I had the one last dream. It was in color. I appeared on the front steps of Mrs. James's house and had finally found her. I put my arms around her and said, "Mrs. James, you were a blessing to me while I stayed with you." That was it. That was the final dream.

I had called Mrs. James occasionally through the years and had spent the night with her when I went back to Emory for my fifth-year class reunion. It was so much nicer staying with her than at a motel. But after having that dream, I called her home again. A stranger answered and told me Mrs. James had passed away some months previously. I'm sure God gave me that dream to let me know she understood everything and to give me a sense of healing in my own heart.

We finally settled on Clarkton, North Carolina. Dr. Bill Keith had his dental practice in Clarkton for a short time but had moved to Elizabethtown, a much larger town, where his practice was much more lucrative. I considered the possibility of using the old Lion's Club building, but its location in the town was not very good, and a fair amount of remodeling would have been required before I could use it as a dental office. I finally settled on the idea of erecting my own office building. How exciting to be in the process of going into practice after all the years of preparation in school! At last I was going to be able to help my people with their dental needs. I loved them dearly, and that way I could repay them for all they had done for me through the years gone by.

Mr. James Green, a prominent merchant in town, sold me a lot for $3,500 right on Highway 211, an excellent location for a dental office, and was kind enough to finance the total amount, allowing me to pay $600 per year plus six percent interest. That was such a great help, too. I don't know what I would have done without all the assistance given me. Waccamaw Bank loaned me the money for the building construction, with Uncle Kevin and Uncle Swift as cosigners. In addition, the bank deferred those payments for a year to help me get on my feet. That note was for $15,000, to be paid at $187.50 monthly for ten years. Thompson Dental Supply sold me my supplies and equipment without collateral, and that money was financed by Wachovia Bank out of Greensboro. The amount of that note was $13,000 to be paid at $330.13 monthly for ten years. It was a wonderful day when those notes were paid in full.

In order to prevent my being idle for several months while the construction of my office building was under way, Thompson Dental Supply located me a position at the state penitentiary in Raleigh. I was to be in charge of the dental clinic, and my salary was six dollars an hour, which for me seemed like a fortune. As I had been accustomed to working in tobacco for five dollars a day or as a cleanup boy and carpenter's aide during my teens on home construction sites for my uncles for less than two dollars per hour, that salary was wonderful. Again I felt like somebody. There was a place there for me, and it was important for me to help those dependent on my knowledge. It was a good feeling.

I began working there in September. That was a totally new experience for me. I'll never forget the first time I went through the cell block to reach the dental clinic. It seemed so sad to see people behind bars like animals at the zoo. Their faces stared out at me so imploringly, and some of them even reached through the bars and tried to touch me. For the first few nights, until I could find an apartment to rent, I was given the privilege of sleeping in the prison guards' locker room. Sleeping was rather difficult, because the guards changed shifts during the night. Their coming into the room, turning on the lights, and talking always woke me. Fortunately, I found a nice room on Boylan Avenue within a week. When I came back inside the prison compound those first few nights after eating supper, the sad haunting melodies floating through the air from the inmates' cells seemed to tell the story of the poor guys locked behind those steel bars. I thought, *Dear God, you can even hear the sadness in their music.*

I enjoyed working there, however. The guys looked up to me, and most of them couldn't believe I was a dentist. "You look too young to be a dentist," they all said. "How old are you anyway?" They were always raving about my clothes and how good my cologne smelled. "You're tough, man," was their compliment. Inmates worked as dental assistants, so I had two of them to help me, and they did their job well. There are a few memories that stand out very sharp in my mind, and I will share them with you.

One of my assistants was doing time for stealing. He loved to brag. One day during a slack period when we had nothing to do, he was telling me about his "stash"of loot: $250,000, or so he claimed. He described exactly where it was buried under the cinder-block foundation of a certain house. Then he went on to describe one of his holdups to me. This is the fun part. He was in a parking lot and saw a well-dressed lady get out of her car. So he went up to her, pulled out a gun, and said, "Ma'am, this is a holdup." She very calmly gave him her pocketbook. He thought to himself, *Man, this is the easiest holdup I've ever pulled off.* But as he turned and walked away, she let out a bloodcurdling scream louder than anything he had ever heard before in his life. He said, "Man, it was so loud it kicked the rocks up off the sidewalk." At that I burst into laughter. But that was just the beginning. "Man," he said, "it peeled the paint off the cars." I was almost hysterical. Then he topped it off by saying, "Man, it frayed the elastic in my underdrawers." With that I lost control. I was laughing so hard I could barely get my breath. Tears were streaming down my cheeks. My stomach muscles were cramping. My cheeks were aching. I had never heard anything so hilarious. Needless to say, he derived a great deal of pleasure from seeing me laugh so much.

Another case involved a man who had been framed for a murder he didn't commit. The pharmacist down the hall from the dental clinic told me the poor man would never get out as long as the people responsible for putting him there were alive. One day he was brought into the dental clinic with chains shackled to his feet and a chain fastened from his feet to his handcuffs. There was no way he could escape. His forearms looked like snakes were under the skin. They were riddled with scars where he had slashed them with razor blades in an attempt to convince the prison officials he was insane. His reason for faking insanity was to be sent to Dorothea Dix Hospital, where escape was much easier than at the state prison. His eyes were coal black pools of hatred. There was no emotion at all in them, no feeling, no life, as if he were dead. He was the only patient who came to the dental clinic for treatment that I actually feared. I knew if he got hold of a gun, he would shoot anything or anybody in his way. It was a relief to see him leave.

Another day, a guy came through the clinic who was most interesting. Without any introduction he announced, "I'm a thief, always have been, always will be, and I don't care who knows it." He also grew up in the same town as I had. His next statement really struck home: "I remember a Howard girl in my class. They had a strange religion. They didn't believe in shaving their legs." I didn't say a word. I didn't want to embarrass him or make him feel uncomfortable. But I thought deeply on what he had said. I thought to myself, *What a pity that our religion is so peculiar that someone would remember it in that way instead of remembering the love and kindness we showed to others.*

One final incident left me with a sad memory. There was an X-ray technician from the medical clinic who enjoyed talking with me. One day we somehow got on the subject of death and hell. Almost jokingly he said to me, "I know I'm going to hell. I'm going to ask old Lucifer to give me a pitchfork so I can 'jugg' them as they come in the gate." I'm certain my face was a picture of shock when that statement came out of his mouth. I couldn't believe anybody would be so flippant about anything so serious. But, looking back on it, I really believe the poor fellow was trying to reach out for help. I assured him that everything can be forgiven except blasphemy. I had no idea what he had done to be put there, and I do so much hope he found peace in his heart before it was too late.

My time spent there among those inmates gave me greater compassion for those who make mistakes and/or do stupid things.

By April of 1967 my office was finished, and I opened my practice. Again my life was not my own. I could not interview applicants to determine the one best suited for the job but was told to hire Judy, Uncle Swift's daughter, knowing in advance what a struggle I would have with her. She had been abused by her mother and, because of that, was very defensive. Any criticism I gave in the process of training her to be a good dental assistant, she took the wrong way. It was a battle of wills, mine against hers. But in the end I won anyway. Judy became an *excellent* chairside dental assistant. I would have put her up against the very best and I am sure she would have come out on top. I don't regret having hired her, for we have many good memories of times, good and bad, that we shared as we worked together. As you can see, however, every aspect of my life was controlled to some degree by Mother.

My family does not show age very much, and neither did I,

apparently. Many times patients would come into the office looking for the dentist. Not seeing any other man in the room, they would look at me rather startled and with disbelief showing on their faces as well as in their voices, would say, "Are you the dentist? You don't look old enough to be a dentist." After hearing that said so many times, I wanted to ask them, "Do you want me to age before I work on your teeth?" Those are very fond memories for me, however.

We had been told in school that in rural areas we would not be able to practice dentistry as we had been taught. For a number of years that proved to be the case. Not all rural patients, but the majority, didn't want their teeth checked or to have them cleaned. Instead it was "I want this one filled," or "this one pulled." Doing fluorides on children's teeth was also out of the question. Rarely would anyone agree to have an X ray made. I had to include it as part of the extraction of a tooth in order to get them to undergo that procedure. But little by little, things began to improve.

The first few weeks I would see a patient and, since there was nothing else to do, would lie down on the daybed in the spare room and take a nap. I remember when we had four patients in the morning: I thought I was really busy.

The most difficult task for me those first few years was charging fees, most especially knowing how to charge my relatives. Remembering what it's like to not have, I always wanted to help the patient out, even to my own detriment. Mother reminded me quite often how much she and Daddy had sacrificed for me to attend dental school and that Uncle Swift and Uncle Kevin had also given her money to help with my expenses. Mother said her dear brother would come to her, get down on his knees, and with tears streaming down his cheeks give her money to help send me through dental school. That alone increased my sense of guilt to charge them for their dental work. Without fail, every time a family member was dismissed from the office there was a struggle inside me to decide what fee to charge. It made me nervous. I hated it. What should I do? What should I charge them? I had to make a living. I had to pay my debts. The struggle was so difficult for me and caused me such emotional turmoil that I actually prayed to God to please help me become financially strong enough so that it would not be necessary for me to charge my relatives for their dental services.

Soon that time came, and for years thereafter I didn't charge them anything at all for routine dental procedures such as examinations, fillings, cleaning, X rays, and extractions. For crowns and dentures I only charged the lab fee. In that way the burden was taken off me. I didn't have that turmoil facing me when they left the office. I had peace inside. I didn't have that dread hanging over me when I saw their names in the appointment book.

Ah, my eyes! My poor eyes! While working in Raleigh, I grew tired of my visual world being so out of focus. I said to myself, I'm going to see better. So I made an appointment with an optometrist there in the city and purchased a pair of glasses. When I walked out of that office and looked around, I couldn't believe my eyes. That time that expression was true for me in a literal sense. I had forgotten how things looked. I could actually see individual leaves and branches on a tree instead of the treetop just appearing as a blur. Cars at night were so shiny and clean. Instead of appearing as a vague oval shape with two gray fuzzy spots in the upper part of it, a person's face actually had eyes in it. From a distance of twenty feet I couldn't recognize who I was looking at without my glasses. It was truly amazing. I would take my glasses off, put them back on, and take them off again. It was incredible. I just couldn't get over the difference. Oh, how wonderful it was to see clearly again!

On the trips I made to and from Atlanta the summer after graduation, I would have to stop and pull over onto the shoulder of the interstate highway a short distance from the large green highway signs. I would sit there and press against the inside of my eyeballs so I could read the exit signs and highway numbers. Without pressing against my eyeballs to help improve my vision, I couldn't read the signs. That's how nearly blind I was without glasses.

I had a dread of facing Mother but had no idea she would treat me like she did. After all, I was out of dental school. I had been faithful in not wearing glasses those four years. In fact, I had no idea where my old glasses even were. My first encounter with her while I was wearing glasses was at Aunt Esther's. Mother was sitting on the sofa talking to Aunt Esther when I entered. That terrible scowl immediately came over her face. "Why did you do it?" she asked.

"Because I wanted to see better," I replied meekly.

"How could you go against the Spirit?" she asked again.

I did not reply to that question, for that was one of those times when there was a big question in my own mind whether God had really told her that I should lay aside my glasses in the first place. She was so cold and hardly talked to me. Later when she had me by myself, she preached to me for hours about the virtues of living spiritually and of trusting God, always making me feel guilty, just like I had committed some awful sin. I couldn't even enjoy being in her presence. Every time I was around her the tension was so great you could feel it in the room, for I knew she was judging me for wearing my glasses. In spite of her attitude and treatment of me, I continued to wear my glasses for a year or two.

Then one Sunday morning in church Mother stood as she quite often did to deliver what she said God showed her. It was 1969. She was once again on the subject of trusting God to heal our eyes as opposed to wearing glasses. She presented before the congregation that if we had faith like we ought to have, God would heal us, leaving us with a deep sense of guilt. I had known for years that God could heal me. Why He had not I didn't know, but it didn't make my faith in Him any less.

At times like that in our church, when ultimatums were presented to us, people were afraid. We were told many times that we either accepted what she brought or faced damnation from God. In an effort to show their eagerness to be obedient to what they believed to be God's will, three members of the church came forward and laid their glasses on the little table at the front of the church. That table was sacred to us. On it lay the Bible that was used by the preacher and anyone else who stood up to give a testimony. A small bottle of oliveoil was kept there, too. It was used to anoint the sick when they came before the church and knelt at the altar to be healed. As I have said before, I was not certain in my own heart whether God *had* brought this to Mother or not, so I didn't take my glasses forward. I did, however, out of respect to the others, lay them aside once again. I felt too guilty to continue wearing mine knowing the others had taken theirs off, even though I also knew their vision was not as poor as mine.

The next day was a nightmare. I'll never forget it as long as I live. We were working in Jim's yard picking up roots so he could level the ground before planting grass. My entire visual world was blurred and totally out of focus. I felt ruined. My depth perception was gone. As I stooped over to pick up roots, it was difficult to discern exactly where the ground was. When I looked off in the distance, everything seemed to be in a haze. I couldn't help but weep as I worked.

Fortunately, my work at the office was easier for me to accomplish than working outside in the yard at Jim's. Astigmatism is made worse by dim lighting, and the office lights were very bright. Needless to say, people wondered why I was no longer wearing my glasses, but they didn't dare ask. I religiously practiced what I had been taught and didn't socialize with anyone. I was barely friendly and kept all conversation on a strictly professional basis. During those early years I was very unapproachable, and I look back on those years with many regrets. I could have been much kinder to everyone, but I had not escaped yet!

What happened between that Sunday and the following weekly prayer service on Wednesday was truly a sacrificial act of love. As I sat in my pew in church that Wednesday night waiting for the others to arrive, my sister Eva came in and took her seat in front of me. The instant I glanced at her face from the side, I noticed how thin and pale she was. It was almost like my heart stopped for a split second. A voice spoke to me saying, *That was for you*. A few minutes after the service began, Eleanor stood on her feet and gave a testimony of what she had done.

She stood and said before everyone present, "It came to my heart last Sunday when Aunt Beulah brought that about us not wearing our glasses to fast for my dear brother that perhaps God would heal his eyes, because I know he is almost blind without his glasses. I haven't eaten anything or drunk a drop of water since I was in church Sunday." As she stood there saying those words, I saw how emaciated she really was. Her already-slender body had wasted away until she looked like a skeleton, and her eyes sat in deep sunken hollows in her thin, gaunt face. Her cheekbones protruded beneath her pale skin. She had absolutely no color in her face. To think that no food or drink of any kind had entered her mouth from Sunday morning when she ate breakfast until that very moment! It broke my heart to think she had done such a thing for me.

There's no way anyone can imagine how I felt as sat listening to her kind, tender, and loving voice as she spoke those words. Had I not been certain her actions were done out of pure love with no strings attached, I would have felt horribly guilty. As it was, I was so humbled by her supreme act of love I just cried and cried. How could anybody have such love? I was amazed beyond words. Thinking of what she had done made me so ashamed for complaining about not being able to see. I felt like an old dog.

Still, in my heart of hearts, I didn't believe it was in God's plan to heal my eyes. I suffered without my glasses for several long months. Then I started wearing them once more, never to lay them aside again.

In order to have some semblance of peace with Mother, however, I agreed to not wear them in church. It was Mother's way or no way at all. She pressured me and gave me a tremendous guilt complex. Every time I was in her presence, I was uncomfortable. I knew she disapproved of my actions, and I wanted Mother's approval more than anything else.

Since I had graduated, Mother had begun a campaign to get firm control of me again, and in the process she began little by little to destroy my self-esteem. While I was going through dental school, my self-esteem had been healed to a great degree from the scars put on me in grade school. I was treated like everyone else, not like some creep whom no one wanted to touch. I felt at home and comfortable among my classmates. I was their equal. They even bragged on me at times, which made me feel so good. But it was as if Mother wanted my identity destroyed. She tried to break my spirit. My title of Doctor was nothing to her. I was called to be a servant of God, and nothing else mattered. My feelings were not considered at all. She shamed me for wanting to be introduced as Dr. Hall instead of just Mr. Hall. With family members I couldn't even practice proper medical procedures such as prescribing antibiotics for infection. It was like being on a string. When I didn't do just as she thought I should, she gave the string a jerk back to the "right path."

Her criticism was relentless and all-encompassing. When I traded cars, she was displeased. I was being extravagant and ungodly. While working in Raleigh, I began to collect antiques for a future home. She rebuked me for buying them. I was supposed to be humble and buy plain and simple things. But it was fine for her to buy whatever she liked. And I wanted so much to share my life with her. I wanted to share my happiness with her. I was finally planning for my future home. My dream for a home was just beginning to take shape. One has to start somewhere. I wanted her to be part of it. But after being treated so coldly over and over again and always being reprimanded for whatever I bought unless she approved of it, I ceased to share anything with her. She had eyes like a hawk; she saw everything. When she came to the house and noticed something new that I had not told her about, she commented on the fact and then began to rebuke me for being secretive with my life. It was a no-win situation for me, damned if I did and damned if I didn't. I dreaded for her to come if I had purchased something new. But that made me sad, for she was the only mother I had ever known and I didn't really want to shut her out, but I had to survive.

I bought myself a horse, and every few days I rode her, putting her through her paces. She was a retired show horse, and to keep her in shape it was necessary to exercise her with small, light chains around her front ankles. After I worked her with the chains on, her legs were accustomed to the extra weight. When I rode her with them off, boy, how she picked up her feet. She was a beauty to behold as she trotted along picking those feet up so high, holding her neck in a lovely arch with her ears pointed forward, with infinite grace and poise. Mother said she had a dream and in her dream she saw my horse with the chains on her. She saw the horse flying through the air and I was worshiping it. How foolish! Then a long sermon ensued about the virtues of being spiritual and not letting the things of the world be a god to me. It seemed to me Mother wanted to destroy any happiness I found anywhere.

She even invaded the realm of music in my life. I was rebuked for taking music lessons to improve my technique. She told me that God wanted me to play only the hymns in the hymnbook. That was a crushing blow. It was like an iron cage had been placed around me. My hands were shackled. Blinders were beside my eyes. My life was not my own. The beauty, joy, and freedom I found playing music were ripped out of my grasp and broken like one breaks a clay pot with a hammer. Deep inside me a light went out. I let her know if I could only play hymns, I'd just as soon not play at all. That day my love for music died in me, and not until many years later and after much more sorrow would it be resurrected.

Not only were we rebuked for having no faith for our eyes, but were also chastised for using medicated Band-Aids, cough drops, alcohol to cleanse a cut, or anything for pain or infection or to help stop diarrhea or vomiting. And I was even given a sermon for suggesting that stitches should be used to close a wound. When she did that, it took a lot of patience not to have contempt for her ignorance. I honestly prayed for grace to overlook it. I said to myself, *They can have all the scars they want, I'll never mention sutures or anything else to them.* Ah, but when Bob, an outsider who had married into the family, cut his leg with a bush ax while helping Mother clean her lot to build her house, who was the one called on to sew up his leg? John. That was done to prevent Bob's going to the doctor. I'll never forget it. There I was in my dental office shaving his leg around the wound site so I could sew it up. Judy, my chairside assistant, helped me. I did a very good job, too. I used resorbable cat gut sutures to pull the underlying tissue together, then black silk thread sutures to close the outside layer of skin. It looked quite neat when we had finished, and I was proud of myself .

Some of the things imposed upon us by Mother's religion brought untold pain and suffering to certain ones who were sick. I remember a cousin of mine who developed an abdominal cyst. I thought the poor woman was pregnant, because she continued to grow larger by the month. She later told me about her experience the night the cyst finally broke through to the outside of her stomach. "John, I've never suffered so much before in my life. I thought I would die. The agony just before it ruptured was so great I thought it would kill me." When it did break through the skin, quarts and quarts of putrid, foul-smelling liquid poured out onto the bed sheets. The stench was almost overpowering. It would make you retch and heave even if you didn't vomit. Dozens of towels were used to mop up the horrible stuff. No one but those directly involved can even imagine just how grisly it was with her lying in bed smelling like something dead. Cynthia's dear sister-in-law, Annabelle, who stayed with her night and day was never given credit for what she did. It was truly an unselfish act of love Annabelle had displayed by staying with Cynthia, keeping the bed as clean as possible and waiting on her day after day. Annabelle truly was not only a dear sister-in-law but also an invaluable friend.

Poor Cynthia had endured the fear of knowing something was seriously wrong with her and all that pain and agony, simply because she feared Mother's judgment even more than the suffering she was enduring. Cynthia knew if she went to the doctor, Mother would openly rebuke her in church and, even worse than that, she would be ostracized by many of the other church members. The opening through which the cyst drained just wouldn't heal. Mother persuaded Cynthia to sell her house out in the country and move into a trailer placed across the dirt road from the church. After lying in bed for years and getting no better, she finally went to the doctor. He was horrified. "Woman, you could have died," he said. Cynthia told him she probably would have had she not been trusting God with her whole heart.

Sure enough, she was set aside as if she were an awful sinner, simply because she had gone to get help so she wouldn't have to remain bedridden for the rest of her life. She was made to move out of the trailer by the church, just like she had turned into some kind of wicked person who would pollute the church grounds being there so close by.

The sadness of all that was that Mother had brainwashed us all to such an extent that we believed we were doing God's will. We believed that if it was God's will to heal us, it would happen. However, for me, I began then to question some of those things in my own heart. But I said nothing to Mother, for I knew she would not listen. With Cynthia, for example, how could she be so wrong for going to get help? It didn't make any sense to me. And as the years passed, Mother became more and more fanatical in her religious zeal.

One would ask, How could one person have so much control over the lives of other people? For Jim and me, it began years ago. When Mother first adopted us, even though she did things to terrify us, we loved her. We were totally dependent on her for our very existence. She was loving and kind to us, too, and we had many wonderful things we'd never had before. Then as religion took its

171

place in our lives, we acquired an awe and respect for her as if she were one of the prophets out of the Bible. Years ago when I was a small child, people needed Mother more because they were inexperienced with many different aspects of everyday life, such as building a home, landscaping, choosing clothes, etc. As the years passed and they acquired information for themselves, became more knowledgeable and thus more independent of her, Mother began to lose control over them, and as she did, she began to use desperate measures to regain that control.

And in those early years, she was more good than bad. People went to her for help with their problems, and she was always so understanding, kind, compassionate, and loving, never hateful, critical, or judgmental. You could tell her anything you had done, and she helped to dispel your guilt and restore your confidence again. She always gave you hope. That kind of love bound her to the church, and they were willing to do almost anything to please her.

The factor most responsible for the extreme degree to which Mother was able to carry her control over our lives was our isolation from the outside world. Religion was all we knew. We had no real friends outside the family. There was no social contact with other people except in day-to-day encounters in the business world. We did not mix with anyone; we didn't visit them, and they of course didn't visit us. We did not participate in any "worldly events" such as sports, car racing, movies, bowling, etc. We ate, slept, worked, went to school, and went to church. That was it, nothing else. Vacations for us were wonderful trips to Gatlinburg, Tennessee. We walked the streets, browsed through the little shops, and climbed the rocks in the cool streams. We knew nothing else to give us fulfillment in our lives.

The fear of hell, too, had been so deeply instilled into our very being that we were willing to do whatever was necessary to escape it. There were times in church when fear was so great it could be felt like a noose being wrapped around the soul or like a deep cold chilling the bones. It even was proclaimed that death was in the camp. People want to live, not spend an eternity in the flames of hell. Without obedience to what Mother brought, we believed that was our destiny. Mother put herself in the place of God to the people.

Over and over she stood before the congregation and proclaimed to them that if they couldn't come to the things in her heart, there was no way they could get to God. To them, she was their means of reaching God, their hope of heaven. They did not stop to think that they had direct access to God themselves. But that's part of the mind control, the brainwashing, that had been done to us. Through the years I heard her proclaim that to the church, but I didn't believe it in a complete sense, as others did. I never knew until years later just how literally some of them believed that proclamation. In other words, without her, they had no way to heaven.

And as children growing up, our lives were dictated for us: exactly what we did; when, where, and how. There was no other choice but to obey. Without obedience, there was punishment and pain. We were even told that we must be punished so we could know pain and would want to escape hell. You have seen previously what happened when Mother merely *thought* I was doing something she disapproved of. She beat me black-and-blue. Because there was no other avenue of expression and no other activities to be involved in, church became the focal point of our lives. It was everything to us.

And as for me, I was a conforming child. I tried to do what I believed to be right. And I wanted to please Mother. She was our spiritual matriarch, the one we looked to for guidance, the one to whom we almost entrusted our soul's salvation. I had more confidence in her at one time than any other living being on earth. No one but her could destroy that confidence, no one. As she continued to exert her powerful influence over me after I became a Christian, slowly, little by little, I became intrenched in her religion and in practicing the things we had been taught, some of which brought pain and grief to others, and for which I have so many regrets. At the time, because we had been taught to put aside ourselves, as Christ taught when he said, "He that would come after me let him first deny himself, take up his cross and follow me," it did not seem to me that I was hurting anyone. I was doing God's will. We were indoctrinated, by the interpretation of that verse of Scripture, to have absolutely no regard for people's feelings. We could be as cold and hard as stone and truly believe we were doing the will of God. Our religion was a legalistic religion, but I would not know that until many long years later. Legalistic religion has no room for compassion and hardly any room for love. I could set people aside and treat them as if they were strangers when they had transgressed one of the laws of our religion, just as the Scripture said: "Treat them as a heathen that they might fear and repent." Ah, but as I had been on the receiving end of that kind of treatment, there is no way in this world I could do that again, not even to a stranger, let alone to my very own kin.

However, through the years there was always a battle waged deep in my heart over some of the things Mother claimed God had shown her were sins. The struggle came about because I had also read the Bible and my own understanding of what it said was in disagreement with Mother's rules or her laws. I would often ask myself, *Is that really what God expects, or is that just what Mother expects?* I knew that God looks on the individual heart, not on the outward appearance of things as people do. For example, wearing glasses, women shaving their legs, men growing beards, wearing a bathing suit to go swimming, women curling their hair, wearing jewelry, going to the movies, watching TV, having a stereo to listen to beautiful music that can lift up the soul, the list of no-nos could go on and on. I had always wanted a Cadillac, but Mother said God wanted us to live a simple life, not be ostentatious; therefore, we were not to drive such cars as that, but my interpretation was that if we do not feel arrogantly proud of such a car, then having one would be no sin. But Mother would never listen to any kind of reasoning. It was her way or no way at all.

The years following my graduation from dental school I became most intensely involved in the church. During those years I was struggling to regain Mother's trust and confidence in me. I wanted her approval again more than anything else. And at the same time Mother was continuing to destroy my confidence, my sense of self-worth; in short, she was slowly and inexorably totally demoralizing me, little by little.

As I have said before, very shortly after I was first saved and became a Christian, Mother began to pressure me over and over again to let God give me something to do. "God doesn't save us to be idle," she would say. If something is repeated to us long enough, we begin to believe it is true. And a child wants to please his parent.

So I began to try to do the things she expected of me. When I complied, then I received her blessing. If I didn't, then she was very unhappy with me. That reward and performance cycle can carry a person a long way, even to the brink of catastrophe. I know from my own experience. The shock jolts us into the reality of what is actually happening to us. Not too far in the future, events would take place that were so shocking to me that I was finally able to break away and escape.

10

The events of 1970 would shake the very foundations of all the trust and confidence I had in Mother. In January of that year, Uncle Swift and Aunt Neville were killed in a terrible automobile accident on Interstate 95 just outside Parkton, North Carolina. Two drunk GIs pulled out from the rest area going in the wrong direction. Uncle Swift was traveling south on the way home from Fayetteville. When he pulled over in the left lane to pass the car ahead of him, he saw the oncoming headlights. A split second before impact he exclaimed, "Oh, Lord!" Those were his dying words. Both cars collided head-on at around sixty-five miles an hour. The two marines and Uncle Swift were killed instantly. Aunt Neville died forty-five minutes later in the emergency room. One of the nurses in the emergency room made the statement that Aunt Neville must have been a religious woman, for she never stopped praying until she lost consciousness. Three of Uncle Swift and Aunt Neville's six girls had been with them, and all three suffered injuries of varying degrees. One lay in a coma for days.

I'll never forget the Saturday night Mother called at Jim's house to tell us what had happened. Betty answered the phone. She returned right away to the den, where Jim, Butch, and I were sitting. She said, "John, you'll have to go see what's the matter. I can't get anything out of her. She just keeps mourning and praying."

I thought to myself, *Dear me, what now?* When I got on the phone, I had to be emphatic and demand to know what was the matter. She wouldn't stop wailing, otherwise.

Then came the shocking words: "My dear brother Swift and dear Neville have been slain on the highway." Immediately my mind returned to one Sunday morning in church when God had revealed a prophecy to me in which I stood as the Spirit commanded me to and proclaimed these words to Uncle Swift's family: "The Lord has shown me that if you children don't change your life,

176

God will take your daddy away from you." Every one of them turned as pale as death. Some of his children were causing him a lot of grief. He would cry and pray for them many times in church. My response to Mother's dreadful news was, "Well, Mother, it's the fulfilling of the Spirit. Remember what the Lord showed me that morning in church." My answer brought her no comfort, however. And even in the face of what I had seen spiritually, it still seemed unreal to me that they were gone.

The following Sunday in church, Mother's proclamation to the congregation concerning the death of her brother and sister-in-law caused the first crack in her religious armor that brought about her eventual downfall. She, the spiritual matriarch of the entire family, stood up before us with the Bible in her hand and said that Uncle Swift and Aunt Neville's deaths were the sacrifice for our sins, that God had let them be slain on the highway in order to bring us back to the Spirit!

Hearing her make such a claim that Sunday in church, I knew she was not speaking the words given her by God. What she had said simply and absolutely was not true. I confronted her with that claim: "Mother, that's contrary to Scripture. Christ was the last sacrifice. If what you said were true, then Christ died in vain." Still she wouldn't listen to reason but steadfastly maintained she was right, even to the point of arguing that "No, God took them because we had strayed away from the Spirit, and they were the sacrifice." That was one strike against her. More would come.

Events related to their deaths became progressively more extreme. It was as if Mother became obsessed with their deaths. Mother proclaimed to the congregation that the blood in the clothes her dear brother and sister were wearing when they died was sacred and must never be washed out. The clothes should be kept as a memorial to what God had done. A member of the congregation was inspired to build a piece of furniture in which to keep the bloodstained clothes. Unless they have been removed, those clothes are still in that chest, sitting in the living room of my sisters' home.

The same was said of the car in which Mother's brother had died. The car must be preserved as a memorial of how her dear brother was slain on the highway before the world, like King Saul in the Bible was slain before the Philistines, the enemies of the Lord. A cement slab was poured, and a building was erected to house the car. It became a shrine. Church members were taken to the car to pray in order that the spirit of my deceased uncle would come there to give them comfort. Other times they were beaten there at the car to drive out the evil spirits from them or to punish them for sins they had committed. It held a lot of power over many for years.

The most destructive element to the church, however, was Mother's bitterness. She became bitter about losing her favorite brother. She wanted others to suffer because she was hurt at losing her brother and blamed them for it. In addition, she took it upon herself to go live with her brother's children and complained about it quite often, yet she denied she complained. She would tell me at times that the other women in the church weren't tied down like she was. "They're footloose and fancy free and can go and do as they please," she said.

"You didn't have to go stay with them. They are old enough to take care of themselves," I argued.

But Mother wouldn't listen. Instead of the loving, caring, non-judgmental mother I had known, she became hard, bitter, accusatory, and unfeeling. She said one thing and did another. She brought emotional chaos and pain to those children's lives. She put such pressure on them to do as she commanded, and if they didn't comply, she beat some of them also, just like she had beaten me and Jim. The baby girl was even told one Wednesday night that if she didn't go to church and let the Spirit bless her, she would be beaten when Mother got her back home. Can you imagine the fear in this girl's heart when she was in the church?

Instead of letting them mature by assuming the responsibility of their household, she took charge and ordered them around.

Their life was miserable. She had an obsession about sex, and it carried over into their lives there, making them very uncomfortable. The baby girl said Mother would feel her buttocks when she left to go to school, checking to determine if she was wearing a girdle. Mother's claim was that nice girls didn't go around letting their butts jiggle when they walked. The baby girl made the statement that Mother, by her treatment of you, would make you think of things that otherwise would never cross your mind. The books they read were censored. If she suspected them of reading love stories, she confiscated the books and burned them. Once she showed me in her trunk a large brown paper grocery bag full of paperback books she had collected from their homes. I'll never forget it. We were out behind the church when Cynthia lived in a trailer house beside the church. I remember thinking to myself, *Mercy, they are just simple stories that give the children an outlet to their narrow lives. What's so awful about them?* I recognized the author of some of them. It was Louis L'Amour, the famous writer of Westerns.

One of her brother's daughters made the mistake of moving in with them when she was first married instead of getting out on her own. Mother had used her power of persuasion, saying it would be more economical for them. But the way Mother treated them, she apparently wanted to police their life. The niece and her husband couldn't even go in the bathroom together without Mother wanting to know what they were doing in there, just like they were having sex on the floor or on the countertop in the bathroom, as if the bathroom wasn't used for washing the body, brushing the teeth, and so forth. Why did she have such a hang-up about sex? She had eloped when she was only fifteen and married a thirty-year-old man. What was the problem? Did she not want them to have pleasure? Sex within the marriage relation was certainly not forbidden by God. And the way she was, if you had children too soon in the marriage, the husband was sorry and self-indulgent; if you waited too long, then both members were classified as being selfish and self-centered. It was impossible to please her.

What was she doing?? I've been there on Sundays when the two would go in their bedroom to take a nap and Mother reacted in the same fashion, very agitated and provoked, just like all anybody did in a bedroom was have sex. Then when we got down to pray, you could tell exactly how she felt about every single person whose name she mentioned in her prayer. Their lives were at times almost intolerable. To get her way she would fall down on the floor in one of her anxiety convulsions. For a while it worked, until Judy, the oldest girl, had enough. She had come to realize it was only Mother's strategy to get her way with them, to manipulate them, to continue to exert her control over them. Judy said one particular morning she just decided to ignore Mother and get on with her household duties and see what Mother would do. So, instead of getting down on her knees beside Mother, Judy simply stepped right over her as she lay there on the kitchen floor, continuing with her household chores of vacuuming, cleaning the bathrooms, and emptying the trash cans. It worked! Within ten minutes or less Mother was up and acted as if nothing had ever happened. Before that, they would have spent hours on the floor praying, with Mother dictating whatever she wanted the girls to do. It was awful.

Lucy, the next oldest girl, and her husband were to live in the family home, but for years Mother rebuked them for anything they did to the house to improve it or, more especially, to decorate it to suit their taste. They were supposed to be thankful and reverence the house and the fact that her dear precious brother had built it with his own dear hands. They were rebuked for cutting down some holly trees in the front yard. It seemed even the trees in the yard were sacred. Mother resented anything they did, anything at all. Poor Lucy shed many a tear there in her daddy's home from the emotional turmoil Mother inflicted upon her and her little family.

Instead of treating them so tyrannically, Mother should have given them advice and let them make their own way; then the hatred and anger toward her would have never taken root later in their lives. But instead she wanted to control everything they did, especially their money. I truly believe her motives were good. She didn't want to see them lose what little they had, but it still would have been much better if she had sat down with them and said, "Children, this is the last thing you will receive from your parents. Take care of it. You won't get any more. If you need help managing it, I will be glad to give you sound advice. If you squander it, you will have no one else to blame but yourself." I'll say again, if she had taken that approach, the anger would never have taken root in their hearts. They would have loved her and could have only said, "Well, we have no one to blame but ourselves." The children would have been better off if she had never gone there.

During this period of time, Mother became obsessed with her brother's children almost to the exclusion of everyone else. Jim and I felt abandoned, like we no longer mattered. We both were struggling with trying to live up to her expectations of us, striving to obtain her approval, to know for sure that she loved us. It was a very difficult time for us both. My integrity was questioned, as well as the integrity of others of the congregation. She would stand in church and tell us if we knew of her brother's children going astray we should inform her. We took her at her word. I did let her know of one such thing, and instead of her appreciating the information as she had said she would, she accused me of being a "gossiper." I was frustrated, to say the least, and told her if I were not interested in their spiritual welfare, I wouldn't tell her anything else if they went to destruction. Other members had similar and equally devastating encounters with her. Most were rebuked and informed that they should find the sin in their own household, and they were simply doing what she had asked of them, not feeling like they were perfect and therefore good enough to see the wrong in another person. She should have loved them and let their faults be between them and God and not attempted to police their actions. Mother meant well, I believe, but if Christ didn't come into the world to condemn the world, who are we to do so?

I remember visiting Uncle Kevin one afternoon and he came and sat in my car and confided in me how Mother had treated him in regards to his brother Swift's children. Uncle Swift and Uncle Kevin had been partners in the home construction business. Mother had accused Uncle Kevin of embezzling money from Swift. He said to her, "Beulah, I wouldn't take anything from those girls for anything on this world. It's all there on paper in black and white."

"Those books don't mean a thing to me," was her cold reply. In addition, she forced Uncle Kevin to buy out his brother's share of the business so Uncle Swift's girls would have some cash. By her doing that, however, she actually deprived her brother's children of their inheritance.

I tried several times to give her some sound advice for them, but she wouldn't listen; she always knew everything. After the accident I tried desperately to convince Mother she should obtain the services of an experienced big-city attorney, one who had previously handled a case concerning the kind of accident in which Uncle Swift had been killed. The lawyer they were using had told Mother the reason the girls didn't stand a chance to collect much was because there wasn't any physical evidence in the automobile that would tie the drunk GIs to their rented car, not even a belt buckle, sock, or anything. That didn't make sense to me, but she

181

wouldn't listen. She knew everything. No one could tell her any-thing. Those girls should have obtained a settlement of at least a million dollars. They had lost both parents, who not only had pro-vided love and emotional support but also had been the girls' means of furthering their education as well. They had suffered a tremendous loss.

As Mother's bitterness drove her to destroy all she had ever built up in the church, she used her power over the people like a great beam to knock down anyone who opposed her. That power had gone to her head. I remember well her telling me that she made one of the men in the congregation get down on his knees in front of her in the bathroom in the church before she would tell him the words she claimed the Lord had given her to bring to him. I thought to myself then, *My God, what kind of person are you anyway? That's putting yourself in an exalted position.* I knew right at that moment that I didn't want to follow in her footsteps. But I didn't voice my opinion, for I had learned years ago to keep silent about certain matters. She wouldn't listen to anyone. She reminded me of a freight train going full blast down the tracks, and neither hell nor high water would stop her.

During that period of time when her brother's children seemed to be her sole preoccupation, when there were church services in which I was cut to pieces and cast down into the very dust in church I would be so hurt inside I could hardly bear it. Still desperately seeking the assurance that she still loved me and Jim, I would go by her car after the service to speak to her and to give her a hug. Time and time again she sat there in that car seat exactly like she was made of stone. There was no response from her either verbally or physically. She did not utter a single word; not even one muscle twitched. If we saw her face, it was just as stony. The dread became so great my mouth would become dry and it was difficult to talk. Even to this day she has absolutely no idea how deeply that hurt us. You, the reader, will probably ask the question, "Why on God's earth did you put yourselves through that ordeal time and time again?" There was an invisible compelling force that drove us to that car. At that time in both our lives, we couldn't do otherwise. We didn't have the emotional strength or maturity. Look at the entire picture. Take these two small children at a very early age, beat them

182

into almost complete submission to your will, brand in their hearts the fear of hell, brainwash them so deeply they believe every word you say is true, instill a deep and profound sense of guilt for ruining your life, and in so doing make them pathologically dependent upon you emotionally; then you have the answer.

We loved her in spite of the fact that we may not have stood in the church and delivered a great message to the people. There are times when we ourselves need to be strengthened, not to strengthen someone else. We desperately needed her acknowledgment of our love and that she in turn still loved us, in spite of her current overwhelming concern for her brother's children. She had said many times that she loved us, but her actions proved otherwise. How could anyone believe he is loved when he is treated colder than a stranger? Just for her to reach out to us, put her arms around our necks and give us a warm, heartfelt embrace would have been the most wonderful thing in the whole world for either one of us. That's all it would have taken to remove our doubts. But it never came, never! We went away with an empty void, a longing, an ache, deep in our heart. The questions were never answered. Did she really care now? Did we even matter to her anymore? We left the little church many a time with our hearts so heavy it was difficult to get on with our lives. You can see how dependent upon her we were for our emotional well-being.

Her relentless criticism made me dread attending church services. I no longer knew what Mother expected of me. If I stood and preached or if I rebuked someone, if what I said didn't meet with her approval she condemned it. She even told me that only two or three times I had stood in the Spirit of truth and brought wonderful words of life. Imagine how I felt. What were all the other times for? That left a message in my subconscious that I had been a failure in church. We can't be the same every time. She condemned others in the same manner as well. Many a time a sincere soul stood up and gave a testimony out of his heart, and if it wasn't said or done to satisfy Mother, that individual's very words were criticized openly. Mother became even more fanatical about the dos and don'ts of our religion. We were not to have radios in our cars. I was preached a sermon because I bought a car on the dealer's lot with a radio in it. Mother really wanted me to take the radio out of the car, but I refused. It seemed ridiculous to me. We were supposed to disconnect our radios. Newspapers became an item of sin. If brought into our homes, they would defile our homes, but it was OK that Mother kept Daddy's *Navy Times* newspaper in the garage and read every word of it. Do you see the damage Mother began to inflict on those who looked to her for strength? And the people weren't stupid! It was obvious to them there was a double standard, one for her and other "precious souls" in the congregation for whom she made excuses in regards to breaking the law of the "spirit." I placed Spirit in quotation marks, used a lowercase "s" because it was her spirit, not the Spirit of God. And she was the spiritual matriarch of the church. These differences she made were so destructive to our emotional and spiritual well-being.

Many a Sunday morning I would be so nervous and upset before I left the house, I would have to go to the bathroom twice. By the time I reached church, I felt weak and purged. I wanted so much to please Mother. As I sat in the church pew, when I felt moved by the Spirit to stand, there was always the struggle going on inside my heart. Should I stand? If I stood, Mother would not accept me. Then if I waited until the Spirit passed by me, the torment of failure gripped me. It should not have been that way. I still had the memory of that encounter in the bus station in Columbia in my subconscious, and I wanted that place back in Mother's heart. Looking back now, I feel so sad that my self-esteem had been so damaged by her that instead of blocking her out of my mind and getting on with my life, I was still desperately trying to obtain that approval. I was that little boy wanting his mother's love so desperately, needing to know that I was OK, that she loved me in spite of my shortcomings.

Many a Sunday when I stood in the church to preach or to give a testimony, I was so aggrieved my eyes were blinded with tears. I needed Mother's support and the assurance that she believed in me. She could either lift me up or cast me down just by the look on her face. One glance into that stony face was all it took to cast me down into the dirt. Sometimes in church she would get up from the altar in disgust and take her seat in the pew while everyone else was still on their knees praying. That cast a pall on the church and made worshiping next to impossible.

One Sunday in particular stands out very clearly to me.

Mother, as I just said, was sitting in her pew with a provoked, stony expression on her face. I needed encouragement so much that day. I felt like a dog anyway. Mother could make you feel like that by the way she treated you. Standing up from among those kneeling around me and with the Bible in my hand, I took one look at her and knew my only hope was God. I stepped to the altar and knelt down with my face to the floor, weeping, before the entire congregation. Putting everything else aside, God came to my rescue. I stood back up and told everyone how Satan wanted to cast me down into a pit. (And as David said in Psalms, "If it had not been the Lord who was on our side . . . then the waters had overwhelmed us, the . . . waters had gone over our soul.") But God had lifted me up. As those words came out of my mouth, a dear aunt of mine shouted all around the altar. As she had been victimized by Mother for years, her experiences let her know exactly what I meant. The church was so dear to me, and when my heart was broken the greatest compassion filled my heart and I wanted just to touch them, to wipe away their tears, to lift them up, for I knew they also felt cast down. The church looked to me for strength, for Mother's bitterness had made her so hard and judgmental toward nearly everyone. They loved me, too, for the compassion I had for them. But Mother was rapidly destroying everything she had built up over the years past.

Other times when I left church Jim had to drive home because I would be so overcome with weeping I couldn't even drive. In spite of all these terrible experiences, it would still be a few more years before events took place to give me the strength to break away, to escape.

11

Well, the year was 1971. I was thirty, time to start a home and I hoped a family as well. In the fall of 1967, while I was working in Raleigh, I had written to Brenda, the secretary at the dental school I had dated a few times, to break off our relationship. I explained in the letter that I thought too much of her to expect her to conform to all the strange religious demands expected of those who became members of our church. It just didn't seem fair, so we parted as friends. One incident I will share about our brief dating period, however. On one of our dates, Brenda and I were going to Stone Mountain on a picnic. When she came out of her apartment, she was wearing slacks. I asked her to please change into a dress. I explained my reason for asking her to change: our religion dictated that it was a sin for women to wear slacks; slacks of any kind were considered men's clothing and were not to be worn by women for any reason whatsoever. Brenda gave me a very reasonable explanation for wearing them: climbing over rocks in slacks was much more modest than wearing a dress. And to me it made perfect sense, but I was still afraid. The religion was too deeply entrenched in me to allow me to follow my own heart. And I knew Mother would preach to me about it also. I had those balls and chains of religious legalism firmly shackled to my ankles. I feared to do anything that would displease God, believing that if I was faithful to all those things we practiced, God would in turn bless my life. She changed into a dress, which gave me relief from the burden imposed upon me by the shackles, but inside I regretted that I had in turn imposed the same conditions upon another person who was totally free from them. It was as if I was bringing her into servitude to my religion. It just didn't seem fair to her. My fear of reprisal from Mother was greater than my sense of reason in my own mind and my own trust in what I truly believed God expected of me. In those years I was still like a bug that was wrapped very tightly in a spider's web. I was alive and still wiggling but unable to wiggle free. That would not come until years later.

One spring evening I entered the men's department in Sears in Wilmington. Immediately my eyes lighted on a pretty girl about the same instant she saw me. We were drawn to each other like steel shavings are drawn to a magnet. Her name was Betty Ann New. She was a pretty little thing, and sweet too. We dated a few times, and I really liked her, but again, religion was the main problem. There was a big age difference, too; I was thirteen years older than she. At the time, I was living with Jim and Betty, where I had lived ever since graduating from dental school. Mother had asked me to stay with Jim and do all I could to help him and Betty. Betty Ann came to the house once and had supper with us. Jim and Betty liked her, too. We went hiking over my property, and I talked about my plans to build a home somewhere in the woods near Jim's house. Betty Ann and I had a few arguments about religion, and she broke off our relationship, saying there was just too many differences between us. There was another interesting fact about Betty Ann. Mother had said on more than one occasion she had no desire to meet her. I guess because she had not been involved in the selection of her as my girlfriend and possible wife for the future and had not chosen her for me.

In December of 1972, I met the new Columbus County extension agent, Glenn Ann Bobo, at the home of my Aunt Maggie. Her daughter, Sue, was Ann's (as they called her) secretary. The two of them were going over the ins and outs of sewing. I had gone out to make some divinity fudge for Aunt Maggie. It was raining that day. I remember Ann's saying to me she had heard you shouldn't make divinity when it rains. I retorted, "Huh, I make it when I get good and ready to." I had never heard that statement before. My fudge turned out just fine.

Ann was a nice girl, jolly and outgoing, but there was no instant attraction to her like there had been to Betty Ann. Not too long after that first encounter with Ann at Aunt Maggie's, Mother said to me, "Why don't you go with Ann? She's a nice girl." So, we began dating. Her favorite expression when I would call and invite her out for dinner was, "Neat." I can just hear her say it, with so much excitement in her voice: "Neat, neat."

187

Our courtship was one of the most unusual of anyone's anywhere, I am sure. Mother had such a hang-up about sex that she forbid anyone to kiss or even hold hands before marriage. It was expected of me to be an example to the others in the church, so I complied. Ann and I never even kissed before we were married. Can you believe that?

Let me diverge a moment. Through the years, we had heard the biblical account of Isaac and Rebecca preached in our ears. The story always seemed so wonderful to me because Isaac fell in love with Rebecca as soon as he laid eyes on her and that gave the story a mystical air to it. Wouldn't it be wonderful to find someone like that and to know she was meant for you?

But our religious practice of being so separate from the world made the prospects of finding a mate very dismal, and for that reason some in the family were attracted to each other. To them it was like if we can't go out with other people, then we'll have to notice someone in the family. I know my sister Eva in her frustration once said, "What's God going to do? Plop them down on my doorstep?"

At that time, I believed in the biblical story so strongly that I believed I could learn to love whomever God chose for me without having actually dated her. The story had been presented to us in such a way that it seemed almost like a fairy tale, as if the right people would suddenly appear in our lives and we would marry and live happily ever after. As if dating someone to learn if you were compatible, etc., was not even necessary. Quite unrealistic! That's how deeply we had been brainwashed. Little did I know I would literally have to put that belief into practice in my own life.

Ann and I had been dating for about nine months, but not anything serious. I was not in love with her. We were just friends. Then Mother stood in the church one Wednesday night during prayer meeting and proclaimed to me that she believed Ann was the right girl for me. At that moment I felt no joy, rather grief. I put my head down on the floor and wept and wept. I realized the gravity of my situation. I was expected to marry this girl I didn't love. Now there was no escape.

Here another very important part of my life was being dictated for me. I had not been allowed to pursue music as a career but had to choose another profession. Next I was refused the chance to join the military and travel to Europe. Then the location for my practice was not my free choice, nor could I hire whom I would have chosen. And now this. I felt trapped, ruined. But as in the previous situations, I had to rise up and face this one with courage, knowing that somehow I had to survive. Later in the next week or so, Mother asked me if I loved Ann. I answered her quite honestly, "No."

"Then why are you marrying her?" Mother asked. "Why do you think? Because you stood in church and told me she was the one meant for me," I answered, with some indignation in my voice too. Considering how she had been the one to perpetuate these beliefs regarding marriage, I was shocked that she had asked me the question in the first place. But I went on to say that I believed I could learn to love Ann, and I have!

Knowing I was supposed to marry her, Ann and I began to plan our wedding. Church weddings were not allowed. In fact, ours was the first actual wedding ceremony held in the family. Ann and I set a precedent for other couples to follow. Many had gone to Dillon, South Carolina, and been married by a justice of the peace. Having a minister from another church marry us would also have been totally out of the question. Mother considered all other ministers to be "wolves in sheep's clothing." To me, having a justice of the peace marry us seemed a bit too impersonal. Mother had me inquire of my personal attorney, Worth Hester, if Uncle Sam, our minister, could legally marry us. Fortunately, the answer was yes. With that hurdle out of the way, we began to get excited about everything, all the preparations, the flowers, the music, the location (the service was to be held at Uncle Swift's home), the food for the reception at Aunt Maggie's home. So, on October 12, 1973, at 7:00 P.M., Uncle Sam performed the wedding ceremony, pronouncing me and Ann husband and wife.

After the reception, we left for Atlanta, Georgia. On our honeymoon we drove down Fairview Road and stopped at Mrs. Buck's. The house had been torn down. Only the vacant lot remained. I pulled up at the curb and sat there a few minutes to reminisce about the years spent on that piece of land, the terrible events that took place there on that spot of earth. A sadness filled me as I sat there with Ann. I shared with her some of the horrors I had endured at Mrs. Buck's. We also visited a beautiful white stucco house standing on a hill on Ponce de Leon Avenue. I had admired that stately mansion through the years as I passed by while I was in dental school and had wondered what it looked like inside. We drove slowly up the drive, noticing the place looked neglected and run-down. When we passed though the front door, which was falling off its hinges, our gaze went straight up. The ceiling was near thirty feet high. The room was huge, and the tall ceiling gave it a lofty appearance, providing a sense of freedom and unlimited space, where nothing could close you in. At that very moment I decided this was the style of house I should build, not the colonial style with a veranda out front like so many you see. This house would be different from any other house around; only we would build a much smaller version. We took pictures and some crude measurements to take to an architect. We still have those pictures and our first sketches of the house. A few years later we would begin construction of our new home.

The first few years of our marriage were difficult for Ann. Many times Mother would come by the house, ask me to go sit in the car with her, and talk to me for hours, leaving poor Ann alone inside wondering what was going on. It was a continual thing, week in and week out, Mother talking to me about living right, living spiritual. My life was not my own. Mother's influence over me was still very strong, and I didn't share much of my heart with Ann. I was not aware of it at the time, but deep in my subconscious I was afraid to trust Ann with my deepest feelings because Mother had hurt me so deeply, leaving a deep distrust of all women inside me.

I had bought some land right down the road from Mother and Jim before I ever met Ann. The years passed quickly. Ann and I had bought a small house in a neighboring town. I commuted to and from Clarkton. She worked in that town. Our architect, Wallace Klontz, had taken our sketches and photos and drawn up an excellent set of blueprints. Ann and I began building our new house. So, on June 7, 1976, which was Ann's birthday, the foundation was dug for our new home. Mr. Vernon Suggs from Elizabethtown was the builder. We paid him a weekly wage and paid the salaries of the two carpenters who helped him. They did an excellent job, too. I also spent many hours alone in the house doing things I couldn't afford to pay someone else to do, such as the wall ornamentations in the living room.

I didn't understand why at the time, but again and again as I was alone in the empty house, before I left to go home to Ann, I felt a compelling urge to go to the organ room upstairs to pray. Looking out the window, I could see my driveway as it wound around in two curves and then disappeared out of sight. That drive always seemed to represent the road to where my real mama was. A deep sadness always enveloped me. More than anything else, I wanted to see my mama again, and I knew I must never forget God and what He had brought me through. I would always kneel down with my face to the floor and, while the tears dropped from my eyes, pray the same prayer: "Dear God, please, please, don't let me ever change. Don't let me ever forget where I came from. Let me never become proud and arrogant. Never let me change." I knew if I wouldn't change, someday at the end of life's road, I could once again see my mama I loved so dearly. And that prayer has been granted me, for I have never forgotten what it's like to not have things and to be in adversity and I have acquired a deep sense of compassion for all those I know.

The house was completed in July of 1977, with the help of so many of my relatives, and we moved in. While the house was under construction, I had promised Mother that when we moved into our new home there would always be a place in my car for her and Daddy to ride to church. By giving them a ride with me, I could, with this simple deed, repay them just a little for all they had done for me through my life.

The experiences of that first Sunday after moving into my new home would be omens of the years to come. I was so happy that morning as we drove up to Mother's garage door. Finally I could do something to repay Mother and Daddy for all they had done for me. I blew the horn. I waited. Nobody came. I blew the horn again. I waited. I asked Ann, "Wonder what's wrong?"

"I bet you they're already gone," she answered.

"No, they can't be," I said. "I told them they could ride with me."

Doubt and incredulity began to creep into my heart. I waited a few more minutes, then went to the garage door and peeked through the little window. What I saw made my heart sink in despair. The garage was empty. The car was gone. I couldn't believe it. My heart sank deeper into a state of emptiness, sadness, and betrayal. I felt numb inside again. It was worse than a slap in the face. Mother had cast away the tender, caring love I had offered to her, love that wanted to repay her for the things she had done for me, love that wanted to do a kind deed for her, to let her save her gas money to help her with their expenses. But my love was worthless. It was like trash. She didn't need it. Once again I had been cast aside, put in the backseat, abandoned. The pain of that day remains forever etched in the depths of my heart. That event was a pattern of things to come in the future. Mother had successfully destroyed my happiness again, even in my new home. But there would be more to come.

Our first Christmas celebration in our new home was also a time of pain and disappointment. We planned a family gathering with my brothers and sisters. It was to be an exciting occasion. At last, the beautiful dream I had years ago was a reality: the room with the tall ceiling, the chandelier, the colors we had used in decorating the living room, everything was the very same it had been in the dream. I was so happy. Now I could share my love with my dear sisters and brothers in my very own home. Looking back, I realize I made the mistake of inviting Mother. But at the time it was another opportunity for me to repay her for what she had done for me, and besides, I wanted her to be part of my life.

We were making the gathering a dress-up occasion, like going to a ball. My sisters wore floor length dresses. They were excited, too, for they had never had an opportunity to wear such clothes. Everyone was busy making last-minute preparations when Mother arrived. She came in unannounced and met me in the small hallway outside the dining room. I went to give her a welcoming hug, but she appeared cold, stiff, and unfriendly. Being the eternal optimist, I pressed forward. "Mother, how are you?" I asked.

Making no effort to at least be polite, she responded with a cold, flat, "I feel out of place here."

I was shocked! Hurt! Out of place! What was she talking about? We were just family members having dinner with one another in the privacy of my home. My sisters had long dresses on, but so what, they weren't out showing off before others, trying to appear proud or arrogant.

Again my heart sank, but this time I felt a stab of bitterness, too. My first thought was to go upstairs, take off my coat and tie, throw them on the bed, and put on the shabbiest thing I possessed and then go back downstairs and ask, "Are you satisfied now?" But I didn't. I just endured the hurt and the disappointment.

At the table there were more hurt feelings. Eva sat directly across from me. She didn't enjoy the meal and could hardly eat for dabbing her eyes to dry the tears. Mother had treated her very coldly and, in addition, had said something equally cruel to her. That fateful night my happiness was turned into bitter disappointment, and the night was changed from a festive occasion into a nightmare. I look back now and am amazed at how well we were able to cope in such adverse circumstances. It wasn't easy, but the fact that we already had a lot of experience with adversity made it less difficult.

I wonder now, too, if Mother was jealous. She certainly wasn't very polite. If confronted about that night, Mother would maintain that God troubled her heart for us and that was the reason for her behavior. She ruined many a gathering for the entire family at large. We would be having a cookout at someone's home. Everyone would be relaxed, the adults talking, the children playing and just having a good time. Mother would drive up and get out of the car, and a cloud of fear and dread would float down over everyone. The whole atmosphere changed. The laughter ceased. The conversation became muted, for fear something might be overheard and misconstrued as unspiritual, bringing open rebuke later in church. Somber expressions came over the faces of all present. We could not feel free and be relaxed. That's how much we were all under her spell. We feared her criticism and rebuke.

The year 1975 was a year to be remembered. I had a rather profound dream, which I told to Mother and Jim. Mother passed it off as if it meant nothing, but I felt sure it was a dream from God. Jim later confided in me that he almost opened his heart to me when I told him the dream. In the dream I appeared in Jim's house. He was standing before the mirror in his bedroom looking at himself, stroking his face with his hand, and as he stood there, he said, "She's going to beat me again." In the dream a revelation then came to me. I realized that Jim had an illegitimate child somewhere, and that was the reason he worked so much. He was supporting the child, but was trying to keep it a secret. In the dream the saddest feeling came to me then, and I felt so much pity for Jim.

Not too many months after I had the dream, Mother called me up to her house. It was January 1976. When I entered her bedroom, I knew there was a major problem. The atmosphere in the room was the same as when the church congregation was called together for a special service and we spent hours and hours on our knees praying, searching our hearts for any unconfessed sin in our lives, or whatever sin Mother claimed we were guilty of, and trying to repent of it. Right away upon my entering the room where Jim and Mother were sitting, Mother asked me if I believed God would bless Jim. I thought to myself, *Why is she asking me this question?* "Of course. He will," I answered.

Then she made a strange statement. She looked at me and said, "God has put it on me to let Jim wear my dear brother Swift's boots, and God is going to bless Jim with Swift's dear spirit to be true and faithful."

Eva was also there, and the minute she left, Jim asked Mother, "Should I tell him?"

Just as soon as those words came out of his mouth, I stopped Jim. "Wait; let me ask you something. Was God trying to show me something when I had that dream?"

Jim's answer was an immediate, "Yes." Then he told me what he had done: he had been having an affair with a married woman for the last five years. The affair began while I was living with Jim and Betty, and I had no idea what was going on. All I knew was that Jim had begun to treat Betty like dirt. I would be so upset at him for his behavior toward Betty. It seemed inconceivable to me for him to treat Betty as he did. She was and still is such a dear person.

After that day, Mother began a desperate and at times very strange "campaign" to ensure that Jim would terminate the relationship with the woman and that he wouldn't backslide into it again at a later date. She did all these things claiming that God bid her do them. First of all, she commanded me to wash Jim and particularly his genitals. That was to cleanse him from the adultery he had been committing. Jim and I chuckled as I washed him. It was amusing to us both. It reminded me of the time I had to stand outside the shower and keep vigil while he took a shower. I honestly didn't see how washing him could make any difference. The change had to come from within, but there was no getting by not doing whatever Mother demanded of us. Next, I was required to go to the church and wash the pew where he sat. More rituals were to follow.

Mother knew exactly how to get what she wanted out of Jim. Sometimes she fell on the floor in an anxiety convulsion. Jim would go into a panic. He would be so frightened he was willing to tell her anything. I think he actually believed God was upon her, giving her directions for Jim's life. The first time that happened, she asked for a writing tablet and a pencil, on which she scribbled that he must go to the church and write a letter to the woman telling her how evil their affair had been and that it was over forever. He complied with that demand. But the nightmare had just begun.

Our lives were kept in turmoil for months and on into years. There were phone calls to the house, to my office, Mother always talking about living spiritually, about Jim, whether he was back with the woman or not. She would call my office, I'd answer the phone, and she wouldn't say a word. "Mother, say something. I have patients in three chairs and a waiting room full of people. I've got to get back to work," I'd say as the stress inside me continued to build higher and higher like steam in a boiler. It was maddening.

I often defended Jim to Mother and tried to reason with her that change had to come from within and that she had to give him a chance to redeem himself. She had to trust him, for he declared again and again that he wasn't seeing the lady anymore. But Mother never let up. Betty even had to keep a diary of the odometer reading on Jim's car in an effort to know where he had driven. Then Mother had another one of those anxiety convulsions and poor Jim confessed to her about some porno magazines he had in his desk at work. She insisted that he bring those magazines to her for her to destroy. Jim was so ashamed for her to see them. He told me, "John, those books are not fit for her to look at. But I knew she would never be satisfied until we brought them to her." Jim wanted to throw them in the ditch on the way home. But knowing how fanatical she was, he was afraid not to bring them to her. Betty told us later that Mother looked at every one of them. She even told me once that "I think it would be better if men didn't wear boxer shorts. You can see their private parts hanging down. They look better wearing briefs. Then they aren't so obvious. I've finally talked Daddy into wearing briefs." Talking about having a hang-up about sex! I never understood her on that subject!

I tried to reason with Mother that doing all those peculiar things to control his life wouldn't help unless Jim was different inside. You can't become a detective trailing your own child. But Mother wouldn't listen to reason. In her continued zeal to eradicate adultery from Jim's life, she went to his house one day while he and Betty were working, took all his cowboy boots and hats to her house, cut them in pieces, and burned them in the fireplace. She told Jim that as she watched the black smoke billowing out of the chimney it reminded her of the awful sins he had committed. When Jim learned what she had done, he was first angry, then deeply hurt.

He also has had a struggle through the years with self-esteem. The Western wear had given him a new identity. Mother had destroyed his "new self." I'm sure the loss of all of his boots and hats was indeed like losing a part of himself, not to mention the loss in monetary value. But we were under her iron thumb, so to speak. And we were conditioned to accept whatever was done to us without showing any resentment or dislike of any kind. We had been rebuked for even shrugging our shoulders. Remember all the beatings Jim had received for doing nothing as a teenager. If he received that kind of treatment for nothing, what would he get if he showed resentment for what she had done? We had learned long years ago to suppress all our negative feelings and emotions. To show any would have brought unmerciful punishment. Bear in mind, too, that Mother did all these strange actions in the name of God. She claimed that God had put it on her to burn Jim's "polluted" boots and hats.

As anyone with a normal childhood reads this account of mine and Jim's lives, I am certain it seems almost unbelievable that a grown man would allow his mother to do such things to him. I do not know if I can even explain it myself in such a way that you can understand why we allowed her to do these things to us. It had everything to do with how deeply we were brainwashed by this woman we called Mother. First of all, we loved her very much and were deeply indebted to her. She was the only mother we had ever known. Our real mama had been taken away when we were very young, especially Jim, who was only two and a half. We both believe the primary reason we allowed Mother to do those horrible things to us was the deep sense of guilt she instilled in us over the years by repeating again and again through the years that if it weren't for us, she and Daddy could travel and be happy. In our subconscious minds we believed that whatever she did to us we deserved. We had ruined their lives. Add to the intense guilt the fear of hell she had also instilled in us, and the fact that we believed she was called of God, and there you have it: an unnatural, unhealthy, and almost total control over both our souls and bodies.

But even then in my life, I was already beginning to have serious doubts about the validity of God being behind the things she was doing to Jim. These strange rituals just didn't make sense, but I wasn't strong enough yet to escape from the web of mind control in which I was entangled.

Mother's bitterness at the loss of her favorite brother and her unwillingness to acknowledge that she had become bitter changed her from a loving person who wanted to lift up the church into a hard, cruel woman out to bring vengeance in any way possible to those she held responsible for his death. In addition to Jim being among those she held guilty for her brother's death, he had also done this terrible thing that Mother hated, committing adultery. Moreover, I truly believe she was angry that Jim was able to carry off the affair for five years right under her nose without her knowing it. She couldn't bear to be "outfoxed," and that's exactly what Jim had done. Right after the affair was exposed, Jim talked about running away and marrying this lady he said he loved. Mother told me she would break both of his legs before she would let him run away. I was shocked. Break his legs! *What kind of Mother is she?* I thought. "*I* certainly wouldn't," I answered. That statement was bad enough, but there was much worse to come.

Mother stood in church before the entire congregation on several occasions and said to my poor brother, "I would rejoice to come upon you on the highway and see every bone in your body broken and to know you could never lead the kind of life you have led for the past five years." How absolutely horrible! That was not even a mother's love and certainly not the love of Christ, yet she claimed to be so spiritual, as she passed such stern judgment on every other person in the church. Some in the family even said that if we were really her children, she wouldn't treat us the way she did. How do you think that made Jim feel? What did that do for his self-esteem? It's no wonder he felt like a dog. Then, in addition, he was told he was responsible for the church failing God and causing the death of her dear brother.

But then the absolutely unimaginable happened. One day she said to me, "If you will help me, I'll fix him so he can never run around again."

I knew she had gone mad. I was horrified. "Mother!" I said "That is horrible! You can't do that! It's against the law!"

"Well, I could do it in the Spirit," she answered.

"No, Mother, that's not the way God works. If it were, in ten minutes He could destroy all the wicked people on the face of the earth and only the good people would be left, but that's not the way God works. He gives us a choice," I argued.

She stood firm by her conviction. "I could do it in the Spirit," she replied.

Can you imagine? Castrating a grown man, and with no medical knowledge, and then attempting to coerce me into helping her commit the crime! To even hint at such an atrocity was ghastly enough, but to actually want to perform the deed as a means of controlling your child's behavior! And to say you could perform the deed in the Spirit of God! That's taking religious zeal to the most extreme measure humanly imaginable, very much like some of Hitler's crimes. I am sure, too, that if I had been willing to help her, she would have taken his scrotum with his testicles attached and shouted all over the room praising God with a loud voice for giving her the strength to deliver Jim from the clutches of Satan.

Another avenue Mother used to destroy Jim was an attack on something very important to his emotional welfare and to his sense of accomplishment and self-worth: his landscape business. She demanded that he sell his equipment and get out of the landscape business. "That's how you went astray in the first place," she would say. Jim had cut down a tree for the lady he became involved with, and that first day at her house the affair began. Mother didn't want him out away from the cabinet shop where he might be tempted to repeat his crime. That's why she had told him through the years to remain at the shop, to work for his people, where he would be safe from the world. He had begun the landscape business as an aside from working at the shop, which he hated. Jim was an outdoor person. He hated the confinement of a desk job. He was very successful, too, and quite professional at it, as well, with many customers.

The little child in Jim still feared his mother and most of all wanted her approval and to know that she still loved him. I attempted, without success, to come to Jim's defense again, explaining to Mother that the change had to come from within and selling his equipment would make no difference unless he changed his heart. In addition, he would continue to have all those payments to make and no revenue coming in to help make them. My intervention on his behalf made no difference whatsoever. Mother was like someone possessed. She presented it to him that he couldn't serve God if he didn't do as she said.

Many Sundays she had stood in church before him with the Bible in her hand and said these words to him as she pointed to her heart: "If you don't come to the things in this old heart of mine, there's no way you can get to God." Jim believed it literally, he feared if he wasn't obedient and did whatever she said he should do, he would surely end up in hell. It was that simple.

She wouldn't listen to anybody, but was hounding poor Jim and Betty day in and day out. I encouraged Jim not to listen to her, not to sell his equipment. "Tell her to leave you alone, that you and Betty are trying to work things out," I said. But at that time in his life, Jim had neither the emotional independence nor the fortitude to tell Mother to get out of his life. It would take years of pain and heartache before he became strong enough to do so. Eventually, with her continual prodding him day in and day out, he sold his backhoe, his dump truck, and some other important pieces of equipment for a "little bit of nothing," as we say in the South. He and Betty paid on the equipment bank notes for years. But it was like something died inside him, as if he were crushed. And he was. The loss of his landscape business wreaked such emotional havoc later in his life, it was almost his undoing. Part of him had been destroyed, simply to satisfy the ravings of a religious madwoman. As you can see, Mother would stop at nothing to achieve her goals.

The next event I must describe is more difficult to relate than all the other events I have described so far. Knowing I actually did such a thing causes me a great deal of pain and remorse. During all the turmoil going on involving Jim and his affair, Mother began to brainwash me, to pressure me to let God put it on me to punish Jim for his sins. She came to me in church again and again while we were on our knees praying and said these exact words to me, "If you'll get your heart like it ought to be, God will put it on you to punish Jim." When she talked to me time and again for hours at her home, she said the same thing, and in addition, she said, "He needs to be punished. If I were strong, I would do it myself, but I'm not able. He needs a strong man like you to punish him." Her goading me about that went on for weeks, just like Delilah did to Samson in the Bible, day in and day out. Now, more than anything in this world, I wish my confidence in her had been broken enough that I would have totally ignored her. Unfortunately it was not, for I began praying to God to help me be willing to do whatever was required of me. You can see how brainwashed I was, *even into my very soul.*

Then one Wednesday night during prayer meeting, the service had become an arena of fear and desperation. It had been proclaimed openly before the congregation that there was death in the camp. Mother told Jim if he didn't come to God that night, he would be lost forever. That alone brought cold chills up our spines, and we became caught up in the emotionalism of fear. At times like that, we all would search our hearts and lives diligently for anything we had done wrong or anything we had failed to do. It was then something seemed to speak to me telling me to take Jim down to Uncle Swift's old car and punish him. I was on my knees at the altar praying. I arose, went to Jim, took him by the hand, and led him outside and down to the old car. He went along with me so willingly. It just breaks my heart to write these words, and as I write, the tears stream down my cheeks. Who on earth was I to punish anybody? I was far from perfect myself. Looking back now, I find it so difficult for me to believe I actually did such a thing. Me, imperfect me, beating another human being for mistakes he had made and, of all people my very own brother! But at the time, I honestly thought I was doing God's will. I truly did. That's the kind of grip a religious cult can exert on its members.

When we arrived at the car, it was only a short walking distance from the church, I told Jim God had put it on me to punish him. He took off his belt, handed it to me, and knelt down so humbly and took the punishment willingly. I still remember the expression on his face and the look in his eyes. They were pools of black liquid, devoid of any emotion, or so I thought. When one is caught up in the throes of such a controlling religious cult, which practices such cruel and judgmental treatment of its members, you are devoid of any compassion when carrying out these deeds. The only thought that pervades your mind at the moment is completing your task so that you do the will of God. During the actual beating, I was crying out with a loud voice to God to deliver his soul. My heart was pounding so hard in my chest I felt I would choke. I can see now that I was possessed with the same spirit as Mother had been when she had beaten my dear brother in her bedroom in Charleston while I played the piano in the living room. She had succeeded in transferring her will into my will. At this moment I am so certain I was completely wrong that, as I have previously said, I would kneel down myself and let someone beat me to death before I would stand on my feet and do such a terrible deed to another person again. When we got back to church, I stood up before everyone and told them I had taken Jim down to the old car and punished him and that it was to deliver his soul from torment. Many shouted for joy, not because I had beaten him, but because they believed it actually did deliver him from hell, as we had been taught. It is still so difficult for me to think about what I did that night. It was simply so horrible. You can truly see the depth of the depravity to which a religious cult can lead its members and the depths to which I had been brainwashed. The first time I told him how very sorry I was, I realized he had never held it against me in the first place. He told me, too, that if he had not believed I was trying to do God's will, he would have taken the belt away from me and beaten me half to death with it. That statement of his explains the look I saw in his eyes that night. It was a look of hatred, for I was doing the same thing Mother had done to him so many times before. But he pleaded with me not to think about it ever again, that he knew my intentions were good, that he never thought about it himself. Still, I have begged his forgiveness many times since, for it has haunted me, knowing I did such a hideous deed.

We were not in control of our own lives during those years and for that reason we were not able to make wise decisions. If we began to do so and our path didn't take the direction Mother wanted it to take, she began to exert her powers over us again in order to control us.

Mother had said, "Jim needs to be punished. If I were strong, I would do it myself, but I can't," *but she did one last time.* That was a day neither I, Jim, nor Betty will ever forget. It was a Thursday afternoon. I had worked until lunchtime and then closed my practice for the remainder of the day.

Mother called me later in the afternoon requesting I go up to her house. We met outside in the yard, and when I saw her face I knew something was wrong. She was in a very agitated state of mind and informed me that God had shown her Jim and "that woman" had committed adultery that very day. "You claim he hasn't been seeing the woman. Well, I've known all along he's never stopped seeing her," Mother said in a rather hateful and accusatory tone of voice. "I want you to be there when I confront him about it."

She went up to Betty's home later in the afternoon. As soon as Jim entered his kitchen door, Mother jumped up from her chair, grabbed the Bible, and began to scream at him with the Bible in her hand that God had shown her he had been with "that woman" that very day and they had committed adultery. At first, Jim was stony and hard, denying the charges, but when Mother began to threaten him with the fire of hell he confessed. Mother could always use that tactic to get anything she wanted out of Jim, for he actually believed she held the key to his access to God and without her he was doomed, cut off, without any hope except to go straight to hell.

I was shocked and disappointed. Betty and I both had been hoping the relationship was over. I had even stood between him and Mother in his defense, telling Mother that she had to give him a chance. "Mother, you have to trust him," I would tell her. But during the past three years Mother had not ceased to accuse Jim of continuing to have contact with the lady. Jim told us later that he grew tired of being falsely accused and decided that if he was going to be accused of it, why not go ahead and commit the act? Poor judgment on his part, he has said.

Poor little Betty fell on her knees by a chair and began to weep. Mother strode over to Betty like some kind of military tyrant and slapped her face, saying in a cruel, bitter voice, "It's not a time to cry. It's a time to fight and pray." She then turned to Jim. "Come on; I've got to beat you," she said to him in a cold, matter-of-fact tone. They went into the bedroom, which was right next to the kitchen, where Betty and I remained on our knees praying. Mother made him take off his shirt and give her his belt, and she beat him with it.

The only sounds coming out of that room were the horrible thud of belt hitting his flesh, followed by muted grunts with an expulsion of breath as poor Jim endured the unmerciful onslaught of a vengeful religious zealot. It was such a sickening sound, almost like death was being played out in that room. Jim remained totally silent, not uttering a single cry of pain. It seemed the horror would never end. After she had beaten him for what seemed like forever, knowing the deep-seated anger and resentment she harbored in her heart for his adulterous affair and fearing she might beat him into unconsciousness, I went into the room, with absolute resolve to carry it out, and demanded, "Don't hit him again. You've beaten him enough." To this very day it's still almost impossible for me to recall that act with clarity. I am sure it was because of the horror of what was taking place and perhaps the deep subconscious fear in my own mind that she would beat me when she finished with Jim. I also realize how traumatic it was for me to hear my poor brother being flogged so unmercifully. Those other times in Charleston, while she was beating him in the distant bedroom, I was playing the piano in the living room and I heard very little. This time the sound of every ghastly blow seared itself on my very heart. She had pushed me to my limit of tolerance. Knowing myself as I do, if she had tried to strike Jim again, I would have taken the belt away from her and might have even attacked her with it myself. Jim has since told me that he will never ever forget the look on my face that day. "I'd never seen that look in your eyes before. It actually frightened me, for I knew you would attack her if she had hit me again," he said. She also recognized my resolve, for she stopped. It was a hellish experience for all three of us.

Betty told me later that when she saw Jim's back she almost

threw up. It looked like ground beef where the belt buckle had cut the flesh. The blood had run down to his trousers. Mother had beaten him with a vengeance that day, wanting to inflict as much pain and suffering as possible, and for that reason had turned the belt backwards allowing the buckle to do its terrible damage. There are scars on his back today from that beating, which he will carry with him to his grave. Mother hid behind the cloak of the Spirit in committing such terrible deeds, claiming God had put it upon her to punish Jim. When I beat him at the old car my desire was not really to hurt him, but to deliver him so he would be free from what I believed were the clutches of Satan. For Jim and me, in order to survive such atrocities we had to push the memories of such events deep down into our subconscious, else we would have hated her. Even after she did such terrible things to us, Jim and I would have forgotten them if Mother had not continued abusing us emotionally and attempting to control our lives. Events were soon to take place, however, that would bring about our final escape from it all.

12

It had been thirteen years since Uncle Swift was killed, and the first cracks appeared in the armor of trust and confidence I had in Mother. A culmination of events or turning points spread out over that thirteen-year period of time brought about the final collapse of the religious beliefs I had once so strongly followed and which were so much a part of me.

As I stated, the first cracks appeared in 1970 when Mother stood before the church proclaiming to the congregation that her brother and sister-in-law were the sacrifice for our sins. That proclamation was brought to us time and time again. No amount of reasoning would convince her to refute that claim, which was really almost like blasphemy, completely contrary to the Scriptures. I tried to tell her that, but she would not listen. Everyone is entitled to a few mistakes, but she continued to make other equally drastic mistakes and, in addition, refused to acknowledge them. Her bitter and cruel treatment of Jim after his adulterous affair was exposed was one of them. I wonder if she ever thought about all the times she had beaten him in Charleston, supposedly at God's instruction, in order to prevent his doing exactly what he did. In addition there was the day in the entrance hall of his home, on our niece's wedding day, when I heard Mother screaming at him. With her voice elevated to a shriek, her eyes cold and cruel, the curses of banishment rolled off her tongue like thunder: "You can't go to the wedding! You can't go to church anymore! You can't go to cookouts! You will be driven out from among your people like a vagabond on the face of the earth!"

Jim was kneeling before her, his hands held up so imploringly, crying so pitifully, begging her, "Please, Mother, please, let me go to the wedding."

She turned to me and in a voice as cold as ice and totally devoid of any compassion or love said to me with contempt, "He's not my child. He's your brother. What would you do?"

The sheer shock of her statement was like a tremendous blow to my senses. It made my blood freeze. I realized she laid no claim to him whatsoever, and probably not to me, either! But *my* reply came immediately, without any thought or hesitation. "I'd let him go," I answered. With that she turned and marched out of the house. That encounter there in his entrance hall made an impression deep in my soul. "He's not my child. He's your brother," would ring in my ears over and over again. I just couldn't believe what I had heard. Her religion truly had become her lord and master, and it was the all-pervading force in her life. Gone were the love and compassion she once had, and in their place was cruel vengeance that she wanted to be measured out to Jim in every way possible. The more, the better. That cold, unfeeling statement in some respects explained her resentment of us children we had sensed through the years. The question "Did she ever really love us?" became a heart-wrenching search in our lives. Many in the family had said if we had been her natural children she wouldn't have treated us the way she did.

The message we received from her statement was, "Do as I say and I will love you; break my rules and you can get lost." Once again, Jim and I had to pull ourselves together and continue down life's pathway. We couldn't wallow in self-pity or weakness, but as one says today, we had to "keep on keeping on," or, "when the going gets tough, the tough get going."

During the previous years I had begun, little by little, to see that many of the beliefs taught us simply were not true. One example concerned women wearing makeup. It was preached to us in church that make-up and Jezebel in the Bible were synonymous, as well as any other ornamentation used to enhance a person's appearance. Any woman wearing makeup was vain, proud, and sinful and certainly couldn't be a child of God. Through having an open heart and mind, I discovered that teaching was far from the truth. Many of the sweetest and dearest ladies I knew wore makeup, and it was no more to them than the clothes on their backs. The inside of a person is where the sin lies, not on the outside.

I questioned the practice of remaining so separate from the

world, too. I began to have a deep desire in my heart to share my life and my home with my patients. I would ponder over it: how could it be sin if I invited someone to my home just to show my appreciation to him for his patronage in helping me to achieve my dreams for a home? That couldn't possibly be wrong in the eyes of God. Always wishing to share my life with Mother, I expressed that belief to her. She issued me a stern warning: "You must be careful. You can't bring the world into your home. The world is your enemy. It will lead you astray." I realized then and there that Mother didn't share my views, nor my love for people. I didn't abandon my beliefs but kept them buried in my own heart, knowing I was going to eventually act upon them. It was just a matter of time.

Mother had led a very secretive life in Clarkton. She wouldn't even let Daddy go to town to buy an ice cream, always making the excuse that he might talk. The poor fellow was so glad to get away from her that he did talk a lot, but that was OK, too. I guess she was afraid she might be exposed. At home she ruled the roost, doing most all of the talking and everything else in addition. Poor Daddy was one of the most henpecked men on the face of the earth. At every single meal Mother said the same things to him without fail: "Now, Earl, don't spill crumbs; hold up close to the table and you won't spill crumbs so easily. Don't eat so fast; chew your food better. That's why you have so much indigestion." Then when he had finished eating she would say, "Earl, go brush your teeth and go lay down and take a nap, but be sure to put a towel on the floor under your head so the grease from your scalp won't soil the carpet."

Once I asked her why she said those things to him. I said, "There are three hundred and sixty-five days in the year and three meals a day. That's over a thousand times you repeat the same things. He's not going to change." But it made her angry. She didn't like anyone telling her anything.

I remember watching her in the rearview mirror as we rode to church, pinching Daddy behind his back so he would hold up his shoulders. She even did the same thing in the church pew. Once I heard her scolding him so cruelly for getting a spot of blood on his pillowcase where he had cut himself shaving. In her hard, impatient voice she said, "Why did you get blood on the pillowcase? It's just more work for these gnarled hands of mine to have to do."

I thought to myself, *Woman, it's not like he cut himself just so he would bleed on the pillow.*

In his old age he loved sweets and chocolate candy to death just like his own father before him. Mother blamed his eating sweets for his need to go to the bathroom at night. She didn't seemed concerned that he was the one getting up but was always saying it disturbed her rest. She was always so self-centered.

Bless his heart, Daddy was foxy. When Mother went to visit Grandmother, he would call Betty at work and ask her to go to town and get him some candy, which he hid in his toolbox in the outside storage building. The only problem with that was he went outside one day and ate a candy bar but didn't know there was a piece of chocolate still clinging to the corner of his mouth, which old hawk-eyed Mother immediately spied. "Where did you get that candy?" she asked.

"What candy? I haven't seen any candy," he replied.

"It's on your mouth. You can't hide it. You're keeping it in the tool house, aren't you?," she continued.

"Aw, shut up," Daddy would always say when he had been caught.

I think years later, when Daddy became ill, Mother had a lot of regrets, but then it was too late.

All her banking, grocery buying, and other business was carried out in Elizabethtown, where I suppose she thought no one knew her. She didn't want anyone to know a thing about her. She wouldn't even go to the grocery store in Clarkton to buy a carton of milk but sent Betty, Jim, or me.

After I was married, Mother didn't want to let me go free, but as she said, "I want to be entwined in your lives." She wanted to be included in everything we did. She wanted us to inform her of our plans for vacations and any other time we left the house. Jim somehow felt obligated to tell Mother when and where every time he went out. I didn't. She made the statement to Jim with obvious resentment that "if John wants to go somewhere, he doesn't tell anybody; he just goes."

I said, "That's just what I'm supposed to do. I don't have to tell her every move I make." Poor Jim lived next door to her, and he couldn't bring himself to do as I did. He was too much in her clutches.

Ann and I had wanted to have children for some time. She had one miscarriage that we are sure of, but finally, in June of 1979, Ann became pregnant with our first child. Mother learned Ann was pregnant while we were on vacation in Gatlinburg, Tennessee. I loved Mother dearly and didn't mind her accompanying us on this vacation, but there were times I wanted Ann and myself to go out together without Mother.

Right away she began to hound us about modesty during the pregnancy. She would call the house to discuss with Ann the making of clothes that disguised the fact that she was pregnant. One night Mother had poor Ann in tears about sewing those precious clothes! Then I stepped in, telling Ann, "Pay no attention to what she says to you. The clothes you have made look perfectly fine." What a comforting thought to Ann. She knew she had my total support in that matter.

Mother had even approached me about the subject, suggesting that I buy the groceries, letting Ann remain home in private. Mother said to me, "Do you believe the Scriptures?"

"Certainly I believe them," I answered.

"Then what are you going to do with the Scripture that says: 'Mary hid herself for six months'?" In exasperation I replied, "Mother, that was a different time and a different culture. That's ridiculous; do you want Ann to get in a box and hide?"

If Mother could have had her way, Ann would have lived with her bottom half surrounded with something like a box for nine months, then stepped out when the baby arrived and said, "My, I had a baby!"

Mother's next point of attack concerned Ann staying home with the baby. Ann and I had planned all along for her to do just that. We both felt it was very important for the children to stay in the home with the mother the first few years until they began school if at all possible. But no, Mother couldn't wait. She had to destroy all our joy in willingly being an example by Ann staying home. Mother got up in church one Sunday and said to Ann that God wanted her to quit her job and stay home, as if we weren't willing to comply without her open reprimand there in the church. Before discussing it with me, poor Ann wrote her letter of resignation and by doing so forfeited an entire month's wages as well as her insurance coverage.

That money would have been a great help too, for we were having a financial struggle at the time, for Mother was on my case all the time about living spiritual, about reading the Bible between patients and not working so much. She would say to me, "I fear you will be a good dentist and fail to be the servant of the Lord I brought you up for." I never reached my practice potential until I broke away and became free from the bondage of her religion.

Not only did Ann stay home with the children, but she became very efficient at running the household. She had to prepare all her Sunday meals on Saturday, for we were forbidden to cook on Sunday. You could make coffee but not cook, wash dishes by hand but not use the dishwasher. Our laws were similar to all the laws the Jews made for themselves after they were taken into captivity. Ann made most all the girls' clothes, and they were beautiful, too. She spent hours reading to them. Her efforts paid off too.

Then Mother jumped on us about a name for the baby. She wanted us to use the name Jody Ann if it was a girl. Jody Ann sounded too diminutive to me. Neither Ann nor I liked the name, so we chose our own, naming her Charlotte. Mother was offended by our refusal to use her name and rebuffed us several times when we met at church or other places in the family. I thought to myself, *If that's the way you want to be, you can help yourself, but I'm not being intimidated by your attitude.* Charlotte was born on March 19, 1980. From the very beginning she was a very loving child, one who liked to be cuddled, very outgoing, and not the least bit shy. She grew quickly and soon she was attempting to use her own little legs. I saw her take her very first steps. We were in the front yard. Charlotte had squatted down to pick a tiny flower in the grass. As I watched, she slowly stood up, her little legs trembling just a bit from the effort. Then, to my amazement, she very deliberately took a tentative step, then another. I was so excited but didn't do as I had seen other parents do, scream with jubilation, frightening the poor child into tears. I just watched with loving joy, knowing my precious child was beginning her long walk through life that very day.

Two years later, Ann became pregnant for the second time. We were both excited again. Mother made no attempt to interfere this time with clothes or names. On January 27, 1982, Emilie was born. She was quite different from Charlotte. Emilie was much livelier, didn't like to be cuddled, was very shy around strangers, was very independent from the very start, and had curly red hair. Charlotte was a blond with perfectly straight hair. I suppose Emilie got her curls from me, as my hair is curly, too. She had been in breech position, sitting on her legs instead of being upside down in the uterus, until two weeks before delivery, which made her feet turn completely inward. She could have never even walked if we had not taken her to an orthopedic specialist, who prescribed using a brace to keep her legs straight at night. Emilie adjusted to wearing the brace very readily. She learned how to stand up in the mornings and would be rocking back and forth on her brace when we came to her room. In six months her legs were perfectly straight.

I have spent many hours with my children, knowing from my own experience that time spent with them, showing them my love, instead of saying "I love you," then doing something that implied quite the opposite, would be more important than anything else I could ever give them. Many parents think erroneously that material things will make children happy, but it doesn't work that way. We have to touch them, play with them, talk to them, hold them, and comfort them when they need it, letting them know through our actions that they are important, that they matter, that they are not just some object there in the house. When the opportunity is gone, it can never, ever again be recaptured, and I absolutely meant that by the grace and help of God I would never, but never, treat my children as I had been treated. If it was at all possible, they would know without a doubt I loved them, and I believe they truly do know it. The Bible says: "Our children are our inheritance." How profound a statement and how true. Mine mean more to me than anything else on this earth.

My dear brother Jim lost both of his children. As I have said before, our religion forbade our seeking medical treatment. Jim's wife, Betty, had their first child at about seven months. Jim was so scared, literally terrified, when Betty went into labor, for he knew it was not time. His fear of retribution from Mother prevented his taking Betty to the doctor and to the hospital. The only help she had was a midwife. The baby was a little boy with a headful of thick, dark, curly hair. They named him Jim Alton, Jr. He only lived for a week. Their next child was still-born. After Jim's separation and eventual divorce from Betty, which had been brought on by his affair, he turned to drinking in an effort to drown the pain of his loss. Many times in his inebriated state he would go out in the country to the graves of his little children. He would fall down at their tiny little tombstones, and his tears watered the grass as he wept his poor heart out with the sorrow of losing them, longing to hold them again in his arms. He grieved for many years until finally time healed the wound. So you see, Jim and I both have truly been robbed of so many precious things in our lives.

The desire to have people visit in my home grew stronger, so I began to invite people to come see the house, not in a boastful way, but just to share with them what they had helped me to accomplish. When Mother heard about it, she stood one Sunday morning in church while preaching and, with the Bible in her hand, said to me before everyone present, "Don't have any more strangers in your home. It troubles this old heart of mine." As she said those words, she touched her chest with her hand to emphasize her heart.

Once again she demonstrated to me that she had no confidence in my spiritual discernment, nor in my ability to make sound judgments. What I believed was not good enough, since it was not the same as her beliefs. It was as if I were not capable of going to God myself but should be seeking her guidance. The real issue was her control, which she recognized was slipping out of her grasp. But my resolve was firmly established. I was not about to stop inviting friends and patients to visit my home, even though her saying that to me in church hurt me so deeply. I knew from that day forward that my life and Mother's would go in opposite directions. If she was opposed to that which I knew was of God and which brought me such happiness, then there was no way I could share my life with her. For that reason and that alone, I was very sad. But I was absolutely certain of one fact: sharing my home with others, to show them my appreciation for their helping me achieve this dream, was not sin. That was turning point number one.

On June 25, 1981, a Thursday morning, my sister Josie lost her only son, Windric, in a car accident. After a night of fun at the beach with his friends, being so tired, he fell asleep at the wheel on the way home, drifting across the center line into the path of an oncoming cement truck. Even though the driver of the cement truck over-

212

turned his vehicle in a desperate effort to avoid the collision, it didn't help. The two vehicles slammed together on the shoulder of the road and Windric was killed instantly.

Mother's attitude during this difficult time of grief was appalling. I canceled my appointments for the afternoon and went to stay with Josie to offer her comfort and moral support. Mother came by on Friday for only a few minutes, bringing along her bitterness and inflicting more hurt and pain on my dear sister. Like a military officer Mother strode into the room where Josie lay on the floor weeping and, without any other greeting or the least hint of compassion for my dear grieving sister, said to her, "I have not shed one single tear for Windric. My concerns are for the church and how we have failed God, and I don't want Carl to allow the world to come into his home." Then she turned and marched out without an embrace or any other display of sympathy for the grief my sister was experiencing. I was shocked! What kind of Christian love was that? We were all left rather numb emotionally.

On Saturday morning, Mother called. I answered the phone. "What are you doing there? My soul is in an awful fix." she said.

"What kind of fix do you think we're in?" I retorted resentfully.

"You don't need to be there consoling the flesh," she continued. Then came the real shocker! "Where are they going to bury him?" she asked me.

"In the churchyard, where do you think?," I answered, shocked that she would even ask such a question. There was a long pregnant pause. Then it struck me like a bolt of lightning. She was thinking of making them bury Windric somewhere else. You see, legalistic religion has no room for compassion and little room for love as well. I was dumbfounded. I thought, *What on earth is wrong with her?* But I also knew there was no need to try reasoning with her, not after she had maintained that my uncle's and aunt's death were the sacrifices for our sins.

I learned later that Mother had called a meeting of some of the elders and if they had agreed with her, she was going to inform Josie and Carl that they would have to bury Windric in their yard if she did not have confirmation in *her* heart that Windric's soul had gone to heaven. I couldn't imagine anything crueler; making people bury their child in their yard instead of the church cemetery! That

213

was turning point number two.

Two years later, in 1983, the third and final turning point unfolded. It involved Mother's treatment of me after the purchase of a *used* 1977 Lincoln Towne Coupe.

I was driving a Chrysler at the time, which I had bought new. It had 84,000 miles on the odometer. I'll never forget the day in 1977 when I went by Mother's home to show her my new car. It was a beautiful canary yellow Chrysler New Yorker. I was proud of it and so excited. Sons often want to share their lives with their mothers, and I was no different. I had brought Mother a lovely arrangement of cut flowers that day, too, because I wanted her to know that I had not excluded her from my heart. I loved giving Mother flowers. I always wrote a note to accompany them trying to tell her how much I loved her and how much I appreciated what she had done for me. I always told her, "When you look at the flowers, remember their beauty represents the love in my heart for you. The flowers are an expression of my love." When she went outside and saw what I had done, she was provoked at my buying the new car and was quite hateful to me. When I gave her the flowers she said to me in a hateful, irritated voice, "I would rather you not give me flowers. I don't even want them. They remind me of a funeral arrangement." It would not have hurt nearly as bad if she had slapped me in the face. At least, as soon as she slapped me the pain would be gone, but the pain of that statement has lasted for years. That was the last time I ever gave her flowers. She killed something inside me by her cruel statement. Needless to say, she did not share my enthusiasm for the new car.

I feared she would not be happy about this used Lincoln either because in 1973 I special-ordered a new Lincoln Towne Coupe. A deposit of $100 was required to order the car. When I told Mother about the car, she rebuked me very harshly, saying God was not pleased with my purchasing such a luxury car, that I should be more humble and only buy a Buick or Oldsmobile. She was very adamant in letting me know that if I followed through with the purchase of the new car, she would never set foot in it. That would exclude her from being able to ride to church with me, and I could not bear the thought of that. I still carried a tremendous sense of debt to Mother and Daddy for what they had done for me. In addition, at that point in my life I didn't have the emotional fortitude to rebel against her. When the car arrived, even though I wanted it so much, I wrote a letter to the Lincoln dealership, giving my apology for not accepting the car, and forfeited the $100 as payment for their trouble. That decision would torment me years later. Once again Mother had managed to destroy my happiness.

A patient of mine, Hubert Lewis, owned the 1977 Lincoln Towne Coupe and had traded it in on the purchase of a new car at the Lincoln Mercury dealership in Fayetteville, North Carolina. I had never stopped wanting one of those cars ever since I had refused to accept the one I had ordered, and knowing Hubert had owned this particular car, I realized it would be in very good condition. I called the dealership to let them know I was interested in the car, and Ann and I went to Fayetteville and purchased it. Mother was on vacation in Gatlinburg, Tennessee, at the time. I wrote her a letter telling her what I had done, because I still wanted that mother's approval. She answered my letter with one of her own. In hers she told me how smitten she was for what I had done, how aggrieved she was that I had gone against the Spirit. The contents of that letter let me know there was a real problem. I just didn't know how extreme it would become. The first time I drove the car to church, Mother came and stood by the car after the service, pleading with me to return to the Spirit. Later that week when she was talking to me again about the car, she told me she had to repent for touching the car on the church grounds. Touching the car! Just like it was a demon or something worse! How absurd! The following Sunday she called me before I left home to ask me not to drive the Lincoln to church but to drive Ann's old blue 1970 Dodge Dart. "It is more humble," Mother said, "more like God's people should drive." That really provoked me, because I knew my heart was not arrogant about the car. After all, it was only a *used car* anyway, not a brand-new Mercedes or Jaguar. That one day I obliged her, but I remember telling Ann, "I'll leave the car home this time, but I have no intention of not driving that car. I didn't buy it to sit at home." Ann supported me in my decision.

Mother had also enlisted the help of another church member in her attempt to break my will. The next Sunday I had driven the Lincoln to church again, just as I had promised myself. As we were

215

on our knees having prayer at the altar as we always did, Aunt Reba came to me and said these words: "John, would you be willing to move your car off the church grounds so the Spirit could bless people?" I was aghast. I couldn't believe my ears. *Move my car? What on earth does she mean, move the car so God will bless people. I prayed, Dear God, I will stay here on this floor until my knees sprout roots and grow into the carpet before I move that car. It has absolutely nothing to do with anyone else in this church except me, and it is no sin to my soul.* The completely ludicrous had happened. There was no longer any doubt whatsoever in my mind that these things were the desperate acts of someone trying to manipulate me to recover her strict control over me. I knew Mother had been talking with my aunt about the car. I knew it, else my aunt wouldn't have said such a thing to me.

Outside on the lawn after the service, Mother was again talking to me about the car, and this time her words were even more pathetic. As she picked at the lapel of my shirt, just as she had done on my graduation day in Atlanta, she said to me, "Son, if you will come to the things in my heart, God will work something out about the car." The events in the church had hurt me deeply and I was crying when she first began to speak, but when those words left her lips every tear in my eyes dried right up. I thought to myself, *Sister, if you think for one minute that I believe God Almighty jerks people up and down on a string like a yo-yo, you're sadly mistaken. You need not think you can intimidate me by using such tactics. If the car was wrong for me one time, it was always wrong.* I realized in that moment many of the practices and beliefs we had been told were from God were actually her own ideas she had imposed upon us in the guise of the Holy Spirit. I, personally, had had doubts through the years about many things. But if we ever expressed doubts about any of these beliefs we were told not to question the Spirit. Now I was convinced that the very things I had questioned in the years past were indeed her ideas and not those of God. Now I could see plainly it was another one of her means of control. All I could do was walk away with a sad heart, but with more determination than ever to follow the dictates of my own heart.

Being the fighter she is, Mother then began a silent battle against me in church in an effort to break my will. She would stand in the church and make derogatory statements about me without calling my name. I was aware of what she was doing, but very few of the other members of the congregation understood the struggle that was going on at the time. I made the decision then in my own heart that I would not do battle with Mother in the church but would remain silent, and if she thought she could destroy me, then let her try. But still it hurt me to know she had turned against me simply because I stood for the truth, not some fabrication to suit my need for control. Those Sundays in church were the beginnings of a trail of tears for me. Why was I being treated so coldly just because I had purchased a *used* car? Sunday after Sunday the tears streamed down my cheeks as I played the organ while everyone walked out of church. More than anything else in the world I wanted Mother to just stop by the organ, put her arms around me, and say, "John, I love you." But it never happened. Some of the other church members realized what was happening. Those dear souls would stop at the organ occasionally to speak to me, letting me know they loved me and understood the struggle I was having. Mother's opposition to me was so great I sensed she wanted to put me aside from my position as church organist in an effort to break my will. I was correct too. I learned months later she had talked with some of the elders, and if they had not opposed her, she was planning to purchase a piano for my brother-in-law to play, and she was going to tell me that I could no longer play the organ because I had rebelled against the Spirit.

During this time in the life of the church, Mother had destroyed so much of the congregation's confidence in themselves. Sunday after Sunday she would stand saying basically the same words. We grew to dread going to church.

Because of all the trauma Jim, Betty, and I had undergone at Mother's hands over his extramarital affair, I had acquired a great compassion for the congregation, for now I knew what it was like to be ostracized from someone you loved dearly. Many times while everyone was on their knees at the altar praying, when Mother had cast a pall of gloom over them, I would get up from my knees, go to the organ, and begin to play very softy and with great tenderness. My playing always moved the people to find peace for their sad, tormented, and pained hearts. The music was a door for them through which they could go to find freedom for a brief moment of time. I suppose my music was like the music David played for Saul, which soothed him, only in our case it comforted their wounded hearts. Many times my dear sister Eva, as well as others, would break down into tears, putting herself completely aside, then be so moved by the Holy Spirit that she would rejoice, shouting praises to God all around the altar. At those times she looked very much like an angel dancing around on her tiptoes like a ballet dancer as she waved her hands back and forth above her head in praise to God and her feet carried her joyfully around the altar. Anyone who has never experienced the ecstasy of the Spirit doesn't know what a wonderful experience it really is. For that brief space of time we are carried beyond the current world into a realm of peace and perfect assurance that cannot be explained. Nothing else on earth matters more than that peace from God. It transcends everything else. It is difficult to put into words. I believe it is truly a touch of what it will be like in heaven. I have experienced it many times, and there is nothing in this world to compare with it. It was so wonderful each time that happened, for the Spirit gave us courage and strength to continue on just like the strength Elijah received from the bread and fish the angel prepared for him when he fled from the face of that wicked Jezebel. Were it not for those times when God Almighty lifted us up above the pain and destruction Mother was inflicting upon us, there would have been no way we could have survived it.

Some would ask, "How did anyone come into the family? Was anyone from the outside accepted into your religion?" Yes, they were, and it was considered a wonderful thing if anyone did bring someone into the church; as he had saved a soul from the world. We had been taught that we were the saved of the world, that everyone else was lost. If one of the family met and married someone from the outside, then they were expected to attend our church, because it was absolutely forbidden for our members to attend church anywhere else. We believed all other churches were "synagogues of Satan." And if any outsiders' families objected to their attending our church instead of his or her own, then it was expected of them to ostracize their own relatives.

To let you understand how deeply I had been brainwashed into these strange beliefs, my own dear wife had to undergo such alienation from her parents. She endured a painful period of separation from her parents for two and one-half years. When I finally realized it was a bunch of hogwash, we went back to see Ann's folks, who, incidentally held no grudges at all. But it was still a while before I accepted them completely, simply because of the beliefs that had been so deeply ingrained into my very soul.

The newcomers in the family had to get saved again, as it were, for Mother didn't respect their salvation as real. In her eyes they were lost. She had to experience the conversion process herself. There were times when our own family members were saved at the altar, but if Mother didn't witness it herself, we had to continue to pray until she said they were forgiven. I said once, "If it took as long to get people saved as it did in our church, then it would have taken several months for the five thousand to be saved that the Scripture speaks about in Paul's writings. When they got saved, they had to be baptized again, too." So you see, it happened so that the monster of control had finally taken over so that no one had freedom to come and worship God. It had to be done Mother's way or it was not accepted at all.

She wanted me to rebuke my sisters for shaving their legs. She tried the same tactic she used to brainwash me into beating my dear brother, but never again. It didn't work this time! I told Mother I didn't want to rebuke them. There was nothing wrong with what they had done; it was only part of a woman's hygiene. Mother didn't like my attitude toward that subject, not one bit. Another Sunday morning while we on our knees at the altar, Aunt Reba came to Ann to inform her that she should make bloomers for Charlotte to wear to church for modesty. Ann asked me that day at home if I wanted her to make bloomers for Charlotte. I replied, "Bloomers! What are you talking about?" Then Ann related what had been said to her that morning in church. I answered her emphatically, "*Modesty!* No, I *don't* want you to make bloomers for Charlotte. If anybody wants to get their jollies looking at her diapered behind, then let them help themselves!" She was wearing four diapers to church anyway, because we had been rebuked for taking the children to the bathroom during the service to change their diapers.

Mother made one last-ditch effort to intimidate me back into her control again. Early one morning Betty, Jim's wife, called me to say Mother was on her way to my house. She had told Betty, "I have to go to my dear boy."

When I opened the door to the side hall, Mother was praying as she entered the house, saying, "Dear boy, God has sent me to plead with you to return to the Spirit."

Only out of respect for her, not because I believed in her anymore, I knelt down at the little love seat by the door. When Mother really began to pray in earnest in a loud voice, beating me on the back with her open hands as was her usual practice, her words brought a revelation of such magnitude that it changed my life forever. My confidence in her was destroyed by one single sentence she said to me. As she prayed, she said, "This is the same stubborn spirit I've labored against many times in the past." It was like a bolt of lightning that illuminated my mind so clearly. Now I knew what had happened in the past. I prayed, *Dear God, that's exactly what happened to all my aunts and uncles who would oppose Mother in something they didn't believe in themselves. Mother would frighten them into believing they would be lost forever, or that God had shown her their names had been blotted out of the Lamb's Book of Life.* That proclamation was enough to bring them back into submission to her will. But not me. I knew God and trusted Him, and I knew my own heart before God, and she didn't frighten me at all. At that instant I questioned everything Mother had ever done supposedly in God's name, and from that day forward I weighed all her actions against what Jesus Christ would have done. When Mother saw she was not able to penetrate my armor, she walked out the door as if to say she had to wipe her hands clean of me. I walked back into the living room, and my poor wife, Ann, was standing on the landing of the living room stairs weeping. I said to her, "Don't cry. I'm certainly not. She didn't frighten me." That very day I began to ever so cautiously open the door of the second chapter of my life. It was only a matter of time before I left the little church I had grown up in, the only church I had ever known for the forty-two years of my life.

As Sunday after Sunday passed and there was no change in Mother's attitude toward me, I began to consider making the most monumental decision of my entire life, breaking away from the church. Attending church had become a dread for me. There was no worship of God in our services anymore. True worship had been replaced with fault-finding, criticism, judgment, and Mother's desperate attempts to crush my spirit so that I would once again bend to her will. All these strange practices were in total conflict with true Christianity. Sometimes the service was like a battleground, like the time Mother told her brother before the entire congregation that he had turned his children over to Satan. He was so angered by her accusation that he wanted to leave church right that minute, but his wife wouldn't leave with him. They never came back. Remember, we had been taught that all other churches were synagogues of Satan, but I already knew that wasn't true. To those who believed it, however, leaving our church was sin enough, but attending another church was certain to send them to hell. But I was not afraid. I had been shown the truth years ago when I entered that beautiful cathedral in Charleston and felt the presence of God so profoundly. God was where we sought Him; we carried Him in our hearts. Our church wasn't the only church on earth where He could be found. I knew with absolute certainty God would go with me; it was just the journey that would be so painful.

I had become friends with Charles Hester, the pastor of Clarkton First Baptist Church. He was the one person I trusted outside of my church in the "world." The very first time I saw him as we passed on the street, I knew there was something different about him. I sensed a wholesomeness about him that I didn't feel from many other people I had met before. I had been taught to be wary of all the people outside our family. They were the "world," and the "world" was dangerous to us, to be feared and to be kept at a very great distance lest it pollute us. So when he came to my office for a dental checkup and I learned he was a pastor, that explained why I felt as I did about him; he was truly a man of God. I remember the very first time I went by his office at the church to talk to him about the struggle I was having. I laid out before him a brief but revealing account of my past life, sharing with him the strange things being practiced and the fact that I was considering breaking away from the church. I let him know what I faced if that became my final decision: I would be ostracized by many of the church members.

Mother wouldn't even call my name when she prayed. I would be treated as if I didn't exist, and once I left, I could *never, never* go back. It was truly a turbulent time in my life. During my conversation I asked Charles if he had ever heard anything like the events I was describing to him. His answer was an emphatic *"No!"*

I continued to seek God's guidance for my life. Charles told me he would also pray that I might do the right thing. My first tentative step outside the realm of safety I had grown up in was to stop attending the Wednesday-night prayer meeting services at my church. On those nights I would slip very quietly in the front door of Clarkton First Baptist Church after service had begun, take a seat in the very back pew, and sit there praying in my heart, pondering my decision, knowing all those present there would pray for me as well. I never participated actively in the service, however, and wanted to keep as much distance between myself and the others as possible. I didn't want anyone to influence me in my decision. I had already had enough of that throughout my life. God was my source of strength, and for once in my life I was relying entirely on Him to help me make the right decision.

I talked with Charles on two other occasions. The last discussion with him helped me to make the final decision. I ended the conversation with the statement, "Well, that's it. I'm not going to church out there anymore."

As I stood up to leave, he said to me, "John, I admire you. What you're about to do takes a great deal of courage. I admire you for that." I told Charles, "Me? I have a lot of courage?" It seemed strange to hear someone say something good about me, to give me a positive attribute. For so long Mother had relentlessly criticized everything about me, and virtually everything I did. It seemed to me that nothing I had done before was ever quite good enough. I was never able to measure up to her expectations. The continual criticism had virtually destroyed all my sense of self-worth. I had been completely demoralized by Mother's continual criticism. Looking back now, I understand what Charles meant about my having a lot of courage. I had no idea whatsoever what I was facing, and had I known, I'm not so sure I could have survived it. For that very reason, I'm sure, God doesn't allow us to see into the future. Charles gave me the assurance that he would be praying for me, and I walked out of his office to begin a new life, one that, initially would cause me great sorrow and pain but in the end would bring me freedom, happiness, and a whole new family of friends.

13

I attended church services at Clarkton First Baptist Church for the first time on Sunday, August 15, 1983, accompanied by my wife, Ann, and my two daughters, Charlotte, age three, and Emilie, age one and one half. About one month had passed since the first time I entered the church for the first time. Ann's parents were down that weekend visiting with us and went with us to church that first Sunday, too. It was a most interesting day. I'm sure God had a hand in my being there that Sunday. Mary Little, the church organist, had cut her leg on an old plow on Saturday while she and her husband, Ben, were chasing stray cows and was not able to play. Spying me among the congregation, Charles came to the pew where I was sitting and asked if I would be willing to play the organ for them. I was delighted! I had already been wishing I could play, since I saw no one was sitting at the organ. That simple request by Charles was a godsend for me. Being able to play the organ for the church gave me a place there and the assurance that I was good for at least one small thing. Having left the only church I had ever known and knowing in my own heart how Mother felt about me for doing that, I had a sense of not belonging anywhere, almost of not knowing who I really was. That heart-wrenching struggle with my identity would become so much more intense and painful in the years to come.

But ah, me, was I nervous that first day at the organ! My heart was pounding, my fingers were cold and sweaty, and my legs were shaking so hard, if my feet had not been resting on the foot pedals, my legs would have been jumping up and down like a jackrabbit. I knew all the hymns by heart but was in a different setting, with new people, and in addition, somehow in the back of my mind I expected to be criticized here as well. It took years and years for my confidence to be restored sufficiently so that I wasn't a nervous wreck every time I sat down at the organ or the piano. Many times as I sat on the organ or piano bench, I would tell God if it weren't that I wanted so much to play for Him and the church, I would not put myself through such emotional torture.

Ah! That very first sermon I heard in Clarkton First Baptist Church proved to me that we had all been told lies through the years. Charles was not a "wolf in sheep's clothing" soothing the itching ears of the unrighteous. Instead he pointed us to the cross and to Jesus Christ and him crucified on that cross for our sins. That made a profound impression on me, for it had not been so in our church. We had been told to follow this dear soul or that dear soul or to pattern our lives after this one or that one, but here I was being told to follow Christ, the one who had died for our sins. It was truly wonderful.

When I left the church of my childhood, there was a mass exodus of most all the remaining members, which left about only twenty-five or so still attending services there, and in a short while that number would dwindle to just a few. Before it fell apart, there were over a hundred there faithfully every Sunday, for we were not excused from Sunday church for any reason. Our church services no longer resembled any kind of worship of God; rather, they had become a time and place for Mother to wield her destructive power over everyone present there. We had become like a flock of sheep milling around trying to decide what to do. The joy of attending church had been crushed, and in its place was a terrible dread. Only because we were so devoted to God and the church did we continue to go.

I was to have been Mother's successor in the church. That's what Mother had groomed me for. Many times through the years Mother had said to me, "My sole purpose in bringing you up was to fulfill the prophecy of your dear mama to be a preacher of righteousness." But for me, as the years went by and Mother continued to harass me about what I should or shouldn't do in the service of the church, what my mama had said so many years ago no longer mattered to me. I knew my mama would not be guilty of such destructive actions as Mother was perpetrating against me and everyone else in the church. I wanted nothing to do with the way she was treating those who loved her so dearly and who trusted her with their soul's salvation. Spiritual survival became the para-

225

mount issue for me, as well as trying to bolster the hearts of the congregation, all of whom I loved very dearly. They had all begun to look to me for courage and deliverance, for they had a great deal of respect for me, and they trusted me, too, because I had been honest with them in acknowledging Mother's mistakes instead of making excuses for her and defending her in that which was wrong.

At one time, too, Mother had planned to put the deed to the church property in my name. As I have said before, it belonged to her and Daddy. She had discussed it with me, but as I became rebellious, as she called it, she let me know she feared to leave it to me, which was fine, for I didn't want the responsibility of owning the church anyway. She thought I would lead the church astray! What a laugh! I could have helped them if she had been out of the picture.

I remember the first time I was at her house after I left the church. She was standing in the back doorway with that dreadful expression on her face and said to me, "I never dreamed you would do such an awful thing. It's the worst thing you have ever done." I just looked straight at her, making no reply to her statement. I knew there was no need to try to explain anything to her. She would never understand.

Within a year or two she sold her home in Clarkton and moved to Whiteville. The home there she remodeled to suit her taste. Everything had to be just so for her to be satisfied. I never thought about it during those years while she and Daddy lived in Clarkton, but Jim and I were obviously not the hindrance to their happiness she had made us believe as we grew up, but rather it was she, herself. She became a slave to the house and yard, and as Mother continued to spend more and more money to improve the looks of the grounds poor Daddy grew to hate the place, for it was his job to keep the yard free of pinecones and tree branches. He longed so much to go on one more cruise on a naval ship. As he had spent thirty years in the navy, his seniority would have allowed him to sail on any of the ships to anyplace in the world. Having tried without success to convince Mother to go on a cruise with him, he begged me to please persuade Mother to take a cruise to Panama. He'd say, "John, you talk to Mother and get her to let us take a cruise to Panama. You can convince her." Dear soul, he thought because Mother and I were close through the past years I could influence her, but I always told him she wouldn't listen to me, either. All she wanted to do was stay home and tend to that precious place. Mother did buy a motor home, and they made a trip to California with Uncle Sam and Hugh and a trip to Newport, Rhode Island, but many of the monies that could have been spent for traveling she used to beautify her yard.

Mother was a very powerful personality and influenced everyone around her. Even though Jim no longer attended church, either, he was still very loyal to Mother, still believed in her, and still visited with her. Right away Mother began using her persuasive powers over Jim in an effort to drive a wedge between the two of us. I realized what she was trying to do, and knew I must be strong both for myself and Jim, knowing I could not lean on him for support. For a while he even grew to distrust me, which hurt me very much, but as I thought on it deeply, I understood why he was unsure of me, and that knowledge made the pain much easier to bear. The control Mother had over Jim's mind was still very powerful, for he could not yet see exactly what she had done to us, nor could he yet believe she was not truly a servant of God who had acted according to His will.

I remember the afternoon Jim dropped by my office to deliver the Christmas presents Mother had given him for my children. There was nothing for me, not even a card. It hurt me and at the same time made me angry. I said to Jim, "You know, this is a slap in my face. Here she's sending presents for my children without even acknowledging me. I was her child before they were her grandchildren. I don't know if I'll give the presents to the girls or not, but if I don't, I will have enough guts to return them and tell Mother in person why I didn't give them to the children. I won't do like she did with the presents Charles sent to us; she put them in the attic, or like the vegetables Uncle Aaron gave her; she threw them away." As I was speaking, I immediately recognized that my straightforwardness made Jim uncomfortable, so I said, "Jim, at least I'm being honest, not like Mother has been so many times, saying one thing and doing another, or not telling us her reason for her actions." I was aware of his loyalty and his feelings for Mother and knew I must be very open, very honest, with him and hope that someday he could see the truth.

Later I pondered over what to do with the presents. I didn't want the children to know any of the bad things about Mother, only to see her as their grandmother, a good person. But there was one single consideration that helped me make my decision; I pictured myself at Mother's door with those gifts, telling her I couldn't accept them, that I had to return them to her. As I put myself in her place, being at the receiving end of my actions, I knew there was no way on earth I could hurt her like that. I knew she loved the girls in her way, and for me to refuse the gifts would be the same as saying, "I don't want your love," which is exactly what she had done so many times to her people. In addition, spurning someone's love is very destructive to that person. I knew, because I experienced it myself. And when you've experienced the pain of being rejected, you cannot put another person through that pain; at least I couldn't. With that very decision, *I began to take the pain of my past experiences and flip it around to make something loving and positive from it, instead of becoming an evil, vindictive person, out to seek revenge for the wrongs done to me. I remembered the hurt and the pain and didn't want to hurt anyone else if there was any way possible to avoid it.*

In the summer of 1984 during our vacation at Sunset Beach I developed viral hepatitis. I realized there was something wrong with me when Emilie, still being a little tot, wanted to sit in my lap all the time, and just the pressure of her leaning against my abdomen made me feel nauseated. Then my urine turned a sickening yellowish-orange. The color was so intense I felt almost like I was emptying out my insides. I knew I had either hepatitis or a severe kidney infection, but there was no fever or any pain, both of which accompany kidney infections. Not wanting to spoil everyone's vacation, I toughed it out until the following Monday morning. After doing a blood analysis in his office, Dr. Phillips came in the examination room where I was lying down from sheer weakness and informed me that I should cancel all my appointments for the next month. Shock! What a shock! Then he told me why! "You have type-C viral hepatitis, which lands many people in the hospital, but since you are in such good health, you can remain at home unless the nausea causes vomiting and subsequent dehydration."

Hepatitis isn't something you would wish on your worst enemy. It makes you feel so yucky. When Ann was preparing meals, the odor of food cooking was almost more than I could bear. One night she was baking some cookies and when the odor wafted upstairs where I was watching TV, I thought I would croak. And it makes you so weak. All I could do was lie around like an old limp dishrag. The least bit of exertion made me pant for breath. But true to what the doctor said, I was out of work an entire month. My first day back at the office I could only last for one half-hour. Gradually, hour by hour, day by day, I regained my strength, and after about six weeks I had returned to my normal self. I was very fortunate.

In September of 1984, we had our first exchange student, Christian Waldow, 17, from Hamburg, West Germany. I had for years wanted to have an exchange student, to have the joy of sharing my home and my life, of giving someone the opportunity to do something he otherwise wouldn't be able to accomplish alone. He lived with us the nine months, attended high school, and graduated with his class. His parents came over for the graduation ceremony. It was quite an exciting event for us to have friends from Germany staying with us. It was a very rewarding and enriching experience, too. I had tried to remain detached from Christian, to accept him as a friend, not as my child, knowing that his leaving us would be very difficult, but it just didn't work that way. He accompanied us wherever we went, and he was just like our own son. Our trip to Disney World in Florida was a memorable occasion for all of us. Our children loved him, too, but he didn't take to children too well. Oh, but we were all pretty devastated when the day arrived for him to return to Germany. We were crying; his mother, being a tenderhearted soul like us, was crying, too. Christian looked at me in disbelief, as if to say, "I can't believe I meant that much to you." But time heals everything, and we soon got over the loss and continued on with our lives. We've kept in touch with Christian through the years and hope to visit him and his family in Germany.

Later that fall the depression first appeared. I had noticed that when I awoke in the mornings, even after eight hours of sleep, I was still tired. Day after day when I awoke, I had a sense of dread hanging over me like a heavy cloud, as if I didn't have the courage to face the day, and wished time and again I could go back to sleep and wake up and that feeling would be gone and I would be better. Being a strong and disciplined person came in good stead for me during those difficult times, for there were days I literally had to make myself get out of bed, put one step ahead of another, and go on with my life. I was determined to survive at all costs. There were too many people depending upon me. I couldn't give up the fight. I learned that by making myself remain occupied, I always felt much better and the cloud lifted. Sitting around pitying ourselves, dwelling on the negative and bad things in our lives, accomplishes nothing. Self-pity is like cancer; it slowly and silently kills. A little is OK, but a lot destroys the person and I wasn't about to let that be my undoing.

One day at the office, since my schedule had fallen apart, I told my staff I was tired of feeling tired all the time and went down the street to the doctor's office for a consultation. I shared with her how I had lost interest in all the things that used to bring me pleasure and how I had pulled out of the church of my childhood and the subsequent alienation from the only mother I had ever known and the feeling of dreading to face the day and being tired all the time even though I had adequate sleep at night. And as I related the events of the past to her, I began to choke up from the emotional pain. Then Dr. Conte said to me, "John, you have classic textbook depression. Let's try medication and see if that will help." I didn't want medication, but I was willing to try. I only took one half of a twenty-five-milligram tablet. The side effects were worse than the depression, so no more pills. Both Dr. Conte and I agreed that medication wasn't the answer.

Then, after I talked with my pastor, Charles Hester, on several occasions about the abuses and pain of the past, he told me my depression was too complex for him to be able to help me work through it, that I needed a professional, and referred me to the Fayetteville Family Life Center, a Christian counseling center associated with the Southern Baptist Convention. My very first appointment there I'll never forget. It was on Tuesday evening at 7:00. I had no difficulty whatsoever talking with my counselor, Dr. Mackey. The horrible events of the past began to float up out of my subconscious like pieces of dead trash surfacing on a pool of dark water that has been stirred with a stick. I was never at a loss for words but simply poured out my life before him, describing the pain and humiliation Jim and I had endured over our past life.

230

At this point let me address the issue of depression to those who read these words and are now or have been the victims of abuse or to those who are suffering from depression or have experienced that pain. My purpose in doing so is to offer those readers moral support and understanding and, for those who haven't sought help, to inspire and encourage them to do so.

First of all, those who have never had depression have no idea what it's like. There is no way anyone can know unless that person has experienced it. I can speak from my own experience, and so can many of you as well. Many of you have had friends say to you, "Oh, just snap out of it!" or, "Don't be depressed," or, "Just don't think about the past," or, "You've got to put that stuff behind you and get on with your life." Those people mean well, but they have never had depression. Everyone at one time or another has had periods when they felt "down in the dumps," but real depression is another thing entirely. First of all, we can't just snap out of it, no more than you can take the part of our brain where all your memories are stored and throw it into the garbage. Our past experiences and the memories associated with them are the sum total of who we are as a person. Those experiences and how we have reacted to them have molded us into who we are. If they were like a wart or even like our external ear or, to seem more desperate, like part of our internal organs, we could have them amputated or cut off and that would solve our problem. But that is not the case. We must learn to recognize the source of our depression and to relate to the experiences of the past and the pain associated with it in such a way that we do not harm ourselves or others and so that we can function as normally as possible in our current situation. The same is true for those who have a chemical imbalance in their blood that causes their depression.

For that reason professional help is so important for us. And the professionals are not "shrinks" in the sense that was used about twenty years ago. There are many good men and women out there who can help. I would recommend all Christians and those who have a strong belief in God seek help from Christian psychologists or psychiatrists. They will understand you better. For myself, I wouldn't have been able to relate to anyone who made disparaging remarks to me about God or Jesus Christ. Even though virtually all the abuse my brother and I endured was done in the name of God, I knew God had nothing to do with it, and I didn't need anyone to tell me otherwise.

Don't any of you be afraid to seek help for your depression. That is *not* a sign of weakness, but rather a sign of great strength. Recognizing you have a problem and then seeking help to solve it shows that you are in control of your life instead of letting life control you.

Just think of it for a moment. Take alcoholics or drug addicts, for example. Until they recognize they have a problem and move out of denial, they will never seek help, let alone get better. It takes strength to admit something like that, because you are admitting you, yourself, have done something to put you in that state of mind and health. But for us, we have done nothing to cause our problem; rather, it may be because of what someone else has done to us. We shouldn't feel guilty or less of a person because of it, or blame ourselves.

Most important of all, we must not blame those in our current life for our depression and the painful emotions associated with it. We must not vent the anger we feel for the person who abused and humiliated us toward an innocent person. That's how relationships are destroyed, placing blame on an innocent person. For that reason alone professional help is so very important. The professional can help us understand our emotions, where they come from, why we feel the way we do, and how to diffuse these negative emotions without hurting others as we have been hurt. Always for me, the paramount issue was that my children wouldn't be harmed by the struggle I was having during my therapy counseling. During the years when they were small, I always kept it hidden from them and never let them know the pain I was suffering. Don't let others convince you that it is weak to seek help or that you can get through it yourself, because the road is so much easier when we seek the help of professionals. They can help us to understand ourselves and all the painful emotions involved with the past so that we can learn to deal with that pain in a rational manner. For myself I knew right away that all the emotions I was feeling related to my past were so complicated I would never be able to unravel it all by myself. And more than anything else I wanted to be free. Everyone deserves to be free. Many times I share bits of my life with my patients at the office. They always tell me that it inspires them to hear my story and how I came through it all and to know the person that I have become because of it. With depression also comes the feeling of worthlessness, that we aren't important, that we don't matter. But that is not true. Everyone has worth and value. I can say that now, but for years I also had a great struggle with low self-esteem, so I understand the problems associated with worthlessness. We deserve more than we have been given. We all deserve to be free.

The overwhelming issue that first day of therapy at Fayetteville Family Life Center was the extreme religious zeal Mother had exercised in order to achieve her control over my life and the pain she had inflicted in doing so. During that first hour session I gave a brief synopsis of my life, relating all the most profound events that came to mind. I'll never forget what Dr. Mackey said to me at the end of that first session. "Well, John, you have three things in your favor: your tremendous will to survive, or you wouldn't be here; your love of music, which has given you an avenue of escape, and your sense of humor." When he spoke about the sense of humor, I laughed and said to him, "Well, I can see how those people who can't make a joke out of life's extremes so they can laugh and release the tension of it all commit suicide, crack up, or have a nervous breakdown, which lands them in Dix Hill," (a common term in the South for the Dorothea Dix Insane Asylum in Raleigh, North Carolina). I've always been able to laugh and make facetious jokes out of the ridiculous things in life we had to endure. Had I not been able to do that, I'd probably be insane myself. Again it seemed strange to hear someone give me positive attributes. My whole life had been one of never-ending criticism. My self-esteem was at an all-time low. I perceived myself as a failure in every aspect of my life: as a dentist, as a husband, as a father, as a member of the church. There was nothing positive in my life that I could see. It would take years of counseling, prayers, support from family and friends, determination, and the grace of God to restore confidence in myself so that I wasn't tormented by that sense of worthlessness.

As I worked through the depression, which Dr. Mackey confirmed was brought on entirely by Mother's control and abuse of me in the past, I began to learn a great deal about myself, specifically why I did certain things the way I did and why other events had affected me so profoundly. First of all, I learned that Mother's relentless criticism of me had destroyed my self-esteem and sense of self-worth. I remember her telling me time and again, "I want you to grow up and be like a man and quit letting people take advantage of you." Mother was always very shrewd in her business dealings, looking out for herself and having no apparent consideration for the other party. But in my sessions with Dr. Mackey I learned that subconsciously I had perceived that kind of behavior as wrong and, without even realizing it, had taken the exact opposite approach. Instead of taking advantage of people, I always looked out for the other person, because I didn't want to treat others as I had been treated. Afterward I always felt better for having treated them kindly instead of having been cold, calculating, and without compassion. I had been victimized and knew the pain of it; therefore, I didn't want to do the same to others.

Very soon, in the first few months of my therapy, I began to share with Dr. Mackey my deep and at times overwhelming sense of pain from having lost my dear, precious mama. I remember during one of those sessions, as I was recounting the days gone by and how hard Mama's life had been, I broke down and sobbed uncontrollably for several minutes. I had been telling him about the times my poor mama would go spend all day in the woods picking berries to preserve for us little children to have in the cold winter months, and as I did so I could actually see her as she walked away from the house with her metal pail in her hand. At that moment I would have given anything in the world to have been able to set her free from that life of toil. I wished so much I could have been there for her when she needed someone so desperately. At those times during my therapy my own children always came to my mind, too, and I would tell Dr. Mackey that more than anything else, I didn't want my children to ever have to know that deep soul-wrenching pain, the pain of losing the dearest person on earth. Neither did I ever want them to know the pain of rejection and betrayal, the pain of feeling like you were never quite good enough, that nothing in your life quite met the expectations of the one person in your life who mattered the most, your parent—in my case specifically, my mother. I wanted to make a pathway for them to be able to follow without having to scale all the obstacles I had overcome. During that same session I also learned why, all through my life every time we sang in church the hymn, "The Last Mile of the Way" my heart would break in two. The explanation: The song told the story of my mama's life. There was a very profound love and pity deep in my heart for my mama, and the words of the song that brought me so much pain were these: "Here the dearest of ties we must sever, tears of sorrow are seen every day, but no sickness or sighing forever, when I've gone the last mile of the way." As I heard those words, it felt like they would tear my very heart out of my chest. It seemed as if in my mind I could somehow see my mama far away and more then anything on earth I wanted to be with her. I wept many a time in church as that dear old hymn was being sung. At the same time in church if Mother appeared meek and humble, then I was drawn to her with the tenderest love, the same love I felt in that old hymn, as if she were my real mama, but when Mother appeared cold and hard, as she did many times, the tender feeling vanished, and she then seemed like a stranger. It was like the umbilical cord that bound the two of us together was cut when she sat in her pew with that stony expression on her face. The times when she was tender and humble, I always went to her, put my arms around her, and with tenderest love tried to tell her how much she meant to me and how much I appreciated all she and Daddy had done for me. I realize now, too, that I had not been allowed to grieve over the loss of my mama and for that reason experiencing the grief as an adult was much more intense, more difficult to bear, and sometimes quite overwhelming.

Not too far along in my therapy, Dr. Mackey pointed out to me that the ground root of my depression stemmed from losing my mama and the subsequent sense of helplessness in my life. Instead of allowing me to develop emotionally by providing me with loving support, Mother had stepped into my life and Jim's as this powerful, autocratic woman who dictated almost every aspect of our lives. Her unnatural and at times cruel domination of our lives actually suppressed us so severely that our emotional development was stunted. I had come to that conclusion on my own even before the depression ever came. Just think of it: We weren't permitted to get out of bed in the mornings until Mother had called us to get up. We never even went in the fridge for something to eat. Remember how she had bragged about the fact that she could hide our Santa Claus in the spare room closet and we never opened any of those doors! She had, by her extremely harsh treatment of us, made us afraid of doing anything with what she had. It was untouchable. And if I didn't like what was expected of me, showing any kind of resentment or dislike was forbidden; therefore I had to learn to suppress all my negative emotions. I remember when she beat me, if I cried, she'd tell me if I didn't stop crying, she would beat me again. And anger, when it is suppressed and held inside and comes full circle back into a person, brings depression also. Mother had humiliated us many times, beating us for nothing, making us wear those stupid-looking clothes, which brought undue ridicule from our peers at school, but yet we could not express any kind of dislike or resentment about them, else she would have beaten us even more severely than she did.

For several years after I broke away from the church, I had an almost obsessive desire to obtain Mother's acceptance of me. The question ever present in my mind was, *Does she really love me? Did she ever really love me?* Being free from the entanglement of Mother's religious control, I could look back and realize clearly that I had never been able to satisfy her, but the little child in me still wanted more than anything else to have her love and to know that she approved of me. I remember when the country song "Love Can Build a Bridge" was on the air, the lyrics in that song would always break my heart. My mind went to Mother every time, and I wanted so much to have that love from a mother. The longing for Mother's love was so overwhelming that for years I could not go by her house without looking up at her window, hoping against hope that I would see her face in the window and she would smile at me and then I would know she loved me again.

It was during another one of my sessions with Dr. Mackey that he posed the question to me, "John, can you pass by her house without looking at it?"

I thought for a second. "No," I answered. As soon as those words came out of my mouth, I broke down again, sobbing uncontrollably for several minutes. Scenes branded on my heart, words seared into my soul, had left me with an empty void in my heart like a great cave, so empty, so lonely, reaching out, aching, pleading, for that mother's love.

In addition to the heart-wrenching question of whether Mother ever loved me, I also struggled with the question, Why would anyone love me? In order to protect myself from being hurt, I would keep a wall between me and those I wanted so much to have as friends. I was safe behind that wall. If I didn't let them like me, then it wasn't so painful to be rejected. If I never let them into my heart, then I wouldn't be hurt. But being alone was not an option I now wanted to pursue, and because I was willing to be hurt in order to love and be loved I gradually allowed the wall to be torn down so that others could get close to me. These events take years to occur, however. It is a long and gradual process of reaching out very tentatively, trying to forget the painful experiences of the past, and little by little allowing others to get close to us. It is so very difficult and requires a great deal of courage, too. It would have been so much easier to have remained behind that wall, but I wanted so much to have friends, because as a child I had been robbed of them. That, too, is part of the healing process. I began to develop many friendships. Friends are so wonderful!

When I would come home from work and the children came running to me with their arms stretched out calling, "Da-a-dy, Da-a-dy," it was almost as if I had to look around to see whom they were talking to, for it couldn't possibly be me. Who would love me? Who would want to love me? And sometimes my younger daughter, Emilie, would say to me, "Smile, Daddy! Smile!" I thought to myself each time my dear child said those words, *Dear God, if only she could look down into my heart, she would see the sadness and know why it's so difficult to smile.* But I would always smile for her and hope she didn't recognize that the smile was superficial and didn't come from deep inside. And I would pray to God, *Please, dear God, don't let this pain and melancholy of mine do any harm to my precious children. Please let them escape this pain and sorrow I have known.* And thank God they have escaped!

I also battled with the issue of identity: who was I and where did I fit in? That would seem to the reader like a joke! Here I was, a man in his midforties, with a graduate degree, a beautiful home, a supportive and caring wife and two dear daughters, a very successful dental practice and a wonderful staff to go along with it, and I was searching for the answer to the question, Who am I? But we have to return to the past to find why I seek to know the answer to that very profound question. Remember when Mother beat me for being humpbacked as a camel, when she beat me black-and-blue for the C in math even though I was doing my very best, when she beat me repeatedly for the "dirty tricks" even though I was telling her the truth, that I had not done anything, that I truly didn't even know what she was talking about. Remember when she put me in the backseat of the car and wouldn't talk to me or let Jim talk to me, either, on the way home from Atlanta, how she demoralized me on graduation day at dental school by telling me she hated my education, thus nullifying all my efforts at doing my best, how she continued to treat me with no respect as an adult even after I was married and had children; then you have your answer. I was a nobody. I was nothing if I didn't measure up to her expectations. I could be replaced with someone else, just like she was planning to replace me at the organ in church because I had become "rebellious to her spirit." It was as if everywhere I turned, she was right there to block me, not to give me credit or recognition for anything positive in my life. Her power over me was so great that at that point in my life I was not able to recognize or accept who I really was. I was still in her web, and unless I fitted her mold of what I should be, then it was as if I didn't exist. Like she had said to me on more than one occasion, "Son, there has been once or twice when you have stood in the little church and the words that proceeded out of your mouth were the most beautiful words I have ever heard. They were the true words of life." Those statements never did anything for me. I always thought, *Well, what about all the other hundreds of times I stood up? What did they count for?* Apparently nothing. They meant more to me than the times when the Spirit of God did truly come to me and gave me interpretations of the Scriptures that were so beautiful, so inspiring, and so uplifting to the congregation. Those other times I simply was standing, giving nothing but the love of Christ to a bleeding, wounded flock of sheep that so desperately needed encouragement and strength. You see, after graduation from dental school Mother systematically, little by little, destroyed my identity just like someone takes an ax and very slowly, bit by bit, chops down a pine tree. I even had a recurring dream in which I would appear in Jim's and my bedroom in Charleston standing at the window looking outside into the backyard. As I looked out I saw two tall pine trees that looked as if someone had taken a spoon and scooped wood out of the trees or as if a beaver had gnawed them down. In each dream the trees appeared to have been chopped down smaller and smaller until in the last dream they were only a few feet tall. Remember when she said to me, "Son, I want you to grow up and become a man and stop being weak, letting others take advantage of you." Again the real me, the one who had perceived that always taking advantage of others was not the way to be a true Christian, was not good enough. Jesus taught, "Love your enemies. Do good to those who despitefully treat you." I had taken those words to heart. When she questioned the purchases I made in furnishing my home, telling me that "I know you. You want only the best, and if you find something better, if you can't sell what you have, you will give it away and buy more." My judgment was questioned and my ability to make wise decisions also. As long as I remained within the confines of the religious web she had wrapped around me, I wasn't able to comprehend what was happening to me.

I placed such a low value on myself that for years it was very difficult for me to receive praise of any kind. I felt as if anyone could do what I was doing. I was always putting myself down. Even the sense of the value of my education had been ripped from my subconscious, for I have said many a time, "Oh, anybody could have gone through dental school." But that's not true. The year I entered dental school, during orientation my class was given a pep talk and the instructor informed us that we 85 students had been selected from 300 applicants, that we were the best of those 300. So you see, one had to be good to even get *into* dental school.

But when people did give me recognition, for me it was as if they had to be talking about someone else. It just couldn't possibly be me they were talking about. Why would I deserve any praise? I should be forgotten or unnoticed. The only reason I should be pointed out would be to receive a reprimand for not doing better. When we have been so deeply demoralized, especially by the most important person in our lives, it takes a very long time to eradicate those powerful negative thoughts we hold so deep in our minds and, yes, in our very hearts. As Dr. Mackey has told me many times, "what we know with our rational minds is completely different from what we feel in our hearts, with our emotions." And sometimes it is very difficult to distinguish between the two. Another very important reason for seeking professional help!

Like the other issues in my life I had done battle with, I fought to conquer this one, too. Another country song that struck a chord deep in my heart and affected me very profoundly and at the time seemed to confirm my status as a nobody was "I'm Going to Be Somebody Someday." Many a time as I was out in the yard pulling up weeds in the flowers, and the words of that song went over in my mind, the tears fell from my eyes watering the ground, and I prayed, *Dear God, please help me to come out of this great pain; please help me to be somebody someday, too.* For years an overwhelming cloud of sadness enveloped my very being each time I heard that song.

I grew to hate myself and the image I saw in the mirror. I wanted to be someone different, as if the person I saw was the bad person whom Mother didn't like and didn't approve of. I grew a beard and for a while that helped. When I then looked into the mirror I saw someone else, as if I had become another person. When I went out in public, particularly to the shopping mall, seeing other men who seemed so confident and self-assured, I would think to myself that I would give everything I possessed to be like them, instead of having to carry around the overwhelming sense of worthlessness that pervaded my being. You can't imagine how painful it is to carry that feeling of inferiority with you every day of your life, yet at the same time wanting more than anything else to be like everyone else. In my own eyes, I seemed so pathetic.

While my children were in grade school and wanted to attend the school basketball games, I took them because I had long ago determined that I would not deprive my children of happy experiences as I had been deprived. But the memories of the emotional abuse perpetrated against me by my peers was so great, it took all my determination to enter the gymnasium that very first time. Taking a deep breath, I walked slowly into the gym. But deep in my subconscious I expected every second to hear the hisses and the boos and the derogatory names I was called on the first day of school when we all gathered in the gym to learn who our home-room teacher for the year was. The memories were so real it was difficult for me to accept that those who had done those terrible things to me were no longer there. So in order to survive, we learn to adopt survival tactics. Only those who have been abused and demoralized by others can understand what I'm talking about, but even the clothes I wore were a survival or escape mechanism for me. Each time when I would go to the gym, I wore my Western outfit, cowboy boots, jeans and the cowboy hat. Somehow I felt safe in those clothes, as if the people who had tormented me would not recognize me. Those were clothes, too, that Mother wouldn't have approved of, either. Each time I went to the gym with the girls the memories faded further and further into the background of my mind, until now they are so faint and far away they no longer present a problem to me, which is so wonderful.

Very, very slowly, as the years went by, I began to feel positive about myself. Finally I was able to accept compliments for playing the organ well in church without always apologizing for my mistakes. After attending Clarkton First Baptist Church for over twelve years, I was finally able to relax and not fear that someone would criticize me for any mistakes I might make. I know that seems incredible to you, the reader, but when a person has been criticized relentlessly for forty-two years, it takes many years to break free from the mind-set that criticism comes automatically, no matter how hard you try. For all those years I had kept up my guard, but now I realize I am truly accepted for who and what I am, mistakes and all. It is a wonderful feeling. Because of my own experiences I can understand and empathize with others who struggle with low self-esteem. It is not an easy thing to overcome. The pep talks our friends give in an attempt to cheer us don't really do any good. At least, they never made any difference to me. Their message was like words meant for someone else. Until the wounds heal and we can feel good about ourselves from the inside, nothing makes any difference. It takes time, patience, and, above all, an absolute determination to never give up trying, no matter how long or how painful the journey is. I know from my very own experience. I've been there.

And as time went by I grew to accept myself for who I was

even without Mother's approval. I realized I was OK even if Mother didn't approve of me. I did graduate from dental school, and that was no small accomplishment, either. I had not done badly in building and furnishing my home or in running my practice. I was not as wealthy as some of my relatives, but I had not had to declare bankruptcy, either. I had been able to make friends, too, many absolutely wonderful friends who have stuck by me through thick and thin. So, very, very slowly, I began to give myself credit for the accomplishments I had achieved in my life, and in so doing I slowly unraveled the web wound so tightly around my life. It was a very long, tortuous, and painful journey reaching that point in my life, however, for deep inside the heart of a man is the longing for his mother's love, approval, and acceptance of him.

I had to learn to accept the fact that I might never receive her approval or her love. But that wouldn't prevent me from receiving the love and acceptance of other friends and associates. Their love, little by little, began to fill the place in my heart that ached so much and felt so empty. There was always a place left for Mother, however. I would always leave the door of my heart open for her. I never gave up hope that maybe one day she would come back to me. I could never close the door of my heart to her no matter what she had done to me and Jim. To close the door was too final. That would mean there was never another chance. I could never give up hope, never. I loved her too much.

As I continued to work and sort through the painful memories of the past, I began more and more to recognize what triggered the pain of the past, and if it was possible, I would avoid those situations. And as I continued to experience particular episodes of grief over the injustices committed against me in the past, I began to more quickly recognize and understand what brought on the grief, and for that reason I am able to cope with it much more easily, not being devastated by the grief as I used to be at times. I can assure you it has been a very painful process. Many times during the deepest pits of my despair over not having been accepted by Mother I believe I can understand in just a very small way how Christ must have felt before he was crucified. Without seeming sacrilegious, there are parallels between my life and his. Think of it: He had performed all those miracles, had healed the blind man, the lame, the woman with the issue of blood, had raised the dead, had taught the people all the wonderful lessons of life, had fed the thousands with only a few small fish and a few loaves of bread, and yet they had him crucified, simply because they were jealous of him and hated him for exposing them before the people. Nothing he had done was ever good enough. He was never accepted. Don't you know it must have been very painful for him to bear, knowing that in the face of all he had done they still hated him? In comparison I am absolutely nothing, but I do believe I understand just a tiny bit of how His grief must have felt. Nothing I had ever done had been good enough, either. I could never live up to Mother's expectations of me. And for that reason it was always so very comforting to know that Christ truly did understand my grief. He had been there himself, only his pain was a thousand times greater than mine. I knew he knew and understood me. Always. There was never any doubt in my mind whatsoever. He was always there for me. His strength helped me bear my own grief. He was the one absolutely immovable point in my life upon which I could surely depend. For me that meant everything, and that is, without doubt, why I am here today. At the time we are going through these terrible events, we don't realize God is there with us. It's only after we look back that we understand without Him we couldn't have ever survived.

A sadness fills my heart when I think of those who put their trust in other religions. What can an inanimate statue do for us? What can a dead person do for us? Nothing, absolutely nothing. But Christ can do for us. Christ lives. He will never forsake us. Our dearest and closest friends and even our families will abandon us at some point. If not of their own choosing, they will abandon us in death as my mama did, but Christ will never ever abandon us, not even in death, because he has triumphed over death as well. That is a very comforting thought.

As time passed by, the periods of deep despair came further and further apart. And little by little that heart-wrenching ache to have Mother's love and approval gradually faded away and life wasn't so painful anymore.

However, other seemingly harmless events in my daily life brought flashbacks from the past. For example, there were times at home when Ann would speak to the girls in an impatient tone of voice and just hearing her speak to them in that manner would bring back memories of Mother's harsh, impatient voice. As I heard that voice, I would stop in midstride, stand there frozen in my tracks. My throat would tighten, my heart would even begin to pound in my chest; I would hold my breath, listening for the kitchen drawer to be jerked open to get the toaster cord out. Any of you who read this and have suffered abuse as a child can identify with that same experience. Rage would begin to well up in me like a volcano, unbelievably violent rage that made my whole body tremble. My first gut reaction would be to race downstairs, seize Ann, and throw her as far away from my children as possible. But I knew the rage was against my own adopted mother, who had controlled, abused, and humiliated me time and time again when I, too, was so vulnerable and helpless. But thanks to God for giving me strength and my having sought professional counseling to understand the source of the rage, as I never harmed Ann.

There were four separate instances when I was not able to contain the rage within me and in venting it I did cause some physical damage, but not to those I love and hold dear to me. I want to share these events with you, the reader, so you can know and understand how I let go of the consuming rage without lashing out at the ones who had triggered it. The first event occurred in 1986 while Robert Hadac, our second exchange student from Germany, was living with us. One afternoon Ann said something to me in the bedroom and the tone of her voice and the way she said it caused the rage to erupt like a volcano. At the moment I wanted her to accept the blame for having caused it to happen, but she was still belligerent. Before I stormed out of the house I said to her, "You know where this is coming from. Why do you say things like this to me? You know the anger is against Mother. It's not fair to you to have to go through this." But at the moment Ann still maintained her hoity-toity attitude, which further infuriated me. By then I was trembling inside and I feared the rage in me. I remembered the feelings I had when Pat Buck choked the little canary, how I wanted so much to karate-chop him right in the neck. I knew if I ever lost control over that beast inside me, something dreadful might happen. So I said to Ann, "I'm getting out of here before I hurt someone." With that I hurried out of the bedroom, slamming the door with all the strength I could muster. Robert told me later it scared him and the girls about to death. They all three decided to go sit down very quietly and wait until things were back to normal. I went outside and walked for about an hour. Then I was OK.

Another time Ann was talking to me while I prepared myself a plate of food for supper. I had an engagement and was trying to make the best use of my time. It frustrated Ann that I didn't stop still and listen to her. She said, "I wish you wouldn't do that." The very instant those words came to my ears, it was if a switch were turned on inside me. Here I was doing something to help her, being independent so I could make my appointment on time, and she was telling me "I wish you wouldn't do that."

I replied, "Do what?"

"Continue doing what you're doing while I'm talking to you."

I was being second-guessed again. "I can do this and hear what you are saying to me at the same time," I retorted.

"No you can't," was her terse reply.

Those words were the breaking point for me. I held a strong oven-proof plastic plate in my hand, which I had been going to use for my dinner plate. "I am sick and tired of this," I said and with that I took the plate and with every ounce of strength I could gather struck it against the corner of the counter-top, breaking it into a dozen or more pieces.

That time Ann did immediately recognize what she had done and said, "I'm sorry. I'm so sorry." And I'm sure she meant it, too, but the fire had come to the top of the volcano and had to be released. Again, as before, I fled outside and got in the car, and as I was driving away from the house I saw Ann running out the door toward me. In that short space of time it seemed to me she represented a beast, and I had to flee from it before it caught me. I knew the feeling of terror that gripped me was because Ann, in that instant, represented Mother to me, because of the actions she had taken. But at the moment I was not able to take the time to sort it out. I just had to flee. Poor Ann was afraid I would leave and never come back. I drove and drove and even thought of going to Lumberton to spend the night, but I didn't want to leave my family. After a while the trembling ceased and I was able to return to the house. Ann and I talked about the event together and came to a better understanding. Each time Ann understood what had triggered the anger and tried to be more careful what she said or did.

The third event was similar to the others in that it was also triggered by something Ann had said to me. I don't remember what was said, and I suppose the reason for that is what happened after it was said. Whatever Ann said made me so angry that I fled out of the house, saying as I left the kitchen, "I'm getting out of here before I knock your head off." When I went out the side door, I slammed the door as hard as I possibly could. The door bounced back open, and the dead-bolt latch sprang out from the first impact against the doorjamb. In my fury I didn't notice the bolt was protruding, and I slammed the door again, equally as violently as the first time, for slamming the door helped me expel some of the rage inside that seemed it would explode me if I didn't release it. The very split second the bolt struck the doorjamb, I heard the different sound it made. I turned around and I saw what I had done. Needless to say, I felt like a complete fool. Here I had allowed my rage to get the better of me and had damaged my beautiful custom-made door. I closed the door gently, went outside, and walked for hours until my body slowly stopped shaking and I could return to the house and my dear family. I've never had the door repaired but left it for a reminder to me of what anger can do.

The fourth event was also a little comical. That time I grew angry at Ann for nagging at me on and on about something concerning Charlotte. When I reached the breaking point, I turned and yelled at Ann, "I can't take it anymore! I feel like I'll go insane!" I raised my hands with balled-up fists over my head, then brought them down as hard as I possibly could against my thighs, letting out a primal shriek at the same time. The sad thing was that my fists hit my testicles a glancing blow and the pain made me right sick. "Oh, Lord, I've hit myself," I managed to blurt out.

"Are you all right?" Ann asked with urgency.

"Yes, I'll survive," I responded. Then I staggered out of the kitchen. Two days later a blueberry-colored bruise appeared on each thigh where my fists had slammed into them with such force. And I don't bruise easily, either. The rage during that episode brought tears, for not only was I angry, but I was also hurt that Charlotte was being treated in a like manner to that I had received as a child.

So you can see how I was able to release the rage without hurting others. I've always known if I ever completely lost control and hurt someone I would never be able to forgive myself. We must put those we love first and pray for strength to handle the situation in such a way that no one gets hurt. During the years while I was dealing with the anger against Mother through therapy, I told Dr. Mackey I knew I must stay away from Mother, because if I would be in conversation with her and she would purse her lips into that thin, straight line and tilt her head the way she did when she thought she knew everything about everything, I would want to slap her face so hard her ears would ring. I was actually afraid of the anger inside me. What if I would lose control? What might I do? I did not really know. There was no telling. I wasn't going to even take a chance. I did not put myself in the place where I might not be able to handle the situation. I knew if I lost control and did something terrible, even as bad as slapping her, it would be extremely difficult for me to forgive myself, even for that, and if I would do worse, then I could never live with myself. So I simply remained away from Mother until I had resolved most of the anger toward her.

During my life I had acquired great experience in self-control. The years I spent in the church setting of my childhood practicing such intense self-control gave me an additional edge. We weren't allowed to cry when we were beaten but had to learn to stifle the tears, for Mother would always say, "if you don't stop crying, I will beat you again." We couldn't laugh and have fun like other children, except when it was OK with Mother, but had to learn to stifle our mirth, too. We had been rebuked for even shrugging our shoulders. Showing any kind of anger or resentment against any of the requirements expected of us would have brought untold consequences. Also, as a child in grade school I was afraid to go to the rest room for fear my peers might humiliate me, so I learned to go the entire day without going to the bathroom. Such control, Dr. Mackey had said, was almost incomprehensible. Think of my willingness to go through dental school without my glasses, another type of control. My willingness to even fast on Sunday in order to not break the

Sabbath. So you see, I was already schooled in the art of self-control.

I can well understand how men and women who have been demoralized, abused, and humiliated again and again can, without having sought help, and who have not had the strength of God to help them understand themselves, go into a fit of rage and without intending to do so commit murder. Then those reading the event in the news cannot understand how someone could do such a terrible thing. And many times the event that triggers the violent outburst seems to the causal observer to be so trivial. You've heard it said many times, "But he just did so and so." But it's like the old saying we have heard all our lives: "It's the straw that broke the camel's back." They don't see the entire picture. It's the years and years of control, of criticism, of humiliation, of never being given credit for having done your best, that builds up resentment inside the person, causing the rage. Then when the child grows up and an event triggers the memory of the abuses of the past, causing that immense anger to burst forth, you have a mature individual with unbelievable strength who can inflict a lot of damage. Men especially are so powerful when that rage fills their very being. It's the "fight or flight" mechanism of the body that takes over. Adrenaline pours into the body, dilating the eyes for better vision, flaring the nostrils to allow more oxygen into the lungs, increasing the pulse dramatically to carry more blood to the muscles that will be used to either fight or take flight. Uncontrolled anger is a very destructive emotion. Even the Bible addresses the issue for us: "Don't let the sun go down on your wrath. Be angry and sin not." Anger by itself is not sin. It's what we do with that anger that becomes sin. We can knock a hole in the wall or split the door as I did or do something to vent our rage, as long as the object we damage belongs to us. So we must let go of the anger and not sin by hurting someone or, even worse, killing someone. And it can be done. I am living proof of that.

These events I have described happened over a period of years, each one being separated from the other by at least a year or more. Each time Ann and I survived one of the outbursts of mine, it strengthened the relationship between us. As I have already explained, I didn't love Ann when I married her but did so in faith that she was indeed the one meant for me, and I took my wedding vows very much to heart. I always told her that it was not her problem, it was my problem, and I had to learn to deal with it. Of course she could help by being understanding, which she did better and better as the years passed. Talking things out together helps, even though it may be painful and difficult to do. Communication in a marriage relation is of paramount importance. If you want it to work, you must invest time, patience, tolerance, understanding, and consideration for the needs and feelings of the other partner. It's best also if we do not put ourselves first, to the exclusion of our partner, or we won't do too well. The more we care, the better we will succeed.

So you can see why I have so much empathy and understanding for all those disenfranchised persons, be they children, adults, or the elderly, but especially children, for they are the most vulnerable and the most trusting. I have been there myself. I know firsthand what it's like. I've experienced it myself. I don't need anyone to tell me. And I can assure you that those who have not experienced it have no idea what it's like. They may say to you, "I know how you feel," or "I know what you are going through," but they simply don't know and can never know unless they have been there themselves.

When our children were small, Ann and I both believed in corporal punishment: we spanked the girls for disobedience but only spanked them, not flogged them as was done to me. But every single time I ever spanked them, a voice always said to me: *What kind of woman was Mother, who flogged us little children like she did, and sometimes for absolutely nothing.* Almost every time I spanked the girls I would cry, too, and tell them to please not do things that we had to punish them for. My children were so dear to me. I remember the time I spanked Emilie with the thin, flexible ruler we used, and as I was giving her a bath I noticed where it had left a bruise on her little behind. That broke my heart. I cried and told her how sorry I was, that I didn't know it had done that and I was going to throw the old thing away, which is exactly what I did. And you know, I never had to spank either one of them again.

I remember at the very beginning of one session with Dr. Mackey, almost before I began to talk, I broke down into tears and asked him, "When will this pain ever go away?"

"John, that may be the price you'll have to pay so that your children won't ever have to know that pain," he said.

"Well, in that case, it's worth it," I answered. And it truly has been worth it for me and for them, for my children have been able to lead a very normal life. That ever-pervading fear has been absent in their lives. Report card day isn't a nightmare for them with their little hearts pounding in their chests with fear and sickening dread; rather, Ann and I have always let them know their best was good enough, not the impossible. They have friends visit them, they visit their friends, they go to camp in the summer, they're able to play sports, to have things like other kids, and don't have to wear freaky clothes like I did, and the list would go on and on. And for those things I am so very grateful.

As I began to reach out to others in the community for support in my times of despair, I made many new friends. Margaret Harrington was one of them. She was the first person to ever baby-sit our children. On her first visit to our house, having been so moved by the way we treated her, she asked me if she might have a word of prayer with us before she left. Of course we said yes, and the dear soul thanked God for us and for the kind way we had accepted her into our hearts and into our home. Then when she got home, she called and was so afraid she had offended us, but I reassured her that she indeed had not, that we were humbled by her prayer. We only treated her like one of the family. Since I broke away from the legalistic religion in which I had grown up, I've always tried to treat others like I wanted to be treated myself.

Helen Brown was another dear friend to me. There are too many to mention here. It gave me strength to have so many friends who I was certain would never forsake me in a time of need.

Mrs. Laura Singletary became one of my very dearest friends during my period of searching for my identity and experiencing the grief of having lost, first of all, my own mama and then discovering I had lost my childhood and many other periods in my life as well. During that heart-wrenching period of time Mrs. Singletary filled the place of a mother in my heart and truly became a grandmother to my children as well. She lived directly across the street from the church we attended and she was one of the persons I had invited to see my home before I left the church of my childhood. She was such a dear lady, so motherly, so kind and good, never judgmental or critical but always loving and supportive. When Charlotte was a little thing, she couldn't pronounce the word *Singletary,* so she would say, "I want to go to Terry's house." She loved Mrs. Singletary. Many times Mrs. Laura would baby-sit the children. She loved for them to come. She said to me once, "Dr. Hall, these are the children I never had. They bring me a lot of sunshine." I won't ever forget her telling me how amused she was the day Charlotte patted her on her breast and said, "Tummy?" Mrs. Laura thought that was so cute of Charlotte. Children have the gift of innocence that lifts the soul and sets one free. How can one abuse an innocent child? It never ceases to amaze me, what adults do to children.

I tried to take Mrs. Laura a plate of food by her house every day, for I knew being alone, she was not as likely to cook for herself properly. Occasionally, when I stopped by to bring her plate of dinner, she would be asleep on the sofa. Not wanting to disturb her rest, I would leave the plate in the chair on the screened-in-porch, knowing she would find it when she awoke. When she passed away, it broke my heart. It was so difficult to say good-bye to her. She had been a true friend to me and had loved me unconditionally; to that kind of love I was not accustomed. As I stood by the grave weeping, a family member said to me, "She's in a better place." I looked straight at her and replied, "Certainly I know she is better off. These tears are for me. It's so hard to say good-bye to her. She was such a dear friend." I was happy that she was in a better place where she didn't have to lie on a nursing home bed in a coma every day, but I knew I was left here to battle life without her loving support and encouraging words.

Later in the fall of '83 after we had been attending church in Clarkton, I felt compelled to write Mother a letter and open my heart to her and let her know exactly how I felt about the things she had done and what I believed about some of the beliefs we practiced. The letter I wrote was originally meant to be only between the two of us, but when I began to hear comments from other relatives that Mother was saying John had written her an awful letter, I knew that in my own defense I must let others read the letter and draw their own conclusion. I had made a copy of the letter before I ever sent it to Mother, for I realized that without a copy of the original it would be my word against hers. All I had done in the letter was I had been perfectly honest with Mother, stating my position on some of the beliefs we practiced, letting her know exactly how I believed, and trying to show her how she and only she had destroyed my confidence in her by claiming the deaths of her brother and sister-in-law were the sacrifice for our sins and by having double standards for different members of the church. It was actually a son's plea to his mother to consider what she had done in the past and how wrong some of her deeds had been. But it only made her angry. It was years and years before she quit letting the contents of that letter eat at her.

To show you just what a grudge she held against me for the letter, I called her one Saturday morning to ask if I could visit her and bring the girls. I wanted them to see her, to keep in touch, and for her to visit us, too. I said to her, "Mother, we have differences of opinion, but at least we can be friends. I'd love to bring the children to see you."

But her answer was a cold, hard, terse, "Well, I'll have to think about it." And so she did, for I didn't hear a peep out of her for three years. By that time the desire to visit her was gone. She did finally come by in August of 1987 to bring the children their Christmas presents from the previous year. When she left Emilie asked, "Who was that nice old woman?" We had to explain to her that it was her grandmother. She gave a surprised, "Oh, really!" I thought, *How sad, the children don't even know their own grandmother, and all because of her own stubbornness.*

During those three intervening years I was having that great struggle with self-identity, I knew it would never be wise to allow my children to enter Mother's world of mind control. I knew her well enough to know she would get down on the floor and pray with them and as she did, in her prayers she would paint me to be an evil person. I also knew if my children would look at me in that light, that would completely destroy me. For my dear little girls, whom I loved so dearly, to turn against me would kill me. I knew that for certain. My spirit would be completely crushed into powder. But somehow I believe Mother knew I wouldn't have let them go to see her alone, for only once or twice did she ever ask, and then both times she said, "You do whatever you feel like you can do."

Every time Mother came by, she and I got into an argument, for she always brought up something about the letter or those ridiculous beliefs she still clung to, for example maintaining that God had shown her a member of the congregation was lost forever and had no hope of salvation. I tried reasoning with her that that was like knowing when the last judgment would be and only God knew that, not even Jesus Christ, and I was absolutely certain God would not entrust such information to us mortals. But she wouldn't budge.

In my heart of hearts I hoped she would change and we could be reconciled and the pain of the past would go away. During this period of time Ann's love, understanding, and support were crucial for me. On one occasion Mother called Ann asking if she could come to the house to visit the children, but she specifically requested that I not be there. Ann was very quick to let Mother know that I was a very important part of the family, that without me the family was not complete, and that if she didn't want me there, she was not welcome herself. She never again asked such a thing. She knew exactly where Ann stood.

For Jim and me both, the fact that Mother continued to maintain that God had put these cruel things on her to do to us kept the pain alive like something eating away inside our hearts. Working through those painful memories helped me to deal with the past and to resolve in my own mind that Mother wasn't going to change. As time went by, the unquenchable longing to obtain Mother's love and approval of me slowly died out and with it the heart-wrenching pain.

The Christmas of 1988 Ann and I decided to have an open house for all my friends and patients who had helped to make my dream for my home become a reality. We sent out dozens of invitations. We began preparations about two months in advance, especially Ann's cooking the goodies. The girls were small, but they helped me all they could by handing me the ornaments for the trees. We had three different Christmas trees. The one in the drawing room we decorated in the traditional American style with colored lights, colored glass balls, and tinsel. In the dining room we used red satin balls, white lights, and rattan ornaments given to us by Christian's parents when they came to visit us for his graduation from high school. There were pinecones, wreaths, angels, apples, and stars, all made of rattan. The living room tree was the tallest, and we decorated it in the Victorian style, with both pink and white satin balls, white lights, all kinds of beautiful Victorian ornaments, and tiny hearts and bows made very lovingly by my dear nieces. It was truly a very festive occasion. The children and I decorated the house, and Ann cooked all the goodies. That night the only illumination in the house was provided by the lights from the Christmas trees and the many candles sitting around in strategic places on certain pieces of furniture. The flickering flames of the candles gave the interior of the house a magical air, like a dream-world, a world of fantasy. That first Christmas open house the night was very cold and sharp to the ears, nose, and fingers of the kind souls who remained outside for a short while at the beginning to help with organizing the parking on the front lawn. As one entered the front door, the crisp, fresh scent of the fir trees filled the air in the living room. In the dining room, where our long table was adorned with about twenty different delicious-looking finger foods, the mouth-watering aroma filling the air invited one to hurry in and taste any or all of the goodies waiting on the table. Well over one hundred friends honored us with their presence that first Christmas season, and my dream had finally come true. My reason for building the house in the first place had been fulfilled. It was truly a wonderful celebration for me, having all the many people come together at one time to share the Christmas season with one another; it was a grand success! Everything else that Christmas season was anticlimactic for us after the joy and excitement of our open house. We received such wonderful comments from so many of those who came, and some even urged us to please continue having our Christmas party every year. For them our open house kinda brought in the Christmas season, so we decided to make it an annual event.

As more of the past surfaced and I continued to work through those events that had scarred me so deeply, I grieved over the losses I had sustained. Before I experienced any of the depression, I had already developed enough insight into my own life to realize that my adolescent years had been lost. That became even more vivid to me when Christian, our first exchange student, introduced me to the world of convertibles. As I flew along the highway with the air blowing through the little hair I had left, I found a freedom that I didn't know even existed, just as if all the walls surrounding me had been torn down and I could escape to any place I chose to go. I could look up to the heavens where God is, and that even made me feel closer to Him. I understand more about my feelings now than I did then, for I realize that after having been in an invisible prison for all those years, the freedom I experienced with the sky above my head and the wind in my hair was almost intoxicating and it was real. Jim and I had never been allowed the simple luxury of riding down the street just for the fun of it, so with the convertible I was able to recapture just a little of that bygone joy.

It's very difficult to explain the sense of loss I felt in such a way that the reader can understand it. During one session with Dr. Mackey, I told him the recurrent dream I had continued to have now and then through the years, in which I always appeared in the house in Charleston. This dream was always in full color, as if all the lights in the house were on. As I searched and searched through the house looking for something I had lost, I wept like a child whose heart had been broken. A profound sadness engulfed me as I searched so desperately for the thing so dear to me that I had lost. The longing to find that for which I searched was like a wound that never heals but remains tender to the touch. I would have those dreams over and over again, and through the years I had pondered their meaning. I was certain it was very profound. Dr. Mackey expounded on the dream to me, and it was simple yet, as I had thought, quite profound; I was searching for my lost childhood. In my subconscious mind was a great void, like a missing link with the past, an emptiness, where there should have been the joys of childhood and adolescence. And indeed Jim and I had lost not only our birth mother but also our childhood and our adolescence. A great part of our adult life had been lost as well, most definitely our freedom to make our own choices in life with regard to many of the things that are so important to the emotional development of an individual: my choice for my vocation, having to accept someone to marry that I had not chosen, having the place for my practice chosen for me, not being able to join the military, the list of losses goes on and on. That explanation made a lot of sense to me, for the grief was so very intense, even in the dreams. As Dr. Mackey said to me on numerous occasions, "You have unfinished business in your subconscious that must be dealt with." And it was not until I had come to terms with that loss that the dreams ceased.

As the memories of Mother's refusing to give me permission to join the military and of her choosing the location for my practice flooded in from the past, I began to hate dentistry. I felt frustrated, trapped, imprisoned. Day after day the dread of going to work hung over me like a dark cloud. If I had not been a very disciplined person, my practice would never have remained intact, for many days I just had to make myself get up and go to work. All sorts of ideas and options for another means of making a living came to my mind, but none was satisfactory. One doesn't pull up and move easily when he has a family to consider. During those years of deepest despair, there were days when several events came close together reminding me of the past and making the depression so intense that even my physical body was affected. My eyelids became heavy, and blinking was slowed. I felt as if my legs were leaden. My low energy level made me tire easily. Keeping my mind focused on what I was doing became more and more difficult. The thought of making any decisions was very taxing. On those days, I found it necessary to cancel all my appointments and go home where I felt safe. During those times my wonderful staff was so supportive of me. Many times my sharing with them whatever had surfaced allowed me to get in touch with my feelings of pain and loss. I always felt sorry for them when I broke down into uncontrollable sobbing, for I realized it put them in a difficult situation, wanting so much to help yet feeling so helpless. I tried to let them know, however, that their having a listening ear and just being there for me was very comforting. Other times when I went to the house I was able to reach someone by phone who was dear to my heart, and by talking to him about the painful events that had surfaced I was able to release the grief bottled up inside me. Sometimes all I could do was to say just a few words, and then I would be overwhelmed by deep, gut-wrenching sobs for minutes at a time. But weeping brought such tremendous relief.

Being able to weep is a gift, according to Dr. Mackey, for many people are not able to release their pain and it remains bottled up inside. I am sure that coping with any kind of emotional pain for them is very difficult. After the pain had been released, I always felt much better, like I had a new lease on life, for inside my heart I was like the dry earth after a downpour of wonderful rain. I was refreshed, restored, and ready to go again. It seemed to give me renewed strength. It was like I had been relieved of something that weighted me down, and truly I had. I have great compassion for all who are not able to release their painful burden. This was a long and painful healing process, which took years to complete. The wounds healed; the scars always remain, but the pain of them lessens as time passes.

Depression at times is incapacitating, for it so pervades your thoughts and your life that performing just the normal functions of life are all you can deal with. Sometimes I became so weary of being strong all the time. Being able to lean on someone else would be the most wonderful thing in the whole wide world. At those times when I felt so tired from the struggle of it all, thoughts of suicide floated through my mind, too. The thought of death was so comforting, so sweet, for then I finally could lay down my weary head and rest. I had no fear of dying; it would be wonderful to go be with God and my dear mama again. But what kept suicide from ever remaining long enough in my thoughts to become a viable option was the reality of what it would do to my family. I always pictured myself going to my garage, where I kept my classic cars, cranking one of them, curling up in a fetal position, and falling into peaceful oblivion. But immediately I would picture my dear wife, Ann, going into the garage looking for me, and I could just see her as she gazed down into my pale lifeless face, and the tears came to my eyes, just as they are doing now as I write these words. That was my answer; no, no, I could never do that to her or to my family. I had to continue to be strong and fight. Giving up was not an option. Suicide would appear to be a plausible solution for many people in similar situations, but that never really solves anything, for as I have read and heard said, "suicide is a permanent solution to a temporary problem." We can always work out our problems. There is a solution as long as we remain here to complete it. No, I loved my family and friends too much to deal them such a cruel blow. I wish others who ponder suicide would have the insight to realize what their actions would do to those they love as well. There would be many more dear souls alive today if they did.

I learned, too, that reaching out to someone else, trying to do a kind deed to lift his spirits, always made my sorrow much easier to endure. Many days when the sadness began to settle down over me like a thick fog, realizing its source my mind would begin to search for someone whose heart I could cheer or whose day I could brighten by some kind little deed. On many an occasion my sadness disappeared completely. It was wonderful. I never have believed in sitting around feeling sorry for myself. That didn't accomplish a thing. One learns quite a lot while working through a past life such as mine.

As I reached out to more and more new friends, my life became fuller and I began to understand just how much I had missed as a child growing up and how much I had lost. The overwhelming sense of loss lessened as the years passed, and the pain of losing Mama also. For years and years I never gave up hope that someday Mother and I would be reconciled with each other, but the reconciliation with my natural father came about first.

My oldest sister, Dana, and my sister Marie, had some dreams. When they told me the dreams, I said those dreams were surely sent from God and the things we had been taught about our daddy simply weren't true (that the only way his soul could be saved was for us children to remain separated from him, pray for his soul, and if he acknowledged that we were righteous and he was a sinner, then God would have mercy on him and save his soul.) So Dana broke the separation and began visiting our daddy. He was so happy to see her but would have never known her again. He wished to see us all, so I invited all my brothers and sisters to my house for dinner one night and Dana made the arrangements to have him come. After we had finished our meal, Daddy told us all how he had prayed for that day, to be able to see us all together again, how that at times he feared it would never happen, but how he never stopped praying for it. But as he was speaking, I realized all the feelings for him inside me had been destroyed; it was just an old man I was listening to; there was no emotion, no bond, nothing, everything, had been destroyed by the brainwashing Mother had put us through, instilling in our very young hearts and minds the fear of our own daddy, as if he were a very wicked person with an evil spirit that would possess us if we got near him. I felt very sad, for at that time there were several cases in the news about children being reunited with their parents after thirty years and they were able to rejoice with tears of emotion and joy, but for me there was nothing. All was dead. Truly such a sad truth.

I also visited Daddy a few times myself, but he talked so little and I was afraid that maybe he still didn't want me in his life, so I didn't go back again until the day before he passed away. It was on a Thursday morning that Dana called the office to let me know Daddy had been on a penicillin drip for ten days for pneumonia, with no improvement, and the doctors didn't expect him to live through the night. He had developed the pneumonia after getting so chilled at his wife's graveside service two weeks previously. I had my staff cancel all my appointments, telling my patients I had an emergency, that I had to visit my daddy in the hospital. I knew it was imperative that I find some kind of reconciliation with my daddy before he died, or I would be tormented the rest of my life. So Dana, Josie, and I went to the hospital to visit him. He was so pitiful sitting there in the chair gasping for breath. As I sat there looking at him, I thought about the years gone by, about the sadness he had no doubt experienced because of his having been ostracized from his own family, of never being able to see us children again. It all seemed so cruel. Mother was responsible for all that, too. I asked Dana, "What kind of Christianity does Mother have that she can't come here and tell her poor brother she had been wrong and to please forgive her?" It is just more than I can fathom.

I told him I loved him and that I was sorry our life had been like it was, not being able to see him, but most important of all for me, I told him when he got to heaven to please tell Mama I had missed her so much and that someday I would meet her again. He nodded his head to let me know he understood. The poor fellow couldn't talk much, for his breathing was so labored, taking all his efforts just to get enough oxygen to live. We stayed a while longer, then said good-bye, knowing we would never see him alive again. He died at 5:00 the next morning with Charlene, one of his five daughters by his second wife, Inez, sitting by his bedside. Charlene told us that just a few minutes before he passed away he asked for a pencil and paper. He scribbled on it the words, "Mama go home." Bless his dear old heart, he was ready to go home.

When I drove up to the funeral home the day of his burial, the director met us at the car to ask how we were related. I responded by saying, "I'm his son." Then it struck me; I had never said that before in my entire life, and I knew in that moment how things would be emotionally when I went inside. It was as if I had found my Daddy at last, and now he was gone. When I stood looking down into his face as he lay in the casket, I became completely and totally overwhelmed with grief. I've never wept so much and so intensely in my life. I felt the tremendous weight of my loss like a ton of cement crushing the very heart out of me. My entire life passed before me, all the days and years Daddy could have held me and didn't, could have told me he loved me and was not able to, could have taken me by the hand to lead me places and was not there. I even felt his own pain at having been rejected by his family, the years he had spent longing for the return of those he truly did love, realizing too late the magnitude of what he had done but not able to rectify his terrible mistake. In those moments it seemed I also felt the pain of all the emotional and physical suffering Mother had inflicted upon each of my relatives. I've never had such an experience before. It was quite overwhelming. For at least five or ten minutes, long gut-wrenching sobs wracked my entire body. As the convulsions of grief gripped me, my stomach would contract until it seemed it would touch my spine. I could hardly even catch my breath between the spasms of sobbing. One wave would wash over me, and then another wave would follow, like the waves at the beach when they seem to almost knock you down with their force and power. Finally, all the grief had escaped like the great flood of water that spills out of a reservoir when the dam breaks and the pain was gone. Then I was able to stand up straight and tall and say good-bye to the dear daddy I never knew. I closed that chapter of my life forever. It was comforting to know his suffering had come to an end and he was in a better place. That was March 18, 1993. From what little I have learned from Charlene, he grieved all through his life because his family had completely and totally rejected him, and I can certainly understand that grief. Only two of his siblings were ever reconciled with him before he died, Uncle Sam and Uncle

Aaron. One of his sisters wanted to visit but was afraid of retribution from Mother. The poor fellow had died hoping to learn that they really cared, but only the two ever showed up at his humble door.

Never having given up hope that Mother would change and feel sorry for the terrible things she had done to us, I was happy beyond measure when I received a letter from her one day in which she expressed regret for the past and said that even if we couldn't visit, at least we could be friends. I shared the letter with some of my closest friends and my pastor, Mike Thompson. Mike cautioned me to be careful, to not build up my hopes too much. "There might not be that much sincerity in her intentions," he cautioned. Still, with hopes of better days my family and I made a visit to Mother's and even ate supper with her. It seemed good to me to be there with her. But, as I continued to develop our relationship, things began to change, and I began to realize she was not basically any different. She maintained that if she had it to do over, she would do exactly as she had done in the past.

During this period in our lives Jim had a very, very difficult time dealing with the reality that she wouldn't change. In his heart of hearts he still loved her so much, but at the same time he had so much anger deep inside from all the abuse, control, and humiliation she had perpetrated on him and me. In his clear state of mind he loved her and felt sorry for her, and it was literally years before he could actually grasp the magnitude of what she had done to us. I had to tread a very thin line between Jim and Mother. Because I had any contact at all with her, that in itself made him suspicious of me. So I chose my words very carefully, knowing I could lose him if I was not wise, but it was not very long at all before Jim began to see through Mother. And she brought about her own downfall in our eyes. Each time Jim visited her, the conversation always turned to me. In her attempt to drive a wedge between the two of us, she usually made disparaging comments about me, which raised Jim's ire, and he began to realize what she was doing. His trust was broken, and once that happened, it never returned.

When he began to drink to drown his pain over losing Betty, the anger and rage from the abuses of the past began to flood his inebriated mind. Then he wouldn't even let me call her Mother in his presence. He'd shout, "Don't call her Mother! She's not our d——— mother. She's a bitch from hell. Beulah White Roberts is our Mother, the one who married that sorry good-for-nothing thing who turned us over to Beulah Howard. And she's a so-and-so." A long list of horribly profane adjectives would follow. As his depression deepened over the loss of his wife, Betty, he began to drink more and more. As his drinking increased it lifted the lid of suppression off the memories of the past he had kept buried deep in his poor heart. Many times he would call me to go to his house; he needed to talk to me. I could always tell he was drinking, for most of the time he would address me on the phone by saying, "John, my dear brother, this is Jim. What's up? How are you making it?" He would talk for an hour or more at the time, pouring out his anger and frustrations at what Mother had done to him and me.

Other times I would go by his house, in his drunken state he would begin by telling me in a very distressed tone of voice, "That so-and-so beat the hell out of you. I can still hear you screaming. You hadn't done anything. I was the mean one."

I would always tell him, "Jim, that's in the past."

Then, describing her with the most horrible language imaginable, he would tell me what he wanted to do to Mother.

Once he said he would love to hang her up by her feet, skin her, and pour salt on her raw flesh and hear her scream. Another time he said he'd love to pluck her eyeballs out, stuff one up each nostril, then tell her to blow her nose. When he said such horrible things to me, I'm sure the expression of shock on my face was so great, for one time he said to me, "Lighten up! Smile. Don't be so damn serious." Then I was actually afraid. His anger at Mother was so intense, and in his intoxicated state he seemed to perceive me as being on her side, and I didn't know what he might do to me. Once while describing how he would love to choke her with his bare hands, he got me by the neck to demonstrate. His grip on my neck was like a vise. I very calmly said to him, "Jim, you're hurting me."

That's all it took. He apologized instantly. "My brother, my dear brother, I'm sorry. I wouldn't hurt you for anything on this earth." And he wouldn't have, either! Sometimes he would rave on about how he could kill her with his bare, bony hands, the hands she had belittled all his life. He told me during one of his tormented outbursts that he would love to take his bare hand, grab her by the throat, snatch her "gousel" out, and cram it up her a——hole. His rage against Mother about his hands stemmed from what she had told us both through the years. She would say time and again, "I've watched them. Men with small hands and small feet are no good. They are sorry. They never amount to anything." She never gave any thought as to how her statements affected our minds and our self-esteem.

Sometimes the poor fellow was so distraught that one minute he was on his knees crying about her beating me and the next minute he was up jumping around like a madman, even tearing his clothes, yelling so loudly it actually hurt my ears. I would have to ask him to not get so close to me for the power of his voice actually brought pain to my ears. It was truly distressing to me the first time I witnessed such behavior, but I could understand his rage. I had been there when he was beaten unmercifully, when he was so humiliated in front of all his classmates by the exposure of his back covered with black-and-blue welts from those horrible floggings. I was there when she made him sell his landscape equipment on the pretext that if he didn't he would be lost. All I could do was pray that one day he would become strong enough to deal with his rage without resorting to alcohol. And indeed, as I continued to become stronger emotionally, so did Jim. His fits of rage came further and further apart. He had met another woman who began to bring him some peace of mind, and to fill the tremendous void left by his first wife, Betty. This woman helped Jim so much and I was thankful for that, so very thankful, for it was a great burden I carried every day in my heart for my dear brother who had been through the same hell I had experienced. When Jim did better, it always made me feel better, too. We both accepted the fact that Mother would never truly change enough to see what she had done. As we rationalized that fact in our minds, the heart-wrenching longing in our souls slowly began to subside and we found peace about it. We just had to get on with our lives without her.

On the morning of December 12, 1994, my younger daughter, Emilie, and I were hanging some clothes on the clothesline. It was very cold that morning, in the twenties I recall. All of a sudden I began to ache right over the area of my heart. I commented to Emilie that I was aching, but not wanting to alarm her, I didn't tell her where. The pain stopped, though, in a few seconds, and I thought nothing of it until I arrived at the office and, after reaching down and picking up a heavy box, the pain returned; only this time it was more severe than the first episode at the house. One of my staff even said to me that my face turned very pale. I knew without a doubt it was my heart, so I canceled my appointments and went straight to the doctor, who did an EKG, which turned out to be perfectly normal. Dr. Bridgers advised me to try to take it easy, not to be too anxious about our open house on Saturday, and to try not to think about the pain of the Christmas season. I was in such good overall health he did not suspect any heart problem, but to be sure, he scheduled an appointment for me to have a stress test done on Thursday in Wilmington.

My staff and I went to Wilmington that afternoon, ate lunch at the Nuss Strasse Cafe, then browsed through the shops in the Cotton Exchange. Then on Tuesday I worked all day as usual without any more episodes of pain, so while Ann was cooking supper I said to myself, *Well, I'll take my exercise like I usually do and see what happens.* I did fine for thirty minutes; then I began to hurt, only this time the pain wouldn't go away. I stopped exercising and began walking around to get my breath. I looked at myself in the mirror, noticing that I appeared unusually pale, then turned to make my way to the balcony over the living room. As I staggered out onto the balcony, I began to call for help, but my breath was so short I couldn't call out very loudly. Charlotte just happened to be upstairs in her bathroom and heard me calling for help. She reached my side just as I was slowly sinking to the floor. I gently told her to call 911, that I thought it was my heart. The rescue squad arrived in a few minutes and transported me to the hospital. My pastor, Mike Thompson, was one of those who came to the house, and the last thing I remember his saying to me as we reached the hospital was, "John, we're going to move you from our stretcher to the hospital bed." The next thing I remember I was in the emergency room full of lights and all those people around me. I begged for water; I was so thirsty from all the sweating I had done. All they could do was dip a cloth in water and let me suck the water out, but oh, it was sooo good. Many years had passed since I had sucked water out of a washcloth in the bathtub in California. I knew something had happened, because I didn't remember being rolled into the emergency room, so I asked Dr. Bridgers point-blank, "Have I had a heart attack?"

"We don't think so. You've danced all around it," he replied. With that answer I gave everybody a good laugh by asking another honest and quite serious question: "Well, can I go back to work tomorrow?"

Everyone within hearing distance laughed heartily.

"No, you won't be going back to work for several days," Ann informed me tenderly.

"Well, OK." But in my mind I still knew there was a period of time I couldn't account for, and the thought came to me, *What if that happens again and I don't wake up. What will happen to my children?* So I closed my eyes and prayed a simple but very earnest prayer: *Dear God, please take care of my children.* Then a great peace came over me, and I didn't worry anymore.

As the doctors worked with me, they explained to me that I had been given the clot-buster shot to help dissolve the clot in my heart and morphine to reduce the pain. On the ride from the house to the hospital, the pain had been so great I continually wiggled my feet to help me endure it. I heard someone in the emergency room ask about my wiggling my feet, and another person from the rescue told then I had been doing that ever since they had picked me up. The pain made me have the urge to get up and walk, but I knew that was impossible. The deep aching in my chest was comparable to the cramp in the butt one gets after sitting for long periods of time without moving, but only a hundred times worse. It was so severe it made me feel sick.

By 10:30 P.M. my condition was stabilized and the cardiac unit from New Hanover Memorial Hospital in Wilmington came to transport me back to their facility. The morphine had sedated me so that my thought process was like that of a child, for I had no idea why I was being sent to the Wilmington Cardiac Center at New Hanover Memorial Hospital. I thought, *Well, if the doctors treating me want me to go to Wilmington, then it's all right with me.* Without the sedation I would have understood my condition, but I'm so very thankful that I didn't know. It would have been emotionally devastating for me to even think I might die and leave my dear children like my poor mama had to leave me, and my recovery wouldn't have been so soon.

I remember leaving Bladen County Hospital but nothing else until I woke up en route to Wilmington feeling very nauseated. I began to plead with those in the unit, "What will I do? I've got to vomit." I was wearing an oxygen mask and knew the mask would pose a problem if I vomited. Before the EMTs knew what was happening, I was vomiting, with the stuff spraying out all of the holes in the mask. They went into action, but immediately after upchucking I went right back out of consciousness and didn't regain it again until the cold night air hit my face as we were entering the hospital there in Wilmington. I remember all the bright lights surrounding the emergency entrance, but as soon as I entered the warm space of the hospital I went out again.

In Bladen County Hospital, Ann had been instructed there was no real need to rush to Wilmington, that my situation was stable and I would be OK. But, just as soon as she arrived at the hospital, her name was being called out on the paging system in a most urgent tone. The cardiologist had been paging her for some time. He showed her my angiogram and explained how the angioplasty didn't work for me. My legs and chest had already been prepped for open-heart bypass surgery, and the minute she signed the release form I was wheeled out and my open-heart surgery began. It was around twelve midnight.

My first fleeting conscious recollection was of a hazy figure standing in front of my bed pulling the curtain aside and a male voice saying to me, "Well, it's Wednesday and your surgery's finished."

I thought to myself, *Surgery! Dear God, what's happened to me?* The darkness of sleep engulfed me again. The next thing I remember, I was trying to cough and realized my throat was full of tubes and I was freezing to death. I mouthed to the nurses, *I'm cold.* Immediately they brought me some deliciously warm blankets, placed them over my body, and gave me some encouraging words: "Oh, the doctor said you would snap right back because you were able to assist us in moving your body before you were even conscious." At

266

the time those words were very comforting, even though the reality of what had happened to me had not sunk in yet. I went right back to sleep.

Some hours later I awoke to find Ann standing at the head of the bed, calling my name, telling me that I'd had a heart attack, that Dr. Hunter had done double-bypass surgery, and that I was doing fine. Then the shocking truth began to sink in. In less than fifteen minutes, the nurses came and took out the breathing tube. What a relief! I spent Wednesday night in the cardiac intensive care unit hooked up to all those machines that monitored my cardiac functions and where the nurses could keep an eye on me every minute.

On Thursday I was moved out of the cardiac intensive care unit and placed in a cardiac step-down room, where I would still be monitored around-the-clock. My chest cavity was draining, so there were two rubber tubes extending out of my chest into a box in which the fluid collected. I could get up and go to the bathroom and walk for exercise but had to carry the draining apparatus with me everywhere I went. As I was fully conscious by that time, the complete realization of my condition struck me, and the shock set in. I felt so completely helpless. *What else can I do?* I thought to myself as I looked down at my skinny little body. I just couldn't believe it; it just didn't seem possible. Here I was, skinny as a pencil, had never smoked a single cigarette, didn't drink, always exercised, and had been watching my fat intake for years, in fact, since medical research discovered fat to be so harmful to the American male. Those first few days I wondered if I would have the courage to fight, but I never stopped trying. My family and all my wonderful friends and loving patients were my inspiration. I wanted to recover for them.

But true to the doctor's prediction, I recovered miraculously and would have been able to go home on Saturday had my chest not still been draining too much fluid. I remember on Thursday, when I first began walking in the hospital for exercise, everyone was so concerned that I would overdo it, but walking was so effortless. I said to those so afraid for me, "What do you want me to do, creep along like a one-hundred-year-old man? All I have to do is put one foot ahead of another and walk, it's really quit easy." They got a kick out of that statement. All my years of discipline in exercising faithfully were paying off for me. So, on Tuesday, the twentieth of December, I was allowed to go home, and what a happy day that was for me. I carried my faithful pillow out to the car, and it went with me everywhere, but, you know, the fear of sneezing or coughing and in the process ripping my sternum apart before it had a chance to heal, somehow suppressed the urge to sneeze. I never had to sneeze until my chest healed well.

We stopped by the post office that day on the way home, and it was then I became so acutely aware of the concern everyone had for me, and that love I felt and support given me was so wonderful in the days and months ahead. Everyone who saw me expressed their concern for my speedy recovery and was so glad to see me out again.

Arriving at the house, I was so very weak I didn't even have the energy to feed myself, which thrilled my girls, who took turns feeding me. When a forkful of food was placed in my mouth, I rested my head in my chin, chewing slowly and methodically, like cows do when they chew their cud. I'd never been so weak in all my life, except perhaps for the time I fainted in church and had to be carried out. The doctors had explained to me in the hospital why I was so weak: I had lost a lot of blood. But they felt it was better to let my body rebuild itself than to give me a blood transfusion. That was fine with me.

Ann had fried some good chicken livers which were sooo delicious. The doctor had said not to worry about cholesterol right now. I needed all the nourishment I could get. By the time I had finished eating, I would get the shakes from being so weak on the way to the drawing room from the kitchen, and my whole body would convulse from the shivers until my chest wound hurt from the effort. After a few days of that, old knucklehead me took Ann's suggestion to wear long thermal underwear, and that solved the problem with the cold. Thank goodness, no more shivering.

For a year those nights during my recovery were like a nightmare in my mind. We had made the drawing room into a bedroom downstairs, for I wasn't allowed to climb stairs for a month. If there was any heat in the room I couldn't breathe, so we cut the heat down to fifty-five degrees at night. Then when I had to get up to pee (I've never had to get up so much at night before in my life), the house was so cold I'd shiver all the while, because my body was wet with sweat. Getting up at night was dreaded, to say the least. I never understood why I sweated so much, but I guess it was part of the healing process, just like my racing pulse. My pulse had been an average of 91–96. Before the heart attack it was around 68–72.

Well, believe it or not, in two and a half weeks I went back to work doing very simple things like checkups, taking an impression, seating crowns, and delivering dentures. I couldn't extract any teeth for six weeks because of the torquing action to my chest. I was doing so well, following the doctors' orders of walking outside in the fresh air every day, even though it was so cold outside the wind felt like it was cutting the surface of any exposed skin.

Then one Friday morning Aunt Maggie called shortly after 8:00 A.M. to see how I was doing. Charlotte was sick that day, and my first thought was to get to the phone before it woke her, so I flew out of the bed like a whirlwind, but as I was sitting up, the thoughts were passing through my mind, *What is the matter with people? Don't they know I'm recovering from a heart attack? Why on earth would anybody call me at this unearthly hour and wake me up?*

The phone was just across the hall from my bed. When I reached the phone, Aunt Maggie asked how I was.

I answered, "I feel fine but I think I'm going to faint."

The next thing I knew I was wondering what was pushing so hard against my chest. Then I realized what it was. I was lying face-down on the rug in the hall, still clutching the phone in my right hand. My weakness made my body feel like it weighed a ton and as if my body were being pushed into the floor. It took all the effort I could muster to raise my body up off the floor, get on my feet, and place the phone back on the hook. I then turned to go back to the bed, but had no warning that time.

When I came to, I first thought I was watching a movie. There was a round pool of blood right in front of my face, my nose was aching, my glasses were thrown aside, and once again I felt like my body was made of lead. In my mind I said, *Am I being tortured or am I watching a movie?* Then it struck me what was going on, and that really frightened me. I managed to push myself up on my arms but apparently blacked out again, for I have no recollection of how I managed to crawl to the bed. But when I regained consciousness the next time, I was on my knees by the bed, my arms stretched out, my head and torso lying across the bed. I was panting from the effort, and in addition I had become completely incontinent. I had wet my robe, and feces were running out and dropping onto the calf of my leg. I thought, *Dear God, am I like some dying animal, lying here messing all over myself?* I lay there on the bed until I could get my breath and then tiptoed to the bathroom to clean myself up. First I thought of getting into the shower, but then I reconsidered: *What if I faint in there?* I could break my neck. So I just cleaned off my leg, went to the phone, called Ann at school and told her, "Ann, something has happened to me. I've fainted three times, cut my nose, and messed myself all up." Next I called Mike, my pastor, who said he would be right over with the rescue squad truck and take me to the hospital emergency room. I couldn't help but cry when they carried me out of the house again to the hospital.

I was taken from Bladen County Hospital back to New Hanover Hospital in Wilmington for the entire weekend. They took blood and took blood and measured my blood pressure lying down, then sitting up on the side of the bed, then standing up by the bed. I jokingly told one of the nurses that if they didn't stop taking so much blood, I wouldn't have any left. The doctors finally deduced that the blood thinner I had been taking caused my blood pressure to plummet to rock bottom when I jumped out of bed so suddenly, and for that reason I didn't need to take it any longer, which was fine with me.

The only lasting effects of the fall were the pain and limited mobility of my right shoulder, which had slammed against the doorjamb as I was falling to the floor the second time. The pain was so great at times I simply couldn't work, and on those days it was so frustrating to think if only I had not been called so early that morning, if only I hadn't sailed out of bed like a whirlwind, I would be doing so much better, because up to that time my recovery had been miraculous, and then to have such a setback because of a phone call! Then I would think, *Maybe I had not been thankful enough and God let it happen to humble me more.* Gradually, very gradually, though, my shoulder began to heal, and I was able to take therapeutic exercise to strengthen it, and soon the pain was completely gone, which was sooo wonderful.

For those who survive a heart attack, the first year is the most difficult. For me I think the problem was more of an emotional one than physical. In addition to eating well to build back the blood I had lost, my cardiologist recommended I walk every day in the fresh air. Those first few strolls down our road I'll never forget. It was freezing cold. The wind felt as if it would cut my skin. Every square inch of skin had to be covered. I wrapped a wool shawl around my neck so that I could wrap it around my face, leaving only my nose exposed. Many times as I walked in the freezing air outside, I wept and prayed, *Dear God, please help me. Please give me the courage to keep on fighting. I must for my children's sake and for Ann, for my friends, and for my patients.* It would have been so much easier to give up, but you can't give up the fight. The strength I had already acquired through the previous years definitely came to my aid during my recovery period. But little by little, my confidence returned and things began to look brighter.

A very profound lesson I learned from my brush with death was the importance of relationships. Nothing is more vital to our emotional well-being than relationships with others. That's what sustains us. It gives us a reason to live. What we have materially will still be here when we're gone, but lost opportunities to spend time with someone can never be regained. What does it matter that we don't have everything in perfect order all the time? It's much better to spend a little time with our friends and family than to put inanimate objects ahead of them. What do we do when they are gone? Then it's too late to go sit and chat awhile. After resolving these issues in my own mind, I was much happier, too. Relationships became my top priority.

Also for me, it seemed that something inside me had healed. I no longer felt driven to achieve this or that or to attempt to do the impossible. For years every time we had a cook-out or any kind of gathering at the house, I felt compelled to make sure everything was neat, tidy, and in order. Somehow, in the back of my mind was the unconscious fear that someone would criticize me if things weren't just perfect. But as the healing took place, I began to realize that my real friends accepted me just as I was and didn't criticize me for what I couldn't or hadn't accomplished. That is one of the definitions of a true friend: "A true friend accepts us just as we are, warts and all." That was such a relief for me too, not only emotionally but for my poor little heart as well, because putting ourselves under pressure to do so much in a given period of time stresses the heart, and that's not good!

Then another crisis unfolded. I slowly became more and more depressed but also realized it was not because of the past. I began to have extreme weak spells that prevented me from working or doing anything except lying down. One morning at the office I called a member of the rescue team over to take my blood pressure. It was 98 over 68. Again I was checked into the hospital to see of I had had another heart attack. Blood was taken over a twenty-four-hour period to check for the enzymes that show up if there has been a heart attack, which was negative. Having paid close attention to how I felt at all times during the day, I had already deduced the problem was Lopressor, the heart medication I was taking. I took it in the morning when I ate breakfast. Within an hour after taking that tiny pill, I would become so weak I could barely stand up. So Dr. Bridgers had me break the tablets into four pieces, taking only one-fourth-tablet at a time, which did just fine. After about one year I didn't need to take even that much but was able to stop taking the Lopressor entirely. All I take now is an aspirin a day, which helps to prevent further heart attacks. Isn't that wonderful? I think so!

At various times my pastor expressed to me the seriousness of my heart attack, letting me know that if I hadn't been where I was when it occurred, I would have died. In other words, God had spared my life. That was very humbling to me, and since I believed it was true, I wanted to do whatever God had spared me to do, be it ever so small. First of all, I knew I had to give Mother another chance, no matter what she had done to me and Jim. Mother called me on Wednesday, the day after I arrived home from the hospital from my heart attack and bypass surgery, to ask if she could come to see me. Of course I was glad that she would come and hoped we could develop a relationship. Deep in my heart I still had not given up hope that we could be reconciled and could share our lives. I knew I had forgiven her for everything even though there was residual anger still buried deep inside me for some of the more humiliating things she had done to Jim and me. When she came into the room where I was lying in the bed, it seemed so good to see her, and I told her I loved her. She said she wanted to bring me something, but I interrupted her to say, "Mother, I don't want anything except your love." We exchanged a little small talk, and then she and Emilie accompanied me that day on my walk outside. The day was beautiful; it was bitter cold even though the sun was shining brightly in the winter sky. As I walked along, I held Mother's hand inside mine, which I kept deep in the secure warmth of my topcoat pocket. It was so good to have her there with me, and my hopes began to build again for the future. Mother came for a couple of other visits to the house during the period when I wasn't able to drive myself and took me to work.

But my pastor and friends warned me to be careful, to not get my hopes too high. They didn't want to see me be hurt again. When I finally recovered well enough to drive, I began to visit Mother in her home. She would call me to go eat lunch with her, which I did several times. It seemed a bit strange at first to be there with her, almost eerie at times as I sat looking in her face, seeing the woman who had grown older sitting before me, remembering the terror she had struck in my very heart in days gone by when she said to me in her cold, threatening, and provoked voice, "What possessed you to do such a thing?" But I tried very hard to push those memories from my mind. At first we talked about small things and avoided any mention of the past, just spending some time with each other. After my going to visit with her a few Fridays, Mother began to call every week for me to go to her house. It was a replay of the past all over again. I began to dread hearing the phone ring on Friday mornings for fear it was Mother wanting me to come to see her. Those phone calls reminded me of the years past when she called every day of my life to talk to me about living right, about being spiritual, about doing God's will. I wanted to be free to decide when I should go and not to feel obligated to go every Friday. After all, I had a practice to run and a family to take care of. But I didn't want to be too unreasonable, so I tried to overlook her ways.

But as our relationship began to take root, there were certain events in my past life I felt compelled to confront her with in order to have an honest, trusting bond between the two of us. I had to know how she felt, to know if she had changed and perhaps was sorry for the things she had done to Jim and me. The memory of those events lay like huge boulders between the two of us, not in her mind I'm sure, but in my own mind. First of all I wanted to know how she felt inside when she told me she would have to think about letting me and the children visit her. When I confronted her with the question, "Mother, when I asked you years ago if I could come visit and bring the girls, why did you say you would have to think about it?" she began to "beat around the bush," so to speak, but I gathered the gist of her meaning, so I asked her point-blank, "Were you still angry with me about the letter and what I said to you about Mary?" I had told Mother that Mary had a sweeter spirit about her than Mother had, and I knew she didn't like that one bit.

"Yes, that was it," she answered.

"I thought so back then," I told her.

But Mother made no apologies about having felt that way or even admitted she had been wrong. Mother did, however, volunteer to say she was so sorry for making Jim wear the handcuffs and for beating me those three years for "the dirty tricks."

Then I embarked on another very profound subject. I asked her how on earth she could be so un-Christian as to not be willing to forgive her poor brother, my natural father, for having refused to have anything to do with him after he gave us up for adoption. Why couldn't she go to him, tell him that she had been wrong, and be reconciled to him before he died? She firmly maintained she had done God's will with regards to my poor daddy. That day I left her house feeling very angry at her and didn't even bother to say good-bye. I just couldn't fathom such unforgiving attitudes from someone who considers herself to be a true Christian, looking askance at everyone else in the world as if they are all sinners and she alone is righteous. I questioned her cruel treatment of Jim and me during our adolescent years. Why? Why? Then she admitted that it was because our daddy had tried to molest her on two different occasions and that made her feel hard and bitter toward us, because we represented him to her. That admission by her explained virtually everything. Dr. Mackey had told me during a session with him that he could almost guarantee Mother had been sexually molested when she was a child. I informed him she had told me my daddy had fondled her through the open bedroom window on two separate occasions. The doctor explained to me that she was taking her anger against her brother out on us, because we represented him. We were males and not just any males, but his male children, which made her resentment against us even greater.

But as I have said before, all those beatings didn't leave us scarred, but the emotional pain she tortured us with left the deep scars. She also continued to stand by her claim that God did show her that a member of the church was lost and would never be saved even though that person was still alive. I tried to reason with her once again, but to no avail. I also tried to explain why Jim had so much anger against her about his lost landscape business, but she immediately took the defensive, saying Jim had made many bad choices in his life and that was the reason he was unhappy, and she denied having forced him to sell his landscape machinery. I asked her about the meeting in the bus station and her not trusting me. The same kind of response: she didn't see that she had done anything wrong. Even after those confrontations I continued trying to let something grow between us, for I knew I could forget the past if she would change and be different herself.

Then one day about three weeks after I had taken the initiative to confront her with the things that had been so painful for me, as we were eating lunch together at her house, she took the initiative and said to me, "I think we need to talk. Maybe it will help us understand one another better."

"That's fine with me," I answered. My optimism made me expect her to express regrets for having mistreated us and for having not realized how those things had affected us, but that was not the case at all!

She lowered the boom like a sledgehammer. "You remember you told me you loved me when I went to see you that day right after you came out of the hospital. Well, from that day to this I've tried to convince myself that you do, but I can't."

By the time those last words had come out of her mouth, my heart was pounding, I was trembling inside, and I stood up to leave, saying to her as I left my chair, "Well, there's no need to continue this conversation any further. It's only a repetition of the past, you falsely accusing me, telling me things that simply are not true. I'm leaving." And what I really wanted to say to her was, "Woman, after all the horrible things you did to me and Jim, if I didn't love you, why in the name of common sense would I be here with you now? Why would I find joy in taking you out to lunch?" I just couldn't believe she had said those words.

Then in a split second she made a complete about-face, changing from someone cold and calculating, calling all the shots, to someone pitiful and pleading. She grabbed me by the arm, begging me to stay: "Please, please don't go. I feel like if you go like this it will be the worst thing that's ever happened."

Looking back now, I realize she recognized the fact that I had the courage to live without her and that I might never return. I can count on two hands the number of times I had visited her during the last thirteen years. She grabbed me by the arm, held onto me rather desperately, and stood there for thirty minutes talking to me about the past, starting with my mama, how hard her life had been, how my daddy wasn't a good provider, how she had taken my mama's place in the church, how God had placed her as a watchman over my soul, and on and on, telling me virtually the same things I had heard over and over before. Out of respect to her, I didn't tear myself away and go running out of the house, which is what I really wanted to do. When I finally left, I wasn't sure whether I would ever go back again.

The experience was depressing and rather upsetting, to say the least. I talked with my pastor about it. It seemed to me that I was at square one again. The message I had received was still the same. She still didn't trust me, no matter what I did. I had told her I loved her and had tried to show her as well, but that wasn't enough. She still wanted to be able to control my life, to dictate when I should visit her and whatever else. Weeks passed before I could bring myself to go back. But I am not one to give up easily. That tremendous will to survive has helped me in so many other situations. Knowing how she had been in the past, I feared she might still be accusatory of me for what I had said, but one Friday morning she called to see how I was doing and the tone of her voice was so sweet my hopes immediately returned. I visited her a few more times, and on one of those visits I said to her, "Mother, my children do quite well in school and sometimes they are highlighted in the paper for their accomplishments. I've wondered if you would care to share their success with them. I've even thought of sending you a clipping out of the paper, but you know how you have always been about the paper." (She had always rebuked the congregation about reading the newspaper. We weren't supposed to read the paper. It was worldly and sinful. We were virtually forbidden to take papers into our homes.) But she made no reply, not even one little peep. Her lack of response sent the message to me that she wasn't interested in my children except in the way she wanted to be, that she didn't want to be part of our family or part of our world. The way I believe, if she were sorry for the past and wanted to share our lives with us, then she would have said to me, "Yes, Son, all that mess about the newspaper was a mistake. Yes, I would love to share in the children's lives. When are these things done? I can't drive at night, but if you will come get me, I'd love to go with you." That would have thrilled my heart. I would have known she had a change of heart. But it began to appear that a relationship as I had hoped for was not possible. It had to be on her terms. She still wanted to be in control. Even the days when I ate lunch with her she tried to insist that I eat whatever she put on my plate instead of my eating what I wanted myself. As I had been so controlled through most of my life, it was just too obvious to me.

Then she said to me during another visit, "You just don't understand; I can't apologize for what God put on me. I can't be sorry for that. You just don't understand; God put it on me to beat Jim." Another confirmation that she had not changed in her basic thinking.

My answer to her statement was, "Well, the God I love doesn't work that way. If He did, then Jesus Christ would have spent his entire life beating people, for he was the only perfect person. But God gives us a choice. We can choose good or evil. If we choose evil, then we must pay the consequences of our evil deeds." But there was no change in her. She held firm to her belief.

That statement let me know for certain that a relationship just wasn't possible, and I realize that even though Mother seems to have changed in some ways, I cannot trust her, for she still believes in virtually all of the terrible things she did to all of us, Jim and me and the rest of the family at large. And I had hoped so much that the memories of her home there in Whiteville would be good ones, but that was not to be, either.

The events surrounding my last visit to Mother's were like a nightmare. She had called that Friday morning for me to come eat lunch with her, and I was hurrying to be there at 12:30. A couple of my own errands had delayed me. When I stopped at Highway 701 just outside Clarkton, I looked both ways and seeing no one, began to pull out. My car had moved forward perhaps two feet when a car came whizzing by at an alarming speed. Goose bumps covered my entire body. My heart almost stood still. *Thank you, dear God for looking out for me again,* I prayed. I pondered all the ten miles to Mother's about that incident, knowing I could have been killed, right there just a few miles from home. I arrived at Mother's without further incident, parked the car, and went inside to eat lunch with her. We were sitting there about half-finished with lunch when the doorbell rang. Mother went to answer it, and I heard her say, "It's probably my son's." As I walked to the door, I thought to myself that maybe I had lost a hubcap off the car. What I saw as I looked out her front door chilled my blood. I felt like it was all draining down into my feet. Sitting in a huge ditch with its nose pointing down and the tail end jacked up in the air was my car. The poor fellow who had stopped to find out whose car it was said it almost hit him as he drove along minding his own business. He told us he thought to himself, *Is that person crazy, backing out in front of me?* But as he stared straight at the car, he then realized it was empty. When the car came to a stop in the ditch, being so relieved that he had not collided with it, he went up to Mother's door to find out to whom the car belonged. As I stood there looking at it, I said over and over, "It was a miracle, an absolute miracle!" The traffic along that highway was very heavy that afternoon, and my car had somehow slipped out of park and rolled down Mother's inclined driveway and across 701 without colliding with another car. My car could have caused a horrible crash, the death of one or more persons, and I could have been sued and lost everything I had ever worked for. As it turned out, the only damage sustained by the car was to the exhaust pipes, both of which had to be replaced. They were bent forward as the car rolled backward into the ditch. I just couldn't get it out my mind what a miracle it really had been. I pondered over it for a long time. Was that incident a sign that I should put an end to seeking for a relationship with Mother again?

I called Mother a couple of times after that frightening day, then decided it was futile to attempt a relationship with her. Somehow knowing Mother still believed she had done God's will in doing all the terrible things to us kept the pain of it and the past alive. Jim and I both can cope with life better by remaining apart from her. In that way the memories remained more submerged in our minds.

Last Christmas, 1997, I felt recovered enough to have our annual open house again, so we sent out the invitations and made the necessary preparations. It was a grand success. It was such a joy and was so good to have everyone in our home again. We are looking forward to Christmas 1998. In fact, we are already making a newer list for invitations. We want to invite some new friends who have never been here before.

Life goes on in spite of our losses and sorrows. We learn to cope. We must never give up, must never let life engulf us, but when we are knocked down, we must just get up, brush the dirt off, and start again. And Jim has done that as well as myself. On Labor Day of last year, 1997, about the time our guests had all gone, Jim came to the house to see me. My pastor and his wife greeted Jim out on the front driveway. I was in the house. Becky, the pastor's wife, came inside to tell me Jim was outside wanting to see me. He had frightened her so much she was concerned for my welfare after they left. She told me later she could see the hatred in his eyes. I told Mike and Becky I would be OK, and they left. I immediately recognized Jim was drinking and was in a very bad way; in fact, he was in the most tormented state I had ever witnessed. His eyes were black pools of vitriolic hatred. He began by begging me to drive him to Gatlinburg, where the bitch was and he would kill her. He said, "I'm willing to spend the rest of my life in prison just to have the satisfaction of knowing I've killed her and she's not here to torment me. I've got the loot." He opened his wallet to show me the wad of money he had to pay the cost of room, gas, and food. He patted his hip, saying, "I've got the heat to do it with. But I don't need a pistol, I can kill her with my bare hands." He raised his hand before my face and said, "You see this bony hand? That's the hands she talked about all through the years. I can take this bony hand and put it around her g——d——neck and finish her off." Then he let out a powerful loud yell, so loud, in fact, it brought pain to me, as it had at other times. "She fucked up our lives; she fucked with our minds. She's a bitch from hell. She needs to be killed. If you will just drive me there, I'll do it myself," he yelled at the top of his lungs.

"No, Jim, you can't do that. You'd spend the rest of your life in prison if you did. Sure, I would testify in court on your behalf about all the cruelties Mother did to you, but that wouldn't get you off the hook. You would spend the remainder of your life behind bars. You've got to forget her. If you did that, she would get the last laugh." Poor fellow, I had never seen him so tormented in all the years past. He would even tear at his own body, letting out those horrible yells, so loud and harsh, "She needs killing, the bitch! She deserves to die for what she did to you and me. I'd love to kill her and watch her die, watch her beg for mercy. Do you reckon she'd be scared?" he said. Then he laughed the demonic laugh of someone tormented.

Ann came out, and Jim told her the same things he had told me. It blew her mind, for she had never had any experience with his drunken fits of rage. I continued to talk very calmly to him, trying to assuage his anger, but he continued to rage on and on. I began to grow weary, for it was getting late. Finally I told him I was getting tired and needed to go inside, and his concern for me prompted him to leave. He went into town to the home of the lady with whom he had the affair and talked to her for hours until his rage at last subsided. She told me about it later, how she informed him that "You'd better either seek professional help or, when you feel the anger coming up, call your brother. John can help you. If you don't, you're going to hurt somebody and end up in prison."

And thank the Lord, I have been able to help him. Every time since that night, if he feels tormented and angry or the past comes back up to haunt him, he has called me and talked out his anger and frustrations. So far I've been able to help him diffuse his anger and help him see things in a positive light.

He's almost quit drinking entirely and is doing so much better. As proof of that, on Saturday, August 22, Mother came to see him. When she was ready to leave she clutched him by the arms and begged him to come to see her. "Mother," he said, "it's like I told you before; I'm trying to survive and I've got to do whatever it takes to do that, even if it means staying away from you. You will never see or be able to comprehend what you did to me and my brother. You may not believe it, and it doesn't matter whether you do or not, but I still love you. I appreciate all you did for me and my brother. I'm getting along real good. I've almost completely stopped drinking, and I can't do anything that will set me back." He told me he choked up a bit when he said that about still loving her, but she didn't seem moved by it; rather, she seemed to become cold and stiff. But it was so wonderful to me that he was able to confront her without having drunk a drop of liquor and without being angry either. He simply told her the truth out of his heart without any animosity at all. He has made tremendous progress. Just last year he couldn't face her without being intoxicated. He didn't have the courage or strength. But thank the Lord for answered prayer.

The hope still lives in my heart that perhaps Mother can read my story and then she can see what she did, not intentionally, for I don't believe she ever meant to hurt us. She was simply too confident, too sure of herself, and not willing to listen to anyone else, and she did exactly what her wise old daddy had told her not to do. She read the Old Testament when she was saved and became confused, and even to this day she doesn't realize just how confused she has been.

Epilogue

As I was nearing the completion of my manuscript, I had a little brainstorm. Originally there were only twelve chapters in it, but that was before I had the heart attack. All of a sudden, I realized one day that for me the number 13 is a lucky number. In 1959 I graduated from high school no. 13 out of a class of 93, I graduated from dental school June 13, 1966, there are 13 foods I am so allergic to I can only eat them every third day, it took 13 years for me to break away from the religious prison I was in after the first cracks appeared in the armor of trust and confidence I had in Mother, and I survived a major heart attack on December 13, 1994. So I decided I must have 13 chapters in my story, and the 13th chapter would relate the heart attack, the recovery from it, and then a sense of closure for my story. That made a lot of sense to me.

Since my heart attack, I have become involved in a couple of volunteer organizations, which bring me a great deal of joy and fulfillment. I am a volunteer Yoke Fellow member at the Lumberton Correctional Institute. We are Christian volunteers who go to the prison each Tuesday from 7:30 to 9:00 P.M. Our mission is to give the Christian inmates a chance to talk with someone other than the prison staff members, so they can develop a relationship that will help them to be able to cope in society and be productive members of it as well when they are released. I also have four guys I'm teaching how to play the piano. I really enjoy those lesson times. It is so rewarding to see the light in their eyes when I compliment them on doing well. They all aspire to play for their church when they are set free and can finally go home.

My purpose in writing my story was never to hurt anyone but to show the reader that there is an alternative to becoming a criminal when one has been abused growing up. We all grow so weary of hearing in the news about a murderer, rapist, or thief who uses his past as an excuse for his current behavior. We each have a choice.

We can choose either to take our painful experiences and turn them into something good, or perpetuate them on others, hurting them as we have been hurt or, as in most cases, hurting others far worse than we were hurt ourselves. My hope, too, is that those who are struggling in the throes of a religious cult can see there is a way out to freedom and a fulfilling life, that we don't have to be controlled by anyone else, that God has made a way for us all to find Him without having to go through other persons. We don't have to answer to anyone except God and His Son, Jesus Christ. We don't need others in order to communicate with God. I hope, too, that my determination to fight, never giving up, never letting life defeat me, can give others courage to do the same; that those who, even today, are being abused by whomever, whether parents, guardians, foster parents, husbands, wives, or even employers, can see that by always trying to do good we can become better persons. Always remember to "do unto others as you would have them do unto you," and you will never regret it. A kind deed will always leave us with peace inside, and many times it will vanquish our pain and even our anger.

I don't regret that my life has been such as it has. I believe it has made me a better person. I certainly hope so. I do believe there was a purpose for all of it and that I will soon see the whole meaning for it all. And the most beautiful, most wonderful thing of all to me is that my precious children will never, never have to experience the pain and anguish of a life such as mine, but through the grace of God, the love and support of all my friends, and my willingness and determination to work through the past, I was able to stop the abuse in myself, take it myself, deal with it, and then get on with my life, so they would never have to deal with it themselves.

Life is quite different for me now. It is a life without constant fear, one of happiness and freedom, knowing that God is the One Who keeps us. We cannot keep ourselves. Most of the time I'm like a bird out of a cage, free to go here or there. I love to laugh and have a good time with those I love. I tell my friends I'm trying to make up for all those years when I wasn't allowed to even laugh. Laughter is good for the soul, too. I don't have the fear of doing something displeasing to Mother but am free to do whatever I can to help those who need it. I have only to answer to God. That is truly a wonderful feeling. I can enjoy the company of all my friends without fear. The good times we share together hold very dear memories.

Mother called again after about a year of silence between the two of us to express more regret for the things she had done to Jim and me than she had ever expressed before, which gave me hope once again. As I said to my pastor, "I will give her another chance over and over again, no matter what she has done to me. What kind of hypocrite would I be if I didn't? Where would I be if Christ had only given me two or three chances?" So I am carefully and prayerfully trying to develop a relationship with Mother while I can, and I hope she will truly see the error of her way.

Jim has married June Hughes, the girl he has grown to love and who has stood by his side over the past eight or so years. Committing himself to her has given Jim great peace. He told me on Father's Day that he had more peace than he ever believed possible and that he was the happiest he had ever been. I am still praying that Mother will see through some of the un-Christian-like behavior she exhibits and will leave Jim with some tender memories before she leaves this world. An example of her un-Christian behavior: She told me the other day she would come to my home any time we prepared for her and eat with us, but not to include Jim and June because Jim is still an adulterer and God had put it in her heart long ago to not eat with those people and that she would rather have her head chopped off than to go against the things God had put in her heart. I was dumbfounded. She is still her controlling, judgmental, self, seemingly so unforgiving, so hard, even cruel. I tried to reason with her that if she loved her child and, to demonstrate her love, she sat at the table to share a meal with him and his wife, there was no way that God would bar her from heaven. Her being so judgmental of Jim is like the attitude of the Scribes and Pharisees in the Bible when they accused Jesus of eating with publicans and sinners. I told her that if she treated Jim in that manner, he would get the message that he was still an outcast. I certainly have no intention of ever telling Jim how Mother feels about eating with him.

But as I described in another place in the book, Jim has come a long way working through the pain of the past and accepting the fact that Mother will never change in many respects. Saturday, two weeks ago, Mother came to see him. When she was ready to leave, she grasped his arms, begging him to come visit her and to bring June with him. Without having taken a single drop of liquor, he had the strength and courage to face Mother and tell her how he felt. He let her know he still loved her whether she believed it or not, but that he had to survive in the face of the terrible things she had done to both of us and that if in order to survive he must remain separate from her, he would do that. If he felt like he could handle it, he would indeed visit her; otherwise, he would remain in his world and let her remain in hers. I am so thankful for his progress. It is truly an answer to prayer.

I realize that the following words seem inadequate to express my true feelings, but I would like to offer a most sincere and heart-felt word of thanks to all those who have stood by me in my hours of sorrow and despair, who never lost faith in me, and who many times gave me the encouragement to accomplish this task. Thank you all from the very bottom of my heart. I love you, everyone!